HEIR OF SHADOW

SARA C. ROETHLE

Copyright © 2023 by Sara C. Roethle

All rights reserved.

No part of this book may be reproduced in any form or by any electronic or mechanical means, including information storage and retrieval systems, without written permission from the author, except for the use of brief quotations in a book review.

Cover art by JV Arts

Chapter art by Hiidra Studio

❦ Created with Vellum

CHAPTER ONE

"So these witches... will they look like you?"

I ignored Tholdri glancing me up and down. He was only joking. I just wished I could appreciate his attempt at levity. As it stood, my stomach was tied up in knots.

I gripped the ends of my reins, peering up at the mountainside. My horse waited close behind me, her lips skimming the ground for something to eat. The witches would have spotted us by now. As instructed by Cael, we had dismounted to show our trust. Now, we would wait.

"It must have taken years to haul all that stone up the mountainside." Tholdri stood casually, though I didn't miss the tension in his jaw. There was no saying how the witches would accept us, two hunters—though we had left our armor behind.

"They had strong magic, once upon a time. Perhaps they used it to construct the fortress."

Because I could see no other way. Imposing stone

towers rose straight out of the steep incline near the mountain's peak. The surrounding walls were higher than those of Castle Helius, which was impressive. From our vantage point, we could see nothing beyond them.

"Do you think they've noticed us, or . . . "

I cut Tholdri off with a sharp look. "Cael said to wait."

"He also hasn't been out here since he was young. That was a *long* time ago." His golden hair fluttered in the breeze, skimming broad shoulders clad in thick blue linen. His fur-lined cloak was draped over his saddle. It was cold in the mountains.

I sucked my teeth, too nervous to give him further assurance. We had arrived at midday. Asher and Cael would be resting for some hours yet. We were on our own with the witches, as planned. Arriving with two vampires would only hurt our chances.

I straightened my green silk shirt, feeling ridiculous for wearing my finest clothing with more simple attire waiting in my saddlebags. The witches wouldn't care what I looked like. They would only care about the blood running through my veins. Blackmire blood. If I weren't a vampire's human servant, they would accept me with open arms.

But I was a servant, *more* than a servant, to an ancient vampire. It complicated things.

A cool breeze gusted us, carrying no sound from the mountaintop. The fortress seemed abandoned, but Cael had warned me it was only an illusion. He had also said that we could only see it at all because we knew what we were looking for. Others might walk by and only see inhospitable mountains.

A throat cleared behind us and we both spun, startling our horses. The woman standing just a few paces away was small, probably a whole head shorter than me. She wore a deep purple gown beneath a long matching coat with a high collar. Black fur bristled beneath the collar against her brown skin. Her silver-streaked black hair fell in tight curls down to her waist.

I stared at her, trying to figure out how she had snuck up so easily. The landscape was barren. There were no places to hide. We should have heard her.

"Am I supposed to believe that you are a Blackmire witch?" She raised a brow at my braid. "The color is accurate, I'll give you that."

I stiffened at her words. "And *you* are?" I bit my tongue too late. Cael had impressed upon me the importance of being polite, but I didn't like being snuck up on.

"Drucida, high witch of the stronghold you've been gawking at." She stepped closer, the movement smooth and sinuous. I placed her around sixty, but she moved like a woman half her age. Her eyes roved over me like I was a prized mare. "Ah, there *is* a bit of magic there, buried deep." Her gaze caught on the hilt of my sword. "And *that's* interesting."

I unclenched my fists from my horse's reins. *Polite*, I was supposed to be polite. I dipped my head in a slight bow. "My name is Lyssandra Yonvrode. My mother was Alicia Bouenoire, and her father was Cedrik Bouenoire."

Her eyes widened briefly. "*Was?* You would like me to believe that Cedrik is dead?"

"Believe what you like. It is the truth."

There was a hardening in her expression. The news of my grandfather's death had unsettled her. She turned her attention to Tholdri, who straightened and lifted his chin under her too-heavy gaze. "And who is this?"

"My lifelong friend, Tholdri Radran."

She laced her hands together, hiding them beneath the black fur at her sleeves, then stared at us for a good long while. Nothing moved except the breeze.

Just when I was at my breaking point, she finally spoke. "What is it that you want, Lyssandra Yonvrode?"

My first instinct was to lie, but Cael had warned me to speak only truth. "An ancient vampire—the *first* vampire—has been released. I would like to learn magic so that I might slay him."

"No," she answered instantly.

"No what?"

"No, you may not learn magic. Cedrik fled this order. He hid his daughter from us, just as he hid you. You are not welcome here, Lyssandra Yonvrode."

I glanced at Tholdri, but he seemed to be equally at a loss, so I handed him my reins and stepped toward Drucida. I had tried being polite, but politeness was overrated. "I apologize, but I am not able to take *no* for an answer." I loomed over her. "I *will* slay Eiric, and you will help me do it, unless you want this land to fall into total darkness."

I was used to smaller people being intimidated by my height, but Drucida didn't so much as flinch. "You believe I care for the fate of the Ebon Province?" She stepped even closer, craning her neck upward. This close, I could see flecks of gold in her eyes. She smelled strongly of sage and woodsmoke. "Have you ever watched someone close to you as they burned alive?" Her voice lowered. "Have you listened as the surrounding cheers drowned out your sisters' screams?"

If she wanted to shock me, she was trying it with the wrong woman. I tilted my head down, bringing us eye to eye. "I never learned why my parents were burned alive. Why I returned home to find nothing but ash and smoldering embers. I didn't hear their screams, but the end result was the same. I might not have known what blood flows through my veins, but I have paid the price many times over."

Tholdri stood back, not saying a word. He knew I was beyond the point of being reasoned with regardless. We had journeyed too far and waited too long to be so casually dismissed.

Drucida narrowed her eyes like she might read my mind. Like she might root out whatever she thought I was hiding. "There is death to you. Not just loss, but death. Necromancy?"

"Guess again."

"You're not a vampire."

I didn't want to tell her the truth, but she would have to know eventually. If me being a human servant was blocking my magic, she would have to know. "I am a vampire's human servant, but I maintain my free will."

"That's not possible."

She really had lost touch with my grandfather. She

didn't know about him making his hunters into human servants. "Everything I have told you is the truth. You may not care for the Ebon Province, but the one I hunt still concerns you. He killed my grandfather, and if he wants something from the witches, he'll kill you too. No one is safe. No one is strong enough."

Her expression softened slightly at my words. "When was Cedrik killed?"

"Not but a week ago."

"And this vampire, the one you hunt. This creature killed him?"

I nodded.

She watched me for a long moment. "Do you know why?"

I hesitated. On that matter, I had only speculation. "I believe it is because my grandfather worked to keep the vampire imprisoned, but I cannot be sure. Perhaps his motive was something other than vengeance."

Her eyes narrowed. "I will hear your tale, but nothing more." She breezed past me toward the distant fortress.

When I turned to keep her in my sights, she was gone.

Tholdri stared at the space she should have occupied. "What exactly just happened?"

I held out my hand for my reins. "I think we just received our invitation to the witches' fortress."

The sun had shifted in the sky by the time we reached the fortress, casting harsh shadows across the rocky ground. I hadn't really expected Drucida to be waiting for us, but I had expected more than the nervous young girl wringing her hands, glancing back at the tall iron gates like they might save her. Bordering the gates were two stone sentry towers. I caught a flicker of movement in one. Someone watching, but remaining out of sight.

The girl seemed relieved when she spotted us, but then her dark eyes grew more pinched the closer we came. Thin, mousy brown hair was cut just below her sharp chin. The rest of her was swallowed up within an oversized midnight blue robe.

Despite all the extra fabric, she shivered as we came to stand before her, leading our horses behind us since the rocky incline had been too steep for riding.

"I didn't think it would take so long or I wouldn't have waited out here all this time." Her wide eyes and hunched shoulders took any possible sting out of her words. She was putting on a brave face, but she was obviously terrified. Just what had Drucida told her?

"My apologies for not scaling an entire mountain more quickly." I smiled, liking the odd girl.

Blinking a little too rapidly, she looked at Tholdri. "He'll have to wait out here."

"Why didn't Drucida say that before?"

She turned those wide eyes back toward me. "It was implied."

I adjusted my sword strap, then crossed my arms. I had donned my heavy cloak during the walk, tossing it back behind my shoulders when I started to sweat.

She blinked at me a few more times. "He can't come in."

I continued staring at her while Tholdri did his best to look harmless. Difficult—since he was a tall, muscular warrior, but he managed.

She glanced at the gates behind her. The sentry in the tower had peeked his head out, but now the young man was pretending not to look at us.

I leaned forward and lowered my voice. "I don't think he's going to help you."

She audibly gulped. "Illya won't like me letting him in," she whispered.

And here I'd thought it was Drucida being difficult. "You just let me deal with Illya."

"Are you really a Blackmire witch?"

It didn't feel entirely like the truth, but I nodded.

"Alright," she breathed.

She waved at the young man, who had finally started looking directly at us. He nodded, gestured to someone else, then a pulley sounded and the gates opened outward.

I wasn't sure what they were all so worried about. We hadn't seen a village in days. I traveled extensively and had no idea such a fortress existed. As far as anyone was concerned, all witches were long gone. They could have no gates and no walls, and still would see no trouble.

The girl turned and hurried through the gates without another word. I realized I had neglected to catch her name.

Glancing at Tholdri, I started forward, nervous but

almost . . . excited. Drucida at least had known the Potentate, my grandfather. With his death, I had thought so many answers lost to me. But maybe they weren't. Maybe I could still learn something more than the scraps of information Cael had divulged during our travel.

The girl led us down a cobbled street, and I found myself once again amazed by the scope of the fortress. *More* than a fortress. It was an entire village protected by high walls, like a miniature version of Silgard. The homes we passed had stone foundations with whitewashed walls built from sturdy lumber—though where they had obtained lumber in the barren landscape was beyond me. Maybe things looked different on the other side of the mountain.

I caught a few people observing us as we passed, and I wondered if they were all witches. Surely there couldn't be so many, hidden away all these years.

Tholdri moved close to my shoulder. "How is all of this here? How can no one know about this?" The sound of our horses' hooves on the cobbles nearly drowned out his words.

Just as well, since I had no answer for him. The only explanation was magic, but I knew so little about it. I had no idea what these witches were capable of.

At one time, fear of the unknown would have kept me away from such a fortress. We were vulnerable, at the mercy of magic wielders. But avoiding possible threats was no longer a luxury I could afford. Not with Eiric free to kill as he pleased. I knew without a doubt that my grandfather was only the beginning.

Our guide stopped at a central home, larger than the rest. She turned toward us and bowed her head. "Drucida and Illya are inside." Her eyes shifted from side to side, then she stood up on her toes to whisper in my ear. "Don't make Illya angry. You'll pay for it." She lowered onto her heels, then took our horses' reins and scurried away, her too-large robe flapping around her.

I gave Tholdri a wary look.

He gestured toward the aged wooden door. "We've come this far, Lyss. No turning back now."

"Easy for you to say. You're not asking to become one of them."

I reached for the door handle before I could think better of it. At least my sword wasn't warning me. No one in the fortress meant me harm—yet. Their opinions of me might change once I asked them to allow two vampires into their stronghold. They would likely cast me out entirely.

But I at least had to try.

CHAPTER TWO

The door creaked open with a blast of warmth. A woodstove pumped heat furiously into the interior. It would need to burn all day to heat the large space. Faded tapestries bedecked every wall, trapping in more heat. While the colors varied from muted greens to vibrant purples, it was clear they had all been stitched by the same hand. Some depicted animals, some valiant warriors, but they all had an air of sameness to them.

I stepped further inside, tearing my eyes from the tapestries to observe the two women seated at a small round table, sipping tea. Drucida had removed her purple coat to reveal the embroidered gown beneath. The other woman had pure silver hair and bright blue eyes, her face deeply lined. She wore a red coat with thick white fur trim over layered skirts. I guessed the extra heat was for her. Even with all the layers, she looked painfully thin and frail.

"Not one hunter, but two." Her quaking voice held no emotion. A simple observation.

I nodded. "I did not feel comfortable leaving him on the mountainside for the wolves."

Her blue eyes looked Tholdri up and down. Intelligence danced in the vibrant orbs. She was aged, but still sharp. "I imagine he can fend for himself. And now, he'll know the layout of our stronghold. He'll report back to your order."

Tholdri said nothing in his defense. He had always been skilled at holding his tongue. It was a skill I admired, but had never developed.

Drucida rolled her eyes a bit. "The Helius Order has not hunted witches in their lifetime." She addressed us with a flick of her chin. "Not since Cedrik."

That was news to me. I had always assumed we stopped hunting witches simply because they no longer existed. But maybe my grandfather had only wanted us to *believe* they no longer existed.

"Cedrik is a traitor," the elderly woman, presumably Illya, snapped.

"*Was* a traitor." I approached their table. "He's dead."

Her expression made it obvious Drucida had not told her the news. I wondered what other reason she had given for letting us into their fortress.

I forged on before Illya could waste more time. The heat was stifling, and I wanted things settled before dark, when Asher would come looking for me. "He was killed by the very first vampire, recently set free. I would like to learn enough magic to hunt him, then I will leave you in peace."

Illya's eyes narrowed to slits. With her aged skin bunched up, it almost looked like her eyes were actually closed. "You are hunters. Hunting vampires is what you do. Why would you need our help?"

"The vampire, Eiric, was able to cloud my mind. I cannot kill something I cannot see."

"And why didn't he kill you?"

I shifted uneasily. "I don't know."

"A lie," Drucida observed.

I fought the urge to wince. Cael's warning had been sound. Drucida could somehow sense lies, and the conversation was moving almost too fast for me to follow. It felt like both women knew much more than they were letting on. "I do not know for sure why he left me alive. Perhaps because I was instrumental in freeing him. Or perhaps because he is my ancestor."

Illya met Drucida's waiting gaze. Silent moments passed.

Finally, Drucida spoke. "If he's Blackmire—"

"Then it's really him," Illya finished.

Hope blossomed in my chest. If they knew about Eiric, they knew how dangerous he was. Any sane person would want him defeated.

They stared at each other for another long moment, then Illya looked at me. "Eiric was Blackmire's responsibility. Lavandriel sealed him away. Her heirs kept him caged. It is not our task to right Lavandriel's wrongs. She should have let her brother die when she had the chance."

"She wasn't the one who made him a vampire," I

argued. It had been Cerridwen. She had used her necromancy to animate Eiric.

Illya snorted. "Good luck convincing the Sidhe to take responsibility."

They really did know everything. They already knew about Lavandriel, Cerridwen, all of it. If only they knew just how poorly *working* with the Sidhe had gone. I tried another tactic. "My grandfather and mother are dead. As far as I know, I am the last living Blackmire witch."

"Hardly a witch," Illya scoffed.

"Which is why I need your help."

"No."

I flexed my hands, longing to grab Illya's shoulders and give her a good shake. The woman was an utter fool. "He is a danger to everyone. I don't know what he wants, but witch blood runs through his veins. If he comes for you—"

"Do not threaten me, girl," Illya cut me off. "If he comes here, we will deal with him. Until then, he is Blackmire's responsibility."

I felt Tholdri's hand on my shoulder, making me realize I had taken another step toward the table. "All the Blackmire witches are dead."

"Except you," Illya repeated. "You are a hunter. *Hunt.*"

I looked at Drucida. She had allowed me to come here. There had to be hope.

She gave me a secretive smile, then said to Illya. "She *is* a hunter. We might not want to send her away so soon."

Illya looked like she'd been slapped. "*That* doesn't concern her."

"Lives have been lost. She is trained to track killers."

I glanced between them, thrown off by the sudden change in subject. I suspected this line of conversation had been Drucida's plan all along.

Illya stood. She was taller than I'd imagined, even taller than me. "Absolutely not."

Drucida stood. Even with her lesser height, she seemed far more imposing than Illya. "I am high witch. Not you."

Illya scowled. "So this is why you brought her here. You want to pass off your burden."

"Would someone mind telling me what we're talking about?" I interrupted, barely containing my irritation.

Tholdri gave me a long-suffering look.

Drucida's smile seemed just as long-suffering, and perhaps a bit sad. "There have been several deaths. Witches killed in horrible ways. We are yet to unearth the culprit."

Thinking of Eiric, my pulse sped. "When did the first death occur?"

"At the solstice. At first we thought it was a lone occurrence, but weeks later, another was taken."

Not Eiric then. He would have still been trapped at that time.

"They were not killed by vampires." Illya's attention rested solely on Drucida. "We've no need of hunters."

"They have hunted other things before," Drucida said calmly. "They will do so again."

Now her saying nothing against Tholdri made

perfect sense. She didn't want to teach me magic. She wanted to hire me. Hire *us*.

But if it would gain me her trust . . .

"I'll do it."

Drucida lifted a brow. "You haven't yet heard the details of the deaths."

"I'll find your killer, no matter what it is."

"This will not inspire us to teach you magic," she warned. "You are bonded to a vampire. That is simply not something we can overlook."

"I will still find your killer." I looked at Illya. "Just as you said, I am a hunter. I *hunt*." I emphasized my final word, because I felt like the woman could do with a bit of threatening.

"This is unacceptable," she snapped. "Hunters must not learn our secrets. They will come for us."

"Someone has already come for us." The sudden power in Drucida's voice made Illya fall silent.

Goosebumps marched up my arms. It was more than just a voice. It was . . . magic.

"I will not lose anyone else," she continued more calmly, and the feeling of power leaked away. "We will give the hunters a chance to do what we cannot. We will allow them to find our killer."

I knew it wasn't possible, but it almost seemed like she had known I was coming. Like she had been planning this conversation for a good long while. So then, why had she tried to turn us away?

Regardless, I wasn't about to question her. She wasn't throwing us out now, which meant I had time to win her over. I had time to convince her to teach me magic.

Only, I had to find a killer first, quickly. While I did not know Eiric's current movements, my gut told me time was running out for us all.

THOLDRI AND I stood together back out on the cobbles as the door closed behind us.

"I feel like I've been hit by a war horse."

I couldn't argue with him. "Drucida knew we were coming. I don't know how, but she knew. She knew exactly what she wanted from us from the start. It was all a manipulation."

The girl who had escorted us through the gates approached, chin down and eyes on her feet, blue robe billowing around her. I noticed a few others wearing similar robes, while most were in common dress.

She reached us, then forced her eyes up toward our faces. "I'm to escort you to your lodgings."

I glanced at the closed door behind us. Neither Drucida nor Illya had stepped outside. "Who told you to escort us?"

She gnawed her lower lip, eyes darting around nervously. "Come." She lifted one hand, crooking her fingers at us before turning away.

I shrugged at Tholdri, then followed. Drucida had strictly forbade the presence of vampires within her fortress. Once we had our lodgings, we would wait until dark, then I would find Asher and Cael out in the night.

The girl led us down a narrow path between several small dwellings, taking us away from the curious people watching us along the wider street. I suspected a few of them had been whispering about the color of my hair.

She stopped at the smallest dwelling at the end of the path. "It might be a bit dusty." She wiggled the handle, but the door didn't budge. She gave the handle a sharp turn, hitting the door with her shoulder. "Hmph. The wood must be swollen."

I motioned for her to step aside.

She seemed unsure, but stepped back next to Tholdri. She startled, looking at him like he had just appeared right next to her, then took another step back.

I turned away to hide my laughter, gave the knob a sharp turn, then hit the door with my shoulder. Wood scraped against wood with a dull shriek, and the door opened.

I stepped inside, coughing as dust stirred. A single broken chair was the only seating. What looked like a single bed was draped with a stained sheet. I was glad there was only one window to let light in upon the tiny stove next to a cracked washbasin. The pots and plates within the basin had been left caked in food and other grime. At least everything in the basin had been rotting long enough to no longer smell.

"We've slept in worse." Tholdri ran a finger across the seat of the broken chair, coming away with thickly caked dust.

He wasn't lying, though I was still dreading how my lungs would feel in the morning after breathing dust all night. I turned toward the girl. "I'd like to ask you a few questions before you can scurry away again."

I might have told her I wanted to yank off her fingernails one by one, for all the horror in her expression. "If you have questions, you should ask Drucida."

"Ah, but I want to ask you." I took a step toward her. She was acting rather strangely. Her fear outside the gates I understood, but what had she to fear now, safe within the witches' fortress?

Her eyes darted around for a path of escape, but Tholdri had casually stepped between her and the open door.

"Why are you so frightened?" I asked.

"I'm not."

"Yes, you are, and I'm beginning to think it's not because of us."

She swallowed loudly, refusing to meet my gaze.

"We won't hurt you."

"I'm not worried about that," she whispered, eyes still shifting around.

I glanced at Tholdri, then back at her, confused. "Then what are you worried about?"

She looked around again, then motioned for me to move closer.

Feeling uneasy, I did. My sword had warned me of nothing. She didn't want me near so she could hurt me.

She lowered her voice to the barest whisper. "My closest friend, Nigella, spoke to an outsider traveling through the mountain pass. Two days later, she was murdered."

I recognized the name. Drucida had mentioned it. She was one of the first deaths.

"I don't know about all the others," she continued, "but Jacques also spoke to an outsider. An elderly man. Jacques bought a hunting knife from him."

Jacques was one of the more recent deaths. Male, twenty-three years of age, descended from witches but with limited magic, which I had learned was quite common. Many within the fortress had little to no magic to speak of.

Tholdri moved closer. "You think they died because they spoke with outsiders?"

"Shhh!" Her cheeks turned scarlet, her breathing ragged. "Both times, the outsider asked for their names, and they got a strange feeling. Two days later, they were dead."

"And that's why you haven't told us your name?" I asked.

Seeming a bit ashamed, she nodded. "It didn't seem worth the risk."

Clever girl. I didn't think her suspicions held much merit, but she was right, it wasn't worth the risk. "The outsider Nigella spoke with, also an elderly man?"

She shook her head, draping her short mousy hair around her face. "No, a beautiful woman. But she sold Nigella a locket, and asked for her name."

I furrowed my brow. "Are there often travelers coming across the mountain?"

"That's the strangest part about it. There are *never* travelers coming across the mountain. Every few weeks, some of us will travel to the villages on the other side of the mountain for trade, but no strangers ever come back. That's why Jacques and Nigella were so excited to tell their tales."

I looked at Tholdri. We knew many legends, but nothing about strange travelers selling trinkets and asking for names. I looked down at the girl. "But you don't know if any of the other victims spoke with outsiders?" There had been six deaths in total, spanning months.

"No," she whispered. "But the two were enough to scare me away from speaking with strangers." She looked at me hopefully. "But you're a hunter, and a descendent of Blackmire. You're not really a stranger, are you?"

"Not the kind you need to be worried about."

She let out a huff of air, relaxing her shoulders. "My name is Teresa. I'm to attend you while you're here. I can fetch you supper shortly, if you're hungry."

Tholdri's stomach growled in answer. We'd had nothing but hard bread and sharp cheddar for days.

I patted the girl on the shoulder. "Thank you, Teresa. Supper would be nice."

Supper first, then I would find the vampires. And after that, we would work on solving the murders.

If only I knew where to start.

CHAPTER THREE

The mountain air turned bitingly cold as soon as darkness fell. I left Tholdri behind to clean up our lodging while I searched for the vampires. No one tried to stop me from passing through the gates. No one spoke to me at all.

I huddled in my cloak, standing at the edge of a rocky escarpment. I hadn't gone far, the fortress lights were still in view, but it was dark enough that no sentries would see me meeting Asher and Cael.

I wondered at Teresa's story as I stared out into the night, squinting against the wind chilling my face. Two different strangers, but similar stories. It was possible that it was only one stranger possessing strong glamour. But what were the chances of yet another Sidhe crossing my path?

I was afraid of the answer.

I sensed Asher nearing, and suddenly the night seemed a little less cold. Warmth bloomed in my chest, and I knew he was standing right behind me, having moved as silently as only the dead can manage.

"You made it into the fortress."

I turned, and the sight of him stole my breath. I had assumed the reaction would wane with time, but I had thus far been proven incorrect. Every night when he found me, I longed for my skin to be pressed against his.

I shook away my thoughts. We had important matters to discuss. He must have thought so too, because he was shielding me from our bond. Everything I felt for him . . . it was all me.

I was embarrassed, and I wasn't sure why. "The witches have not yet agreed to teach me magic, but they are allowing Tholdri and I to stay until we can solve a string of murders."

He closed the space between us, lifting one long-fingered hand to lightly stroke my cheek. "Murders?"

I closed my eyes for a moment, enjoying the soft touch, then told him everything Drucida and Teresa had divulged, including the grizzly details of how the bodies were found. Skinned alive. Internal organs missing. My stomach turned at the mental image I had formed. I was used to seeing death. Torture was another thing entirely.

His brow furrowed. "I do not know of a creature that kills in such a way."

"I would have suspected it was one of their own if it weren't for Teresa's story."

"It still could be another witch, casting illusions."

Asher had been alive a long time. Long enough to

have met witches before they went into hiding. "How similar are illusions to glamour?" I asked.

"Quite similar, but easier to break if you know what you're looking for. Glamours can trick all the senses. Illusions are made only to trick the eye. But why change appearance when the only witnesses are dead?"

I shrugged. "At least two of them told their tales. Maybe the killer wanted to prolong the game as long as possible. If my friend died after speaking with a beautiful woman in the mountain pass, I would surely avoid speaking with a beautiful woman in the mountain pass. Teresa was reluctant to even tell us her name."

"And what of the objects they purchased?"

"I'm going to ask Drucida about them in the morning when I view the bodies."

His eyebrows rose. "They were not burned?"

"Preserved with ice made by magic, which I'm almost as interested in as the bodies. There is ample evidence that the high witch knew we were coming, though I do not know how."

He casually rubbed his hands up and down my arms, like it was comforting just to touch me. Maybe it was. I knew I didn't mind it. "In the olden days, some of the most powerful witches possessed a second sight. Sometimes they could see the future, the past, or even things currently happening far away."

Well that explained it, but, "Does that mean she could possibly be looking at us right now?"

He continued slowly rubbing my arms. "You did not tell her you travel with vampires?"

"I told her. You're not allowed within the fortress, but she knows you exist."

"Then what is the issue?"

My cheeks burned. If Drucida really had been watching me . . . If she had seen Asher and I—

I cut off my thoughts again. In all likelihood, she had just had a premonition that hunters would arrive. Witches weren't as powerful as they used to be.

"Where is Cael?" I asked, wanting to change the subject.

"I requested that I meet with you alone."

A pleasant tingling started in my gut at his words. "Alone?" My voice came out hoarse.

His lips curved into a knowing smile. "Unfortunately, not for the reason you are thinking. At least not for *just* that reason."

Disappointment washed through me. We'd had no time alone since we started traveling. Other than stopping in Bordtham to send a letter to Steifan detailing our plans, we had been traveling under the stars and resting by day.

"I believe Cael is struggling to maintain control." His words jolted me out of my thoughts.

Ever since Cael had revealed his true form, he had maintained it, at least around me. He looked like a younger version of my grandfather. Flowing red hair, a neatly trimmed goatee, a strong, tall, body. There was still a deeply disturbing sense of evil to him, something lurking just beneath the surface, but on the outside . . .

"He warned me that he needed my help to stay himself, but he never told me what that meant."

"I believe he needs that help now. It may just be the recent lack of blood—"

I frowned at the thought. I didn't like considering Asher's eating habits. He was ancient. He could go a long time without feeding, but not forever. The same applied to Cael. Although . . . he wasn't ancient. Powerful, but not ancient. Maybe he needed blood more frequently.

"He can't feed from any of the witches. They already barely trust me."

He nodded. "I agree. And lack of blood may not even be the issue. It has been over a week since your grandfather was killed."

"And my grandfather kept Cael under control." I swiped a palm across my face, remembering what he had been like before. *Monstrous.* A desiccated corpse with living shadows clinging to every bit of him. "I don't need yet another issue. I need to focus on the murders."

"I apologize, but I thought it important to tell you."

I forced a smile, not sure when I first started caring about his feelings. "I know. I'm just complaining. I will speak with him tonight, see if there is anything I can do."

"I do not think it likely he will be honest about his issues. He doesn't want to burden you."

I remembered how animalistic he had appeared just after my grandfather's death. From monster, to beast. It had nearly driven him mad, but once I had agreed to watch over him, he had maintained himself. Was it all just an act for my benefit?

"Then what am I supposed to do?"

"I thought you might ask the witches."

I laughed, I couldn't help it. After how they had reacted to me being a vampire's human servant, I knew they wouldn't want to help me. "I will think on it. Maybe I can find someone who likes me better than Illya and Drucida, the two witches I met with today."

"I'm sure you will. You are, after all, polite and charming."

I wrinkled my nose at the laughter in his voice. "You aren't exactly a joy to be around either."

"Touché." He touched my arms again, this time to pull me close.

My heart sped as he looked down at me, tucking a stray lock of hair behind my ear. In the cold moonlight he was ethereal—too perfect for words. And it wasn't the bond clouding my judgement, it was just him. "You know, this is the first time we've been alone since—"

I swallowed the lump in my throat, thinking of the night by the stream. "Yes, of that I am painfully aware."

"Does that mean you desire a repeat . . . occurrence?"

My heart fluttered. He was so close. I could just remove his coat, tug his shirt free from his pants— "It's absolutely freezing out here. And you don't exactly offer much warmth."

"Are you *just complaining* again?"

I nodded, and he lowered his mouth to mine, just a tender brush of lips.

But I wanted more. I pressed against him, deepening the kiss.

His hands found my waist, pushing under my silk

shirt to knead the flesh beneath. His hands were cold, chilling my already icy skin. His heart was still beating—he had some warmth to give—but the longer he went without feeding, the colder he would become.

I broke our kiss. "You said Cael might be struggling with lack of blood. Are you in the same position?"

His silver eyes searched my face, his hands still circling my waist beneath my shirt. "I was under the impression you did not like to hear about such things."

"If you are in danger of starving, I should know."

He was suddenly shielding so tightly, I couldn't feel a thing. "It is . . . difficult. I am not as strong as I could be, but I am in no danger of withering away."

"When was the last time you . . . " I removed one hand from his shoulder, twirling it in the air as I searched for the right word.

"Fed?"

I looked away from him. Why was I being so silly about this? I had seen vampires feed many times. Most of them I had killed afterward.

"Shortly before we ventured to Evral's lair."

I whipped my gaze back up, meeting his eyes. "You can go that long?"

"It is unpleasant, but yes."

"And when you do feed? How does that occur?" Why was I asking? I really didn't want to know, but I couldn't help myself. I didn't like thinking of what we had as a relationship. I had never wanted a true romantic bond . . . but then what were we doing? Saving each other's lives and having sex? It was more, and I knew it. I just didn't want to admit it.

He searched my face for a long, quiet moment. Finally, he asked, "Are you sure you want the answers to these questions?"

I looked down again. "No. Yes. I don't know, but I do find myself wondering. Our relationship . . . It is not like other relationships."

He placed a finger beneath my chin and applied gentle pressure until I met his eyes again. "My choice would be to keep nothing from you. To shield, nothing. But you must decide what you want. I believe you may need more time to do that."

I frowned. "How can you always be so rational about things?"

"Lyssandra, I have been alive a rather long time."

I knew it. I knew he didn't think like me, but it was still mind-boggling at times. "Alright, maybe I don't want answers yet, not to all of it. Just one. How much longer can you go without feeding?"

"I will be fine for some time yet."

He was still shielding tightly, and I had a feeling he wasn't telling me the complete truth. A more practical woman might have offered her own blood, but I just couldn't. I had done it once when he was near death, but that was different. Then, I didn't feel like *food*. Maybe I was only practical when it came to hunting—to *killing*. I had been willing to sacrifice my life on many occasions, but apparently there were still some things I wasn't willing to give up. My blood being one of them.

"Your thoughts betray you." He smiled to soften his words.

"Don't read my emotions," I grumbled.

"I am not. That doesn't mean I can't tell what you're thinking." He tilted his head, and I thought he might say more, but instead he looked over his shoulder. "Tholdri approaches."

I pulled away from him. Tholdri had no reason to follow me, unless something had happened.

I heard his soft footsteps moments before I spotted him in the dark.

Noticing us in turn, he walked toward us. "You know, it's unnerving when you both watch me like that."

"Like what?" I asked.

"A pair of wolves."

I stepped around Asher, regretting the loss of his touch. "Why are you here, Tholdri? Was the dust too much for you?"

He reached us, shaking his head. "I wish it was that, Lyss. There has been another death. We're needed."

The breath left my body. Another murder, right under our noses. I glanced at Asher, giving him an apologetic shrug. Alone time would have to wait.

SEEING the fresh body made me wish I didn't have to view the others. The young man was sprawled across his bed. I wished he looked like he was sleeping. But most people don't sleep without their skin.

Tholdri held a hand over his mouth. If I didn't know any better, I'd say he was about to be sick.

I knelt beside the body, observing the wounds in the lantern light. The skinning was far too perfect. I didn't see how it could have been done with any normal knife. It would have taken hours, maybe days, and the young man had been seen alive an hour before his corpse had been discovered.

"Who found him?" I asked.

Drucida stood near the door, as far from the corpse as she could get. "His mother. She is with Illya now."

I stood, avoiding any observation of the face. The lidless eyes were just too unnerving. "I'll need to speak with her."

"Illya gave her a sleeping tonic. It will have to wait until morning."

I turned toward her. "Do you feel any magic in this room?"

Her eyes widened a bit. "No more than usual? Wylan had magic, but not much. Not enough to protect himself."

"Had he met any strangers lately? Purchased any strange objects?"

"Why would that matter?"

I hid my surprise, sealing the information away for later. For some reason, Teresa had not told Drucida her suspicions. Unfortunately, that meant if trinkets had been purchased by any of the others, no one had taken note of it.

I glanced around the small room, looking for anything out of place. If Wylan had also spoken to a stranger, maybe whatever he had purchased was still in the room.

I noticed nothing. He had few belongings, and the room was tidy. Maybe the killer took the trinkets back, along with the victims' skins and internal organs.

"Have you ever seen anything like this?" Drucida asked.

"No, but I've seen a lot of strange things this past year." Sidhe, Natmarra, a summoner, and now whatever this was.

She scrutinized my face, hardly glancing at Tholdri. "You may as well view the other bodies now. I assume you are *accustomed* to staying up through the night."

I chose to ignore the subtle insult. Who says I can't be polite? I gestured toward the door. "Lead the way."

CHAPTER FOUR

Tholdri's breath fogged the air around his face. His honey-brown eyes searched the small chamber, awestricken. "This is incredible."

I couldn't argue with him. Outside, the building was unremarkable. Inside, the walls were solid ice, thick enough that I couldn't see the wood on the other side. Only the door was was somewhat visible, the wood caked with thick frost. I suspected the building had been a home at one time, but all the furniture had been cleared away. The woodstove and washbasin were two solid ice cubes in one corner of the room.

The bodies were all lined up on the floor, so thick with ice it was going to be a task to not slip and fall on top of them. They lay on their backs, skinless arms crossed over their hollow chests.

Illya had joined us, though she looked none too happy about it. She had layered a thick winter cloak over her fur-trimmed coat. I suspected the cold hurt her old bones.

I counted six bodies. Soon there would be seven.

I turned my back on the two witches. "What inspired you to keep the first body?"

"What do you mean?" Drucida asked.

I shrugged with my arms wrapped tightly around myself. Even with my cloak, my teeth were chattering. "I can see why you'd want to preserve them *after* the first few deaths, but why keep the first? What did you hope to learn about it?"

Alright, so maybe I was not so subtly prodding for an admission of her spying on me, but it was still strange. Vampire victims were usually held until a hunter could investigate, but these were not vampire victims.

I glanced back when she didn't answer.

She gave me a tight-lipped smile. "As you are well aware, our secrets are closely guarded."

Keeping my arms crossed, I turned and jutted my hip. "Do you want me to solve your murders, or not?"

Illya glared daggers at me, but kept quiet.

Drucida's eyes darted toward Tholdri, then back to me. "I suppose no harm can come of it," she sighed. "Sometimes, more powerful witches are granted premonitions. The first came on the night of the first murder. I saw more deaths to come, but no way to stop them. Then, on the night the second body was found, I saw two shadowed figures. I didn't know who was coming, but I knew they would help us. I created this room after the first body, because I knew there would be more. And I maintained it all this time, because I knew you would come."

I narrowed my eyes. "But you almost turned us away."

She looked like she tasted something sour. "Perhaps I did not want to believe that help would come in the form of two hunters, but you persisted. I knew then that you were needed."

Tholdri moved closer to me, pressing his shoulder against mine, though neither of us had much warmth to give after a few minutes in the ice chamber. "How could you know we were coming, when we hadn't yet decided ourselves? The second murder took place well before we chose to come here, before we even knew this place existed."

Drucida shrugged. "It is not for us to know how the light works. Only that it guides us as it chooses."

I didn't like her answer, but we could debate it later, when we weren't soon to be as frozen as the corpses. "You said you created this room. How?"

She held out her hand, palm up, sweeping it across the room. I could have sworn the space grew even colder. It was then that I realized she was the only one of us not shivering. "We all have certain affinities, even those with weak magic."

My eyes widened. I had seen magic, felt it. But I had never seen anything like *this*. "And what can she do?" I nodded toward Illya.

Drucida's eyes took on a mischievous glint. "You saw her tapestries earlier."

Illya's jaw fell open, then shut with an angry click. "You may share your secrets all you please," she huffed. "But do not share *mine*."

"My apologies." Drucida didn't seem even slightly remorseful. She enjoyed getting a rise out of Illya.

I glanced at the corpses, though really, I was wondering about the tapestries. They were strange and beautiful, but didn't seem magical. "I think I've seen all I need to." I turned back toward the witches. "What was done with the victims' belongings?"

"Why?" Illya asked.

I sighed. Families of vampire victims were so much easier to work with. They never questioned me poking through journals and other belongings.

Drucida watched me, her expression thoughtful. "The belongings were either distributed or disposed of by family members, but one victim had no loved ones. His cottage has not yet been cleared out."

I gestured once more for her to lead the way.

"It's the middle of the night!" Illya cried out.

"No one asked you to come, Illya," Drucida was already walking toward the frosted door.

I gave Illya a wide berth as I stepped around her, wondering at the rivalry between the two witches. Once I had the chance, I would ask around.

I didn't think either of the witches was the killer, but I'd keep my options open. If only witches were being targeted, with the deaths occurring in their well-guarded fortress, the killer was either a witch, or working with one.

WE RETURNED to our cottage with roughly an hour of darkness left. I thought about finding Asher, or Cael, but decided I would enjoy my first opportunity for a soft bed in over a week, even if I'd have to share the small mattress with Tholdri.

The first thing I noticed as I opened the door was that there was significantly less dust. The stained sheet was gone from the bed, and the moldy dishes were nowhere to be seen. Tholdri had been busy while I was away. Even a table and two chairs had been added beneath the largest window.

"Teresa helped," he explained when I raised a brow at him.

"Did you learn anything new from her?"

"No, but you might. Her magic is weak, but it's there. She wears those blue robes because she is an apprentice. To *Illya*."

My brows lifted further. "That poor girl."

"Yes, she doesn't seem entirely pleased with the arrangement, but she is excited that she has enough magic to develop. Few do, apparently."

I walked toward the bed. If all else failed, perhaps Teresa could teach me a few things. Even if she only knew the basics, it was more than I possessed. Cael had been able to tell me a few things in theory, but with no access to his natural magic, he couldn't actually show me. Necromancy was entirely different. Even with my connection to the undead, I could not attempt necromancy unless I died too.

I was hoping to avoid that.

"I imagine you inquired about an extra bed?"

Tholdri stepped up behind my shoulder. "And miss the opportunity to sleep next to you?"

I rolled my eyes, though he couldn't see it. "You're incorrigible."

"And you prefer the lower body temperature of vampires. Did you have a good meeting out in the darkness?"

I stepped away from him. "It was good until you interrupted it with your loud clumsy footfalls."

He followed me toward the bed. "I'm not loud. You just spend too much time with dead things."

I turned and wrinkled my nose at him. "Better dead things than idiots."

He lifted his palms in surrender. "Hey, to each their own. Now who has to sleep next to the wall?"

"You do. I'll protect us if anyone breaks down the door."

"Now that's what I like to hear." He stepped around me and flopped onto the bed, taking up far too much room.

I sighed dramatically, but deep down, I was glad he was there. As much as I hid my reaction, I had found the bodies deeply disturbing. Not to mention, we were about to sleep in a fortress full of witches.

Sleep would not come easy, and when it did, my dreams would surely be haunted by skinned corpses. And by the image of what my great uncle could become if I didn't figure out a way to help him maintain control.

If he became nothing but a monster, I would be

forced to kill him. And even if I managed such a seemingly impossible feat, I would be losing the only family I had left.

CHAPTER FIVE

I woke with Tholdri's arm across my face, and his heavy leg wrapped around me. Scowling at the sunlight streaming through the window, I gave him a shove, but he didn't move.

"Get off me you foul ox."

With a huff of annoyance, Tholdri rolled onto his other side.

I sat up, wincing at a sharp pain in my skull. Tholdri was always able to sleep no matter the circumstances. I, however, had hardly gotten a wink. Every time I closed my eyes for too long, I thought about how it would feel to be missing my eyelids like all the corpses.

I stood, stretching stiff arms over my head. First, food. Then Teresa. Now that I knew she was Illya's apprentice, I had some new questions to ask her.

Moving sluggishly, I pulled on my boots. I had slept in my green silk shirt and breeches, and they would do for the day, but at some point soon I needed to find myself a bath. Cold streams just didn't quite do the trick.

Curious, I checked the only other door in the house, finding a small water closet, but no bath. I did at least find a fresh pitcher of water, a rough towel, and a chamber pot—enough to get me ready for the day. As Tholdri had pointed out the previous night, we had endured far worse.

With my cheeks numb from cold water, I took my sword and left the cottage, leaving Tholdri to his slumber. Teresa had delivered a modest supper, but according to her, most dining was done communally. A perfect opportunity to question the other witches.

I walked down the narrow path leading to the main street, casually observing the other lodgings. Some were in disrepair like mine, but others were clearly occupied. And yet, I had seen none of the occupants. Vegetables grew in small gardens, well maintained, and the windows were clean, the whitewash on the walls fairly fresh. They should have been bustling with life, but they were eerily silent. It was strange, but not primary on my list of concerns.

I reached the main street, and three women in blue robes fell silent. They all turned to stare at me.

It seemed word had spread. I wondered if it would make the questioning easier, or far, far worse. Even though the women were too young to have ever been hunted by the Helius Order, I couldn't blame them if they still bore a grudge.

I approached them, meeting each of their stares with a challenging stare of my own.

One woman with olive skin and startlingly bright grey eyes looked me up and down, clutching her blue robes close around her. "She doesn't seem terribly impressive."

A blonde woman with plump cheeks and an upturned nose shrugged. "I wouldn't say that. She does carry a sword, just like a *hunter* would."

I gave each of them an equally assessing once-over, then turned to the third woman. I guessed she was a few years older than the other two, who were merely teenagers, and her green eyes held more curiosity than disdain.

"Since it seems like you all know who I am, I'll skip the niceties. I'd like to ask you a few questions."

"Why us?" the blonde asked.

I ignored her, keeping my attention on the third woman. There was a hint of red in her brown hair, coiled into a tight bun at the nape of her neck. "Can we speak alone?"

Her brows lifted, but she nodded, gesturing for me to lead the way.

We walked away from her friends. I tried not to take pleasure in their stunned silence. Then I failed, and allowed myself a moment of delight.

We walked further down the cobbles, drawing a few stares as we went.

"Since I imagine you already know my name, would you mind if I asked yours?" I was really starting to catch on with this politeness business.

"Ophelia. Why did you want to speak with me specifically?" Once again, I sensed only curiosity from her. No fear, nor disdain. My sword was silent, though there was a feeling of *waiting*, almost as if it also wanted to hear what this woman might have to say.

"Call it intuition, but I don't think I would have gotten far with your friends."

"They're not friends. We apprentice under the same witch."

She stopped us at a small bench, and we both sat.

"Which witch?"

"Elanore."

I didn't know who Elanore was, so that wasn't helpful. "Don't take this the wrong way, but you seem older than the other two, and the only other apprentice I've met is far younger . . . "

"We apprentice for many years. Most of us hardly have magic at all. It is difficult to develop, sometimes impossible."

I looked directly at her, but she was watching a young boy hanging linens on a line across the street. "You're answering my questions quite easily."

She turned toward me, and my heart skipped a beat. Some dark emotion had crept into her eyes. *Haunted* was the only way to describe it. "Jacques was my twin brother. I want the killer caught."

She was in pain, so I tried to hide my excitement over happening upon just the person I wanted to speak with. If Teresa's suspicions were true about the strangers, the purchased items might lead us to the killer. But we only knew what two of the purchased items were—those belonging to Jacques and Nigella.

The alleged knife and locket were my best leads. "Do you know what happened to the knife he purchased?"

"Knife?"

My excitement waned, but I forged on. "I was told he purchased a hunting knife from an elderly man two days before his death."

Her eyes narrowed. She licked her lips, considering her answer. "What man? Why is this the first I'm hearing about this?"

Why indeed? "I cannot say if the tale is true, but your brother told someone that he met an old man in the mountain pass. The man asked your brother's name, and sold him a knife. I believe it may be connected to your brother's death."

Her eyes darted aside before quickly returning to mine. Almost like she was hiding something, but what? "Did Drucida tell you this? I know she likes to keep secrets, but I should have been told anything that might concern my brother's death."

"I agree." I stayed calm, because she most certainly wasn't. "But the knife? Do you know of it?"

She took a deep breath, letting it out with a loud huff, then seemed to consider my words. After a moment, she frowned and shook her head. "No, I don't remember seeing any knife, and I don't know why he wouldn't show it to me and tell me his tale himself."

I had already been thinking the same thing. It seemed like Ophelia and her brother had been fairly close. Why would he tell his tale to Teresa, and not his sister? "Do you still have his belongings?"

She nodded. "There weren't many. Most of us don't have much, but I can show you what I have."

"That would be helpful." Although if there was no knife, I wasn't sure what else I might hope to find. "Can we go now?" My stomach was begging for a hot meal, but it could wait.

She seemed hesitant, but nodded. "Elanore will understand if I'm late."

"A little more forgiving than Illya?"

She laughed, seeming to relax a bit. "Oh light, yes. I see she has managed to give you an accurate impression of herself in the short time you've been here."

I grinned. "I was hoping I was mistaken."

She stood. "No. She's even worse than she seems. My lodgings are not far. I can take you there now, but we should hurry. I don't want to be *too* late."

During our short walk, I learned that Ophelia could create weak illusions with her magic, she could heal minor wounds, and that was about it. But even that seemed impressive to me.

Her cottage was similar to mine, but cleaner, larger, and filled with furniture and a few trinkets. She knelt on a faded rug to pull a small wooden crate from beneath her bed. "This is all that I kept." She looked down at the box, tucking a stray lock of hair behind her ear. "I haven't had the heart to look at any of it again." Her voice thickened with unshed tears. She quickly stood and stepped away, avoiding my gaze. "You can go through it. I'm going to make some tea."

I nodded my thanks and asked no further questions. If she didn't want me to see her cry, it was fine by me. I sat on the floor, giving her my back as she filled her kettle from a large pitcher.

I pulled the crate toward me. Nothing jumped out immediately, so I started taking the items out one by one. A comb, a few quills, neatly folded handkerchiefs . . .

The items piled up, but no sign of a knife. At the bottom of the crate I found a bound stack of letters. I lifted them from the crate, but was reluctant to undo the twine with Ophelia in the room.

I held the letters up and glanced back over my shoulder. "Are any of these recent?"

She had been sprinkling herbs into her kettle. She stopped mid-motion, eyes wide like I had caught her in the middle of a criminal act. "No. Those were letters that our adoptive parents wrote to each other when they were young. I was honestly surprised he kept them."

"Adoptive?" It really wasn't my business, but many of the witches were related. Maybe those targeted were of the same family line.

Her brow creased. "Yes. We were abandoned as babies. We were lucky to have survived."

"Did they live apart? Your adoptive parents?"

She nodded, turning back to her task. "My mother was a witch. My father wasn't. They met when my mother traveled through my father's village. Her family traveled with a small caravan, always on the road. She would send my father letters whenever she could, but his return letters for her would pile up all year long until her family would return in the winter. They communicated that way for years, until they finally ran away together. My mother couldn't have children, so when a distant friend showed up with two babies, she jumped at the chance to raise us."

"What happened to them?"

"Dead. It was a few years ago. Drucida found us, brought us here."

I knew it was none of my business, but I had never figured out the details of my parents death. If they were killed because my mother was a witch . . . "Who killed your parents?"

She had finished with the tea, but she still wasn't looking at me. "Not the Helius Order, if that's what you're worried about. But they are not the only ones who hate witches."

The words were on the tip of my tongue—the details of my parents' death. But I didn't actually know Ophelia. I didn't know if I could trust her. And so I turned away, looking once more through the contents of the crate before replacing everything how I'd found it.

I stood. "I don't see anything here that will help me, but my search has just begun. I *will* find the killer."

She finally looked at me. "How can you be sure?"

"Because I always do."

She stared at me for a moment like she could see my very soul, then nodded. "In that case, I can be a little later. Let's sit and have some tea."

I wasn't about to refuse. Though I needed to solve a murder, I also needed allies. Ophelia already had someone teaching her magic, Elanore. I didn't care whose student I became, as long as I was able to learn.

I LEFT Ophelia's home with a promise to see her before suppertime. She had agreed to arrange a meeting with Elanore, a full-fledged, powerful witch. Things were looking up.

Tholdri found me on the path leading toward our cottage. He was always slow to wake, but no longer appeared groggy, so I knew he had been up for a while. He rubbed his stomach through his blue linen shirt. "Where have you been? I'm starving."

"I've been doing *our* job. No one is stopping you from finding food."

He frowned. "None of the witches will talk to me."

I laughed. Tholdri could charm the gills off a fish. It was a rare occurrence when *no one* would talk to him. "I know where the dining hall is, but we'll be late. Perhaps there will still be some leftover scraps for us." I debated telling him about the pastries Ophelia had shared with me, but decided against it. He was cranky enough as it was.

Following the route Ophelia had detailed, we made our way toward the dining hall. I told him everything I had learned, which wasn't much. Without Jacques' knife nor Nigella's locket, our only clues were the victims' corpses. When I met with Elanore, I'd ask her if she knew of any rituals involving skins. There had to be a reason the killer had taken such great care in claiming them. Ophelia had heard of no such rituals, but she admitted herself that she knew very little in comparison to Elanore.

We reached the dining hall, its stone foundation taller than either of us. The white wash on the boards leading up to the thatched roof was more faded than most we had seen. Probably because it would take two ladders strung together to reach the top. The scents of baking bread and roasted meat had mostly dissipated. We might have missed our only opportunity for a meal before supper.

"It's worth a try." I approached one side of the double doors, turning the handle and pushing inward.

The space inside was so dark and quiet, the occasional clank of pots in a washbasin seemed louder than it should. Tholdri and I walked past deserted tables, each already wiped clean, following the sound of someone washing dishes in another room.

I knocked on an interior door. Receiving no reply, I entered.

A young man with dark eyes, a wide mouth, and jet black hair spun toward us, eyes wide. He held a wooden spoon in one hand, dripping soap and water down his arm. The hem of his white shirt was damp from leaning against the basin. He assessed us for a brief moment. "Um, who are you?"

I walked further into the small space. Ceramic dishes and iron pots lined several tall shelves. The washbasin in front of the boy was massive. Dirty dishes were piled high on the counter to his left, while clean ones dried on several wooden racks to his right.

"Surely you've heard of the red-haired hunter?" I crossed my arms, then leaned against the nearest countertop.

He took a step away, spoon still lifted as he glanced between me and Tholdri. "I've heard whispers. Nothing definitive."

Curious, since Ophelia had known exactly who I was. "Well now you have living proof. Living proof in need of a meal. There wouldn't happen to be any food left over from this morning?"

If he hadn't already proven otherwise, I would have guessed he didn't understand a single word I had said.

Tholdri fiddled with an ancient kettle at the top of a shelf. "I think you frighten the boy, Lyss. His words have escaped him."

The boy blinked a few times, lowered his spoon, then shook his head. "It's not that. It's just your energy. It's strange."

I furrowed my brow. "Strange *how*? What do you mean?"

His already flushed cheeks grew redder. "My apologies, I guess you don't know. Everyone has their own type of energy gathered around them. I can see that energy. Most of the time it's just light or gentle color. But yours . . . it's like you have two. I've never seen anything like it."

Tholdri gave me a knowing look. I had heard of energy readers before. Some thought they could see the color of people's souls. I thought it was more simple than that. I could sense when someone was good or evil. Noble, or a bit shifty. It made sense to me that some people might be able to sense such things in different ways, namely through sight.

"What color is his?" I nodded toward Tholdri.

The boy looked at him, narrowing his eyes for a moment. "A soft gentle pink, like a sunset."

Tholdri frowned and I laughed. "It makes sense. He's quite a softie. What's your name?"

The boy didn't quite seem to comprehend why Tholdri looking like a gentle sunset was amusing. "Ian. And my apologies again, but I really haven't heard much about you, including your names. The witches, they keep their secrets from the rest of us."

"So you're not a witch?" I asked.

His shoulders hunched. "No. I never even knew witches existed until Drucida found me. No one in my village understood my gift. They thought I was strange. She brought me here where people would understand, but I don't have any other magic. I'm not like them either."

So not only had Drucida found Jacques and Ophelia, she had found Ian too. "Does Drucida make a habit of scouring the countryside for witches and other . . . oddities? No offense. I'm just not sure what to call you."

"Oddity is fitting," he laughed, relaxing further. "And yes. She believes we are stronger together."

She wasn't wrong. It was exactly the belief of the Helius Order. I extended my hand toward him. "Well, Ian. It's nice to meet you. It would be even nicer if you could find us some food and sit with us for a nice chat."

Even if he wasn't a witch, he might know something. Like Ophelia, he seemed more friendly toward us than most others. And I still had several hours before my meeting with Elanore.

He didn't seem to know what to do with my extended hand. After what seemed like great debate, he gave me an apologetic wince. "Apologies, again. But touch... it makes me see more than I would like."

"No apologies necessary." I glanced at Tholdri, knowing he was thinking exactly what I was thinking. If Ian could see more than just colors around people, he could prove invaluable in rooting out the killer. I smiled at Ian. "Something tells me we will become great friends."

Maybe his skills wouldn't be of use, but even so, if I could learn more about Drucida, the fortress, and magic —along with getting a meal, there was no way I could ignore the opportunity.

CHAPTER SIX

We were on our way to meet Elanore when my sword awoke for the first time since we'd arrived at the witches' fortress. It wasn't exactly a warning, but it was close. Someone was watching us.

I slowed, ignoring Tholdri as he looked a question at me. It was difficult to tell just who my sword was worried about when everyone we passed either openly stared, or pretended not to stare.

"Why are you suddenly on guard?" Tholdri muttered through clenched teeth.

I nodded subtly toward my sword hilt as I veered away from the street toward a small shade tree. "We are early yet. Let's take a rest."

We weren't early, but Tholdri followed me without question.

As soon as we stepped into the shade, I missed the warm sun on my face. It made sense for the witches to choose such an inhospitable environment—no one in their right mind would travel across these mountains—but they could have at least chosen somewhere warmer. Most of the Ebon Province was now only at the peak of the growing season. Here, it was more like late autumn.

I watched a few people milling about the cobblestone street, waiting for another warning from my sword.

The warning came a moment later in the form of a light shiver up my spine.

I scanned the street again, my gaze catching on Teresa as she spotted us, then turned to hurry in our direction.

Though she still shuffled awkwardly in her billowing blue robe, the fear was gone from her eyes, and she smiled as she reached us. "There you are. Illya sent me to find you. I've been looking *everywhere*."

She blushed as her gaze lingered a little too long on Tholdri, and I realized where her fear had gone. An evening spent cleaning with a handsome, charming hunter could work wonders.

"What does Illya want?" I asked.

My question seemed to startle her. Tholdri's charm could work wonders, but it could also cause problems. It was the latter more often than not.

Blushing furiously, she smoothed her hands over her short hair, attempting to compose herself. "She wants to know how far you have come in your investigation."

"We answer to Drucida, not Illya."

Her shoulders hunched with my words. She wrung her hands. "I apologize."

I inhaled deeply. Wouldn't do to ruin all of Tholdri's

good work with my demeanor. "Don't apologize. It's not your fault. But we are already late for a different meeting. Illya will have to wait."

Teresa gnawed her lip, looking at us both pleadingly.

I sighed. "You're going to be in trouble if we don't come, aren't you?"

She sucked her bottom lip so far into her mouth that it disappeared, then gave us the barest of nods.

Tholdri gave me an equally puppy dog-like expression.

"Oh not you too," I groaned.

"We can't have her getting in trouble. Illya is awful."

I agreed with him. Teresa had been dealt a cruel hand with Illya, but I really wanted my meeting with Elanore. At least my sword had stopped warning me. Whatever the threat was, had passed.

"Fi-ine." I extended the word dramatically. I looked at Teresa. "Take us to your mistress. Hopefully Elanore will give us another chance."

I glanced up at the sun as Teresa led us away. Just a few hours until dark, and we were no closer to finding the killer. Just as we were no closer to finding any powerful witch allies who might help me with Cael. All we had were a couple of witch apprentices, and a boy who could see energies.

At least it was more than we had started with.

Teresa led us to the building we had visited the previous day, where I had met with Illya and Drucida. I wondered where Drucida was in all of this—if she knew about this meeting, or if Illya had gone behind her back.

Teresa reached the door first. She had already gripped the handle when I smelled the blood.

"Wait." I moved more quickly than any human should, and it showed by Teresa's wide eyes as I gripped her wrist. I looked at Tholdri. "Blood."

He unsheathed his sword, for what good it would do. I was pretty sure the threat was already gone. It was deathly quiet on the other side of the door.

I finally released Teresa's wrist. "Find Drucida. Bring her here."

"But—"

I gave her a look I usually reserved for my enemies, but it was for her own good. I didn't want her seeing whatever was on the other side of the door. There was too much blood for it to be a minor wound. "*Go.*"

She tucked her chin, shielding her face with her hair, then she ran.

I drew my sword, nodded at Tholdri, then opened the door. We had gained the attention of a few passersby, but I had no time for them. I did a quick scan of the room, then stepped inside.

I found Illya sprawled across one of her tapestries. She had pulled it down when she fell, probably right after someone disemboweled her, judging by the blood spray.

At least she still had her skin.

Finished checking the rest of the space, Tholdri came to stand at my shoulder. "Always fun when we have two different murderers."

I sighed, then sheathed my sword. He was probably right. Our primary killer had taken the skins of seven victims. I didn't see why he—or *it*—would stop at Illya. One of the other victims had been around her age, so that wasn't a factor.

Hurried footsteps sounded outside, then Drucida ran into the room. She halted as she saw Illya, then held trembling fingers to her lips. "Oh, *light*."

The gentle swaying of her long curls warned me just before she fainted. I managed to catch her, lowering her gently to the ground. Hushed whispers drew my attention next. Drucida had left the door open, and several people were peering inside, including Teresa.

So much for sparing her the visual.

"Shut the door." I said to Tholdri.

He stepped around me, not speaking to anyone before shutting the door in their faces.

I left Drucida where she lay, returning to more thoroughly observe Illya. The death was fresh—too fresh. We had only just missed the killer, but I didn't see any clues hinting to where they had gone. The door hadn't been locked. The killer could have just hidden their knife and walked away.

Finished observing the wound, I straightened. "We need to question everyone outside. Maybe they saw someone leaving."

Tholdri sheathed his sword. "I'll go. You have a sniff around and see if you can notice anything else."

"I'm not as good as a vampire."

"No, but you're all we've got." He walked past Drucida toward the door, then slipped outside.

I paced around the room, immediately regretting letting Tholdri go instead of me. If the killer was still out there, I might smell Illya's blood on them. The wound was violent. It would have been difficult to avoid the spray.

I inhaled deeply, looking for clues, but all I could smell was Illya's blood. Her tapestries haunted my every step. If only I hadn't argued with Teresa. We might have made it in time.

Did the killer know we were coming? Was that why they risked killing Illya in broad daylight?

I stopped in front of one of the tapestries. A quaint cottage stood in the center of a meadow with blue mountains in the background. I looked a little closer at a figure standing in front of the cottage. The detail in the tapestry was incredible. I had never seen anything like it. I stared at the red haired figure unblinking. She had my face. *Lavandriel.*

But she had lived in another century. There was no way Illya could have known her.

I started looking at the other tapestries. They were remarkably detailed, but none stood out like the cottage scene.

I caught a whiff of blood on the other side of the room from where Illya had been killed. The scent was strongest near a tapestry of a deer bleeding out in a forest. A shadowy hunter held his bow, standing over the animal. I lifted the tapestry, somehow already knowing what I would find.

A hunting knife pierced the wall. Whoever had stabbed it into place had been incredibly strong to drive it so deeply, unless they had used a mallet. The blade dripped with Illya's blood.

I was careful not to touch the knife as I observed it. I wasn't good enough to track such a subtle scent, but Asher might be able to, if Drucida would allow him within the fortress.

I gently draped the tapestry over the knife, then walked back toward Drucida. She was still out, but her eyes were shifting beneath their lids. Maybe now she would answer more of my questions. Someone had come for the witches. Maybe two someones.

And no one was safe.

I DIDN'T MISS my meeting with Elanore after all, but if I thought I was getting any of my questions answered, I was a fool. Once Tholdri's pursuits had proven fruitless, Drucida summoned Elanore and one other witch, Charles. His presence answered at least one burning question of mine. Some powerful witches were male.

Charles was around forty, with the pure white hair of a man much older. A heavy mustache hid his upper lip, the edges growing into a neatly trimmed beard. He'd parted his hair deep to one side, swooping the bulk of it artfully across his forehead. Despite the detailed attention paid to his grooming, his clothes were plain. A close fitting dark gray coat fell almost to his knees, his legs clad in muted blue breeches. His body was slender, but fit.

Elanore was the youngest of the trio. Hazel eyes,

smooth tanned skin, and russet curls. She looked almost like she might be related to Ophelia, though I knew that wasn't the case. I wasn't sure if she had dressed up for the meeting I had abandoned, but she seemed somewhat uncomfortable in her green silk gown and matching velvet overcoat.

Or maybe she was just bothered by the corpse in the room.

We had left Illya where she lay while we debated the most pressing topic. Would an ancient vampire be allowed into the witches' fortress? We had been sitting around the small table for over an hour, and no decision had been made.

"It's absolutely out of the question." Charles' stiff posture and grim mouth made it clear he was not accustomed to being argued with.

Elanore sat straight for just a moment, then quickly wilted. "Illya was alone for mere minutes. Whatever killed her . . . " She took a shaky breath. "We have no idea what we're dealing with. If a vampire can help us find it, I say we let him in."

Charles picked imaginary lint from his sleeve. He didn't seem overly concerned with Illya's corpse staring blankly at the ceiling. "Why do you assume the killer is an *it*? She was killed with a hunting knife." His eyes rolled toward the tapestry still covering the murder weapon.

I had shown it to them. I might have threatened to break Charles' arm if he touched it. Things had not gone smoothly after that.

Elanore looked at me pleadingly. "You know about

these things. Don't you think it's something more than human?"

I wished Tholdri was part of the conversation—his patience lasted longer than mine—but he was outside guarding the door. "Not necessarily. The killer would have had to move quickly, and it would have been difficult for them to avoid being spotted, but even humans get lucky."

She deflated further with my words. She wasn't exactly what I'd expected from Ophelia's description, but I supposed her level of confidence wasn't important. I didn't need her confidence. I needed her teaching.

Because I doubted I'd be getting it from Drucida. She had been staring at me like I was the one who had killed Illya ever since I suggested bringing Asher into the fortress. She suspected ulterior motives, and she was right. I wanted the murders solved, because Eiric wouldn't wait forever. How many had died while I floundered in my task of learning magic?

"Even the hunter admits the killer is likely human." Charles extended his well-manicured hand in my direction. "Which means it is one of our own."

"You believe someone within the fortress, someone most of us have known for years, casually decided to not only kill their friends, but skin them?" Elanore looked like she might be ill at the thought.

"Not all of us consider everyone a *friend*," Charles said pointedly. "You're living in a fairy story if you believe otherwise."

Drucida scooted out her chair and stood. "Whether the killer is one of us or a stranger is not relevant. The question is whether we let a vampire in to hunt them. While it goes against my every instinct, I am inclined to allow it."

Finally, something said in the long discussion surprised me. "You are?"

She pursed her lips, studying me. "I saw you coming for a reason. I would be a fool to hinder you."

Funny, because it felt like she tried to hinder me plenty.

Charles stood abruptly, mirroring Drucida. "This is ridiculous. The vampire will kill us all."

She pressed her palms against the table, leaning toward him. "We are already being killed, Charles."

A loud huff of air bristled his mustache, but he didn't seem to have anything to say to that.

"I would appreciate your support, Charles."

I sat up a little straighter. I had been wondering why the *high witch* was bothering with asking permission in the first place. Perhaps her power was not absolute.

Charles gave Elanore a venomous look. "I suppose *you* will support anything she says?" He nodded toward Drucida.

Elanore gave him an apologetic shrug.

He swiped a palm over his face and shook his head. "You are both fools, but I will support you, if only to maintain this weak façade of unity." He stepped away from the table, then looked down at me. "You had better be worth our trust." He turned and walked toward the door, never once glancing at Illya's corpse.

Eleanore jumped as the door slammed behind him.

"Façade of unity?" I asked.

Drucida shook her head minutely, staring toward the closed door. "Not your concern. I will alert the sentries. At full dark, you may bring your vampire within our fortress." She finally looked at me. "Don't make me regret this."

I stood. With how she was looking at me, I was surprised my sword issued no warning. She clearly did not have the warmest feelings toward me, even though she was giving me what I wanted. "I have one last question."

She seemed to suffer a brief internal debate, then nodded for me to continue.

"Illya's tapestries. Do they depict things she saw?"

"In a way."

"But Lavandriel lived countless centuries ago, perhaps more than a thousand years." I pointed at the tapestry with the cottage scene. The dwelling was primitive, nothing like the homes within the fortress.

Drucida rubbed her furrowed brow. "I didn't say she saw them with her *eyes*. Now leave us. Elanore and I have much to discuss."

I wanted to press for more information, but I knew I wouldn't get anywhere, and I didn't want her to go back on allowing Asher into the fortress. And yet . . . something about the tapestries bothered me. There was something important about them, I just wasn't sure what.

I eyed the scene still hiding the knife as I walked toward the door. Though I could not see his face, the shadowy hunter seemed to watch my every step. The deer just looked dead. Like Illya.

CHAPTER SEVEN

We spent the rest of the day questioning witches about Illya's death. Trying to question witches, at least. Even fewer now would speak with us. Their distrust of outsiders was strong. Their distrust of hunters, even stronger. We didn't run into Teresa again, and I wondered where she had gone.

The heaviness of dusk pressed down on my shoulders as we neared the gates. Darkness always meant danger, but now, if Asher wasn't shielding, it also meant freedom. I could always feel it when he woke. I had thought myself the one in the cage, but I wasn't trapped when the sun was out. I had been servant to a vampire for only years. He had been trapped by the sun for centuries. Feeling his emotions had given me some perspective, to say the least.

"You know, I won't be sleeping on the floor just because Asher is now allowed inside the walls." Tholdri's words drew me out of my thoughts. He strode confidently, golden hair flowing in the cool breeze.

I scowled. "He will be leaving the fortress before the sun rises. I won't have him vulnerable when so many of the witches hate us. They could harm him to get to me."

"And what about Cael?"

"I don't know."

Darkness slowly crept in around us. Asher had been keeping an eye on Cael, and I didn't like the idea of my great uncle being without his company, not if he was starting to lose himself. But if there was any trace of lingering scent on the murder weapon, I needed Asher to track it.

"Do you really think it's wise to leave him out there alone?"

I had told Tholdri Asher's worries. He knew the danger of what Cael could become. He had seen it himself. "I don't know."

"What *do* you know?"

We neared the gates. I would make a judgment on Cael once I saw him. "I know that I already have enough on my mind without your pointless questions."

"Maybe if you were more forthcoming with your thoughts, I wouldn't have to ask my *pointless questions*. We are supposed to be a team, Lyss."

I stopped walking and turned toward him. I was still irritated, but— "You're right. I apologize. I just don't know what to say." My mask of apathy crumbled. "I'm worried, Tholdri."

His brow lowered. "You really think he is that close to losing himself?"

"Asher wouldn't have said anything if it wasn't a very real possibility, but I will make that judgment once I see him."

"And if you think he will become a danger?"

I didn't want to consider it. He was already a monster in many ways, but he was also the only family I had left—and our greatest weapon against Eiric. My grandfather had trusted him to protect me. He had bade me to find him, and to keep him close. "If the situation seems dire, I will ask Elanore for help. Cael was a witch, once. Maybe she can aid him in collecting the remnants of his former self."

"And if she can't help, or if she won't help?"

I turned away. "Don't ask questions you don't want the answers to." I started walking before he could press me further.

He caught up, wisely asking me no more questions.

We waited in silence as the gates were opened for us, then we stepped out into the night.

I held my cloak tight against a sudden gust of icy wind, then started walking. We would return to where I had met Asher the previous evening. I already knew he would be waiting. I could feel his anticipation like a warm stone in the pit of my stomach. Or maybe it was *my* anticipation.

Probably both.

I hated how much I wanted to see him. It was a weakness I could ill afford, and one I was still somewhat conflicted over.

Tholdri stuck close to my side, his attention on

potential threats. But I didn't sense anything, nor did my sword. The only threat was the icy wind chilling our bones. I wondered if the killer was hiding somewhere, sheltering from the wind, or if they were still inside the fortress.

I stepped wrong on a patch of loose gravel and skidded sideways. Tholdri gripped my arm, keeping me from falling.

I took a moment to calm my racing heart. "This mountain is a death trap."

Tholdri smiled, still gripping my arm. "I know. I've seen the corpses."

"Hah *hah*." I rolled my eyes and kept walking.

We found Asher and Cael waiting, just where I knew they'd be. Cael seemed his normal self, not worried, but was it all a lie?

I searched his handsome face as we neared enough for me to see his features. His jaw was relaxed, his crimson hair well kept. No hint of the withered creature that was his other form. No trace of the ghouls he could summon to do his bidding.

It was a good act, but one thing had shifted. Had it been there all along, with Asher's warning finally prompting me to notice it? That look in his pale eyes . . .

He looked at me like I was his salvation.

And I didn't like it one bit.

I schooled my expression into apathetic lines, addressing first him, then Asher. I told them both what had happened.

"Asher is now allowed within the fortress," I

finished. "But just for tonight. I need him to trace the scent on a murder weapon." I shrugged apologetically at Cael. "It was the best I could do. I fear if they learn what you truly are, my chances of gaining their trust will severely dwindle."

Was that pain in his expression? Whatever it was, it quickly disappeared. He bowed his head. "Of course. Anything to speed your progress with them. I will stay out here. Perhaps I will find signs of these mysterious strangers selling trinkets."

While he could probably scare them to death without lifting a finger, I didn't like the thought of him facing an unknown threat alone, and Asher was giving me a look that said, *Don't be a fool.*

Had Cael gotten worse since the previous night? I wished there was some way for me to ask, but we needed to get back to the murder weapon before the scent could dissipate.

Asher eyed me intently.

Oh light, it was worse. Asher's silent communication told me that Cael was close to slipping.

"On second thought, maybe you should come."

All three men looked at me like I'd suddenly started speaking gibberish.

"They already agreed to let one vampire in." I looked between the two of them, settling on Cael. "No offense, but in your current form, you're actually less imposing than Asher."

Cael seemed perplexed. "But my necromancy, they will sense it."

An idea was blossoming in my mind. I had

convinced Drucida that a vampire was useful. Why not a necromancer? The claiming of skins and organs *did* seem like a death ritual.

Tholdri looked at me like he could read my thoughts. "They'll never go for it."

"We can at least try. If they turn us away, then so be it."

He knew what was at stake. I knew the witches hated necromancers. They might even think Cael himself was the culprit. But Drucida knew we had only just arrived. And . . . he was Blackmire, just like me. As twisted as he had become, she could not deny that he had a right to be there, as did I.

Perhaps it was time to stop taking no for an answer.

"It's settled, then," I said when no one argued with me. "We'll return to the gates, see if we can't all get inside."

Cael still seemed confused, and a little wary. Did he suspect that I was worried about him? Did it matter?

I decided it didn't. I was in charge here. It was time to start acting like it.

DRUCIDA HERSELF WAS SUMMONED when we tried to enter the fortress. She met us outside. She wore no coat over her gown, though now I understood it wasn't necessary. Not if she could withstand the ice box she had created.

She looked at each of us, careful to not directly meet

the vampires' eyes. "I have allowed you one vampire, not two."

I'd told her my theory about Cael's necromancy being helpful. She would figure out what he was sooner or later. Maybe it would pay off to be truthful from the start.

"Drucida—" he began.

She lifted her hand to cut him off. "No, Cael. Cedrik, I understood. But how could you—" She looked him up and down, quickly giving up on finding the right words. "How could you do this to yourself?"

I realized then that they knew each other. I should have assumed as much from the start. She'd known my grandfather, after all, and he and Cael were twins. Perhaps Cael had *other* reasons for not wanting to return to the fortress.

To his credit, he did not cower under the pressure of her judgement. In fact, he stood a little straighter. "What would you have done if your loved ones were leading the fight against the vampires? Eiric has inspired a war. He is killing off the ancients."

"Yes," she snapped. "Lyssandra has told me these claims. That Eiric spoke into the minds of the young ones, inspiring rebellion. But it is no business of ours. We are different. Separate. You and Cedrik should have stayed with us. This girl," she gestured toward me, "could have had a far different life. Now she is shackled to a vampire."

Maybe she was right. Or maybe if my mother hadn't married a hunter, I never would have existed at all.

Either way, she was arguing ancient history. I was more worried about the present.

I stepped between her and Cael. I towered over her, but I knew better now than to use my height in an attempt to intimidate her.

She glared at me.

"Look," I said, mustering every bit of patience I had, which wasn't much. "We can stand here arguing all night while the murderer's scent fades, or you can let us help you. Honestly, I have never met someone so willing to cut off their own nose to spite their face. *We are here to help*. We will find your killers and clear up this whole problem for you."

Her eyes narrowed. "You don't care about helping us, Lyssandra. You just want us to help *you*."

I loomed over her. Maybe she wasn't intimidated, but the height was a good tool. It was a pity to waste it. "Whether you like it or not, magic is my birthright. You took in Ophelia, and even Ian, but you would turn up your nose at me? All because of the decisions of my grandfather? Why? Why do you hate me so much? It isn't fear of vampires. You are standing in the presence of an ancient, and you don't seem in the least bit frightened."

She blinked at me a few times, her mouth opening and closing.

I had a feeling I had somehow hit upon the truth of the matter. "It's my grandfather, isn't it?"

She recovered quickly, lightly shaking herself, then settling her skirts. "You didn't tell her?" she asked Cael without looking at him.

"I did not think it my story to tell," he answered.

It was difficult to be sure in the night, but I thought she might be blushing. "Fine. You can all come in. Just for tonight. But I want the killer's head by morning." She looked at Cael. "Tell no one what you are. If any learn I let a necromancer within our gates—" She shook her head. "Just keep quiet."

He nodded. "Very well."

I wondered if she would still speak to him in such a manner if she knew exactly what he could become. She had known him, and it made her bold, but she had no idea what she was actually dealing with.

When no one else spoke, Drucida turned around and marched through the open gates.

I stared after her, then looked at Cael. "They were lovers, weren't they?"

"Not my story to tell," he whispered, then walked after Drucida.

I couldn't help my smirk as the rest of us followed. I had wanted to learn more of my family history, and here it was playing out right before my eyes.

Asher walked close, seeming at ease, though I knew his keen eyes saw everything. Just as I knew that he was pleased about me wanting him within the witches' fortress, even if it was just to sniff out a murderer. His pleasure bubbled in my chest. I might not be groping him in front of everyone, but I was willing to display our bond, at the very least. He had probably thought he would never see the day.

I knew I most certainly hadn't.

It was early enough in the night that several witches

were out, the glowing street lanterns making them look ghostly in their flowing robes and heavy cloaks. They stared more openly than before, unable to help themselves now that two more strangers had entered their remote village.

"I'm surprised there are so many without magic," Asher said lowly.

"You can tell?"

"One gains a sense of such things over time."

I considered his words. "And can you sense *my* magic?"

He frowned. "I'm not sure. You have always felt . . . *different*, but I assumed it was your hunter blood. The innate resistance to vampire wiles feels like a sort of magic."

I lifted a brow. "Vampire wiles?"

He flashed me a quick, secretive smile that made my toes curl. "Yes, vampire wiles, many of which you are yet to experience."

Blushing, I turned my attention forward as we continued walking.

Cael seemed a little stiff, like moving through the fortress physically pained him, and I was reminded of his need for blood. I hoped I hadn't just made a horrible decision bringing him amongst so many humans.

We reached the site of Illya's murder. Drucida stood outside the door, arms crossed. Two men I did not recognize stood with her, huddled in heavy coats. I wondered what made them *special* enough for her to trust them with guard duty.

Wordlessly, she opened the door and stepped inside.

Illya had been moved to the ice chamber. There shouldn't be much blood to tempt Cael, but—

I turned toward him. "Will the blood bother you?"

He winced. I could tell he wanted to say no, but finally, he relented. "It might."

Mistake. I had made a mistake bringing him here. I had gotten used to his façade, forgetting he was dangerous.

Tholdri stepped up beside Cael. "I've seen the knife. Cael and I can wait out here."

The tension between the four of us dissipated. *Tholdri. Pain in the neck, and wonderful best friend.*

I looked at Asher and nodded toward the door. "Let's go."

Together, we walked after Drucida, ignoring the fear wafting off the two guards. They clearly knew what Asher was, though he often passed for human. I wondered how many others Drucida had told. Or perhaps it had been Charles.

The two men started whispering once the door shut behind us, not realizing we could hear them. At least they let me know it had indeed been Charles to share the news, and not happily.

A lone lantern glowed on the table where we'd sat discussing Asher, not long ago. The wood stove was dark. The heat of the previous day was a distant dream.

Asher inhaled deeply, probably smelling the blood even though most of it had been cleaned.

Drucida stood near the tapestry of the hunter and his kill. She pulled the tapestry aside, then looked at us expectantly.

Asher approached the weapon lodged in the wood, eyeing it from a few different angles. He inhaled deeply again, but he was shielding. I had no clue what he was thinking.

"Well?" Drucida asked. She sounded tough, unafraid, but the effect was somewhat dulled by her avoiding Asher's gaze.

He stepped away to stand beside me. "There are two scents. One is strong within this chamber." He glanced around at the tapestries.

"Illya," I explained. "She made them."

"Remarkable."

"Can you track the other scent?"

"It is also strong within this room. Only slightly fainter than Illya's."

I lifted a brow. "Does that mean the other person spent a good deal of time here?"

He nodded. "Yes, recently."

"*Excuse me?*" Drucida gasped. "What do you mean?"

Asher tilted his head, surprised by her surprise, maybe. "Illya's killer knew her well. They spent much time together. In this room."

"Are you sure?" Her voice came out a harsh whisper.

Asher shrugged. "Unless someone else touched the knife. It is a faint scent. It would be difficult for me to remember if I didn't have a more saturated example of it within this room."

Drucida swallowed loud enough for me to hear. "Few people willingly spent time with Illya. I will bring them here, tonight. If you could wait, I would have you identify the culprit."

She looked positively ashen. I couldn't blame her for being shocked. These people were her friends and close allies, and one of them had murdered Illya in cold blood.

I would be interested to find out who.

And more importantly, *why*.

CHAPTER EIGHT

It was a pleasure seeing Charles with his hair mussed and face puffy, thick coat covering his silken night garments. He had refused to sit in the presence of a vampire, so instead he stood with his back against the wall, pinning one of Illya's tapestries with his shoulders.

I wasn't sure what good he thought the distance would do. Asher could still rip his throat out before he could blink.

Elanore was the same as before, still in her lovely but less than comfortable gown and velvet coat. She had her arm around Teresa, the young girl trembling despite her fur-lined cloak. There were two other young women I didn't know, one willowy with deep brown skin, and one short, stout, and blonde. They wore the blue robes of apprentices beneath their coats. Illya's other unfortunates.

Asher stood at my shoulder as Drucida explained the situation to everyone. The three young girls' eyes bulged upon learning that Asher was a vampire. Teresa stared openly, both terrified, and maybe a little bit captivated.

I observed each of them, wondering who had it in them to commit murder.

Finished with her explanation, Drucida turned away from all the worried faces to look at Asher. "Before you are all the people who have spent time in this room recently. Illya's three apprentices, Eleanor, Charles, and myself. Do you recognize the killer's scent?"

Asher didn't move.

"You all sort of mingle together when you stand so close," I explained. "He will need to approach each of you individually."

Elanore blinked at me. "You can smell us too?"

I wrinkled my nose. I could often recognize scents, especially of those close to me, but they took time for me to learn. "Not as well as a vampire." I held out a hand toward Teresa. I didn't want to suspect her, but she had been the last one to see Illya alive. "You first."

She hesitated, glancing at Drucida, who nodded.

Eyes on her feet, Teresa approached. She trembled as she reached us. She was young and inexperienced. As interested as she might be, she had never actually seen a vampire before. It was like seeing a wolf in the wild. You wanted to look, but mostly you just didn't want it to eat you.

Likely sensing her fear, Asher knelt before her, careful to not make any sudden movements. He held out one slender hand.

Still not looking at him, Teresa placed her hand in his. His long fingers made her hand seem tiny.

Asher made no other movements. I couldn't hear him breathe. But I knew so close, he could easily tell her scent from the others. He released her hand and stood. "Not her."

My shoulders relaxed. No normal person would have suspected Teresa, but, well . . . I had been fooled before. I was glad to have my initial instinct proven correct.

Asher held out a hand to the next girl, the blonde.

Elanore gave her a little nudge, then she approached just as Teresa had, eyes downcast.

Asher cleared her name quickly, and the final girl after her. He had already stated that the scent did not belong to Drucida, so it was either Elanore or Charles. And he already knew which. Men smelled different from women. Since he had taken time to rule out each woman, I already knew who it would be.

Eyes wide, Elanore approached, and I found myself wishing the killer was Charles. Though I didn't know her well, I liked Elanore, and Ophelia liked her too. I didn't want her to be the killer.

She reached Asher, then looked down at his waiting hand before turning toward me. "I touched the knife!" she blurted. "But I didn't kill Illya, I swear it."

Charles stepped forward. "Explain yourself."

Her expression crumbled. Tears welled in her eyes. "The knife belonged to my apprentice's brother. She thought it was the reason he was killed. I asked her to keep it quiet while I looked into his death."

Asher had moved between me and Elanore, like he expected she might attack me.

Irritated, I stepped around him. "You mean Jacques?" I pointed toward the knife behind the tapestry. "Is that the knife he bought from a stranger two days before he was killed?"

"It is," she admitted, seeming surprised that I knew. "Amelia, one of the earlier victims, had told Lorena," she gestured toward the blonde apprentice huddling with the other two, "a story about meeting a stranger, and buying a locket. Lorena was too frightened to tell Illya, so she came to me instead. Jacques had told his sister a similar story, but with a knife. When Ophelia found the knife in her brother's belongings, she brought it to me."

"And why didn't you tell anyone?" Drucida demanded. "Both of these stories could have helped us."

Elanore looked like she might collapse. She turned her pleading eyes toward me. "I suspected the killer was one of us. It could be anyone. What if I told someone about the knife, and ended up losing my own skin over it? I asked both the girls to keep quiet for the same reason."

It all made sense, except one thing. I held up my hand before Drucida or Charles could ask more questions. "If you came upon this knife as you say, and kept it entirely hidden, then how did someone else find it? If you really didn't kill Illya, then you must know who else had access to the knife."

She shook her head over and over again. "That's just it. It was hidden in a warded chest. No one else knew about it, other than Ophelia. When I saw the knife in the wall, I was so shocked, I didn't know what to do."

I glanced at Asher, who nodded slightly. Few people could lie well enough to hide it from a vampire. For most people, their pulse would quicken, and they would start to sweat. She was panicked regardless, so it might be more difficult to tell, but Asher didn't think she was lying, so she most likely was not. I wished my senses were as fine as his, because then I would have known Ophelia was lying to me about Jacques' remaining possessions.

"We cannot simply take your word for it," Drucida stated, though her expression as she observed Elanore was more thoughtful than condemning. "We will need proof of your whereabouts during the time of the murder."

Elanore nodded too quickly, raking her fingers absentmindedly through her russet hair. "That's right, I wasn't alone. I was actually waiting for Lyssandra." She gestured toward me. "Ophelia was with me."

I cringed. "You mean the only other person who knew about the knife?"

Her shoulders slumped as her hand lowered from her hair. "Oh. Well yes. But that's good, isn't it? That proves neither of us took it to use on Illya."

"Or it proves both of you did," Charles muttered.

I looked at Drucida. She was already watching me, not Elanore or Charles. Understanding passed between us. In all likelihood, Elanore's story was the truth. Which meant we were no closer to finding the actual killer. There was no other scent on the knife.

It would only be a matter of time until the next body was found.

DRUCIDA PERMITTED Asher and Cael to stay within the fortress until just before dawn, when they would have to seek shelter elsewhere. Our next stop was the ice chamber. Now that Asher had proven himself useful, she actually wanted him to take a look at the bodies. I wasn't sure what he would be able to see that the rest of us could not—long frozen and without skins, the bodies had little to no scent—but we'd exhausted too many other options. The bodies, and now the knife, were all we had to go on.

I would speak with Ophelia in the morning to confirm Elanore's story, but for now, Asher's belief that she was telling the truth was good enough for me. And what was good enough for me, seemed to be good enough for Drucida. Imagine that.

No one guarded the ice chamber when we reached it. Just a simple locked door. Drucida had a lot more faith in people than I did, it seemed.

She set her lantern on the doorstep, then produced a keyring from a pouch at her belt, sorting through the keys until she found the right one. When she did, she held it up to the moonlight. "Enchanted," she said to me. "If anyone tries to open the lock by any other means," she smiled coldly, "they will sorely regret it."

I nodded at her explanation, hiding my surprise. When we visited the chamber before, she had simply unlocked it without explanation. I glanced back at Cael as she opened it.

Seeming to understand my confusion, he gave me an encouraging nod. Somehow, his presence had altered Drucida's attitude toward me. It was my instinct to question it, but I left it alone. It was a first for me.

Drucida had stepped into the ice chamber with her lantern while I hesitated. I hesitated a moment longer, not looking forward to the cold already fogging the air around us, then stepped inside.

The bodies were exactly as we'd left them. Except for Illya's.

She no longer had her skin.

DRUCIDA STAGGERED BACK against the wall, her lantern knocking against thick ice. "It's impossible." Her words fogged the air around her face.

I ignored her. I could only tell the additional corpse was Illya's based on its placement. Eight corpses, one in a new spot. It had to be hers. The height was another indication.

I paced around the small chamber, searching for any additional routes of entry, but even the shuttered windows were blocked by a thick layer of ice. None of it had been broken.

Cael and Asher looked down at the bodies while Tholdri attempted to calm Drucida.

"No," I heard her rasp. "It's simply not possible. No one could break through my enchantment."

But they had. Unless Drucida herself had skinned Illya, there was no other option.

Finished with my brief search of the room, I returned to Drucida and Tholdri. "This enchantment, what would happen if someone broke it?"

"Well first off, I would *know*," she huffed. "I would feel it. Second, whatever part of them was touching the door would be frozen solid."

"And what if someone left the room from the inside?"

She opened her mouth, then shut it, considering my words. "The enchantment only works from the outside."

Tholdri watched me closely. "What are you thinking, Lyss?"

I shrugged. "If it was impossible for someone to break in, maybe they were already in here. Who delivered Illya's body?"

"I don't know. Elanore arranged it. I can find out."

Back to Elanore. Interesting. "That would be helpful." Maybe Elanore was a better liar than I thought. I looked at Asher and Cael. "Notice anything of importance?"

Asher was already looking at me. Cael was staring at the bodies. I hoped he wasn't hungry.

"Cael?"

He shook his head slowly, his skin looking ghostly pale in the lantern light. "This is not necromancy. I do not know what this is."

I stepped toward him, casting shadows around the room. "What makes you think it's not necromancy?"

"Necromancy is power over death. We animate dead

things. Control dead things. These things are simply . . . dead. A necromancer would have no use for dead skin and organs. This seems more like the work of a madman."

"Perhaps," I agreed. "But if the killer is mad, they are also brilliant. I don't know how they have gotten this far without being caught."

"I highly doubt this thing is human," Cael said.

I looked back at Asher, wanting his opinion.

He peered down at the bodies with a look of distaste. "I am inclined to agree. It's difficult to tell with the ice, but I do not believe these bodies were skinned with any normal knife. They are too . . . perfect."

I paced around the bodies, careful to not slip on the ice. "So we have at least one thing that is not human, and at least one thing able to travel by day. Illya's killer is not a vampire, but they may be working with one."

"Neither are vampires," Asher corrected. "I would smell them."

I nodded, having forgotten that aspect. "So neither killer, if there are two, are vampires. They can skin bodies without a knife, and slip in and out of enchanted rooms without being detected. What could they possibly be?"

"Another witch," Drucida said gravely. "They have to be. No scent, no tracks, mysterious strangers in the mountain pass. Magic is at work here."

"Maybe." I looked at the bodies again. "Sidhe can work glamours strong enough to conceal scent. I've experienced it before."

"The Sidhe are extinct."

I gave her a bitter smile. "Trust me, they are not. I know of at least one who is still living, though I do not think she did this." No, Ryllae was a liar and a coward, but she wasn't a killer.

For once, Drucida seemed at a loss for words. Finally, she asked, "What do we do now?"

I was almost as shocked as I'd been when she explained her enchantment to me. I resisted the urge to glance at Cael again. "I think the vampires and I should walk around the fortress, see if anything draws our interest."

She looked like she might be sick. "That doesn't sound very promising."

I let out a snort of laughter as my teeth began to chatter. "You'd be surprised what things you can find by simply poking your nose where it doesn't belong."

Still looking ill, she nodded, and I realized she was glancing past me at Illya's corpse. They hadn't exactly been friends, but it was still unnerving seeing someone alive one day, and without skin and organs the next. I wished I could promise her it would be the last time it ever happened.

But I was afraid it would be a lie.

CHAPTER NINE

We walked around the fortress until nearly dawn, gaining nothing but a better understanding of its layout. No scents. Nothing strange. It was like the killer could appear and then vanish into thin air. I would be meeting with Drucida and Ophelia this morning to confirm Elanore's story, but I believed her. I wasn't going to learn anything new.

Asher walked to my left, and Cael to my right. Tholdri had long since gone to bed.

Cael peered at the eastern sky, though the sun was yet to show any signs of itself. "I fear you will not find any more clues until the next victim is claimed."

"I know." I shivered, and not from the cold. There would be more deaths, and soon. I felt it in my bones. Call it hunter's intuition.

We walked toward the gates, where they would both be forced to leave me. Asher's apprehension of that moment was practically choking me. I glanced at him, and though his face was unreadable, I knew exactly what he was thinking. I wasn't sure if he was intentionally showing me, or if I was just getting better at sensing beyond his shields.

"Do you have something to say?" I asked.

My question seemed to startle him. He stopped walking. This late—or this *early*—there was no one else in the street. "What makes you believe I have something to say?"

Interesting. So he wasn't showing me intentionally. "Your apprehension is so thick it's making me dizzy."

His eyes widened briefly, then he schooled his face back into its normal calm lines. "I hadn't intended for you to feel that."

"Why?"

"You usually become angry when I am protective over you."

Cael cleared his throat at my back. "He is afraid to leave you unguarded within the fortress, Lyssandra. We have no idea what sort of killer we are dealing with."

I stiffened. I couldn't exactly blame Asher for feeling that way, but it still irritated me. I could protect myself—most of the time. I met Asher's pale gaze, his eyes looking almost white in the fading moonlight. "I cannot leave."

"I know, but that does not prevent me from fearing for your safety." Even with Cael watching us, he was bold enough to step forward and cradle my jaw. "I cannot lose you, Lyssandra. Not now."

There was so much in that little statement that I didn't want to analyze. I knew *exactly* what he felt for me. There was no lying about it, no hiding it. "I have no intention of dying."

"Few ever intend it." His small smile was bitter. I was once again reminded that he had lived for centuries. He knew about my losses, but I knew nothing of his.

"I don't know what you want me to say."

His fingers pushed further back into my hair, pulling me close.

I went to him stiffly, feeling uncomfortable with Cael watching us. The darkened street, though there was no one out, didn't feel private at all.

Asher's cheek pressed against my hair. "There is nothing to say. I know you will not leave the fortress. But you cannot stop me from worrying, and from wishing that you would."

Embarrassed as I was, I relaxed against him. He simply had that effect on me. I *wanted* his arms around me, even with Cael watching. I inhaled his scent, now as familiar to me as Tholdri's. There was the turned-earth scent of vampire, but beyond that, there was *him*. Something softer and warmer. "I'll be careful."

"That is all I can ask." He pulled away enough to look down at my face. "If your sword warns you, listen to it. Flee immediately."

I furrowed my brow. "You know, my sword has hardly warned me of anything since I've been here. Yesterday it woke up, but it wasn't exactly a warning of intended harm. Just . . . caution. If the killer has seen me, it is yet to consider me as a victim. And none of the witches have meant me harm either. They've been curious, and rather judgmental, but not malicious."

"That makes me feel slightly better, though you do have a tendency toward making new enemies."

I smirked. "A hazard of my personality." I tensed as the first hint of purple light crept over the horizon. "You both need to go. I'll be fine."

I tried to pull away, but Asher tugged me close and kissed me, right in front of Cael. I still would've pulled away, but I knew he was worried something would happen, and he might never see me again. I understood the worry. I felt the same way, though I wouldn't be continuing on without him. No, if he died, there would be no time for me to mourn.

And so I kissed him, enjoying the feel of his mouth on mine, though his skin was too cool. He needed to feed, and so did Cael, and we hadn't had a moment to discuss it.

I pulled away with a gasp. "We still haven't figured out the issue we spoke of before." I wasn't sure how else to say it in front of Cael.

"We will figure it out tonight." He stroked my cheek, then they were both gone in the blink of an eye.

I stared at the empty space before me. The sentries had been instructed to open the gates for them. They would be fine.

They were probably much safer outside the walls, than any of us within.

I LET Tholdri sleep during the morning meeting. He needed more rest than I did. He couldn't help it. He wasn't a vampire's human servant.

I was glad for once to meet somewhere other than the building filled with Illya's tapestries. I was even gladder when my nose told me there would be food.

I knocked on the door of the building Drucida had pointed out to me last night.

Ophelia opened it. Her wide green eyes darted away from my face, then she stepped back to let me in, swishing her blue apprentice robes around her legs.

I walked past her. If she wanted to apologize for lying, she could do it later. I wanted her to confirm Elanore's story first. Then we could talk about the knife, and try to figure out how it was stolen.

An open fireplace pumped heat into the small home. A few candles in the center of a tall wooden table helped to illuminate a spread of fresh bread, boiled eggs, and vibrant fruit. Drucida and Elanore both sat at the table, watching me expectantly as Ophelia shut the door. Drucida gestured for me to take a seat.

I shucked my long charcoal coat, draping it across the back of the nearest wooden chair before sitting. My mouth watered as I eyed purple grapes and soft, fuzzy apricots. "I've seen the gardens and the chickens, but no fruit trees." I lifted one of the apricots from its bowl. "Where did they come from?"

Drucida buttered a slice of bread. "Villages on the other side of the mountain. They mostly trade with Ivangard in the North, but we have a long-standing arrangement with them."

I had never been to Ivangard, but I knew the city at the edge of the Ebon Province was even larger than Silgard. "Do the villagers know of the fortress?"

Drucida placed her bread on a small pewter plate without taking a bite. "We have a few trusted allies. Rottertham, the largest village, maintains an open port. When my mother and I arrived from Wendshore, a family there took us in."

"Wendshore?" I asked, surprised they had traveled so far.

"The witch hunts in the Ebon Province were atrocious, but they were nothing compared to Wendshore. Most did not escape. My mother and I were lucky."

I remembered her mentioning the screams of her sisters, but I was not callous enough to ask about them. I glanced at Elanore, who smiled at me softly, then back at Drucida. "Why are you suddenly being so forthcoming with me?"

Instead of answering, she looked past me toward Ophelia. "Sit, girl. You are not in trouble."

Ophelia shuffled forward, taking the last chair. She still wasn't looking at me.

Still ignoring the food on her plate, Drucida splayed her hands across the table, draping her long curls around her shoulders. "The trunk where Elanore hid the dagger was enchanted, just like the room that holds the corpses. No one else should have been able to open it."

I crossed my arms and leaned back in my seat. The position tugged up my cream-colored linen sleeves enough to reveal the edges of my wrist sheaths. "But someone did, if Elanore's story is to be believed."

Drucida glanced at the woman in question. "I would have had trouble believing it, but Illya's skin was stolen. I spoke with the men who helped deliver her. Elanore used my key to unlock the room, and they all saw the door shut afterward. My key was returned shortly after that. There would not have been time to skin her."

"That doesn't explain why you're being nice to me." I rolled my eyes down toward the food.

She sighed, then leaned back in her seat. "The only explanation is strong magic, strong enough to overwhelm our enchantments. The killer is another witch. One of us. Just as you are one of us."

"I'm still not quite grasping what you're saying."

Elanore gave Drucida a patient smile, then turned toward me. "She is saying that if she can't trust her own people, she will have to trust you. She's asking for your help."

"She already asked for my help, and I already agreed to give it." I looked at Drucida. "Your attitude changed after you saw Cael. Why?"

"You just can't let things go, can you?" Her chin dropped as she shook her head. "Very well. Seeing Cael . . . seeing what he sacrificed just to protect you." She exhaled loudly. "I cannot judge him for what he is when he was willing to sacrifice everything for his family. I was angry at Cedrik for leaving—for hiding what he was to join the Helius Order. They had *hunted* us. It was absurd." She finally met my eyes. "Cedrik and Cael left after a vampire killed their sister. They hunted the vampire, and it said something had spoken into its mind. The voice had ordered it to abduct a red-haired witch, and to bring her somewhere. But she fought, and the vampire lost control and killed her."

A chill crept up my spine, though I had already heard the story. Cael had told me during our travels. "It was Eiric. Even back then, he was speaking into the minds of young vampires." And he had wanted their sister—my great aunt—brought to his tomb, just like me.

Drucida nodded. "That's what they believed. Their plan at first was to hunt vampires so they could not be controlled. I don't know when that plan changed."

I slumped in my seat, pinning my sword awkwardly. "So you understand why they both did what they did. You already knew why they did it."

"They feared their loved ones would be hunted. Cedrik hid his identity, and his daughter's identity, because he didn't want Eiric to find them. He changed your entire life so that none would know you were a witch. Just so you would no longer be a *target*." She leaned forward. "Cedrik knew the terror of his loved ones being hunted. I love many here, so now I know just what that feels like. I still do not agree with his choices. Necromancy and vampires, they *are* evil. But I understand why you are what you are. I understand why the light sent you. I had hoped I was strong enough, but you are the only one who can save us. Stop this thing, and I will teach you magic, if I can."

I took a moment to absorb her words. More succinctly put, she had been mad at my grandfather and took it out on me. But now that I had been useful—now that a necromancer and a vampire had been useful—she could put her old anger aside. I was irritated, but she was giving me exactly what I wanted. It would do no good to argue about it now.

"I already agreed to find your killer, but I now have one condition."

Drucida's eyes darkened. "Go on."

"You start teaching me magic now. Whatever this creature is, I have encountered nothing like it before. I will need every tool at my disposal to find and destroy it."

Elanore sipped her tea. "Your bond with the vampire may prove an issue. You may not be able to learn."

"I broke the seal on Eiric's tomb. Witch blood still runs through my veins."

Drucida and Elanore both looked at each other, then back at me.

"Very well," Drucida agreed grudgingly. "We will start by learning your affinity."

I lifted my brow. "Affinity?"

"Mine is ice." She gestured toward Elanore. "Hers is air. Not all affinities are elemental, but they do make for the most powerful witches."

"And how do we find out mine?"

Her smile was a little cruel. "We make you bleed."

CHAPTER TEN

Blood dripped from my fingertip into a small copper dish. The puncture was deep, letting out enough blood to pool in the bottom of the receptacle.

"That's it?"

Drucida stood across from me, watching my blood filling the small dish. "Yes, that should be enough."

I gave my finger a shake, then stuck it in my mouth. "When you said you would make me bleed, I was expecting a bit more." My words came out garbled from my finger still in my mouth.

Drucida frowned. "Most people are averse to having a dagger's tip shoved through their skin."

I removed my finger from my mouth. "Remind me to show you my scars sometime."

She shook her head. "*Hunters.*" She lifted the dish from the table.

We were in her personal quarters. Dried flowers hung from the low rafters, swaying with our passing movements. As was already evident by her clothing, Drucida enjoyed rich colors and fine fabrics. The rug beneath my boots swirled with saturated blues and purples. A tapestry, not one of Illya's judging by the style, depicted a sweeping ocean scene at sunset. Velvet curtains blocked out the harsh midday light.

Elanore and Tholdri sat stiffly on a small sofa with their shoulders nearly touching. Elanore shivered lightly.

I smiled to myself as I watched Drucida carrying my blood to a little altar covered in candles and jars of herbs. She had no fire in her hearth—she didn't need it. And she didn't care if the rest of us were freezing our toes off.

"What will you do with it now?" I approached her back.

She was pouring the blood into several smaller dishes. She'd tied back her hair to keep it out of the way. "We'll test the major affinities first, though I doubt any will match. Then we'll go through a series of minor ones." She glanced over her shoulder at me. "We may need more blood for those."

I lifted my hand and wiggled my fingers. "Nine more, ready for the ultimate sacrifice."

Tholdri snorted behind us, then looked down at his lap when Drucida scowled at him. Elanore lifted a hand to hide her laughter.

Drucida turned back toward the blood. "It won't take long to determine if you can learn magic at all."

"You mean if I have no affinity, I cannot learn?"

"Yes."

I stared at the back of her head, willing her to tell me more. She knew what had happened with breaking Eiric's seal. If there was no trace of magic left in my blood, it shouldn't have been possible.

"How likely do you think it is that I cannot learn?" I pressed.

She crumbled a small piece of dark red resin into one dish. "You said you became a human servant at nineteen?"

I nodded, but she couldn't see me. "Yes, somewhere around there."

"Your magic should have presented earlier than that, unless your mother did something to interfere."

I stepped closer. "Cael has mentioned nothing in that regard."

"He might not have known." She glanced back at me. "If your mother was powerful enough, she might have prevented you from accessing your magic, for a time. She wouldn't have been able to stunt you forever."

This was all news to me. "Did you know her?"

"No." Her tone was cold. "Nor do I know who your grandmother was."

I didn't press her. There was an old ache somewhere in her heart, and it wasn't any of my business.

She crumbled a large dried leaf into the final dish of blood. Nothing happened.

"You do not have any major affinity." She stepped back. "We'll need more blood for the next batch of tests."

I looked down at the unremarkable dishes, and the unremarkable ingredients she'd added. "You just crumble in leaves and resin, and that's supposed to tell you something?"

She rolled her eyes. "Leaves and resin with magical properties. Like attracts like. If your blood held those properties, it would have reacted."

It made sense, though the whole thing still seemed a bit too... mundane. "So now we prick another finger?"

She nodded. "Elanore will test the next ones. Her air magic can separate more subtle affinities."

"Couldn't she have just tested the first dishes before you added your magical components?"

Drucida smiled. "Yes."

I huffed as I followed her back to the table with the dagger, glancing at Tholdri as I went.

He grinned at me.

Drucida could torture me all she pleased. I grew up in the Helius Order. I had been put through far, far worse.

I chose my next finger to suffer the dagger's sharp point. She could slice every single one if it meant I could gain power against Eiric. Because there had to be *something* lurking in my blood. I had come this far. Failure was not an option.

AFTER STABBING my finger a little too gleefully, Drucida left us for what would apparently be a rather lengthy testing process. Elanore's affinity was air. Her magic could mimic many different forms, each of which would be used to test my blood for a reaction. But it would take some time for her to cycle through each of them.

I sat on the little sofa watching Elanore as Tholdri built a fire in the hearth. Hopefully Drucida wouldn't be too upset. The stones were blackened. She *had* made fires for other guests at some point.

Elanore pursed her lips as she peered down at the dish of my blood, the nearby lantern making her look ghoulish in the dim, curtained room. She'd stayed at the small central table, needing none of Drucida's herbs or resins.

"Anything yet?" I asked.

She shook her head, her eyes still on the dish. "Nothing. It's odd though. When I add a touch of magic to your blood, it's almost like it . . . rejects it."

"That's not normal?"

She shook her head. "The blood either reacts, or it doesn't. It's not quite reacting, but it's doing *something*."

A trickle of smoke filled the space as Tholdri got a small flame going.

I stood, approaching the other side of the table. The blood appeared unremarkable to me. A pure crimson that I had seen far too much of in my lifetime.

Elanore hovered her hand over the dish, as she had for each new affinity.

"What are you testing now?" I asked.

Her eyes were hooded as she concentrated on the dish. "It's a form of air, the same type of magic Illya possessed."

"Which was?"

"Seeing different times, different places. Sometimes

portents of the future." Her eyelids drooped so much they were almost closed. "Although, *seeing* isn't the right term. She couldn't see them. They would just come out in her tapestries. She would weave, and an image would form, unbeknownst to her until it was finished."

Remembering Lavandriel near the cottage, I leaned closer. "So a scene from the past could simply play out in her work without her knowing what it was?"

Elanore nodded minutely, then lifted her hand from the dish. "Yes, but this gift is not yours."

I couldn't help my relief. It seemed a rather useless gift to possess.

She lowered her hand, then looked at me. "I have tested everything I can think of. Nothing has reacted, but," she shook her head, "I know there's something here. I have done this test many times, and blood has never reacted in such a way."

Done with the fire, Tholdri came to stand at my shoulder. "Could it be her bond with Asher?"

Elanore pursed her lips again, peering down at the blood as if willing it to tell her its secrets. "Maybe. I've never done the test on a human servant. But . . . I just don't think that's it." She glanced at the hilt of my sword over my shoulder. "You say the sword glows for you?"

I nodded.

"I don't know much about it, but such relics usually only react to magic in the blood."

I stared at her for a moment, really wanting to trust her. She meant me no harm, my sword would have warned me, but . . . trust did not come easy to me.

"I have another relic," I sighed, hoping I was not

making a mistake and endangering Asher and Cael. "It is a ring that can drain the life force from a vampire. I've never tried it, but I saw it used by a necromancer."

Her eyes widened. "Can I see it?"

I hesitated, then nodded. I kept it on my person at all times. I couldn't risk it falling into the wrong hands. Hopefully I was not placing it in the wrong hands *now*.

I lifted the leather cord I used to keep it around my neck, then pulled it over my head, handing her the ring.

The cord dragged across the tabletop near my blood as she took it, then held the ring close to her face. "Remarkable. Where did you get this?"

"I killed the necromancer who tried to use it on Asher."

Her mouth formed a small *oh* of surprise. "I see. Do you know where it came from before that?"

"Lavandriel created it. She used it to weaken Eiric before sealing him away."

Her expression was studious. If she was forming any nefarious plans for the ring, she was good at hiding them. "Do you mind if I . . . soil the ring a bit?"

I lifted a brow, glancing at Tholdri. "*Soil* it?"

"I want to dip it in your blood."

Perplexed, I gestured toward the bowl of cold blood. "Have at it."

Holding onto the cord, she dipped the ring into the bowl. Nothing happened. My blood slowly absorbed into the cord, creeping up the length.

Disappointment washed through me, and I wasn't sure why. I didn't know what reacting to the ring might mean.

I felt so defeated that at first I thought I was only seeing what I wanted when the bowl started trembling.

Then it shook more violently. The blood sloshed within the small receptacle, then started steaming. We all leaned forward, awestricken, our faces far too close as the blood exploded out of the dish.

I closed my eyes just in time as hot blood hit my skin. I stood perfectly still as it began dripping down my face. Entirely stunned, I lifted my sleeve to wipe the blood away from my eyes so I could look at Elanore and Tholdri.

Both their faces were speckled with blood, their eyes wide. The ring lay unharmed within the now empty bowl.

It took me a few tries to find my voice. "What in the light just happened?"

Elanore blinked at me. She looked down at the bowl, then back up to my bloody face. "I have absolutely no idea."

DRUCIDA STUDIED the ring in the bowl. She was yet to touch it, but had been peering at it for a good long while. Finally, she looked up at the three of us. We had wiped off most the blood, but I still had some in my hair. It was odd, for once, being coated in my own blood rather than someone else's.

I fidgeted under the intensity of her gaze.

"And your sword?" she finally asked. "What happens when it touches your blood?"

"I don't make a habit of bleeding on my sword. It is used to make *others* bleed." *And* I had used it to make another hunter my servant. Cael thought I should keep that part to myself.

I agreed. I didn't need witches thinking I could do the same to them.

Drucida watched me expectantly.

When no one else spoke, I sighed. "I guess this means we're going to try it."

Tholdri and Elanore both took a step back.

I glanced at them. "Cowards."

Drucida tensed as I unsheathed my sword, then relaxed when I placed it on the table, sending a few new candles flickering. The eye in the hilt remained shut, as if it was sleeping. It had been uncharacteristically dormant since I'd entered the fortress.

I took up the dagger on the table, then smiled at Drucida as I pricked another finger. I set the dagger aside, then let a few drops of blood fall onto my sword's blade.

The eye snapped open.

Elanore gasped.

The eye rolled around until it found me. We stared at each other.

Drucida stepped closer, leaning over the sword. "The blood is gone."

And so it was. Where my blood had fallen, the blade shone, perfectly clean. "I still don't understand what this means."

Drucida pursed her lips. "It means a blade created to destroy demons likes your blood."

"So there must be *some* magic there," Tholdri commented behind me.

"Perhaps." Drucida paced to the head of the table, lifting the bowl still containing the ring. Careful not to touch the magical object, she gripped the end of the leather cord and set the ring aside, then handed me the bowl. "One more time. I have an idea."

Her threat to make me bleed had proven true after all. I was running out of fingers on my non-dominant hand, and the puncture I'd made for my sword had already stopped bleeding. Choosing my thumb this time, I quickly made a new wound, then held it over the bowl. Blood welled, dripping into the copper dish.

"That's enough," Drucida said after just a few drops. "Just one last test."

I held the bowl out to her, but she took the dagger from my other hand instead, then motioned Tholdri forward.

Looking uneasy, he obeyed.

Drucida snatched his hand, turning his palm upward. She lifted a brow at him. "May I?"

He nodded.

She pricked his skin, then guided him finger-first toward the bowl in my hand. She squeezed Tholdri's flesh until a drop of blood fell into the bowl. The droplet steamed as it hit, and my blood in the container roiled.

I stared down into the bowl, more confused than ever.

"Blood magic." Drucida stepped back, dagger still in hand. "*That* is your affinity."

My heart fluttered in my throat. "Something tells me that isn't a good thing."

Drucida and Elanore kept their distance, making me increasingly wary. They exchanged a dark look, then Elanore explained, "There was a time when those with blood magic were put to death without a trial. Lavandriel put an end to it."

I forced my breathing to slow. This was no time to panic. "Why? Why did she put an end to it?"

"Because it was her gift as well," Drucida answered. "It is a magic known only to Blackmire witches."

"Then is it that shocking that blood is my affinity?"

Elanore and Drucida exchanged another look I couldn't quite read. Elanore frowned. "As we have said, it is a rare ... gift."

I shivered. I didn't like it, but we had to move forward. "Does this mean you can teach me magic?"

Drucida's mouth formed a grim line.

Elanore at least looked slightly apologetic. "*Can*, yes. Will? No. No witch in her right mind would teach someone to use blood magic. You would be too dangerous. But—"

Drucida cut her off with a sharp look.

I set the bowl of my blood aside, wishing my magic could have been anything else. I would even take tapestries. "I have to learn. I *must* defeat Eiric."

Drucida stepped a little in front of Elanore. "No one here will teach you, Lyssandra. You should go."

"Go?"

She nodded sharply. "We will keep your secret. The others ... they cannot find out. Some would hunt you."

Indignant anger swelled in my chest. "I can't *go*, you foolish woman. Even if some may hunt me. Something far worse is already hunting *you*."

"You don't understand, Lyssandra." Tiredness showed in her expression, and underneath that, fear. I could smell it on her.

"I don't have to understand. I must catch your killer, and I must learn magic. There is no other choice." I thought of how Eiric had clouded my mind so easily. He had even gotten past Cael and Markus outside the crypt. I needed something more to fight him with. Something he wouldn't expect.

Elanore and Drucida both looked at each other again. Their unspoken words were beginning to annoy me.

I was about to argue further, when a knock on the door made all four of us jump. Elanore hurried to answer it.

Ophelia stood outside. Tears streaked her face. "Lorena is dead. Her skin is gone, just like the others."

I couldn't help the cruel look I gave Drucida. Or maybe I could, but I didn't want to. She couldn't turn me away. She couldn't make me leave. She *needed* me.

Her shoulders slumped in defeat, but she didn't say anything.

I looked at Ophelia. "Take us to the body."

CHAPTER ELEVEN

"A death every day." Elanore's voice trembled. "At least in the beginning, we had a reprieve in between bodies."

We huddled together in the small room. The ring was back around my neck, its weight seeming heavier than before.

I looked down at the skinless corpse, remembering the stout blonde girl from the previous day. The height was right, and these were her quarters, so it seemed safe to assume it was her. "The killer is escalating things. It's almost as if they want to get caught."

"Then why haven't you caught them?" Drucida stood back near the door. She had hardly even glanced at the body. Maybe she was getting tired of looking at them.

I knew I was. "There's something here that we're missing. Where is the knife that killed Illya?"

"Hidden," Drucida said simply. "This time, only I know where it is."

"Drucida—" Elanore began.

Drucida cut her off with a sharp shake of her head. "No. It's not worth it." They had exchanged a few more glances on the way over. There was some silent argument happening between them, and I wanted in on it.

Elanore's cheeks flushed. "How many must die to make it worth it?"

"What are you both talking about?" I interrupted, turning my back on the corpse.

The sun was slowly sinking. It would be night soon, and I would request that Drucida allow the vampires within the fortress again. They could search Lorena's chambers.

Elanore turned toward me. "If you really have blood magic—"

"No," Drucida cut her off again.

But Elanore forged on, pushing her russet hair out of her face to give me the full force of her gaze. "If you really have blood magic, you could use it to track the killer."

Drucida stepped between us, facing Elanore while giving me her back. "We will *not* teach her. As high witch, my word is law."

Elanore flinched, then shook her head. "You know that's not true. You need my support, and Charles'. Just as you needed Illya's before she died. If you will not teach Lyssandra, then I will. I will not have the blood of future victims on my hands."

"And what about *her* victims." Drucida spun, whipping her hand toward me. "What about what she does after she solves these murders?"

"What are you talking about?" I demanded again as the door opened, revealing Tholdri.

He had been searching for clues outside. He took a quick glance at each of us, Elanore with her red cheeks and Drucida with fire in her eyes, then slowly backed out of the room. I wished I could do the same. I was tired of their bickering, but I needed answers.

"If this concerns my magic, I have a right to know."

Her shoulders stiff, Drucida fully faced me. "Blood magic corrupts the user. It always does. The power becomes too intoxicating."

I crossed my arms, unfazed by her warning. "What did Elanore mean about me using it to track the killer?"

Elanore stomped around Drucida. It was the most assertive I had ever seen her. "The taking of life leaves a stain. For a time, the killer is connected to its victim, metaphysically speaking. They have taken blood, and blood connects them. You could use Lorena's death to track the killer. But it must be fresh. The connection will fade quickly."

I ignored Drucida's outraged expression. "Tell me how."

Instead of answering, Elanore looked at Drucida. "You know it's our only option. Whatever this is, it's worse than Lyssandra could ever be. You know I'm right."

Drucida's scowl slowly broke down. First the mouth, then the wrinkled nose, and finally the eyes. They softened, showing what was really beneath. She was haunted by the deaths, and terrified of what might come. "If we teach her, she will be *your* responsibility."

Elanore nodded sharply. "I accept that."

They both looked at me.

Drucida crossed her arms. "Well, Lyssandra. Prepare to bleed *again*."

I winced, already knowing that this time, it would be more than a few pricked fingers.

I STOOD ABOVE THE CORPSE, unnerved by its lidless eyes staring back at me. This time I held one of my own daggers, with my discarded wrist sheath shoved in my coat pocket. The blade was poised over my forearm, my sleeve rolled up to reveal the flesh beneath. "So I just slice my flesh and let it . . . drip on her?"

Elanore stood close to me, her face pale. "Your goal is to establish a connection. While rituals help, most magic is about will. You must will the connection into place."

I remembered Ryllae telling me something similar once, when I wanted my sword to show me its memories. It had worked, then, but I had a feeling this task would be a little more complicated.

Drucida and Tholdri waited in the far corner of the room. Tholdri stood ready to hunt a monster, should I actually succeed. And Drucida . . . I had a feeling she was just waiting for me to fail.

I felt darkness closing in. Asher would be awake soon, and I wondered if he would feel what I was doing.

I sliced the blade across my skin. There was no use stalling. The wound stung, quickly welling with blood.

I knelt beside the corpse, ignoring the bile creeping up my throat. Her death was worse—so much worse than anything I'd ever seen. My blood dripped across her skinless, hollow chest. I focused on building some sort of *connection* with her, but I wasn't even sure what that meant. She just felt dead. There was nothing left.

"Nothing is happening." I realized my eyes had closed, but it wasn't helping.

"I—" Elanore swallowed loudly. "I don't know. It is a different form of magic from any I've worked with. Most magic is partnership, symbiosis. Blood magic is more . . . aggressive. *Taking.*"

I heard footsteps, but I didn't move. I was afraid to stop trying.

"*Will* your blood to claim her," Drucida instructed. She had moved closer than I'd realized.

I could feel my blood dripping around either side of my forearm, the twin streams meeting again at the bottom before trickling down. "Claim her?"

"Just as the killer claimed her. It took what did not belong to it. In a way, you must do the same. It will connect you, for a short time."

"I don't know how to claim anyone." My voice trembled.

"Don't you?"

At first I thought she somehow knew about Markus, then I realized she was referring to Asher. Our bond went both ways. He was as much mine as I was his. But . . . I hadn't created *that* bond. Markus on the other hand . . .

I placed my bloody palm on the corpse's chest, still

keeping my eyes closed. The exposed muscles were smooth and cold. I had willed Markus to live, and it had resulted in him becoming my human servant. I didn't want a corpse as a servant, but maybe the process was similar. She would become mine, for a time.

I couldn't protect her, and I couldn't bring her back. But I *could* avenge her. With my blood and my will I swore to avenge her, because vengeance could connect two people just as much as anything else. Sometimes *more* than anything else.

I felt it as my sword awoke, drawn by what I could only think of as magic. *My* magic. Because my connection with my sword was no different. We were connected through blood and violence, but also vengeance. We hunted the monsters and we made them pay. That was why my sword liked me. Why it had chosen me.

The fresh bond I had created through blood and vengeance snapped into place, stealing a gasp from my lips. I couldn't feel much from Lorena, she was well and truly gone, but Drucida was right, I could feel something on the other end. Another connection not so different from the one I had just created.

I stood so abruptly that I swayed on my feet. It was Tholdri who stepped forward to keep me standing. I opened my eyes to find Elanore and Drucida had both moved out of reach. They watched me, wide-eyed, waiting to see what I would do.

Let them be frightened. I knew I was. "I know where to go. You two should stay here. Tholdri and I will hunt it."

Drucida shook her head minutely. "I'm coming. I owe Illya at least that much."

Judging by the fear in Elanore's eyes, I would have guessed she would stay behind. But she took Drucida's hand, then gave me a hesitant nod. "We will follow."

I didn't question them further. Afraid of losing the connection, I went for the door. Everyone followed me out, leaving Lorena where she lay. There was no saving her, but I could avenge her. I would find her killer. He, she, or *it* . . . whatever it was, its death would not be quick.

Wind whipped my hair back from my face, tugging at my coat. I hadn't had time to gather any warmer clothing. I hadn't even bandaged my wound, but I thought it had mostly stopped bleeding. It was difficult to tell with my sleeve soaked in older blood. I would have drawn my sword, but with the wind, darkness, and uneven footing, I was more likely to impale myself than anyone else. Tholdri climbed next to me, both of us helping to catch the other whenever we slipped.

Elanore and Drucida were not fairing quite so well. Drucida might have been immune to the biting wind, but cold tolerance did not make her any more agile, and she and Elanore had fallen behind.

I didn't like leaving them vulnerable, but I could sense the killer somewhere ahead, higher up the mountain. The lights of the fortress were a distant glow behind us. We were on our own, but not for long. Full dark had fallen. Asher and Cael would find us soon.

"How much farther!" Tholdri had to shout to be heard over the howling wind.

I shook my head and kept climbing. Sharp rocks jabbed my feet through my boots. I could tell we were close, but this way of tracking was new to me. I had no idea what it would feel like when we found the killer. Whatever it was, it was an agile climber to have made it so far in such a short span of time. Lorena's body had just started cooling when we found it.

We reached a small plateau of level ground and I took a moment to catch my breath. My lungs burned, and my wounded arm ached. My sword echoed a warning in my head.

I gripped Tholdri's arm. "The killer knows we're here!" I didn't like shouting about it, but I wanted to make sure he heard me over the wind.

I glanced around, finally spotting a dark spot in the side of the mountain. A cave. No light emanated from within.

I had only taken one step when Asher found us. Suddenly he was right beside me, gripping my injured arm at the elbow to lift it in front of his face. He pulled back the sleeve, frowning at the slowly healing wound. A normal human would have needed the wound stitched, but I healed too quickly for it to matter.

"There's no time to explain." I didn't have to shout it this time. Asher would be able to hear me.

His white hair whipped around him as his eyes turned toward the cave. Silently, he nodded, releasing my arm. I hoped Cael was with Drucida and Elanore, but I didn't ask about it. There was nothing I could do if he wasn't.

I drew my sword, and with a nod toward Tholdri, I approached the cave.

I wasn't sure what I had expected as I reached the opening. Perhaps the smell of rotting organs and stolen skins. What I got was pure blackness, and no sounds to be heard over the wind.

And yet, my connection with the killer pounded in my skull. It was near.

I stepped into the darkness. My sword had only glowed on a few occasions. Once, in the presence of beings from another realm, then when I bound Markus, and again in the presence of Cael. I wasn't sure why it had glowed each time, but I willed it to glow now. I willed it to show me what hid in the darkness.

At first it was only a dull light, but within a few heartbeats my sword shone like a beacon. Eternally grateful for the bit of light, I stepped into the cave with Asher and Tholdri on either side of me. Tholdri's sword glinted dully in the unearthly glow.

A few more steps revealed that the cave was more expansive than I had initially assumed. I watched my steps, wary of a sudden fall. I could still feel my connection to the killer—so close—but it seemed like there was nothing here.

Asher tapped his nose, then pointed to one dark corner.

Understanding that he had smelled something, I approached the area he'd noted, realizing there was a small secondary cavern. I stepped inside, shining my sword in every corner. Someone or something had been here. There was some shredded bedding, and a few odd trinkets and coins. A dark, soot-stained lantern waited beside the bedding.

My skin prickled. There was no immediate danger, but the lingering energy in the cavern—it was *evil*. That was the only way I could describe it. I knew evil was not just dark or light. Some beings, like Cael, could be both, but this thing . . . was stealing skins. I couldn't believe there was anything good about it.

Footsteps in the main cavern sounded thunderously loud. Low voices helped me realize Drucida and Elanore had reached us. Cael had shown them the way.

I scanned the room again. There was nothing here, but I could still feel the killer. I felt its heartbeat pounding in my head. I approached the bedding, still holding my sword out before me. I observed tarnished coins, scraps of parchment—useless odds and ends.

I was ready to dismiss my new magic as faulty, when a glimpse of gold caught my eye. I used the tip of my sword to move aside one fold of bedding, revealing a shining locket on a long, delicate chain.

I couldn't say why, but the locket made my heart catch in my throat. I only distantly registered that Drucida, Elanore, and Cael had entered the smaller cavern behind us.

Moving my sword to a one handed grip, I knelt down, reaching my free hand toward the locket. The next thing I knew, Lorena was right in front of me, lunging toward me.

I rolled backwards, too stunned to threaten her with my sword.

She shrieked, a bone-chilling sound that set my teeth on edge as I got to my feet, following her movements with my sword. Her blonde hair streamed behind her as she rushed everyone blocking her path. Her blue robes billowed around her, tattered and stained.

She was fast, as fast as any vampire. Unfortunately, she was trying to evade an ancient. Asher managed to grab her before spinning her around, pinning her arms behind her. She thrashed wildly, then abruptly went still.

The smile she gave me turned the blood in my veins to ice. Suddenly she was gone, and Asher was gripping empty air.

He and Cael reacted more quickly than the rest of us. They both rushed out of the cavern, leaving Tholdri and I blinking stupidly at each other.

"What in the light just happened?" Elanore pushed wind-whipped tendrils of hair from her face.

"I have no idea." Gripping my still-glowing sword, I walked past them, following in the direction Asher and Cael had gone.

I found them standing out on the mountainside, peering into the darkness.

"What happened?"

Asher turned to give me a grim look.

Cael shook his head, still staring into the darkness. "She—*it*—it turned into a mouse."

I shook my head, now more confused than ever. "It

was a locket before. It doesn't sound possible, but it was."

Asher's brow creased with worry. It was never good when ancient vampires were worried. "I had thought they were mere legends. Children's stories." He raised his voice enough for me to hear it as the others reached us.

"Asher," I said, moving closer. "What is it? What was that thing?"

"A skin changer. In my village, when I was young, the elders would use stories of skin changers to frighten us into behaving." His eyes were haunted.

I had never heard him talk about his childhood before. It was such a long time ago, I hadn't even known if he remembered it.

"Why didn't you think of this before?" I asked. "When the skins were stolen?"

"It was a children's tale, Lyssandra. I would never have believed what happened here tonight if I hadn't seen it with my own eyes."

I glanced at the others, then back at Asher. "Well now that we know what it is, how do we kill it?"

"I don't know."

"What happened in the children's tales?" I pressed.

He furrowed his brow, looking out at the darkness. "Everyone died."

CHAPTER TWELVE

Our progress back down the mountain was slow. Elanore and Drucida were both pallid and winded by the time we reached the fortress gates. And we had seen no further signs of the skin changer.

We couldn't even track it by scent. How could you track something that could turn into seemingly anything?

Well, maybe not anything. The stories we had heard involved a locket and a knife. We had met the locket, but the knife was still hidden somewhere within the fortress.

"We will all go with you," I said to Drucida as the gates opened. "It's too dangerous for you to be alone with that knife."

"We don't know that it's another skin changer, if that's even what that thing was."

I crossed my arms. The blood had dried on my sleeve, leaving it crunchy and stiff at the same time. "We don't know that it isn't. I would like permission for both the vampires to enter the fortress once again until night is through."

She gave me a look that said she wasn't even sure if she wanted to let *me* within the fortress.

"Drucida—" Cael began, his tone reasonable.

She cut him off with a sharp look. "Don't. You *knew* she might have blood magic." She jutted her chin toward me.

"She is Blackmire. We all knew it was a possibility."

I had filled Asher and Cael in during our arduous journey. I hadn't thought Drucida had been able to hear me.

"Do you think her mother suppressed her magic for that reason?" she pressed.

The wind near the fortress was low enough for me to hear his heavy sigh. The sentries above watched us curiously, waiting for us to enter the gates. "Alicia was angry with Cedrik for bringing them both into the Helius order. If she had sensed Lyssandra's magic, she told him nothing of it. At the time, he had assumed the bloodline was too weak within her. It is not uncommon."

Elanore looked a bit wild with her wide eyes and windswept hair. She also looked like she had suffered just about enough of Drucida's worrying. "Look," she said. "We may not have caught the thing, but we know far more than we did when starting out. We know what it is, and how it's getting in and out of the fortress, if it really can look like anyone or anything."

"And how does that help us?" Drucida snapped.

"How can we find it again? How do we know one of us isn't dead in that cave, and the skin changer isn't now standing among us?"

"Ian," I said at a sudden thought. "Ian, your pot-washer, he can see energies."

Drucida crossed her arms and seemed to shiver, though I knew it wasn't from the cold. "So?"

"So, while he can't be everywhere at once, he might at least be able to tell if someone is a skin changer in disguise."

Her eyes widened with realization. "You're right. And he's not the only one. Ophelia can see energies as well."

"We will wake them on our way to check on the knife," I decided.

Drucida glared at me from beneath her lowered brow.

I crossed my arms and glared right back. She might not like my magic, or my company, but I was now more sure than ever that she needed me.

"Fine," she said finally. "Elanore can wake Ophelia. The rest of us will go to the knife."

Elanore didn't seem to mind being volunteered for the task. Maybe she didn't want to experience another scene like we'd had in the cave. I didn't blame her.

The sentries looked relieved when we finally entered the gates. *All* of us.

Elanore quickly branched off without a word. Tholdri and Cael walked just behind Drucida, while Asher fell into step beside me, bringing up the rear as the gates closed behind us.

"You and she are quite alike," he muttered lowly.

I rubbed my sore arm. My bond to Asher meant the wound would be healed by morning, but new scars were never comfortable. "What are you talking about?"

"Drucida. You only seem at odds because you are too similar."

I smirked, still rubbing my arm as I walked. "You noticed that, did you?" I was at least self-aware enough to have already realized it. But it didn't make dealing with her any easier. And it didn't make me have any more sympathy for those who had to deal with me.

Asher took my arm from my grip as we walked, rubbing the dry, blood-soaked fabric between two fingers. "It was a deep wound."

"We were running out of time. I wanted to make sure I did it right. Do you know anything about blood magic?" I didn't look at him as I asked it. I wasn't sure if I wanted to know more myself.

"No. The witches have always guarded their secrets closely. But, if this is something you had in common with Lavandriel, perhaps you could learn more from your sword."

"Maybe." The first memories my sword had shared with me had unraveled my entire identity. I supposed nothing could be worse.

But I was wrong more often than I liked to admit.

We reached Drucida's quarters, waiting while she withdrew her little keyring and unlocked the door. We entered to find all the materials from testing my blood just as we had left them. The fire Tholdri had made had dwindled into nothing. The fresh candles had burned almost to nubs, their flames the only warmth in the darkness.

Cael hesitated behind me in the doorway.

I looked back at him. His cheeks looked more cavernous than before, and his eyes more hollow.

Oh light, he was smelling my blood everywhere. He had probably been smelling it on my sleeve too as we walked.

Quickly comprehending the situation, Asher gave me an abrupt bow of his head, then quietly went outside with Cael, shutting the door behind them.

Drucida looked curiously at the shut door, then steeled her expression as she looked at me and Tholdri. She had a small block of wood in her hands. I wasn't sure where she had pulled it from. I had been distracted by Cael.

She ran her fingers along the edge of the wood, and a seam appeared. I watched unblinking as the solid wood became a box, no, a small trunk. She opened it, but there was nothing inside.

"This cannot be," she gasped.

But I had already expected it. "No one stole the knife from Elanore the first time. It transformed into the skin changer and left on its own."

Tholdri stroked his chin thoughtfully. "So it can become both the locket and the knife?"

I shook my head. It didn't quite add up. "I don't think so. I believe there are two of them. One became the knife that killed Illya, while the other used the knife, left it in the wall, then became something else, hiding itself on her person. That was how it got into the ice chamber to steal her skin. It knew it wouldn't have time before being discovered otherwise."

Drucida watched us, utterly horrified as we puzzled everything out.

"But why leave the knife?" Tholdri asked. "Why was Illya's death different than the others? Why did the skin changers risk being discovered?"

"Her tapestries," Drucida muttered. "She had started a new one just that morning. What if she saw the skin changers?"

I looked at Tholdri. I suspected Drucida was right, but there was more to it. Judging by the way they were living in the cave, the skin changers were more animal or monster than human. They were clever enough to not get caught, but I wasn't sure how far their intelligence extended.

Eiric had convinced many vampires to target the ancients. Could he have done the same with the skin changers? Speaking into their minds from his tomb, convincing them to kill the witches? The deaths had escalated since our arrival. But why?

We all jumped at a knock on the door.

Muttering under his breath, Tholdri went to answer it. A moment later, Elanore and Ophelia joined us. Ophelia was lightly trembling. Elanore must have explained what she had missed.

I truly hoped she could spot a skin changer, because if she couldn't, we were out of options.

After Drucida woke Ian, we spent the rest of the night searching for the other skin changer within the fortress. The sentries had been instructed that no one else was to go in or out. At the very least, we could prevent the skin changer we had encountered in the cave from returning.

With not much of the night left, I managed a moment alone with Asher, Cael, and Tholdri. We shut ourselves away in my and Tholdri's cottage. I hoped nothing would happen while we were preoccupied, but the issue of Cael needed to be addressed.

And I wasn't sure how to address it. We all stood around the lantern I had placed on a small table, and I had no idea what to say. Tact had never been a strength for me.

But blunt honesty? Now that I could do. Hopefully my great uncle could meet me halfway.

I looked at him. His face had returned to normal, but I could sense his desperation. "How long has it been since you last fed?"

He frowned. "That is not relevant."

"Does not feeding make it more difficult for you to maintain your current form?"

His brow furrowed, but he didn't answer.

"I will take that as a yes."

He looked at Asher. "What have you told her?"

Asher's shrug said everything and nothing all at once.

"It doesn't matter what he has said," I interrupted. "I will have the truth now. What will happen if you don't feed?"

He glanced at the men on either side of me. "We have greater concerns to worry ourselves over."

"*What* will happen?" I demanded.

Cael's mouth formed a grim line.

"I believe eventually he will not have a choice," Asher answered for him. "He wishes to be what you need him to be, but that is no longer what he is."

"This is not your business," Cael snapped.

Asher moved closer to me. "*Anything* concerning Lyssandra is my business. I will not have you become a danger to her simply to spare your pride. Are you truly so foolish?"

I stiffened at Asher's words. I was not *anyone's* business, but we could argue about it later.

Cael turned his face away. The room fell silent.

I could have cut the sudden tension with a knife.

Eventually, Tholdri cleared his throat. "How about this? Let's end this conversation here. I'll donate a bit of blood to keep our friend himself, and we can all go back to hunting skin changers."

I blinked at him, stunned. "I cannot ask you to do that."

Tholdri shrugged. "You didn't ask. And it's only blood, Lyss. I've bled plenty over the years." He glanced at Cael. "Although, I hope you don't have to drink directly from the . . . source?"

Cael's expression crumbled. He was very carefully avoiding looking at me. "Any receptacle should do."

That he agreed so easily let me know just how desperate he was. I glanced back and forth between them, settling on Tholdri. "Are you entirely serious?"

He grinned. "Be reasonable, Lyss. I've had time to think this over. He's not going to take blood from you, and I doubt any of the witches will volunteer. Which leaves me, and I don't mind. You sliced open your arm to track the skin changers. How is this any different?"

It *was* different. It simply was. But I couldn't think of how to say so in front of Cael without being insulting.

Asher gently gripped my arm, probably thinking I didn't have the restraint.

I let out a long breath. "Thank you, Tholdri."

He nodded, then grinned at Cael. "Shall we? I'm sure we can find a bowl around here somewhere."

Cael still wasn't looking at me. "Not in front of Lyssandra," he muttered.

I wasn't sure what to say to that, so I said the only thing I could think of. "Asher and I will step outside."

I looked at the vampire in question. He nodded. Together, we went outside.

My spine was stiff as I walked down the narrow lane between dwellings. I was still yet to run into any occupants. That being the case, I walked through someone's small garden and sat on a little wooden bench.

Asher sat beside me. "Tholdri is a good friend."

I buried my face in my hands, shivering against the cold. "Too good. Will this be enough for Cael?"

"For a time, I believe."

I kept my face hidden. "And you?"

"I will be fine."

I lifted my face, forcing myself to look at him. "Are you lying?"

He arched one white brow. "Can you not tell?"

"You are shielding. *Tightly.*"

His expression gave me nothing. And I couldn't sense a single emotion. "Are you worried about me?"

"Would saying yes earn me an honest answer?"

He sighed, leaning his back against the home behind us. He lifted my arm from my lap, observing my bloody sleeve. "You have bled enough, Lyssandra."

"I wasn't offering."

"Oh? And you would offer Tholdri instead? He should not be bled twice in one night."

I frowned. "Are you teasing me?"

He pushed back my sleeve, then gently rubbed the developing scar, somehow knowing that the quick-forming tissue was uncomfortable for me. It was a sensation he wouldn't understand at all. The dead didn't scar. Dried blood flaked off my skin, staining his pale fingers.

I found myself at a loss for words. Tholdri had made it seem so simple. We both bled all the time. But with Asher . . . it would be different. It just would.

"Would you take my blood if I offered?" I bit back my words, but it was too late.

He watched me, still rubbing my arm. "You will only have an answer to that question should such an instance occur. But I would never ask it of you."

Curse it all, I was making it an even bigger deal than it already was. If things grew desperate, and I was the only option . . .

But I couldn't think about it now. I had too many other pressing issues to consider.

I looked down at my lap. "You *will* tell me if it

becomes a necessity." I didn't say it like it was a question.

"As you wish."

Normally it annoyed me how calm he always was about everything, but at that moment, I appreciated it more than anything else. "Tholdri is safe in there with Cael, right?"

"I would smell it if too much blood was spilled."

I left it at that. Bone-achingly tired, I leaned against his shoulder. "I'm worried, Asher. I don't know how to fight these things."

He shifted enough to put his arm around me, saying nothing. He didn't tell me to not be scared, or that everything would be alright. Neither would have been helpful.

But his arm around me as we waited for Cael and Tholdri...

It was enough.

CHAPTER THIRTEEN

I managed a few hours of sleep after the sun rose while Tholdri kept watch. My dreams were filled with skinless bodies and blood. I sat up in bed, squinting my eyes at the harsh light coming in through the window.

Tholdri sat by my feet, leafing through an old book. Sunlight cut across his hair, making it shimmer like spun gold.

"I'm surprised Drucida let you borrow that."

He looked over his shoulder at me. "Why? Because the witches guard their secrets so closely?"

"No, I'm surprised she thought you knew how to read."

"Hah *hah*."

Smirking, I climbed out of bed. The history book wouldn't reveal any magical secrets. Of that, I was sure. Drucida didn't share anything important, if she could help it. I paced toward the window, moving the thin curtain to peer outside. I would be meeting Elanore for my morning meal. She had agreed to teach me what she could, and I would hold her to it—especially if blood magic might help me track the skin changers again. It was our only hope, for now, unless Ophelia or Ian managed to spot them. While word would be spread of the skin changers' existence, the possibility of Ian or Ophelia being able to notice them would remain a secret. We didn't want to make them both targets.

The bed frame creaked, then I heard Tholdri's footsteps behind me. "What do you think the chances are that we'll find another body today?"

"Too high if one of the skin changers is still within the fortress." I let the curtain fall closed. I started to step back, then staggered, clutching at a sharp pain in my chest.

"Lyss?"

I fell to my knees, breathing ragged. "Something is wrong. It—" Unbearable pain choked off my words.

Tholdri knelt beside me, gripping my shoulder. "Lyss, what is it?"

But there was no time. "Help me up!" I rasped.

He obeyed, aiding me as I staggered toward my sword.

"Is it Asher?" he asked, catching on quickly.

My sword glowed as I wrapped my hand around its hilt. Suddenly, I was able to breathe, but something was wrong with the bond. That scared me almost as much as the pain.

"We need to find him," I panted.

"You can't climb a mountain in your condition."

"*Now*, Tholdri."

Shaking his head, he let go of me enough to grab my boots from the floor. I slumped onto the bed, still tightly gripping my sword. It wasn't warning me, and I didn't understand why. Unless whoever was hurting Asher wasn't doing it to kill me.

Tholdri laced my boots a little too tightly, then helped me stand. "Do you know where he's resting for the day?"

"No, but I can find him."

Tholdri helped me into my coat, then we went for the door, opening it just as Elanore was about to knock from the outside. She took one look at my pained, sweating face, then stepped back. "What has happened?"

"No time." We pushed past her, heading down the narrow path, then onward toward the gates.

I could hear her following us down the cobbles, but my attention was on the pain in my chest. It was less now, and the chilly mountain air felt good on my hot skin. Once I was steady enough, I pushed away from Tholdri and broke into a jog. There were few witches in the street. Most of them were probably hiding in their homes, worried they would be the next victims of the skin changers.

As we reached the gates, I remembered Drucida's orders that no one was to go in or out. The stabbing pain was now a dull ache in my chest. Curse the light, I needed to make sure Asher was safe.

Elanore ran up behind us, breathing heavily. "What's —*huff*—going on?"

"We need to get through the gates," Tholdri explained.

The sentries were peering down at us, looking worried and unsure. If anyone who looked like Elanore, Drucida, or Charles instructed them to open the gates, they were supposed to find the other two to verify the individual's identity. It had seemed a wise plan the previous night, but right now, we didn't have time for it.

Comprehending the issue, Elanore nodded. "Prepare yourselves. I can only hold them open for a moment."

My eyes widened, but I was too panicked to ask for an explanation. Tholdri helped me toward the gates. The sentries spoke in panicked whispers above, unsure about what to do.

Tholdri and I turned back to watch Elanore.

Her eyes were closed, palms outstretched. So close to the gates, the wind picked up around us. No . . . it was coming from Elanore.

A sudden gust of wind lifted her hair and billowed her long-sleeved gray gown around her. The wind hit us next, staggering us backwards. Tholdri jerked me to one side as the wind howled around the center of the gates. Slowly, they creaked open.

"Go!" Elanore shouted.

I pulled away from Tholdri and lunged through the gates, barely making it before they slammed shut behind me with a deafening *clang*.

"Lyss!" Tholdri had tried to come after me, but the gates shut too quickly. He gripped the thick iron bars as if he could pry them open. "Lyss, don't you dare run off without me."

Elanore had collapsed to her knees on the cobbles.

She hung her head, her face hidden by her hair. I had a feeling she would not be able to open the gates again.

I gave Tholdri an apologetic look.

"Lyss—" he warned.

"Sorry, Tholdri." I finally took the time to strap my sword on properly, then I turned and ran.

I didn't know exactly where Asher was hiding, nor if he would be with Cael, but I could feel him. The pain in my chest was still there. We were still connected. But something was wrong.

My boots slipped across loose rocks and I had to slow my pace as Tholdri shouted after me. I hated that I had to do it, but I shut out his voice and focused on the bond stretching between me and Asher.

My feet led me without thought, down the mountain instead of up it. Soon Tholdri's voice was swallowed by the wind, and the fortress became smaller behind me. He would find Drucida and the others eventually to let him out. I could only hope he wouldn't be *too* angry with me when he found me again.

The cold wind died down the further I descended, my eyes scanning the bleak scenery for Asher's hiding place. Vampires didn't always need to breathe, and they were physically capable of climbing almost anywhere. It could be nearly impossible to find their hiding places. Impossible for anyone but their human servants.

My steps slowed as I sensed him nearby. I glanced around, confused. I saw nothing but bleak, gray, rocky earth. I closed my eyes, stilling my other senses so I could properly listen.

There. Water flowing somewhere beneath the earth. There was a cavern nearby.

"It was bold of you to come alone."

I spun, already knowing who I would find. I recognized his voice. "Xavier."

He stood with his hands in his pockets. A long, tan coat draped his fit body. His shaggy hair fell into his eyes.

"Why are you here?"

"You foolish girl. You're walking right into his trap." He pinched the bridge of his nose, just above one of the lumps that showed it had previously been broken, then shook his head.

I reached for my sword, but hesitated. It hadn't warned me at all. Now that Eiric was free, Xavier had no reason to kill me. "What have you done with Asher?"

"I hurt him just enough to draw you out here. You should never have let him go so long without feeding. It has weakened him."

This time, I did draw my sword, but it remained silent. "I will ask you one last time. Why are you here?"

If he was worried about the threat I posed, he didn't show it. "I've come to warn you. You are playing right into Eiric's trap."

"You are his human servant. Why would you warn me?"

"I think you are well aware of how I feel about my predicament."

I held my sword out in front of me. My hands felt clammy around its hilt. "You would not be here without his permission."

"I cannot disobey any direct orders. Other than that, I am free to move about as I wish. During the day, at least." He took a step toward me and I tensed. He looked me up and down. "Your sword would warn you if I intended you harm, correct? I have been directly ordered *not* to kill you, or permanently disable you in any way."

"But you hurt Asher."

He lifted his hands, palms out. "No lasting damage. And look at you, entirely unscathed."

"You are splitting hairs."

He smiled. "Splitting hairs is the only way I have managed to see you at all. I cannot disobey orders, but I have not been ordered to stay away from you. I imagine after this, I will be." His smile wilted. "You must not learn magic, Lyssandra. It is exactly what he wants."

I lowered my sword a fraction. "Why?"

He pursed his lips and wrinkled his nose.

"You've been ordered not to tell me."

He nodded.

"And how do you know that I'm learning magic?"

"Because that's exactly what he planned. And his plans rarely fail."

I lowered my sword the rest of the way. Asher's pain lingered in my chest. He was unbearably weak, and he had hidden it from me. "Did Eiric manipulate the skin changers? Did he make them attack the witches?"

Again, the pursed expression.

"I'll take that as a *yes*." My heart beat loudly in my ears. Eiric was behind it, but I still didn't fully understand his motive. "Why would he *want* me to learn magic? My aim is to defeat him."

"I cannot tell you. All I can say is that in learning, you are digging your own grave. You are digging *everyone's* graves." His face twisted, and he clenched his gut like he was in pain. "I must go."

"Wait." I removed one hand from my sword to reach toward him, but he was already gone, moving just as fast as a vampire.

Cursing under my breath, I looked around for the underground cavern's inlet. I walked until I found a small rocky entrance. My breath shuddered in my lungs. There was no way to see where it led, or how steep the fall would be. But I needed to make sure Asher could last until nightfall.

Wishing I had Tholdri and a long length of rope, but knowing I could not afford to wait for either, I got on my hands and knees, lowering one leg into the cavern. I lowered the other next, until most of my body was hanging into the hole, my feet searching for a place to touch down.

Fighting against the feeling of panic creeping up my spine, I kicked one foot back. The toe of my boot scraped across solid rock.

I pushed both feet against it, lowering myself further. With my footing steady, I crouched into the cavern, glancing around in the darkness. "Asher?"

"You shouldn't have come."

His voice sounded soft, weak, but it could have just been because it was daylight outside. He was ancient enough, and powerful enough, that he could move around some during the day, but not into the light, and not far.

I crept further into the cavern, giving my eyes time to adjust to the near darkness. I spotted him, lying on his back across one smooth expanse of rock. A little stream of water trickled past my boots.

"Where is Cael?"

Asher didn't answer me, but I didn't see the other vampire, so he must be resting elsewhere. With the mountains being made mostly of rocks, which had crumbled and fallen countless times, there had to be hundreds of caverns across the range.

I crept closer, smelling the sharp scent of blood. Rage washed through me when I saw what Xavier had done. A dagger protruded from Asher's chest. A fraction higher, and Xavier would have hit his heart.

Asher took a ragged breath as I knelt beside him. "He didn't hurt you."

"No, but he did hurt you." My hands fluttered around the dagger. I needed to pull it out, but I was afraid of damaging him further. "My sword should have warned me." I forced my breathing to still. I understood why it hadn't warned me. Xavier meant me no harm at all. In fact, I knew he wanted me to kill him.

"I'm going to pull the dagger out. Will you—" I didn't know what to say. His pain was still just a dull ache in my chest. "Are you shielding me from it?"

His chin lowered slightly, the barest of nods.

"You should have told me how weak you had become. You're just as bad as Cael."

When he said nothing, I leaned closer. My nerves

made my hands tremble. He needed blood. My squeamishness had made it possible for Xavier to attack him.

I was a fool. I had never let him bite me, but I had given him blood once before, when Amarithe had weakened him. This was no different.

So why did it feel different?

Shaking my head at my own thoughts, I drew my sword. There was just enough light shining from the cavern entrance for me to see that its eye had opened. My movements awkward, I managed to push up the sleeve covering my dominant arm. I slid my skin against my sword's sharp edge, creating a new slice to mirror the healing wound on the opposite arm.

Setting my sword aside, I crouched over Asher, holding my bleeding arm above his mouth.

His eyes finally opened, a flicker of silver in the darkness. "Lyssandra."

"No. Just take it. You'll need your strength to heal when I remove the dagger."

He hesitated a moment longer, then slowly lifted one hand to take my arm. But he didn't pull. It was more my action than his as my arm lowered toward his mouth. He closed his eyes and began to drink.

I looked away. While we had done things that most would consider far more intimate, this was what I shied away from. Needs laid bare.

His shields came down as he drank. This was what he wanted from me—a completed bond. But he knew I did not give it willingly. And that wasn't what he wanted.

He released my arm abruptly, and I knew with

sudden surety he hadn't meant for me to feel his emotions. I turned my gaze back toward him and we stared at each other in the darkness.

I gripped the dagger and pulled it from his chest.

He grunted and closed his eyes. With my blood in him, he would be able to heal the wound, but it was a serious injury. Even if he could heal it, it still hurt.

I started to retract the dagger, but he grabbed my wrist before I could move away. He sat up slowly, his face creased with pained lines. "What did Xavier want from you?"

"He wanted to warn me. Eiric sent the skin changers to hunt the witches. He wants me to learn magic, but I don't know why. Xavier couldn't say."

"I had worried that was a possibility."

My brows lifted. "You *had*?"

"It was one of many that I considered. In a way, the skin changers hunting the witches worked out in your favor. Their presence gave you something to offer." He leaned closer, still lightly gripping my wrist. The new wound wasn't as deep as the other. It had already stopped bleeding.

"How long will the blood last you?" I asked.

"Long enough."

"That's not a real answer. Having you weak, weakens me."

"I will not take again what you are not willing to give. I would rather travel over the mountain to one of the distant villages."

"Why haven't you?" I asked.

"You have needed me every night since we arrived."

I blushed. That hadn't exactly been true. The first night, I had simply wanted to see him. Then there had been more deaths, and the skin changers. Too many things to worry about.

A question scratched at my throat. I didn't want to know, but I *had* to know. "What would it mean to you for me to give my blood willingly? Not like this." I gestured to my wrist still loosely gripped in his hand. "But if I—" I swallowed the lump in my throat, looking down at my lap. "You know what I mean."

"You are not a woman to blush easily. Why does this one thing unsettle you so?"

His words made me look at him. "You can't tell?"

"You have become highly adept at shielding." He gave me the barest hint of a smile. "It is troubling."

"Is it difficult for you to still be awake now? With the sun up?"

"It is . . . painful, but your blood helps. Please answer my question, Lyssandra."

The way he whispered my name elicited a tug low in my gut. "I would think you knew me well enough by now to figure it out."

"You are not a *simple* woman to read."

"You answer my question, and I'll answer yours." He still hadn't told me exactly what it would mean to him if I shared my blood willingly.

He finally released my wrist. I set the dagger on the ground beside us, then turned back to him.

He met my gaze, unwavering. "Normally, when I take blood, it is simply food. I bespell my . . . victim, and they remember nothing. It is a means to survival, nothing more."

I narrowed my eyes at him. "But . . . "

"But with you, it would mean more. Blood does not only have to be about survival. It is at the root of our bond."

"And yet, you will not ask for it," I said lowly.

"I will not." He leaned back against his hands, his shoulders hunching. There was a darker black stain on his black shirt, blood from his wound.

"Will you be able to heal?"

"It will be easier come nightfall."

My fingers lifted to the top button of his shirt before I could think better of it. If the wound would take a while to heal, it should be bandaged. I froze with my fingers near his collarbone. "May I?"

He nodded.

I used both hands to undo his buttons, revealing the wound. It was cleaner than I'd expected—the dagger had been wickedly sharp. But it was still bleeding. He was a vampire. He should have been healing faster than me.

"The blood wasn't enough, was it?" I kept my eyes on the wound as I asked it.

"I was already weak. More weak than I realized."

I was such a fool. This was all my fault. "You'll take more then."

"Lyssandra—"

"Do not argue with me." Tears that would never fall made my throat tight. I was frustrated, tired, and scared.

"Your wound has already begun to heal."

"Then I'll make a new one." I forced myself to meet his gaze. Funny, how I could go from being entirely objectional about donating blood, to trying to force it on him.

He only stared at me.

I lifted Xavier's bloody dagger from the stone beside me. It would be easier to use than my sword.

"I will take no more from you. I will rest, and recover come nightfall."

"This is no time for either of us to be weak." I removed my sheath and coat, then lowered the collar of my shirt. I drew the dagger along my collarbone, wincing at the sharp sting. "No more arguments." I crawled toward him, straddling him, careful to not touch his wound.

He looked at me wide-eyed. I didn't think I could have shocked him more if I had sprouted a second head. The stunned look on his face almost made everything worth it. It wasn't often one was able to shock an ancient vampire.

"The wound will not stay open for long." I leaned my chest closer.

His throat bobbed as he swallowed. "Are you sure?"

"Don't I look sure?"

His silver eyes glistened, the most visible part of his face in the near darkness. He lowered his mouth to the fresh wound, but instead of drinking, he ran his tongue along my skin.

I shivered. I might not be ready for all forms of intimacy, but sex? Well, we had already gone there, and I had no complaints.

He licked my wound again, and I pressed closer, forgetting that I might hurt him.

His response showed that he was either in less pain now, or he no longer cared. He pulled me against him, pressing his mouth over the fresh cut. His hands lowered to my hips, grinding me against his lap.

I moaned in response.

He pulled his mouth away from my collarbone to kiss me. The coppery tang of my blood lingered on his lips. I kissed him harder, deftly running my tongue along his fangs.

His hands pushed underneath my shirt, warmer now than they had been in days, but not warm enough. I couldn't give enough blood in a single day to fully restore him, but I could do as much as I was able.

I tilted my head back, inviting him to drink more.

He spoke as he laid kisses along my throat. "The wound has stopped bleeding, Lyssandra. But it was enough. I will survive."

My body reacted to each kiss, wanting more. "I don't believe you."

He pulled away enough to slip my shirt over my head. "Then I will prove it to you."

Several thoughts warred in my mind. Skin changers. Elanore's lessons. Tholdri searching for me. They all dissolved as Asher removed my undergarment and cradled my breasts, kissing his way down my sternum.

"Do you believe me now?" he breathed along my skin.

I rolled my hips, moving against him. "More proof is

needed." Despite my words, I knew he was still weak, and I didn't want him to overexert himself.

I stood, having to crouch a bit in the low cavern. I removed my boots, then my breeches and undergarment in one smooth motion.

He gave me a knowing look. I might blush about blood, but the rest of it was no issue. I knew exactly what I wanted. I would have liked to stalk toward him, but the cavern was too low. Instead I got on my hands and knees and crawled.

Any hint of amusement wiped clean from his face. His eyes held only heat as he watched me crawling toward him. I stopped halfway up his legs, undoing his breeches. His shirt hung open around his chest. The wound still hadn't healed, but it was no longer bleeding.

He moved enough for me to pull down his pants, but he otherwise lounged like a contented cat.

I looked up at him through a loose lock of my hair. I knew he could see me better than I could see him. "You're enjoying this far too much."

"I am very weak, Lyssandra. I cannot help myself."

I smirked, admiring the full length of him for only the second time. I wrapped fingers stained with my own blood around him and he gasped. "Neither can I," I whispered.

I climbed on top of him, gently pushing his chest to make him lay on his back. After just a few kisses, my body was more than ready. I reacted to him like no other. I slid onto him, moving slowly, bit by bit, watching his face as he entered me.

He cupped my jaw and pulled me down for a kiss.

His mouth still tasted like my blood. I became highly aware of his injury and his weakness, and wasn't sure how much I should move.

His hands slid behind my neck, then trailed down either side of my bare back, ending up on my hips, guiding me gently. I pressed one hand against his shoulder, sitting up so I could watch his face. Cold stone ground into my knees on either side of him, but my body felt impossibly warm. I could feel the blood in both our veins. I could hear our heartbeats in my ears.

Something welled up inside me, and it wasn't just sex or blood. It was molten heat. Power I didn't fully recognize.

Asher pulled me down for another kiss, then whispered against my lips, "Your magic dances across my skin."

I didn't have to ask him what he meant. I could feel it too. I could feel my blood within him. Even more, I could control it. I took the warm feeling in my chest and pushed it into him.

He gasped, tilting back his head. I willed my heat into him, using the connection in my blood to warm us both.

His fingers dug into my hips as he rolled me over, careful to not scrape my skin on the hard stone. He thrust into me, stronger than before.

I ran a hand down his chest, wiping away the lingering blood. The wound was gone.

He gripped my hand, holding it against him as he thrust into me again. My pleasure built with the rhythm of our flesh, but my dizziness was distracting. Pushing my warmth into him had left me lightheaded.

He slowed his rhythm, releasing my hand to lean over me, pressing our bodies together. He was warm now, so warm.

I closed my eyes and fell into that warmth, stroking my fingers back through his silken hair as I kissed him deeply. His fang nicked my lip and I didn't care. I kissed him harder, my blood lingering between our mouths.

His fingers kneaded the back of my neck almost painfully as pressure built again between us. Molten heat tipped me over the edge, my hips lifting to meet him. My body reacted so overwhelmingly that I raked my fingernails down his back. He finished seconds later, sending another pulse of heat through my body.

We were both left warm and panting, unable to speak for several long moments.

Still cradling the back of my head to keep me off the hard stone, he kissed lightly down my jaw. "How did you do that?"

His words sent a delicious shiver down my spine. "I don't know. That's never happened to me before."

He rolled off me, then cradled me against him before I could think to move.

I looked over my shoulder at him. "You feel warm. Is your wound entirely healed?"

His eyes searched my face, his expression almost . . . awestricken. He leaned back enough for me to observe his chest. It was stained with blood, but his skin was entirely smooth. "I had assumed blood magic was more," he pursed his lips, searching for the right word, "*destructive.*"

I shivered. "I could feel my blood inside you. I was in control of it. I could have just as easily used it to harm you."

"A frightening gift indeed."

I stiffened at his words. "You're afraid of me?"

He stroked my hair, soothing me. "I have already offered you my life, Lyssandra."

I relaxed against him. He might not fear me, but the power I had felt . . . I supposed I now feared myself. I could understand why Drucida was hesitant to teach me.

"I should find Tholdri, but I am reluctant to leave you unprotected."

He almost smiled. "If Xavier were to return now, he would not survive. Whatever you have done, it is more than blood." He tilted my chin toward him, then kissed me softly. He pulled away and whispered, "You have my thanks."

"Don't mention it."

He settled back in against me. "Have there been any more signs of the skin changers?"

I shook my head. "I don't know what Eiric will have them do next. Perhaps they have served their purpose."

"Is that just wishful thinking?"

I managed a small smile. "It most certainly is." I sat up. "I should go. Elanore was supposed to start teaching me today."

"It seems you might already be far ahead of whatever she planned to show you."

"I'm going to need a lot more than that to defeat Eiric."

He watched me, almost sorrowful. So much between us still left unsaid.

But at least he was strong again. He was going to need that strength. Apparently, I was playing right into Eiric's trap, but it was too late to turn back. If he wanted me to have magic, then I would have magic. And I would use it to boil the blood in his veins.

CHAPTER FOURTEEN

Tholdri found me as I hiked back up the mountain. I was surprised to see he was alone. He lifted a brow at my disheveled, bloody clothing as he reached me. "Do I even want to know?"

"No." I kept walking.

He turned and caught up to my side, his boots crunching over loose, jagged stones. "I am assuming Asher is well?"

"He is now. Xavier attacked him."

He grabbed my arm to stop me from walking. *"Xavier?"*

I told him what I had learned about Eiric and the skin changers. I'd had some time to think about it as I walked, but I still didn't understand why my enemy would want me to become stronger. Why he would want me to have powerful witches as allies.

Tholdri let out a low whistle. "Eiric is clever, I will give him that."

I pushed my hair back as a gust of wind blew it into

my face. My braid had unraveled during my . . . *activities* with Asher. The new wound on my arm still stung. The slice across my collarbone was hidden by my shirt. "Whatever Eiric is planning, Xavier wants to stop it. We might be able to use him against Eiric."

"But how?"

I shook my head. I hadn't gotten that far yet. Mostly because I couldn't stop thinking about what happened with Asher. My blood . . .

It was like what had happened with tracking the skin changers. I could will my blood to do what I wanted. But there had to be more to it than that. If blood magic was so dangerous that the users were once executed, there had to be more. I wanted to speak with Elanore about everything, but then I'd have to reveal what happened with Asher.

"Care to share any of the thoughts knocking around in that thick skull of yours?"

Another blast of icy wind gusted us. I looked at Tholdri. "In the interest of us being *partners*, I'll tell you. But no teasing."

He lifted one hand, palm out. "You have my solemn vow."

"I am definitely going to regret this." I turned and started walking again as I told him *everything*. We were halfway up the mountain by the time I finished.

While Tholdri seemed suitably stunned, he was also grinning. "When exactly did you start having more fun than me, Lyss?"

"Fun. That's one way of putting it."

He peered up at the fortress as we continued walking. "Cavorting with witches and getting naked with vampires. Sounds like fun to me."

"And you sound like you never swore oaths to the Helius Order."

His mood quickly sobered. "It *is* strange, isn't it? So much that we were taught to fear, to *hate*."

"Many vampires are still deserving of those sentiments." I slipped on some loose gravel that wouldn't have been an issue if my legs weren't still feeling wobbly. Everything seemed just a little bit surreal.

"But doesn't it make you think more about it? While it's true that we hunt vampires after they have claimed lives, sometimes we face more than one. I can't help but wonder if some of them were like Asher."

I had thought the same many times. Even before Asher, I had thought it. Some deaths still weighed heavily on my conscience. "I'm just glad we were never involved in any witch hunts."

He stopped walking, turning to face me. "Could you have done it? Killed someone like Drucida or Elanore?"

"If they were actively attacking me, yes."

"And if the Potentate simply told you they had killed someone? Could you have hunted them?"

I crossed my arms against the cold wind. We weren't far from the fortress now. "Why all these sudden questions?"

He frowned, pushing his golden locks back from his face only to have them gusted forward again. "I don't know. Just being here, it makes me think."

"Did it really not bother you to donate blood to Cael?"

He shrugged, averting his gaze. "Maybe a little, but it was an easy decision to make. He's . . . I know what he can become. He's terrifying. But, he's still a person, an ally. And he needed my help."

"I'm sorry you were put in such a position to begin with."

His grin returned. "I like all *sorts* of positions, Lyss. Perhaps you and Asher could teach me some new ones."

I rolled my eyes. "You're incorrigible." I moved to continue on, but hesitated, turning back toward Tholdri. "For what it's worth, I'm glad you came with us. I only tried to leave you behind to keep you safe."

"You know, Steifan would have felt the same as me. He was probably devastated when he got the letter saying you wouldn't be coming back."

"He's better off."

"Oh most certainly." He leaned close to my face. "But was that really your decision to make?" He turned and started walking again before I could answer.

I stared after him for a moment before catching up to his side. Perhaps I had robbed Steifan of the luxury of choice, but I would do it again. He would survive, and that was what mattered. Markus, I felt a little bad about. His life was tied to mine, so perhaps he deserved the opportunity to defend it.

I shook my head and kept walking. Too late now. As much as the idea appealed, one could not walk into the past, or stay rooted in the present. I could only walk forward. So that was what I would do.

Elanore, Drucida, Charles, and Ian were all waiting inside the closed gates upon our return, watching us through the iron bars. Elanore looked like she hadn't slept in a week. Dark smudges marred her eyes, her skin almost seeming to sag from her bones. She hadn't been like that before she opened the gates for us.

Ian narrowed his eyes, looking me up and down before moving on to Tholdri. After a moment, he nodded. "It's them."

I had been worried that what I had done with Asher might have changed my energy in some way, but it seemed I was the same. It was a small relief.

We moved aside while the gates opened, then we stepped through.

Elanore lifted a brow at the state of my clothing. "I take it you found your vampire?"

I frowned. I would not blush. I would not—curse it all, I was blushing. I avoided Charles' scornful gaze. "I did."

Drucida's mouth pursed then curled down at my curt response, but what was I supposed to say? That they had lost many lives because of me? There was no way I could tell them the reason they were being targeted. They would toss me out in an instant, believing that with me gone, the skin changers would leave them alone. But I didn't think that was true. If Eiric had what he wanted, distracting me further with the skin changers was pointless.

"I'm ready for my lessons now." I hesitated at Elanore's weary expression. "Unless you are needing to rest?"

Drucida stepped forward, smoothing her sapphire blue skirts. "I will be teaching you today." The look in her gold-flecked eyes said she wanted to peel away the layers of my skin until she found my secrets.

I straightened. "Very well."

Charles' mustache bristled furiously. If looks could kill, Drucida would have keeled over then and there. "She will be the ruin of us all. And it will be *your* fault." He stormed past her, stomping down the cobbles leading further into the fortress.

Ian stared down at his feet.

"I take it you told him about the blood magic?" I asked Drucida.

She nodded once, her attention now on Ian. "You will speak of this to no one."

His head bowed further. "I wouldn't dream of it. May I go now?"

I waited as Drucida dismissed him, and he hurried after Charles.

"He's always been a timid boy." Drucida watched him walking away as fast as he could without actually running. She turned toward me. "And yet, he seems to like you. Imagine that."

"Most people do." I smiled sweetly at my lie.

Drucida scoffed, then looked at Elanore. "Go get some rest."

Elanore gave me an apologetic smile, then went in the direction Ian had gone.

Finally, Drucida acknowledged Tholdri. "You'll come with us. We need someone to watch the door. Make sure there are no interruptions."

"Ah, yes, door watching. I've been doing a lot of that lately."

Ignoring Tholdri's sarcasm, Drucida scrutinized every inch of me. "Let us go. You can tell me what happened with your vampire as we walk."

My stomach dropped. Cael had hinted that Drucida could sense lies. And yet, I most certainly couldn't tell her the complete truth. I would have to tell her just enough to satisfy her.

I forced myself to relax as we started walking. If Drucida and I really were alike, half-truths would never do. I could only hope she wouldn't resort to *my* favored tactics for mining information. We might very well kill each other if she did.

I JUMPED as Drucida slammed the door behind me. Her quarters were no less cold than the previous day, but this time I didn't mind it. My blood still felt warmer than usual, like I was radiating heat from the inside.

She walked past me, using a half-burned candle to light a few more on the central table. She'd cleared away the dishes of my blood, and all her herbs were back in their little jars.

I had told her about Eiric's human servant attacking Asher, and that it was all part of some devious scheme. Fortunately, she assumed I had no idea what that scheme was, because she didn't press me for details.

Only now I feared she was going to come around to

it again. She glanced past me toward the closed door. Tholdri waited on the other side.

She let out a shaky breath, then collapsed into the nearest chair. "I suspect Elanore knows more about the skin changers than she is letting on."

It took me a moment to comprehend what she was saying. I took a step toward the table. "Elanore? Why would you think that?"

She sunk further into her chair, bunching her fine gown up around her lap. Her eyes were distant, seeing something that wasn't in the room. "When we went into that cave, she didn't seem afraid. Nervous, yes, but not afraid. And when the skin changer transformed," she swiped a palm across her face and shook her head, "her reaction simply wasn't right. I don't know how to describe it."

I adjusted my sword, then took the seat across from her. "Why didn't you mention this last night?"

"I tried to talk myself out of it. I was frightened and tired. I wanted to believe my own emotions were altering my perceptions. But I can't get the idea out of my head." She looked at me solidly. "I've known Elanore most of her life. She has suffered great tragedy, but she has also done great things. I would like to believe the best of her."

I understood her situation far too well. So many times, I had wanted to believe the best of others. But people just kept disappointing me. Most of them, anyway. "Why are you telling me this?"

She straightened enough to lean forward. "I want

you to watch her. Test her, if you must. See if any of her reactions seem off."

"I can do that. But what about my lessons?"

She lifted a brow. "Lyssandra, the stink of blood magic is all over you. You're lying about how much you know."

Wonderful. She knew I was lying about something, but she had it wrong. And yet if I corrected her, she would be looking for a different lie. "Some things have come to me, but there is still much I must learn."

"Find out what Elanore knows, and I will teach you."

"You can't just keep adding new tasks in order for you to teach me. If Elanore is somehow involved in this mystery, I *will* discover her role, but I need help."

She scrutinized my face, her entire body suddenly tense. "You must understand, teaching you goes against everything I believe in. All magic has a price. You saw what summoning that wind did to Elanore. But blood magic." She shook her head. "It exacts that price from others. Since the user never has to pay, they are not limited in what they can do."

I watched the candlelight play across her face. She and Elanore had alluded to much, but I still felt like I knew nothing. "I understand how to control my own blood, in a way. I can sense it, at least. I understand the connection. But I have to open a vein to do it. Is that not a price to pay? I only have so much blood."

She leaned back in her seat, looking horribly tired. "Those of your kind always start out using their own blood. But the true power of blood magic is using that of others."

I stared at her. "Can I really do that?"

"Only time will tell if you are able to learn, but what you have displayed so far shows promise." She seemed to think for a moment. "You have spilled blood before..."

I furrowed my brow. "Quite a bit, yes."

"Did you ever feel drawn to it?"

I opened my mouth, then shut it, thrown off by the odd question. "I don't think so." I had been covered in blood many times, but I'd never felt magic like I had been experiencing recently. I thought about it. "The first time I felt anything like magic was when a Sidhe taught me to see through glamour." I hesitated. "Or maybe it was before that, with my sword. Sometimes it can speak into my mind."

Drucida pursed her lips for a moment. "While I would be interested to hear more about this Sidhe, the experiences you are describing are different. I am trying to figure out why your blood magic has unlocked now, and not any time before. If being a human servant hasn't cut you off from it, you should have had it all along. So what changed?"

I sifted through my recent memories, trying to pinpoint where things might have changed for me. My grandfather had died, but I had bound Markus as my servant before that. *That* definitely qualified as magic. Maybe even blood magic. And before that—

My jaw fell open. I should've thought of it before. "The necromancer I told you about—Amarithe. She suppressed my bond with Asher while she tried to kill him. There was a short period of time where I was no longer a human servant. Right after that, my sword glowed for me. Amarithe claimed that could only happen if I had access to magic."

Drucida smirked.

"What is it?" I asked, feeling vaguely offended by her reaction.

She shook her head, smiling. "The first witch with blood magic in decades, and you only have access to it because a necromancer tried to kill you."

"Tried to kill Asher," I corrected. "And once she realized I could access my magic, she manipulated me into freeing Eiric."

"Perhaps Eiric knew all along what was needed to free your magic. He needed you to have magic to break the seal, so he ordered her to free you from your bond."

I blinked at her, realizing I had said too much. If she figured out that Eiric still wanted me to learn more about my magic, she would be even more reluctant to teach me.

She stood, then paced toward her altar, giving me her back. "There is more at play here than either of us comprehend. I do wish I could have seen Illya's final tapestry." She looked over her shoulder at me, reminding me of a raven halfway hidden in its feathers. "I will not give you my blood to experiment with, Lyssandra, but I can try to help you discover more tricks with yours. If only to use such skills against the skin changers."

I nodded, still feeling slightly shaken. "It's a start."

She smiled softly. "I hope you have more blood to spare after what you gave to your vampire."

I swallowed the lump in my throat. I hadn't told her any specifics, so how did she know? "I can spare a bit more."

"Good." She lifted the dagger from her altar. "Let's get started."

CHAPTER FIFTEEN

I left Drucida's home at dusk with several new cuts and a pounding headache.

Tholdri waited for me outside, leaning against the nearest wall, looking bored. He glanced me over, pushing away from the wall. "I was going to complain about how long that took, but the look on your face has me reconsidering my complaints."

I flexed my hands, straining the bandages on either forearm. "Blood magic is not a pleasant affair."

He fell into step at my side as I started walking. I was weak, tired, and absolutely starving.

"But were you able to learn?"

"A bit." I still couldn't help my disappointment. I could do a few new tricks manipulating my blood in a small dish, like heating it after Drucida turned it to ice, but everything I had learned didn't seem helpful.

"Do you have any new ideas on tracking the skin changers?"

I shook my head as we reached the main street and

headed toward the dining hall. I stumbled several times, and I wasn't sure if it was from practicing my magic, or from healing Asher. Maybe both. Drucida claimed blood magic had no price, but it did. I was practically asleep on my feet. "We will search the mountain for their new lair tonight."

"And if the knife is still within the fortress?"

I shook my head again. "I don't know. Whether it's a knife or masquerading as someone here, it has no scent. I still have hope that Ian or Ophelia can help, but only if they come close enough to the skin changer to notice its energy." My toe caught on a cobblestone, nearly tripping me. I cursed under my breath. Food. I needed food.

"What about the other bodies in the ice chamber?" Tholdri asked. "Can you cast another enchantment to track the killer through the victim's death?"

"I'm not sure if enchantment is the right word for it." Although, I didn't know what other word to use. Ritual? Spell? Nothing seemed right. "And Elanore seemed to think the death needed to be fresh." I still hadn't told him about Drucida's suspicions. I wasn't sure what to think of them.

"Well we have nothing else to go on."

He was right. I just didn't like the idea of bleeding on the icy corpses. Not to mention, I'd already lost a lot of blood. Losing more might weaken me too greatly.

We reached the dining hall. With no deaths that day, many witches had grown brave enough to leave their homes. The hall hummed with hushed voices and warm light.

I looked up at the double doors, one side slightly

ajar, and didn't want to go in. I looked awful and felt worse. I didn't want to hear any more whispers about me. "Let's find Ian before we eat," I decided. "See if he's noticed anything strange."

Tholdri nodded. He tried to hide it, but I didn't miss his worried look. Maybe I seemed even worse off than I thought.

I forced myself up the steps, my muscles burning. All I wanted was a full belly and a warm bed.

Tholdri reached the door ahead of me and held it open. Every face in the large chamber turned to look at us as we entered. I tried not to wilt under the pressure of so many questioning gazes.

My sword woke up as I walked between the long tables. Witches clutched plates and bowls, glancing at me out the corners of their eyes. While my sword whispered no warning, it was on alert. Something had unsettled it. Unfortunately, with every single person now pretending not to look at me, I couldn't tell who was thinking potentially treacherous thoughts.

I continued walking without a word to anyone, eventually pushing my way through the partial doors into the kitchen. I peered through cloying steam and woodsmoke, searching for Ian.

A young woman rushed forward through the haze carrying a massive platter. She saw me at the last moment and skidded to a halt, but her momentum was too much for the platter of food. It went careening forward.

Tholdri lunged around me to catch it, but he was too

late. Hot soup scalded my chest and stomach before seeping down across my breeches.

I just stood there for a moment. Normally I could have reacted in time, but blood loss does terrible things to one's capacity for strength and speed. I took several deep breaths. The poor girl looked like she thought I might kill her.

"A towel?" I asked through gritted teeth.

Ian came forward through the fog. He assessed the situation, then shooed the girl away. He and Tholdri starting cleaning up the mess.

I left them to find my own towel, passing massive tureens of soup, and racks of baked bread. Trade with the villages over the mountain must have been good for such a surplus.

I found a rag hanging from a hook next to a few clean aprons. I patted at the soup staining my clothing, but it was no use. It had all soaked in, leaving me reeking of garlic and leeks. At least it made the blood and dirt less conspicuous.

Tholdri and Ian found me, then escorted me to a small adjoining storeroom.

Ian stood close, not as frightened of me as most of the others seemed to be. Light cut in through the door left partially ajar. His copper skin shone with sweat from the hot kitchen. "Sorry about Mona. She never looks where she's going. You're not the first one to experience a hot soup bath."

I flicked my hands down my shirt as if I could brush off the soup. "My clothes were ruined anyway."

"I noticed the blood when you arrived at the gates. Your energy seemed different too."

I straightened, forgetting my ruined shirt and burned skin. "Different?" When he'd confirmed we weren't skin changers, I had assumed I was unaltered.

He nodded. "The two energies around you were equal when we met. Now one is shining much brighter than the other."

I glanced at Tholdri, then back to Ian. "What do they look like?"

His brow wrinkled beneath his shaggy hair. "I'm sorry, it is not easy to explain. While I do see the energies, it is more about how they feel. His for example," he gestured toward Tholdri like he was a prized mule for sale, "feels safe and relaxing. The colors of sunset, but also the *feel*."

"Sunset is not a relaxing time for many of us," Tholdri muttered.

Ian grinned. "It is for those who do not hunt vampires." He turned back toward me. "Your energies are both darker."

"Darker?" I wasn't sure what I had wanted to hear, but it wasn't that.

"Not in a bad way, just more . . . muted. Calm. One is *very* calm."

"That would be the vampire," Tholdri whispered conspiratorially.

I scowled. "And the other?"

Ian looked up and stroked his chin, thinking. He jumped as a few pots clattered in the kitchen, then shook his head. "The other energy feels like a rumble beneath the earth. Imposing and a bit ominous, but also," he extended one hand, as if grasping for the correct word, "it's like it's supposed to be there." He snapped his fingers. "I've got it. It feels like thunder. A bit electric."

I frowned at him. "Lovely. Tholdri is a sunset, and I'm thunder."

Tholdri waggled his eyebrows at me. "Sunset doesn't seem so funny now, does it?"

I ignored him. "This isn't the reason we came here. Have you seen or sensed anything unusual? The skin changer can look like anyone."

He shook his head. "No. I've been peeking out in the dining hall every so often. Everyone seems like themselves. Can these things really do what Drucida said?"

I nodded. "Yes, and so you must speak of this to no one. I don't want you to become a target."

He shivered. "Yes, I rather like my skin."

"We'll leave you then. We have to search the mountain tonight, so if you see anything, keep it to yourself. Tell only me, or Drucida." I left out Elanore, just in case Drucida was right about her.

"Of course." He bobbed his head slightly. I started to walk past him, but he turned. "Oh and one last thing."

We both looked at him.

"It may be nothing. She's been this way since I first met her."

"Go on," I pressed.

"Well Teresa, she has no energy at all. Nothing that I can see, at least. But like I said, she has always been that way. Nothing about her has changed."

I turned fully toward him. "She has *no* energy? What does that mean?"

He shrugged. "I told Elanore about it once. She didn't seem concerned."

I pursed my lips. Elanore again. I really would have to take a closer look at her. "Thank you. We'll see you again soon."

I left the little storeroom with Tholdri at my heels. We would abscond with some bread, and maybe some cheese. There was no time to sit and eat with witches to question, skin changers to hunt, and vampires soon to be waiting for us in the dark.

I WAS STILL WORKING on my enormous sandwich as we waited for the vampires out in the night. Ian had caught up with us, offering cured venison and fresh, soft cheese. Normally my appetite wasn't quite so voracious, but I had eaten nearly the entire loaf of bread.

At least I was feeling better, more like myself. We had stopped for me to change clothing on the way, though to the vampires, I would still probably smell like soup. My coat had actually missed out on any blood or soup stains. It was the only piece of clothing I was able to reuse.

With the food making me feel better, I had only stumbled a few times as we walked through the encroaching darkness.

We reached the place we had met the vampires on previous nights, and I settled in with the rest of my meal, shifting until I found a comfortable position where sharp rocks weren't digging into me from every angle. The fresh wounds on my arms no longer stung. I had worried that being as drained as I was would slow the healing process.

I was licking the last crumbs from my fingers when Asher and Cael found us. Before I could blink, I was on my feet, and Asher was moving his hands from my waist to my arms. He pushed up the sleeves of my gray linen shirt and darker gray coat, frowning down at the bandages.

I tugged my arms away. "Magic practice with Drucida."

"She cut you?" His silver eyes met mine.

"Many times."

His frown deepened. I turned toward Cael. "Xavier didn't find you too, did he?"

He shook his head. He'd tied his red hair back from his face. I'd almost gotten used to seeing another person with the same vibrant red as mine. "It was an error to rest in separate locations."

Tholdri gave me a knowing look and I blushed. Today, at least, it had been a good thing that Cael wasn't with Asher. Of course, his presence might have prevented him from getting stabbed to begin with. Cael wasn't nearly as old as Asher, but he was powerful in a different way. He might have been able to stop Xavier, even during daylight.

"Nothing to be done about it now," I muttered, avoiding Asher's gaze. "And I fear I have little else to report. I thought we could check the mountain to see if the skin changer has a new lair."

Cael tilted his head. "But without a blood connection, how will we find it?"

"I don't know, but we have to try. We haven't found the other skin changer within the fortress."

Tholdri stepped closer. "I thought Lyss should try bleeding on the other victims. Maybe her magic is stronger than Elanore realizes."

I glared at him. "I assure you, it's not."

"And Lyssandra has lost enough blood today," Asher cut in.

"Oh, don't I know it," Tholdri chuckled.

Cael frowned at all of us. "We should split up. I will search the mountain." He looked at me. "Asher can search the fortress with you. I prefer you to remain out of Xavier's reach."

"He won't hurt me," I argued. "He can't."

"That is no reason to tempt him."

I opened my mouth to argue further, but Tholdri interrupted again. "It's a good idea, Lyss. I can search with Cael. You and Asher search the fortress."

Drucida would be waiting with Ophelia to let us in, but, "We've been searching the fortress tirelessly. We haven't found—" I cut myself off, thinking of Elanore. "Actually, there is something I'd like to look into."

"It's settled then," Cael said.

I hesitated. I wanted to question Elanore, but splitting up made me nervous. Of course, Cael was more than capable of protecting himself. He could probably kill all three of us if he wanted to.

But, Eiric wanted me alive. That meant he needed to keep Asher alive too. Cael and Tholdri were fair game.

"We'll be fine, Lyss," Tholdri assured. "You can't watch over us all the time."

"If you see Xavier, do not confront him."

Tholdri held a hand over his heart. "We promise."

Shaking my head, I started to turn away, but hesitated, glancing back at Cael. "You are well now?"

He nodded.

I nodded in return. It was one less worry, but Tholdri's blood would not last him forever. I didn't like it, but perhaps a trip over the mountain was in order.

My own thoughts turned my stomach. I couldn't believe I was actually considering setting Cael loose on innocent people, but what other choice did we have? Tholdri and I could only bleed so much.

Asher touched my arm gently.

I nodded. "Yes, let's go."

I left Tholdri and Cael out in the darkness, sorely hoping I would not regret it. As Asher and I walked back toward the fortress, I told him of Drucida's suspicions. It was no small hint for her to believe Elanore, one of her closest allies, was hiding something. Unless it was Drucida hiding something, making false claims against Elanore to throw us off.

My stomach growled as we neared the gates. "Really?" I muttered under my breath.

Asher lifted a brow at me.

"I just ate on our way out here, but I'm already hungry again."

"It smells like you wore more of your soup than you ate."

I scowled. "I was spilled on, thank you very much. I haven't had time for a bath."

He smirked, then his expression softened. "You exerted a great deal of power today. It makes sense that your body wants to replenish itself. You should listen to it. Did you tell Drucida what happened?"

I glanced toward the gates. We weren't close enough for anyone to see us, but on windy mountaintops, words could carry. I stepped closer, lowering my voice. "Just enough. I didn't tell her why Xavier came."

He leaned forward so his cheek was next to mine. I could still feel more warmth from him than he should have. My skin prickled at his nearness. "She will discover the truth eventually. Are you sure it is wise to hide it?"

I shook my head, brushing the side of my face against his soft hair. To anyone watching, we were simply sharing an intimate embrace, not muttering secrets. "If I tell her, she will exile me."

"And what will she do if she finds out you lied?"

"Do you think I haven't considered it?" I stepped back, giving him the full force of my angry gaze. I didn't like lying to Drucida, but I knew what would happen if I told her.

We would be tossed out. Maybe I already knew enough blood magic for Eiric to get what he wanted from me, but I most certainly didn't know enough to defeat him. We really would be giving him exactly what he wanted. I needed time. Time to learn how to use his own blood against him.

Asher watched me for a long moment, then nodded. "It is your choice."

"One you don't agree with."

He smiled ruefully. "When has that ever stopped you?"

I couldn't exactly argue, but his words still stung. I wasn't *that* unreasonable. I simply did what needed to be done. And I mostly just risked my own neck in the process. "I'm doing the best I can."

"I know." He tilted his head. "You always do, don't you?"

"It's the way I was trained, ever since I was a young girl."

Wind gusted his hair across the lower half of his face. He made no move to push it away. "No, it is simply who you are."

I wasn't sure if I believed him, but I couldn't argue. There was no saying who I would have become if my life had been different. If I hadn't been trained as a hunter from such a very young age. "It's getting late. We should find Elanore before she goes to sleep."

He watched me a moment longer, then gestured for me to lead the way.

We approached the gates. On the other side of the iron bars there was a lantern glowing along the cobbles at Drucida's feet, illuminating the hem of her sapphire gown like fire near water. Was she really going to stand there all night until we returned? I would have at least leaned against the wall.

Spotting us, she held out a hand and Ophelia appeared. *She* had probably been leaning against the wall.

Ophelia looked us both over as we reached the gates. She scrutinized us for a moment, then nodded.

Drucida gave the sentries above her a wave, then returned her gaze to us. "I did not expect you to return so soon. Where is Tholdri?"

I slipped through the partially open gates, stopping in front of her. "Searching the mountain with Cael."

Her expression shifted ever so slightly at my great uncle's name. Almost a flinch, but it was gone too quickly to read. "Will you be following up on what we discussed?"

I nodded. "I'll let you know what I find."

"We will wait for Tholdri, then."

I glanced at Ophelia, huddling in her coat. I could tell she wanted nothing more than to find her warm bed. "It might be a while. You should find a more comfortable place to wait."

"We're fine." Drucida stood stiffly, watching Asher. Her eyes were narrowed, *cautious*. "Lyssandra's magic still lingers around you. Do you fear it?"

He gave her an odd, close-lipped smile. "You mean, do I fear she will become stronger than me? Able to control me, and not the other way around?"

Drucida nodded.

Asher laughed, surprising me. "That you would ask such a question shows how little you know her. Perhaps you should take more care next time you slice into her skin."

Drucida's eyes widened, just a touch.

"And with that, we'll be leaving." I grabbed Asher's arm, giving Ophelia an apologetic smile as we walked past Drucida.

Once we were out of earshot, I muttered, "Probably not wise to antagonize the high witch."

Asher slid his opposite hand across my fingers where I still gripped his arm. "She fears you now."

"She fears blood magic. They all do."

"Be careful. Fear is far more dangerous than hate."

I kept my hand around his arm because it felt nice there. And I was still tired and hungry. "Yes, that is a fact with which I am intimately acquainted."

He smiled, keeping his hand on mine. "Will you use it to your advantage while questioning Elanore?"

My smile was just as cold as his. "Of course. A hunter always uses all tools at her disposal."

"Practical to the very end."

My smile broadened. "Hey, it got me this far."

ELANORE PUTTERED around her simple home, making tea and fussing over a small tray of biscuits. She hadn't been sure what to offer Asher. Fortunately, he quickly put her out of her misery by claiming I would eat enough for the both of us. His comment, of course, had irritated me. It irritated me even more that it was true.

Finally finished, Elanore carried a platter with the biscuits and two cups of tea to the small round table where Asher and I were both seated. Her soft pink dressing gown pooled around her as she sat. She took up one mug of tea, cradling it in her bony hands. "I apologize for not being better prepared. I've been resting since earlier."

I had intended to jump right to the questioning, but another thought came to me as I reached for one of the biscuits. I broke it in half, finding cranberries baked into the dough. Before I knew it, the first biscuit had disappeared.

I reached for my tea, wanting to fill my hands before I cleaned her entire platter. "Drucida explained to me that calling winds like that takes a great deal of energy. Do you find yourself needing more food after such expenditures?"

Her eyes widened as I took one hand from my teacup to grab another biscuit without thinking. I hesitated, then went for the biscuit anyway. Pretense was overrated, and I was *hungry*.

She gave me a small smile. "No. Usually I just need to sleep. My appetite remains roughly the same."

I bit into the next biscuit and frowned. "Interesting."

"Blood magic is different though." She glanced at Asher. "And your bond may alter things further. Vampires are known for their ... hunger."

Asher's brow twitched, and some of his emotion leaked through. He was finding the entire situation terribly amusing.

I looked at my empty hands, shocked I had already devoured an entire second biscuit. I licked the crumbs from my fingers, then returned both hands to my teacup. The tea was strong and dark, and would probably only make me hungrier.

"On to my next question then. Why does Drucida think you're hiding something?"

She stared at me, forgetting the tea in her hands long enough to tilt her cup. Hot liquid dripped across her fingers and she gasped. Shaking her hand, she set her cup aside. "What are you talking about? Why would you think that?"

I placed my cup on the table, then leaned back in my seat and crossed my arms. "I think it because it's true. She believes you're hiding something. Now, why would she think that?"

She glanced back-and-forth between us. "I don't understand."

"What do you know about Teresa?" I asked, wanting to keep her on her toes.

She blinked a few times, her green eyes not entirely focused. "Teresa?"

"I'm told she has no," I swirled one hand in the air, searching for the right word, "energy."

"Well yes, but she's always been that way."

I lowered my hand. Ian had claimed he'd told her, but I hadn't expected her to admit it so easily. "You knew?"

"Ophelia is my apprentice. She told me about Teresa when she first came here. When Ian mentioned later on, I was not surprised. But what does that have to do with anything?"

I glanced at Asher, surprised by her reaction. "But isn't it strange?"

"It is, but sometimes things simply have no explanation. Everyone is different. Ophelia tells me she can see *two* energies swirling around you."

I took up a third biscuit without thinking. "Does Drucida know about Teresa?"

She nodded. "She does. Now why do I feel like I'm being interrogated?"

I swallowed my next bite before answering. "Because you are. I like you, Elanore, but I'm still a hunter. Your high witch suspects you of something, and so it is my task to find out what that something is."

"Drucida doesn't trust me?"

I shrugged. "She *wants* to."

Her mouth sagged. "You're serious?"

I nodded.

She crossed her arms, finally starting to look upset. "As if Drucida doesn't keep countless secrets of her own?"

I fought to hide my smile. Finally, we were getting the reaction I wanted. "Secrets?"

"She leaves for months at a time searching for new recruits. Teresa was one of them, along with Ian, Jaques, and Ophelia. Ophelia and Jacques I understood. They had witch blood along with the ability to see energies. Ian is simply an anomaly. He doesn't really belong here. So why did she bring him?"

So Drucida had recruited three different people who could see energies, one who wasn't even a witch. I had already known as much, but I hadn't stopped to ask *why*. And she had recruited Teresa too, a witch with *no* energy.

"Do you believe Drucida has only accused you because she fears I will uncover *her* secrets?"

"You mean, is she trying to distract you?"

I nodded.

She sunk down in her seat. "Perhaps. Drucida *sees* things, more than the rest of us. She knew you were coming. Not exactly you, but someone like you. She wants you to hunt the skin changers, of course, but I think there's more to it than that. I think she has seen things she hasn't told the rest of us."

It was an interesting theory, but not really a surprise. "Why do you think the skin changers are hunting witches?"

"I believe they want our magic. Everyone killed so far has had unusual gifts."

I pursed my lips in thought. "If that's the case, you would think both you and Drucida would be primary targets."

Her eyes widened.

"Surely you thought of it," I pressed. "If you really believe that's how the skin changers are choosing their victims."

She opened her mouth then shut it, glancing at Asher as if he might help her. Finally, she turned back toward me, her expression resolute. "I am a powerful witch, as is Drucida. So far, the targets have been those less able to defend themselves."

If she had already thought that far ahead, she would have answered immediately. There was something she was hiding. For some reason, she didn't think she was a target. She hadn't been as surprised or frightened as she should have been when we entered the skin changers' lair. And now, she had let slip that though those with special gifts were being targeted, she didn't believe she would be taken.

Her face remained stiff, no flicker of hesitation. It was a good lie, as far as lies went. Mostly because I couldn't understand her motive.

I stood. "Thank you for the biscuits. That will be all."

Her expression crumbled. She reached a hand toward me. "I really am telling the truth. I don't know why Drucida and I haven't been targeted."

I glanced at Asher, still reclining in his seat. He gave me a half shrug. He couldn't tell if she was lying. She was already panicked, and maybe there was just enough truth in what she said to cover up the lies.

"I want to believe you, Elanore, and I want to believe Drucida. But I'm wondering if you *both* have ulterior motives in keeping me from my magic."

Her eyes shifted. "Drucida taught you today. I would have done it myself if I'd had the energy."

"Parlor tricks. Nothing useful. Nothing I couldn't have figured out myself."

She finally stood. "True blood magic is *dangerous*, Lyssandra. I taught you how to track the skin changers. That should be enough."

Enough once we have another victim, I thought. "Nothing is as dangerous as these creatures. At least not when it comes to those within this fortress." I wondered how many times I would have to repeat that fact before someone was actually helpful.

"I'm going to the ice chamber," I decided. "Perhaps the dead will be more useful than the living."

"They've been gone too long. You won't get anything from them."

She'd said so before, but now I found myself not entirely trusting it. Maybe I could use the other bodies to track their killers. What I would do with them once I found them was another question, but one step at a time.

"Good night, Elanore."

Asher stood, and she watched us walk toward the door, her expression a combination of worry and indignation. I hadn't learned much, but I *had* learned I couldn't fully trust her.

"Drucida will never teach you what you want to know."

I turned with the door slightly ajar. "Then I'll find someone who will."

Asher and I stepped out into the darkness, closing the door behind us. I was about to speak, when I caught movement out the corner of my eye. Someone darting away from the other side of the cottage. Asher was gone in a flash.

Already knowing it was futile—I couldn't outrun a vampire—I hurried after him.

CHAPTER SIXTEEN

I ran after Asher, deeper into the fortress. My footfalls echoed between the cobblestones and the surrounding buildings. It was early enough that there were still a few onlookers turning with startled faces as I ran by. They probably hadn't even noticed the vampire. Maybe a flicker of movement, then gone.

I followed him by sense. He was still near enough that I could feel him. Tholdri and I had explored much of the fortress, but hadn't lingered in an older area with a decrepit temple. Not unused, just decrepit, the stones so old their edges had begun to crumble.

There were no lanterns to light my way, but the moonlight was enough. I found Asher standing near the temple, his back to me. The ends of his white hair swirled around his shoulders in the breeze.

He didn't startle as I approached him. He already knew I was there. I stood on my toes to look over his shoulder, noticing that he was holding something. A thin, black feather.

He turned toward me, extending the feather. "It was the other skin changer. It turned into a bird. I lost sight of it."

I shook my head in disbelief, taking the feather from his fingers. "If it can fly, then it can easily leave and reenter the fortress."

"I don't think it can. The walls are warded. I believe that's why it has needed to take skins to walk out each time, leaving before the victims are found, using the names it asks for before killing them."

I looked down at the feather. It seemed entirely ordinary. "Something as small as a mouse could easily crawl through the gates. And a bird could fly high above them."

"Do you not feel the shift in the wards every time the gates are opened? Old magic protects this place. Coming and going is not as simple as transforming into an animal. It is why Elanore was so exhausted from opening them."

I looked at him. He didn't often show emotion, but now he seemed worried. I could tell, even though he was trying to shield it from me. "I'll ask Drucida about the wards."

"I am right. Can you really not feel them?"

I furrowed my brow, feeling wary near the old temple. It had an eerie feel, the interior cloaked in shadows, a few crumbling statues dotting the yellow grass around it. "I can feel that there is magic in this place, and magic in the walls, but nothing so specific."

He turned fully toward me. "It is odd. You quickly learned to shield yourself from our bond. And you can sense vampires easily. Your reflexes are more a matter of intuition than reading external indicators."

I narrowed my eyes. "So what are you trying to say?"

"That you should be able to sense the wards around the fortress. You should innately know what they do. I have no magic, just centuries of experience. *You* come from a powerful line of witches."

I lowered the feather to my side. It wasn't like I couldn't sense *anything*. I could feel the magic, I just couldn't exactly tell what it was meant for. "I'm still not following what you're trying to say."

"I don't think it is our bond that blocked your magic, nor lack of knowledge. I believe it's something else."

Goosebumps prickled my arms beneath my shirt and coat. He was saying something simple, but my gut told me it was important. There was something I was missing. "Drucida believes my mother could have suppressed my magic for a time."

"But she died when you were young."

I had told him about my parents' death the night we met. I had been drunk and truly pathetic. And he had remembered every word I'd said. "That's right, so she couldn't have suppressed my magic for the next decade after that. But what does that have to do with sensing wards?"

"I think you blocked your magic yourself, Lyssandra."

My jaw fell open. "That's not possible. I didn't even know I had it. And my sword started glowing *after* Amarithe suppressed our bond. So it was the bond keeping my magic away."

He stepped closer, but didn't touch me. "Or was it mere coincidence? You were about to die, and your sword glowed out of necessity. It might have glowed before that, had the need arisen."

I shook my head. It simply wasn't possible. I had faced death many times where magic could have saved me. But it never happened.

"You became one of the most skilled hunters at a very young age."

I could feel the emotion draining from my face while the wall I kept around my heart strengthened. "If I'd had magic before, I would have used it to prevent Karpov from ripping out my uncle's heart."

His expression softened. "Karpov was powerful. You never should have been blamed for your uncle's death, magic or no."

I clenched my hands into fists, pushing away the memories of my parents, then my uncle, then the Potentate—my grandfather. "Amarithe unleashed my magic. I did not have access to it before then."

He had started reaching toward me, but let his arms fall at my words. I could tell he was frustrated, but he let it go. "What do you think of the feather?"

"What of it?" I snapped. I wasn't angry, not really. But anger was easier than what I really felt deep inside.

"It is a part of one of the skin changers. Might it be used to track it?" His words were calm, as always. He had seen far worse of my anger.

My eyes widened. I would have thought of it sooner if I weren't so wrapped up in my own issues. "You're right. We should wake Drucida."

He stopped me with a hand on my arm before I could turn away. "Are you sure you should continue trusting her? Whatever is between her and Elanore—"

I shook my head. "I have to trust someone. At the very least, I know she wants me to stop the skin changers. If I can track them through this feather," I held it up, "she'll help me."

He nodded, and said nothing else.

I was grateful. I knew there were many things he wanted to say, none of which I wanted to hear. Maybe I really was as difficult as everyone liked to point out. Maybe if I were more open to my emotions, I would be better off—*stronger*. But *maybes* were as intangible as black feathers floating on the wind. They did no good unless you put something into action. So I would stop worrying about my flaws, and I would focus on what I was good at.

Hunting.

MY PLAN WAS THWARTED when we couldn't find Drucida. Asher had followed her scent from her home to the northeastern end of the fortress, but it was as if she had disappeared into thin air. And with Cael and Tholdri somewhere on the mountainside, we were on our own.

We had returned to the temple, the last place we'd seen the skin changer. If Asher was right, and it couldn't actually fly over the walls, it was still somewhere within them.

I held a dagger in one hand, and the feather in the other. All my previous wounds had finally ceased their aching, and now here I was making a new one.

Asher watched me from a few paces away, his brow furrowed. The moonlight was so strong near the temple, he almost seemed to glow. "Are you sure you should do this again so soon?"

Never mind that he was the one who'd suggested it. I supposed seeing me about to slice my flesh had made him reconsider.

My palm sweated around the hilt of the dagger. "We need to catch it while it is still on the run, before it can claim another skin."

And yet, I hesitated. I didn't want to use my magic again so soon, especially when I wasn't sure if it would work. All of Asher's *theories* swirled in my mind, confusing me. I had no idea what the truth was. I might never know.

I pushed up my sleeve, revealing my scarred skin. I had removed the bandages, and the recent wound looked pink and angry. I made a new slice right next to it, hissing through my teeth to distract myself from the sharp pain. My blood welled, drained of color in the moonlight.

Not knowing any measure of ritual, I did the only thing I could think of. I dripped my blood onto the feather, willing my magic to claim it—to create a new connection with the killer.

I closed my eyes, concentrating, but my thoughts were muddy, my body tired. My mind kept drifting to the divine idea of a hot bath.

I felt Asher's hand on my shoulder, and my thoughts calmed. He'd known I was struggling, and was willing to lend me his serene energy.

I took a shaky breath. The feather pinched between two of my fingers dripped blood down to my palm. I focused on that blood, willing it to do what I wanted. It shouldn't be any different from what I'd done with the corpse.

The night air cooled my blood. I felt unsteady on my feet. I swayed, shutting my eyes tightly, maintaining my focus on the feather and the creature it had come from. A wicked creature, hunting innocents. And *I* would protect them at all costs.

A new bond of sorts snapped into place. My eyes flew wide. I could feel the skin changer. And it wasn't far.

I gave Asher a meaningful look, then I crept toward its energy, somewhere beyond the temple. My boots hissed through the grass. The statues were just dark blurs in my vision, because I wasn't seeing only with my eyes.

We left the temple behind, proceeding across a small expanse of open grass. Beyond the grass were gardens bordered by blackberry bushes.

Still clutching the feather, I approached the bushes, smelling the sweet fruit. It was here somewhere, *close*.

Asher yanked me backwards as something erupted from the other side of the bushes. It was a young man in shredded clothing, but he wasn't coming for us. He ran past in the other direction.

We both darted after him, continuing on as he once

again took on the form of a blackbird. The bird soared overhead, a dark speck against the moonlight. But Asher was right. It wasn't flying as high as it potentially could have. The entire fortress really was warded. It couldn't get out.

Which meant it couldn't escape us.

I lost sight of it, but it didn't matter. I could still feel a connection to it through the feather. I ran toward that connection, past the temple and down the street. I kept running, my lungs burning and my fresh wound aching, until I skidded to a halt in front of the dining hall. The skin changer was somewhere within. I had no doubt.

I drew my sword, then hurried up the steps and opened the door. Odd, that I had still received no warning. The skin changer really didn't want to hurt me, which meant Xavier had been telling the truth. Eiric had sent them, and he wasn't allowing them to claim me as one of their many victims.

I stepped into the dark, quiet interior. All the long tables had been cleared, their dull surfaces wiped clean. I walked between them holding my sword out ahead of me with the feather pressed against its hilt, using only the moonlight through the windows to guide my way. The floorboards creaked under my weight.

Movement caught my eye and I turned.

Ian had exited the kitchen, and was rubbing the sleep out of his eyes as he peered at us. "What are you—"

A dark form dropped down from the rafters, knocking him to the floor. It was the skin changer, back in the form of a young man. The creature hissed, swiping down at Ian with a hand turned bestial, tipped with long jagged claws.

Ian screamed, and I lunged forward, but Asher reached them first. He grabbed the skin changer and threw it against the wall.

It hit hard enough to rattle my teeth. There was no way it didn't have broken bones. It slid down the wall, landing in a heap.

Ian sat up, then half-crawled further away from his attacker.

I didn't have time to see if he was alright. Sword extended, I approached the skin changer. It was making a strange sound, still crumpled in a heap.

By the time I stood next to it, I realized what the sound was. It was laughing, but something was wrong with it. If I had to guess, I would say a broken rib had punctured its lung. The laughter was wet and gurgling, punctuated by raspy inhales.

I pointed my sword down at it. Asher would be ready if it tried to transform into a bird again, though I didn't think it would be able to fly unless the transformation healed broken bones.

"I hardly find this situation amusing," I said to it.

It rasped again, letting out another choking laugh as it struggled to climb to its hands and knees. Shaggy hair shadowed most of its face.

"Amusing—" *Rasp.* "Yes. So amusing." It teetered to one side, bracing itself against the wall as it slid into a seated position. The eyes that looked up at me held nothing human. "Amusing—" *rasp*, "that you would slay your saviors."

I lowered my sword's point to its throat. "What are you talking about?"

"Blackmire." *Rasp*. "Blood of my blood. We shall reign." It coughed, its entire body trembling. Blood flew from its mouth, splattering the floor around it.

I stepped back just in time to miss the spray. "What are you talking about?" I demanded.

It continued coughing. More blood spurted from its mouth.

"Answer me."

It laughed again, wheezing heavily, more blood pouring from its mouth. It writhed on the floor, taking in one final aching gasp, then went still.

I could sense Asher just behind me. "Its heart has stopped beating. I apologize, I should not have thrown it so hard. We might have learned more had we captured it."

I glanced back toward Ian now huddling near the entrance of the kitchen. "You saved Ian's life," I said softly. "It had to be done."

I walked toward the boy in question, but his wide eyes were on the dead thing in the corner.

"Did you recognize it?" I asked.

He placed one trembling hand over his mouth, as if his answer was too awful to be said out loud. He stayed that way for a long moment, then nodded, lowering his hand. "Jacques. That was Jacques, Ophelia's brother."

"It wasn't really him. Just his skin."

He nodded too quickly, his eyes still wide. With his shallow breathing, I started to worry he might faint.

"What was it doing in here?" His words were barely above a whisper.

"We chased it here. What were *you* doing in here?"

"Sometimes I sleep in the storage room. It helps being far away from people, so I can't see their energies." He swiped his hand across his face, shaking his head. "It helps me sleep."

I nodded. "Fair enough. You may go back to sleep now, if you are able."

"I don't think I'll ever sleep again."

I felt for him, but I had more important matters to attend. I turned away, walking back toward the dead skin changer. It still looked the same—like Jacques. It seemed death would not reveal its true appearance.

Asher stood near my shoulder, looking down at the creature.

"One less monster killing people," I sighed. "But we still need to find the other one."

He nodded. "We should burn it. We do not know how well these creatures die. It might be able to reanimate."

I blinked at him. "You know, that's not a bad idea."

"I hope you're not thinking what I *think* you're thinking."

"Cael," I said. "He's a necromancer. Maybe he can . . . I don't know. *Do* something with it."

"Necromancers may have some power over death, but they do not bring back the truly dead."

I shook my head. He was right. But what the skin changer had said . . . I needed to know more. "We can at least try. If he can't do anything with it, we'll burn it." I resheathed my sword. For once, I hadn't needed to use it.

Maybe the trend would continue.

But probably not.

I wasn't sure how many times I would forget that we couldn't simply leave the gates, but the occurrences were beginning to add up. Asher carried the skin changer's corpse like a sleeping child. It seemed well and truly dead.

Panicked whispers erupted from the sentry post as we neared. It wasn't every day one saw an ancient vampire carrying the corpse of someone who looked like a friend. Those watching us from above the gates had probably known Jacques, and there was enough moonlight for them to easily recognize him.

I prepared myself for the explanation I would need to give before anyone would help us find Drucida. Hopefully, she had reappeared from wherever she'd been hiding.

The whispers above us abruptly cut off, and I turned to find the high witch herself approaching. Either she hadn't been outside the gates when we'd searched for her, or she had returned long ago.

She'd changed into a simple green gown, the color muted like midsummer grass after it had lost the vibrant hues of spring. Her silver-streaked curls trailed over the shoulders of a matching short jacket. She seemed unworried and well put together.

She reached us, her eyes glued to the corpse in Asher's arms. "I am assuming this is one of the skin changers?"

"How did you know where to find us?" I asked.

"I've been waiting out here all evening for Tholdri. I left for a short time to dine and have a bath."

I glanced at Asher. She hadn't been doing either of those things when we'd searched for her. She was nowhere near her chambers, nor the dining hall.

I found myself overcome with disappointment. I had really wanted to trust her. "We first spotted it spying through Elanore's window. We eventually tracked it to the dining hall where it attacked Ian. We were forced to kill it."

She lifted a brow. "Did it say anything before it died?"

I shook my head. Maybe she could sense lies, but could she really tell just from the shake of a head? I supposed we would find out.

"What are you going to do with it?"

"Burn it." Again, not entirely a lie. We would burn it eventually.

She tilted her head. "What are you hiding, Lyssandra?"

I crossed my arms. "I could ask you the same question. We searched for you earlier. We could have used your help."

She opened her mouth to answer, then looked past us toward the gates.

Asher had already turned at the sound of their footsteps. Tholdri and Cael I had expected, but the others?

I stormed toward the gates. "What are you doing here? I warned you to stay away."

Steifan flinched at my anger, taking a step back, though I couldn't reach him through the bars of the gates regardless. Markus simply stared at me, chin lifted.

Tholdri stepped in front of them. "Now Lyss, is that any way to greet them when they traveled this far to see you? We found them wandering this way. It seemed they couldn't actually see the fortress until we pointed it out."

I glared at Tholdri's smiling face, then turned to Markus. He must have used our bond to track me. "Why are you here?"

"We've news from Castle Helius. Important news."

Drucida approached my back. "More hunters. Lovely."

Tholdri had noticed Asher, and was staring at the corpse in his arms. "Is that—"

I glanced back at him. "One of the skin changers, yes." I turned toward Drucida. "Can we open the gates to discuss this somewhere more private?"

Drucida pinched her brow. "I'll never hear the end of this once Charles wakes up." She tilted her chin skyward. "Ophelia!"

I was pretty sure every single one of us flinched, including Asher and Cael. The door of a nearby home opened, revealing Ophelia looking half asleep. She bundled a blanket around her shoulders, then shuffled toward us. Her jaw fell open as she realized what was in Asher's arms.

Oh light, the skin changer still looked like her brother.

She stood in stunned silence for a heartbeat, not even seeming to notice the new arrivals outside the gates. She opened her mouth and inhaled as if she might speak. Instead, she screamed.

We all flinched again. Asher turned away with the corpse.

"Jacques?" She hurried after the vampire. "Is that my brother?"

I grabbed her arm before she could reach him. "You already know what became of your brother. Think about it."

She looked at my hand on her arm as if it burned her. I realized I still had blood on my fingers, though she probably didn't notice. She stared at me, blinking away tears. "I—" she looked at Asher, then back at me. Her tears began to fall. "Is that the thing that killed him?"

I nodded, still holding onto her in case she entirely lost her wits and rushed Asher.

But all the fight had gone out of her. Tears dripped down her face.

Drucida hurried to her side, pulling her away from me. She muttered softly to her, words that probably only Asher and I could hear. And maybe Cael. Light, maybe even Markus could hear them.

I tuned them out, turning back to the new arrivals outside the gates. "You still haven't told me why you're here."

"There is trouble within the Helius Order," Markus said coolly. "You need to know about it."

Wonderful. *More* trouble. I looked at Cael. So much for asking him to do the impossible and re-animate a corpse. We wouldn't have the chance now.

Drucida had escorted Ophelia back to the door she'd come out of. I heard her telling the girl to wait for her, then she shut her inside. Drucida returned to us, shaking her head. "My apologies. I should have considered her reaction. It's been a long day." She gave me a meaningful look. "For *all* of us." She raised her voice. "Open the gates!"

The only response from the sentries above was silence.

She sighed. Our idea to control the gates really had been more of a hindrance than anything. "Open the gates, *now*, or I will come up there and do it myself!"

A lock clicked, then a pulley whirred. Slowly, the gates opened.

I watched Markus more than Steifan as they all entered. Trouble within Castle Helius, bad enough for Markus to be willing to find me. I wasn't even sure I wanted to know. I had left the Order behind but . . . they were still important to me. If there was something I could do to help, I would. I just wasn't sure how I would find the time.

CHAPTER SEVENTEEN

The corpse lay on the table between us. Asher and Tholdri had volunteered to keep watch outside, leaving me, Drucida, Steifan, Markus, and Cael to discuss things. But already Markus was glaring at Drucida, and her hackles were raised toward *everyone*. It had been a long night. I mentally prepared myself for it to be much longer.

At least Cael and Tholdri had already caught Steifan and Markus up on the matter of the skin changers. And the matter of Eiric, they knew about already. They had been present when he was released. If anything, perhaps they could help me convince Drucida of the threat he posed.

"So there is another one of these things?" Steifan asked.

I nodded, peering across the corpse toward him. We'd only lit a few candles. I didn't think anyone wanted to look at the dead boy. The skin changer didn't seem so harmful now that it was gone, and still wearing the skin of one of its victims.

"They have been hunting us." Drucida leaned forward, the candlelight casting a harsh glow across her tight features. "We do not know why, nor how. As you experienced, our fortress is only visible to those who know what they're looking for."

I was surprised Markus was yet to chime in with an unhelpful comment about witch hunts. Instead, his attention was solely on me.

I shifted in my seat. Our bond wasn't quite like the one between me and Asher, at least not from my side of things. He felt compelled to find me—that much I knew. I could sense him when he was near, but felt little beyond that. I had no idea, however, how Markus *felt*. I didn't think he *wanted* to be near me, but the draw was there. He was compelled to protect me. And that was something I was not comfortable with at all. I didn't think he liked it much better.

"We still have one more to find," I continued. "We think it is hiding somewhere outside the fortress. We managed to catch this one within once we realized what we were dealing with." I gestured toward the corpse.

"And just how did you catch this one?" Drucida asked. "We've been searching for it for days."

I stared at her, for once wishing she really could read my mind. I wasn't about to tell Markus and Steifan about my blood magic. Too many people knew about it already.

Her eyes narrowed, but she gave me a subtle nod. Maybe she *could* read my mind. How . . . unsettling.

I turned back toward Markus, Steifan, and Cael. "We will continue our search for the other one in the morning. Now what is this business with the Order?"

Markus' jaw tensed. His eyes flicked toward Drucida.

I should have thought of it before. He wasn't going to reveal anything in front of a witch based on my trust in her alone. It might have been enough for Steifan, but not for Markus. And I couldn't even blame him. I thought the same way.

I sighed, looking down at the corpse. "We will discuss it later."

Just as I would discuss possible uses of the corpse with Cael as soon as I could get him alone. I also wanted to tell him what the skin changer had said before it died. Maybe he would be able to make sense of it.

We all stared at each other, at an impasse. The hunters would not discuss hunter business in front of a witch. I wasn't even sure they would discuss things in front of Cael, based on the wary glances they gave him.

"We should burn the corpse," Cael said finally.

I visibly winced before I could stop myself. If we burned it, there were no . . . possibilities.

"There is another option," Drucida said, surprising me. "These creatures seem somewhat animalistic in nature. I would guess they are either a mated pair, or siblings. Either way, one has a strong connection to the other." She looked at me. "That connection may be useful."

I appreciated her not directly saying I should use

blood magic to track the other skin changer. I felt silly for not thinking of it myself. "We could do it tonight."

She shook her head. "No, Lyssandra. You need your rest." She gave me a look that said she knew exactly what I had done to track the skin changer, and just how much it had taken out of me. Especially after what I had done with Asher, followed by practicing with her.

"I suppose you're right," I admitted.

"We will place the body in the ice chamber for now," she continued. "It will be kept under guard. We can track the other one in the morning."

"Going in the morning means no help from vampires," I countered.

She lifted a brow. "Surely *four* hunters can get the job done."

I wrinkled my nose. "Of course. And what of those other hunters?"

I ignored Markus' scrutinizing gaze. I knew exactly what he thought of me, cavorting with vampires, necromancers, and now witches. He could maintain his prejudices. I thought it simply made me more practical.

"They may stay within the fortress, for now. You have done us a great service in killing this predator. I can allow you a bit more freedom because of it."

I lifted a brow. "You mean because Charles won't be able to argue?"

She smiled. "Something like that. Now if I could request help in moving the body, the lodging to the left of yours is vacant. You may use it as you see fit."

I stood. I was getting my way, and I knew I should just go with it, but I was so very bad at not asking questions. "I noticed that all the cottages on the row seem empty, yet some are well-maintained. If it weren't for the lack of occupants, I would have guessed they were all filled."

She stood. "At one time, those lodgings were reserved for Blackmire witches. Strong enchantments remain on a few. I'm surprised you haven't noticed them."

I blinked at her, wishing I hadn't asked. "And my cottage? It was covered in dust and grime."

Her smile widened. "I said the enchantments remain on just a few. Some enchantments wear faster, depending on who created them."

Ah, so she'd given us the pig sty on purpose. *Of course*. And the cottage next to mine, the one she had allotted for Markus and Steifan, did not appear much better.

I turned away before I could say something I'd regret, looking down at the body. "Let's get this thing moved. I need a hot meal and a bath."

I turned enough to see Drucida incline her chin, a small smile still curving her lips. "Of course, Lyssandra. You have surely earned it."

I didn't know what to say to that, so I looked over at the three men in the room. "Well? All of those muscles aren't just for show, are they?"

Steifan was the only one to show his disappointment. For a hunter, he really hated corpses and getting bloody. But now that he had found me again, he would surely get used to it.

Once the corpse was moved and Steifan and Markus were settled into their new lodging, I did one last patrol of the fortress with Asher. Dawn was still aways off, but I knew once I sat down with the other hunters, the rest of the night would go by quickly. Steifan and Markus had offered their aid, but I told them to rest. Mostly because I didn't want Markus seeing how close Asher and I had become. Silly, but true.

Asher walked at my side, gazing up at the moon. "Drucida told me where she was earlier."

I stopped walking. "She did? Why couldn't we find her?"

"She has permitted me to show you."

I pursed my lips, observing him closely. "Why are you smiling?"

"You'll have to come with me to find out." He offered me his arm.

I stared at it. I had taken his arm before, but I was still mildly uncomfortable with the showing of affection. At least there was no one out in the streets at such an hour.

I gave him a wary look, but took his arm. "Lead on, I suppose."

We walked deeper into the fortress, past the dining hall, then uphill toward the temple. I was worried for a moment that we were headed back toward the eerie space, but we continued on past it, further uphill. Eventually, we reached the sheer rock incline at the back of the fortress. The walls were built directly into the mountain, using the expanse of natural stone as part of the fortification. We had explored the area before, but there was little of interest save a few storehouses.

"She was here?" I asked, confused. We had tracked her scent to the area, but had found no sign of her.

He reached into his coat pocket and withdrew a little silver key. I recognized it as one from Drucida's ring.

"Another enchanted key," I sighed. "Of course."

He approached the solid rock wall, searching along it with his palm.

"What are you doing?"

He kept his back to me. "Patience, Lyssandra."

I put my hands on my hips and waited, bone-achingly tired and ready to have the night over with.

He found whatever he was looking for, and inserted the key into the solid stone.

My interest renewed, I stepped closer. He had found a tiny keyhole, but I could have sworn it wasn't there before. He turned the key, then stepped back, leaving it in the hole.

For a moment, nothing happened, then stone grated against stone. A seam formed, then spread, creating the shape of a door just barely taller than I was, but twice as wide. We waited as the stone pushed outward.

Once it had stopped moving, Asher placed his fingers against one edge of the seam and opened the strange door. I closed my eyes as steam wafted out, but soon realized it wasn't some sort of defense mechanism. The steam was warm and soothing, scented with lavender and vanilla.

I opened my eyes and looked at Asher. "All right, you're really going to have to explain what's going on now."

"This is why we couldn't find Drucida earlier. She really was taking a bath."

I lifted a brow. "A bath?" Now the steam made sense.

He gestured for me to walk in ahead of him.

I glanced at the dimly lit entrance. There were candles somewhere within, or a lantern, but the space was surrounded by solid stone. The door was just as solid. "Are you sure Drucida isn't hoping to lock us inside?"

He stepped around the side of the door, retrieving the key. "The enchantment should only work from the outside, but we will bring this just in case." The silver key in his fingers glinted in the moonlight.

I hesitated a moment longer, but my shoulders were *horribly* tense. I smelled like blood and dirt—and probably soup. And we still had an hour or two until dawn.

With a heavy sigh, I walked into the side of the mountain. My steps slowed as I beheld the interior. The walls were natural stone with jutting ledges at several levels. Each ledge was bedecked with glowing candles. I looked up, but I couldn't see the ceiling. The stone beneath my boots was swept entirely clean, not a speck of dust to be found. I flinched as the door closed behind us, sealing us in.

I turned my attention back to the candles. "If Drucida lit those while she was here, they should have burned halfway down by now."

"Another enchantment," Asher explained, walking

past me. "An old one, according to Drucida. Created back when the bloodlines were still strong."

I walked closer to the candles. "And it's still active after all this time?"

I turned to find him right at my back, close enough to touch. "The witches were incredibly powerful, once."

I tensed as he reached toward me, but he simply plucked up my braid from where it rested on my shoulder. He undid the leather clasp, then started untangling my hair.

"What are you doing?"

He continued fussing with my hair. It sorely needed a thorough brushing. "Do you not intend to wash your hair in the bath?"

Ah yes, a bath, that's why we were here.

I pulled away from him, running my fingers through my hair to unravel the rest of my braid. I continued untangling the dirty locks as I walked away from the wall, toward a massive natural pool in the center of the space. Steam wafted from the dark, serene surface. At one edge were little glass bottles, presumably filled with scented oils. More candles lined the rock wall behind them.

Asher approached my back. "The natural spring was already here when the fortress was built."

His hands alighted on my shoulders.

"When did Drucida have time to explain all this to you?"

"While you dealt with the corpse."

Of course. She had given us the key to the ice chamber. Tholdri, Steifan, and I had moved the corpse. "But why? Why did she have you bring me here?"

His hands started kneading my shoulders. "I believe she was trying to do something nice."

"People don't do nice things for no reason."

His hands paused, and he leaned in near my cheek. "Are you sure about that?"

His breath on my cheek made me shiver. He was still warm enough, but not as warm as before. I looked down at the steaming water before us. "Are you planning on joining me?"

"If you wish."

I turned toward him. I still didn't believe Drucida was being nice for no reason, but I would surely take advantage. My fingers went to the buttons of his shirt.

He smiled, grasping my fingers in his hands to lower them. "No, Lyssandra. Last time, you took care of me. Now it is my turn."

I furrowed my brow. "I'm not good at being taken care of." Even when I had come down with a dangerous fever shortly after my parents' death, I had refused any offers of help. The most I allowed was Tholdri bringing me damp cloths and cold soup.

He held my fingers against his chest. "I know, Lyssandra. But please, grant me the chance."

I frowned. He was letting some of his emotions peek through. For some reason, this small gesture meant a great deal to him. I might not have given in had I been in full health, but the day and night had worn on me.

"Alright," I breathed.

With a small smile, he released my fingers, then

stepped a bit closer to remove my coat. As he unbuttoned my shirt, I allowed the scented steam to relax me. Sealed away in the candlelit space, my troubles seemed distant. The icy corpse of the skin changer could wait until morning. My shirt dropped to the stone at our feet.

Next, he knelt before me, removing each of my boots as I leaned on him for balance. Soon I was nude before him, and he took my hand to lead me into the water.

I looked disapprovingly at my hand in his. "I'm not some quaking maiden. I can step into the water myself."

"Humor me."

"Fine, but you'll owe me."

"Of course. We can bathe in our victims' blood *tomorrow* night."

I smirked, then stepped into the water. The surface was too dark to see its depths, but I found stone steps leading down. I hissed as the hot water closed in around my legs, then lowered myself further.

Asher kept hold of my hand until I was seated on a stone ledge, the water coming up to my shoulders. He finally released my hand, then moved away. Once upon a time, I might have been motivated to watch his every movement, but not now. He could do as he wished. The hot water was absolutely divine.

I closed my eyes, sinking down further. I heard the light clink of glass bottles, then Asher sat behind me, his legs on either side of my shoulders, dipping into the pool. He'd removed his boots and pushed up his pants enough to keep them out of the water, but he was still fully clothed.

"What are you—"

I smelled warm vanilla and mint, then his hands smoothed the scented oil over my shoulders. The rest of my words were stolen away as he kneaded my stiff muscles. I leaned back against the stone, enjoying his touch.

"Can I ask you a question?" My voice had gone low with pleasure. There was so much steam around me I could barely see.

"Of course."

"Why do you never speak of your past?"

His hands ceased their kneading. I tensed at his sudden stillness. "It was a long time ago, Lyssandra."

"And what difference does that make? My parents' deaths seem a long time ago to me, but you know of the occurence."

"You only told me because you were drunk."

I pulled away enough to look back at him, but I could barely see his face through the steam.

"Do you truly wish to know?" he asked before I could press him further.

I was embarrassed, because yes, I actually did want to know. I could fully admit now that whatever was between us was not just sex. I wanted to know more of who he really was. Maybe it was only because he knew so much about me, and I wanted to even things out. I couldn't say for sure, but I had been thinking about it for quite some time.

He gently guided me to lean back against the stone.

He continued rubbing my shoulders, dipping his hands down my arms, expertly kneading each sore muscle. "What exactly would you like to know?"

I thought about it. "You mentioned your village before, after we found the first skin changer. That was the first time you had ever mentioned it."

"I had not thought of it much in decades. The skin changers revived some old memories."

I closed my eyes again, leaning back between his legs. "Such as?"

"It was a different time. Witches were to be feared, and vampires, but many other things lurked in the shadows."

I tried to picture the place he was from, making up things in my mind. In my lifetime and those before me, many creatures had been hunted to extinction. In the time Asher lived . . . I thought of the Nattmara, skin changers, Sidhe . . . And no hunters. The Helius Order wouldn't have existed yet.

"I see you understand."

I realized I hadn't been shielding, but I couldn't bring myself to care. The hot water and his hands on my shoulders simply felt too good.

"But it was a simple life," he continued. "Not bad by any means. I had a mother and two brothers. My father died from a fever when I was young."

I sat up straighter and turned to look at him. I expected some sort of emotion on his face, but there was nothing.

"When I was nineteen, there was a war between the

provinces. Raiders had devastated nearby villages. I felt it my duty to fight. To protect my homeland."

I turned fully and pressed closer, watching him, though he wasn't meeting my gaze, and he was shielding tightly.

"I saw much death, and blood. Horrors to rival the stories the elders told to scare us as children. It all started to seem pointless. It didn't seem like we were making a difference. I was ashamed, but I went home."

I gripped his knee, dampening his rolled up pants.

He glanced down at me, then looked away. "*You* would have continued fighting."

I kept my hand on his knee. "Yes, probably." I wasn't sure what else I could say. There was no judgment in my words, simply a difference in personality.

"When I returned home, there was nothing left. Raiders had burned the entire village."

A lump formed in my throat. I wasn't sure if it was my emotions, or his.

He finally looked down at me again. "When you told me how your parents were killed, I understood exactly how you felt." He smiled softly. "Although I imagine had you known who the culprits were, you would have hunted them."

"I was just a girl at the time."

"My statement stands."

I laughed, then shrugged, my wet hair dripping water down my shoulders. "Fair enough. What did you do after that?"

"I started walking. I had no home, no place to go. Eventually I found another village and settled there.

The land had been ravaged by war. There were many other survivors in the village. I met a woman there from similar circumstances. In the coming years, we built a life together. We had hoped to someday form a family of our own, once the affairs of the land were more stable."

My chest constricted at his words, which was ridiculous. His story had occurred centuries ago.

He smiled down at me, sensing my emotions.

I glared. "Continue with your story, please."

Steam swirled around the tendrils of his white hair, the strands beginning to grow damp. He pulled me closer so that my ribcage was against the edge of the pool, my arms draped over his knees. "Her name was Faele. She was killed by vampires. I don't know why they chose to take me and not her."

My chest constricted for a different reason. I had endured much loss, but *that* type of loss, the loss of your chosen person—it was different.

He stroked my hair, and I knew that it meant something to him that I actually cared. "I remembered pain, and then the silence of death. I thought for a time I was actually dead, but trapped in my body. Then I awoke."

"What happened to the other vampires?"

He sighed. "Once I realized what happened, I fled. I was on my own for many years, but eventually I hunted them down and killed them."

"Then we're not so different after all."

"Death changes a man." He looked down at me with a small smile. "Has your curiosity been satisfied?"

I still wanted to know more, but for tonight, it was

enough. The darkness outside wouldn't last forever. I used the ledge I had been sitting on to raise partially out of the water. Rivulets dripped down my body, drawing his eyes. "My *curiosity*, yes."

The water had made my recent wounds feel better, but they were all angry and pink from the heat. He took up my wrist and leaned his head forward, gently kissing the most recent scar. With his lips still against my skin, he asked, "And there are other things you would like satisfied?"

"Most certainly, but there is one last thing." I waited until he looked up at me. "I do not think less of you for abandoning the war. You were hardly older than a child."

"I was the same age you were the night we met. And you had already been hunting monsters for years."

"That doesn't mean it was how things should have been. I shouldn't have lost my parents when I was a child. I shouldn't have been raised to become a killer, even if I was good at it."

"No. You should have been given the chance at a peaceful life." He reached out, his hands skimming my waist.

I glanced around the steamy, candlelit space, ending with my eyes on him. I gave him a small smile. "But my life now," I shrugged, "it's not so bad."

He pulled me closer. Heat danced in his eyes, wiping away the emotions of the past. "No?"

"No."

He kissed my collarbone, leaving a trail of kisses

down to my breast. His hands went to my hips. "Come here." He teased my nipple with his tongue.

My breath caught in my throat. "I'm going to get your clothes wet."

"They will dry," he whispered against my skin, then used my hips to lift me out of the water.

He leaned back across the damp stone, pulling me up until I was situated over his face.

The movement had happened so quickly, I let out a gasp. "Somehow, the vampire strength still manages to surprise me."

He laughed just beneath me, pulling another gasp from my lips. Before I could say anything else, his tongue found me. With my body already so relaxed from the hot water and scented oils, I was nearly brought to the edge right then and there.

He caressed me with his tongue and mouth, slowly at first, sensing me already at the edge. Steam seeped from my skin up into the haze around us. For once, there was no danger of anyone finding us. Except perhaps Drucida, but we had her key.

Asher's hands circled my waist, holding me above him, and my thoughts seeped away as easily as the steam. His tongue slid over the most sensitive part of me. Since he could feel my emotions, he knew *exactly* what felt best.

I threw my head back, still exhausted, but in a more languorous kind of way. His lips and tongue were a new source of heat, stealing moans from my chest. His mouth on me brought me to the edge again, and then over.

Heat spilled from within me. It would have been too much if the evaporating water wasn't cooling my skin. He held me easily just above him, taking the weight off my knees as my body tried to writhe against him. My groans of pleasure echoed from the stone walls, leaving me shaking and weak, and still his mouth fed at me, sending rippling sensations through my core. Panting, I leaned forward, my entire body trembling as I braced my hands on the stone above his head.

He gave me a final lick, then brought me down enough so that I was straddling his hips. He propped one hand beneath his head.

I straightened to look down at him, though it was an effort to not simply collapse onto his chest.

He looked at my body like he would memorize every curve. His free hand skimmed up my stomach, his fingers tracing the line of one particularly nasty scar. He looked at me curiously.

"The first time I was seriously injured during training," I explained, referring to the scar. "Another hunter managed to strike me with a dagger."

"How old were you?"

"Fifteen." I began unbuttoning his damp shirt.

He lifted his brows at me.

"We can't let all of this nice steamy water go to waste."

"I can feel how exhausted you are."

I leaned closer to his face. "Well then you'll just have to keep me afloat."

He traced a finger across my cheek, then down the

side of my neck, the gesture so tender I had to look away. "With enough time, your scars will fade."

"Do they bother you?"

"No, but they are reminders of your pain."

"I highly doubt I'll live long enough for them to fade."

His hand froze on the side of my neck.

I finally looked down at him, but couldn't read his expression. The story he had shared with me came to mind, and I wondered if my death would hurt him as much as Faele's had. I would do everything in my power to thwart Eiric, but even I had my limits.

He pushed his hand back through my wet hair, cradling the nape of my neck. He pulled me forward, then wrapped his other arm around me, holding me against his chest. There was tension in his body now—an air of desperation.

I stayed that way, perfectly still, unsure of how to read his mood. After a few heartbeats, I said, "Hugging isn't exactly what I had in mind."

"Shh, Lyssandra."

I frowned, then relaxed against him, deciding hugging wasn't half bad, even if I was nude and straddling him. Eventually my heartbeat slowed. My mind calmed, and his body relaxed in turn.

We stayed that way for a long while, breathing in rhythm, feeling safe. It was a new feeling for me, though part of me knew it was a lie. We were far from safe.

Eventually, with the heavy weight of dawn all too near, we made use of the steamy water.

When we left through the enchanted doorway, the

sky was growing light. Asher was forced to leave me with hardly a goodbye. He would barely have enough time to make it through the gates, even with the sentries instructed to let him out.

As I stood alone out in the cold, watching the first purple hints of sunrise, I couldn't quite settle my thoughts. Somehow, knowing Asher's past made me feel more vulnerable, not less. It hadn't leveled the ground between us at all.

For the first time in a long while, my heart ached with the thought that I might not survive. And not just for myself, because I understood something now.

My death wouldn't hurt Asher as much as Faele's had.

It would hurt him *more*.

CHAPTER EIGHTEEN

Tholdri caught me as I was sneaking into the dining hall. I had hoped for a quick meal before facing Markus and Steifan.

He grabbed my arm before I could step inside. "I don't think so, young miss. Where have you been?"

I turned and gave him my best withering glare. "Watch yourself, or I'll chew your arm off."

"That hungry?"

"Starved."

He grinned. "*Activities* with Asher again?"

"Food first, or I'm not telling you anything."

Laughing, he released my arm, then gestured toward the open door of the dining hall. "I was just coming to fetch food for everyone. Drucida thought it best for Markus and Steifan to remain hidden until she can speak with Charles."

We walked up the steps together. "I apologize for making you deal with everything on your own."

"I'm not one to throw stones if you were having a

good time." He frowned as we entered the dining hall. "Although, Cael was worried when he couldn't track you. You might want to use that apology on him."

Guilt slithered through my gut as I searched for an empty table. "We hadn't intended on being gone so long."

Tholdri pointed out an open expanse of bench at the end of one long table. As we walked toward it, he asked, "So are you going to tell me what you were doing?"

"Absolutely not." We both sat. An older woman seated next to me pretended not to see me, but I didn't miss how she scooted closer to her companion.

Tholdri leaned away enough in his seat to look me up and down. "Well, you're clean. So that's my first hint."

I was frowning at him as a young girl came toward us with a full tray of food. She nearly stumbled as she looked me in the eye. It was the same girl who had spilled soup all over me.

I forced a smile, and we were soon rewarded with two plates heaped with fried eggs, roast turnips, and a buttery sauce. Everyone around us had the same thing. One couldn't be choosy when there were many mouths to feed.

I lifted the fork that had come with my plate and started shoveling food into my mouth. It was piping hot, and I didn't care. I hadn't gotten any sleep and it had made me even hungrier.

Tholdri's first bite remained on his fork as he watched me devouring everything on my plate. "An enormous appetite. Second hint."

I scraped the side of my fork across my plate, scooping up the last remnants of sauce. "It's from the magic," I said caustically, then popped my fork into my mouth. I pointed to his plate, then spoke around my utensil. "Are you going to eat that?"

He slid his plate toward me. "I think you need it more."

I nodded my thanks, then dug into the next plate. I had never eaten so much in my life.

"While you feast, I may as well tell you the news Markus and Steifan came to deliver." He leaned a little closer and lowered his voice. "It seems Steifan's father has stepped in until a new Potentate can be decided upon."

"Of course he did," I said with my mouth half-full. "He practically funds the entire Order himself. No one is going to argue with him."

"Yes, and that's an issue, because Steifan and Markus believe Eiric is controlling him."

My fork clattered to my plate. I turned to stare at Tholdri. *"What?"*

"Everything is being swept under the rug, so to speak. Markus, Steifan, and Isolde tried to convince the other hunters of the threat Eiric poses, but Gregor Syvise is claiming that Eiric doesn't exist, and that *you* made up such a wild story to cover your tracks after killing the Potentate yourself."

My stomach fell to my feet. I swallowed back the urge to gag. "Why would he say that?" I rasped.

Tholdri gave me a sympathetic look. "Markus and

Steifan believe Eiric is controlling Gregor in order to isolate you from possible allies."

I had seen the level of mind control Eiric could implement from within his tomb. Now that he was free, he was most certainly capable of controlling Gregor, but— "Why though? Xavier already made it clear that Eiric knows I'm here, far from the Order."

Tholdri shrugged. "I'm not sure any of us can understand the motives of such a creature, but Steifan feels his father is not himself, and I believe him."

I nodded, feeling numb. "I believe him too, of course. But what does he expect me to do about it?"

"He doesn't expect you to *do* anything, Lyss. They both came to warn you."

"Warn me?"

"Most of the Order believes you killed their Potentate. What do you think they're going to do about that?"

My eyes widened. "They're going to hunt me."

The nearest witches were glancing our way, and I realized I had been speaking too loudly. I pushed away the extra plate of food. "Let's find Ian and see if he can bundle up some extra supplies."

Tholdri watched me as we stood, his honey-colored eyes seeing far too much. "Are you alright?"

"I already knew I could never go back."

"This is different."

"I know." I turned away from him and walked toward the kitchen, feeling sick and unsteady on my feet.

I had spent almost my entire life hunting for the

Helius Order. And now, the Helius Order was hunting me.

I TOSSED a sack of supplies onto the table between Steifan and Markus. "You both need to leave, *now*." They wore plain clothes, no hint that they belonged to the Helius Order, but they were hunters through and through. They were bred for it.

Steifan turned earnest hazel eyes toward me. "Why? Is it the witches?"

I stormed toward the table. "If the Helius Order is hunting me, you're making yourselves targets."

Tholdri remained silent at my back. He hadn't argued with me when I told him my plan. While I appreciated Steifan and Markus coming to warn me, I wouldn't let them ruin their entire lives for me. If I was being hunted, and the Order knew they were helping me, they would both not only be exiled, they would become targets.

Markus' jaw twitched, but he otherwise remained calm. "We knew exactly what we were doing in coming here. If the Order is under Eiric's control, they are no longer our allies."

I gripped the edge of the table hard enough to make my knuckles turn white. "If Gregor is the only issue, there is still a chance of making the other hunters see reason."

Markus shook his head slightly. "Isolde will continue to try, but I know when to forfeit. As long as

Gregor is in control, they are lost to us. They all believe you killed the Potentate."

I flinched at his words. That was the worst part, that they thought *I* had killed him. "You can do no good here."

Markus narrowed his eyes, and I knew I was about to get a speech about his *usefulness*, but Steifan stepped forward.

"This is my father, Lyss. We may not always get along, but he's still my father. If the only way for me to save him is to hunt Eiric, then that's what I'll do. Whether you like it or not."

I stared at him, remembering Amarithe shoving a dagger into his gut, his blood leaking across the ground. "You almost died last time," I said weakly.

He lifted his chin. "Yes, last time, when you made me remain at Castle Helius. I am no safer there than anywhere else, Lyss. At least with you, I can do some good." He stepped closer. "Do not turn me away. I can *help* you."

My shoulders hunched. "You don't understand. You have no idea what it's going to take to defeat Eiric."

"Blood magic?" His voice hitched. "Witchcraft? I don't care, Lyss. I still want to help."

I looked over my shoulder at Tholdri, betrayed. I hadn't wanted anyone else to know about the blood magic.

Tholdri lifted his hands, palms out. "It wasn't me, Lyss."

"Cael told us." Steifan said, drawing my attention back to him. "He doesn't want you to isolate yourself."

Angry thoughts churned my gut. "That was not his secret to tell."

"He was only looking out for you."

I stepped closer. He was only a few inches taller than me, so we were practically eye to eye. "Do you even realize what he is?" I had kept my letter vague. They didn't need to know everything about the creature that was my great uncle.

"We know everything," Markus said coolly. "And we have made our choice. So stop arguing with us."

I spun toward him. "It is not your choice to make."

He stepped closer, and I gasped. Suddenly, I could *feel* him. I could feel the bond between us, not quite like what I had with Asher, but similar.

"This is one of the few choices I *can* make." His voice lowered. "I *will* help you, Lyssandra. I will keep you alive. I will keep *both* of us alive."

I lifted my chin, meeting his angry eyes. "This is a fortress for witches. You've been trained your entire life to hate magic."

"So have you. We'll get over it."

I swallowed the lump in my throat, then shook my head. "You're both fools."

He leaned his face down toward mine. "Perhaps, but that is for us to choose."

I took a deep breath and let it out.

We all turned at a knock on the door.

Tholdri answered it, revealing Elanore and Ophelia waiting outside. I was once again stricken by how similar they looked to each other.

Elanore stepped across the threshold. A long, heavy

winter coat swirled around her ankles, the deep gray color seeming at odds with the warmer tones of her hair and skin. "Drucida is missing. We can't find her anywhere."

I patted my coat pocket with the key to the secret spring. She likely wasn't there, but maybe she had another key. I glanced at each of the men. "We'll search the fortress, then meet at the ice chamber."

Elanore trembled slightly. "You believe the skin changer took her?"

We had killed one skin changer, leaving the other, likely its sibling or mate, alone. We should have predicted it might act.

"It's likely."

Elanore clutched the collar of her coat, glancing at Ophelia. "We'll continue our search, then we'll meet you at the ice chamber. If your magic can track the other monster, we'll trap it together."

I nodded, steadying myself. I could continue trying to make Markus and Steifan leave later. For now, we had work to do.

With so many bodies on the floor, there was barely enough room for all of us to stand within the ice chamber. It was lucky that we still had Drucida's key from the previous night, or we wouldn't have been able to access them.

Tholdri and Steifan stood on either side of me. Steifan

had seen the bodies the night before, but he still looked green around the edges. And maybe a little blue. It had only taken a few minutes for our teeth to start chattering.

Elanore, Ophelia, and Markus stood on the other side of the bodies. There wasn't enough room for us to all stand together.

Tholdri handed me his dagger. "Sharpened this morning."

I appreciated the gesture, but I was becoming a mass of cuts and deeper wounds. A sharper blade here and there didn't make much of a difference. On cold skin, it was going to feel like a viper bite either way. I pushed up my sleeve, then took the dagger.

Markus watched me silently from across the small room, like no one else existed. I couldn't shake the surprise I'd felt when his shields had come down. He had learned to keep me out, all on his own. Well enough that I hadn't even been aware of it.

I peered down at the skin changer's body. I stood close enough that the tips of my boots were nearly touching it. It still looked like Jacques. We might never know what the creatures actually looked like in their original forms.

Ophelia let out a small noise of protest when I knelt beside the body.

I ignored her. It wasn't her brother, it was a monster. And its partner had taken Drucida. My gut told me that it was the truth. She wasn't just taking a private bath somewhere. I sliced the blade across my skin, letting my blood drip over the corpse.

Even that small act made me dizzy. I had given too much the previous day and night. I was exhausted.

A hand gripped my shoulder, steadying me.

I glanced back at Steifan. "I appreciate your help, but I don't think you should be touching me while I do this."

His eyes clouded with worry, but he nodded and stepped back.

I returned my attention to my blood dripping on the corpse, willing a new bond to life. I swayed again, my body trembling. If I had been standing instead of kneeling, I would have fallen.

I watched my blood pooling across the corpse, soaking into its ragged clothing, and nothing happened. I could taste my heart in my throat.

"Why isn't it working?" Markus asked.

I looked past the corpse to his waiting gaze. His eyes were too wide, his entire body tense. I knew with sudden surety that he could feel exactly what I was trying to do, and he knew it wouldn't be enough.

"I've lost a lot of blood lately. I haven't had time to recover." I closed my eyes before he could respond. Being too weak wasn't an option, not when Drucida might yet be alive. We had to find her.

I searched through my body for any last hint of strength. My bleeding had slowed, but I had spilled plenty. There should be enough to make a connection. I took a deep breath and re-doubled my focus, giving it everything I had.

My breath shuddered out of me. There was nothing but a cold, dark pit in my chest.

I searched inward for warmth, light, *anything*. When

I found nothing, I searched outward. Suddenly, my body warmed. Fresh energy seeped into me, making me feel more steady. But that wasn't right. Asher was asleep for the day, he couldn't help me.

Elanore gasped.

I opened my eyes to see that Markus had fallen to his knees. Fresh energy coursed through me. *Strong*. I felt strong again.

Markus gritted his teeth. Veins bulged across his forehead. "What are you doing to me?" He fell onto his side.

Ophelia knelt over him, but seemed reluctant to touch him.

"Lyss," Tholdri said at my back. "What are you doing?"

But it was too late. It was just like when Asher lent me his energy, but this energy was not being given willingly. I was *taking* it. And I couldn't seem to stop. My sword awoke, but not with warning. It was urging me to continue. It wanted me to be strong, at whatever cost.

Markus' life force filled me, and the new bond with the other skin changer snapped into place.

I could sense an invisible tether connecting the corpse below me to the other monster. It was somewhere out on the mountain. I could feel its bloodlust, and its triumph. For some reason, it thought it had won. The bond was stronger this time, letting me know something else. The skin changer had kept Drucida because of me. It wanted me to find it. It was willingly solidifying the bond.

I staggered to my feet, holding my bloody arm away from my body. "I know where it is."

Markus had curled up on the icy floor. He managed to lift his head, and his eyes were filled with hatred. "You're a monster," he rasped.

I didn't know what else to say to him, except, "You're probably right."

For a heartbeat, everyone looked at me. And they weren't just stunned, or confused.

They were afraid.

CHAPTER NINETEEN

We all made our way toward the gates, everyone but Markus. I had taken too much from him. He could barely move. We had helped him back to his cottage, leaving him behind. Other than that initial look of hatred, he had not acknowledged me again.

Everyone else was quiet as we reached the edge of the fortress. The sentries took one look at us, and the gates opened. No questions asked. I had briefly considered fetching our horses, but the skin changer was somewhere higher up the mountain. The footing was too rocky and steep. The horses would never make it with riders on their backs.

My wounds stung as my sword whispered into my mind. The skin changer knew I was tracking it, and still, it would not harm me, not unless I forced it to.

I almost wished it would. What I had done to Markus...

I shook away the thought. Time for that later. I

started hiking up the mountain with Tholdri and Steifan close behind. Ophelia and Elanore brought up the rear. I hadn't offered for them to stay at the fortress, not this time. We were on our way to save their high witch, and I would not risk Steifan and Tholdri in the process if magic could potentially protect them. I had seen what Elanore could do with her winds. She could prove useful.

"It's higher up," I muttered. "Almost at the peak."

The invisible tether stretched between us, guiding me ever upward. My boots slipped across sharp stones, but I maintained my footing easily. I still felt strong, while Markus could hardly move.

"I don't understand how you can tell where it is," Steifan panted. He had known what I planned when we went to the ice chamber, but there hadn't been time to explain the finer details.

"I just know. We will need to be prepared when we reach it. It can change into a mouse in the blink of an eye."

Cold wind whipped across our faces. My cheeks were growing numb.

"What do we do if it turns into a mouse?" he asked.

"Stomp on it, stab it. I don't care. Just don't let it escape."

Tholdri glanced behind us. "Elanore is struggling to keep up."

I shook my head. "We can't wait for her. We can only hope she'll reach us in time to help."

We labored onward as the mountain's peak drew closer. The wind became painful, stinging all exposed skin. The loose rocks which were once treacherous, became deadly, each stone slicked with frost.

But we couldn't rest. Some hidden instinct deep in my gut told me we couldn't rest. The skin changer did not have control of its impulses. It would never be able to keep Drucida alive for long.

My breath fogged the air in front of my face with every exhale, each following inhale painful, like breathing in broken glass. At least my body was warm from exertion, though I knew once I stopped moving the cold would clamp around my bones.

I was focused on my labored steps for so long that I didn't notice as the storm closed in, blotting out the sun. Dense gray clouds filled with ice hung low around us.

"We'll freeze to death if we get lost out here." Steifan's teeth chattered.

"You either go up or down," I huffed. "Nowhere to get lost."

My thighs and calves burned with every step. My feet were numb, the chill in my other extremities leeching away my stolen strength. But we were close. So close. I could feel it not far above us. But how had it carried Drucida all this way?

I resorted to using my hands to help myself upward, and soon Tholdri and Steifan did the same. Ophelia and Elanore had fallen far behind us.

"I smell smoke." Tholdri muttered.

I had already noticed it. Someone had a fire burning nearby, likely within at least partial shelter to protect the flames from the wind. There were enough small, spindly trees for fuel, although I couldn't tell which branches had been broken by hands, and which by the elements.

I pulled myself up over a boulder, then collapsed to my knees on mostly solid ground. The mountain's peak loomed just overhead, shadowing a small cave with smoke trickling from its depths.

We had found the other skin changer. The cord between us held taught. But there was something odd about it. The connection on the other end felt spread too far.

Cold crept up from the ground into my knees. No time to consider it.

Steifan and Tholdri pulled themselves up on either side of me, the latter flopping onto his back as he tried to catch his breath. But the cold wouldn't allow it. Every breath hurt. The tips of his golden locks were frozen white. I could feel ice on my eyelashes.

"Why did it bring us all the way up here?" Tholdri panted.

"It didn't want us able to go for help." I staggered to my feet, overcome by an eerie sense of dread. What if it was angry that I had stolen its partner, and now it wanted to steal something from me? It couldn't kill me, but it *could* hurt me.

"I'll check ahead. We need to know what we're going into." I started toward the cave.

Tholdri and Steifan quickly caught up with me.

"We'll freeze to death," Tholdri said. "You won't get rid of us that easily."

"You won't freeze that quickly."

Tholdri kept walking at my side. "We are stronger together, Lyss."

I wanted to argue, but he was right. I had no idea what we were going into. It was stupid to go in alone just to protect them. Though I almost wanted to risk it.

Together, we approached the cave. And despite my dread, part of it felt right, going into battle with my two closest allies. They would *always* have my back, and I would have theirs.

We stepped through the entrance. Tholdri was the only one that had to duck, but he was able to straighten as we walked further inside. The smell of woodsmoke was strong, almost strong enough to cover up the scent of blood—but not quite.

And underneath the blood was the scent of rot. The other lair we had found was only temporary. This was their true den. And we had been wrong. There hadn't just been two skin changers, there had been three. The connection feeling spread out now made sense. We had killed one, leaving two more.

I didn't recognize the pair who greeted us, a man and a woman, both a few years older than me, if I was judging their age correctly. And their hair ...

Bright crimson. Like mine.

I stopped at the center of the cavern. It was a large space, only one side illuminated by a roaring fire. The ceiling was high enough that the smoke didn't choke us. My bones thawed with the fire's warmth, but the blood in my veins was ice. I knew the curled up lump in the corner was Drucida. Her chest shifted slightly with her breath—she was alive—but in bad shape judging by the smell of fresh blood coming from that corner of the cavern. In other corners were piles of trinkets, and other things I didn't want to think too long upon. The smell was enough to inspire nightmares.

The two skin changers waited while we took it all in.

Finally, I observed them. They were similar enough that they had to be siblings, perhaps even twins. High cheekbones, long noses, thin lips. Their skin was a healthy olive tone, contrasting with the hair. Their clothes were little more than tattered rags. I had to wonder if they even felt the cold.

"You should have come alone," the male said. I had expected his voice to be more guttural, something monstrous, but he sounded like a normal man. "Our message is only for you."

I flexed my hands, trying to loosen the stiff joints enough to grip my sword. "You could have just written a letter."

The female wrinkled her nose. "But you *killed* our little brother. We can't hurt you, but we don't have to make it easy on you."

"What do you want?" I demanded. "Why take Drucida?"

The male furrowed its brow, and I realized it didn't know her name.

"The woman?" The female crossed her thin arms and nodded back toward the corner.

"Yes."

She smiled, thin lips nearly reaching the tip of her strong nose. "Oh, she came to us. So convenient. We never have enough time to do things properly."

I glanced at Steifan and Tholdri. I could feel them both ready to go for their swords, but it would be easier if we could buy time for Elanore to reach us. Her magical winds could prevent the skin changers from transforming and escaping.

"You're lying."

Her tongue darted out across her yellow teeth. "Not lying. She found us. Used magic to track us."

I shifted uneasily. Could it be true? Was that the real reason Drucida had given Asher the key to the secret spring? She wanted us distracted? "Why did she come?"

The female tilted her head, taking a hesitant step toward us. Her feet were bare and stained with dirt, soot, and blood. I got the feeling she was trying to contain herself, while she wanted nothing more than to *taste* each of us. "She wanted answers. Thought she was stronger than us." The skin changer smiled again, raking long fingers through her matted hair. "Proved her wrong. We told *him* what happened and he said to wait. He said you would come."

My heart pounded in my chest like a caged bird. "Eiric? Why did he send you?"

"He says you already know."

We were right then, right about everything. Xavier had been telling the truth. "Why does Eiric want me to learn magic?"

The creature only smiled. "He wanted us to tell you that you have until the equinox to prepare yourself. Prove yourself useful, or he will kill you."

The equinox? That was less than two weeks away. "What does he want to *use* me for?"

Both skin changers continued smiling. I realized they had edged a few steps closer.

I drew my sword. "Do not move."

The male eyed my weapon before lifting his gaze to meet mine. His eyes were a solid, crisp green. "Blood of our blood. Our quarrel is not with you."

Footsteps behind us made Tholdri, Steifan, and I move aside. The skin changers were already looking past us as Elanore and Ophelia staggered into the cavern.

"You must—" Elanore braced her hands on her knees, trying to catch her breath. Her hair was entirely white with frost. "Stop this," she managed to finish.

It took me a moment to realize she wasn't speaking to us. She was speaking to the skin changers.

She finally straightened. "My children, you must stop."

Ophelia didn't seem surprised by her words. She stood at Elanore's back, looking cold and miserable, but not surprised.

I, however, wasn't sure who to point my sword at. *"Children?"*

Elanore wrapped her arms tightly around herself, even though she was the only one of us dressed properly for the cold in her heavy gray coat. "You must understand, Lyssandra."

Tholdri and Steifan had both moved to guard my back from the skin changers so I could face Elanore and Ophelia.

I lowered my sword slightly, but kept it out. "Must understand what?"

She took a step toward me, hands reaching out pleadingly. "I didn't know it was them at first."

I lifted my sword, and her hands fell. "They're your children."

Her chin lowered. Loose tendrils of her russet hair draped down her cheeks, the frost melting away. "Yes. I have five children. *Had* five children."

I looked at Ophelia as a few of the pieces fell into place. "You're one of them, aren't you?"

She nodded. "And Jacques."

"Does Drucida know?"

Elanore's shoulders slumped. "Only in part. She believes my first three children are dead, and that I left the other two behind to protect them, which is the truth."

I glanced at the skin changers. They were both staring hungrily at their mother. I had a feeling they didn't think fondly of her. "Protect them from what?"

She gestured at the pair of murderers. "They were not always this way. I did not want the same fate to befall Jacques and Ophelia." Her eyes welled. "I had never meant to become pregnant again, and with a second pair of twins, no less. I carried the children to term and was forced to leave them. When Drucida found them so many years later." She exhaled loudly. "I was relieved, and terrified. I only told them who I was to get them to leave, but they refused."

"How did you know they were yours?" I asked.

She held one hand over her heart. "I am their mother. I knew."

"You were afraid the skin changers would hunt

them?" I had to assume that's why they had targeted Jacques.

She shook her head. "No, I was afraid if Alexander learned I'd had more children, he would curse them too."

One of the skin changers snorted. I wasn't watching them, so I wasn't sure which one it had been. Likely the female, judging by her demeanor.

"Who is Alexander?"

She eyed me solidly as she said, "He was a witch from the Blackmire line. A witch with blood magic, like yours."

I tightened my grip on my sword. "You're lying."

"Not lying," the female skin changer interrupted. "We are Blackmire, just as you."

I glared back at her. "You're not witches. You're monsters."

"Alexander cursed them," Elanore explained. "He altered the blood in their veins. Altered what they were."

My stomach churned. Suddenly the cavern was too hot. "Why? Why would he curse his own children?"

"Because I took them from him, and I ran. He cursed them to punish me. He could have killed me, and it would have been a far lesser punishment. He knew this."

"He made us stronger," the male skin changer snarled. "He gave us a gift."

Elanore swiped a palm across her face, shaking her head. "He twisted them. But you must understand, I could not kill my own children. I—" Her mouth trembled. "Once I understood what they had become, I ran from them. I hoped I could eventually find a way to change them back, but I never did. A few months after Jacques and Ophelia were born, Drucida found me. She brought me to the fortress. When she eventually found my two younger children—" She shook her head again. "Maybe she knew they were mine. Maybe she thought she was doing me a service. That within the fortress, we could protect them. She never said one way or another, and I never admitted the truth to her."

"This is why you wanted me to learn blood magic," I realized. "You were hoping I could change them back."

She nodded. "I am sorry, Lyssandra. I wanted you to be able to track them, and I hoped I would have time to convince you to change them back, but you didn't learn your magic quickly enough."

My head spun from her elaborate tale, but there was a more pressing matter at hand. "Why did you follow us up here?"

"Please, I know they are monsters, but do not kill them. They will give Drucida back."

I narrowed my eyes at her. "They *killed* your other son. What makes you think they will give her back willingly?"

Ophelia's jaw stiffened at my words. She knew why her brother had been killed. Maybe not from the start, but either her mother had admitted it, or she had figured it out.

Deeming her the more reasonable of the two, I looked at her. "Would you have your brother's murderers go free?"

She glanced at her mother, then lowered her eyes, shaking her head ever so slightly.

"Ophelia!" Elanore gasped.

When Ophelia lifted her eyes, they were filled with rage. "They killed Jacques. They killed my twin brother. I loved him more than anyone else. I want them to pay."

Elanore held a hand to her chest and took a step back, stunned. "I thought you came up here to help me."

"I came here to stop you."

Tholdri cleared his throat, gaining my attention. The skin changers had edged closer. If they turned into their other forms, we might not be able to catch them without Elanore's help.

"If they move again," I said, "kill them."

We were going to kill them regardless, but I wanted more answers first. If they really were Blackmire...

The female took another step toward Steifan. He lifted his sword and she snarled.

"It's not their fault," Elanore pleaded. "They act only on instinct. They must steal the skins of others in order to maintain their own. Without the skins, they grow weak. They are like animals, trying to survive."

"They are killers," I countered, "and you are complicit in every death they have caused."

She took another step toward me. "They are your family too, Lyssandra. Alexander's father was your grandfather's cousin."

I had already been considering how we might be related. It came as no surprise, and it didn't matter in the slightest.

"Distant relations, at best. I know who my true

family is." I knew because they were both standing right behind me.

I lifted my sword. I had learned enough, and I was done talking. "They must pay for what they have done. I can go around you, or through you. Your choice."

Ophelia's eyes widened. She might have been willing to go against her mother, but I doubted she would stand by and let me kill her. That made her another enemy to contend with. Four against three. Against normal opponents, I would have liked our odds, but Elanore was powerful, and we still didn't fully know what the skin changers were capable of.

Not that it really mattered. There were no choices left to make.

Elanore edged further into the cavern, standing between us and the skin changers with just the fire between them. "You will not have them, Lyssandra. I will give you one last chance to walk away."

"And what of Drucida?" I asked.

"I will save her if I can."

I had little skill for sensing lies, but I saw her mistruth for what it was. She would never be able to free Drucida from her monstrous offspring. I gave Steifan and Tholdri a slight nod. We would need to be quick, before the skin changers could transform and escape. My sword finally warned me. If I intended to kill her children, Elanore would see me dead.

"I see you have made your choice." She extended her arms.

Unearthly wind kicked up from nowhere. The fire

was out in an instant, leaving us in near darkness with the storm brewing outside.

"Get the creatures!" I shouted, not daring a glance at Steifan and Tholdri.

I lowered my chin, squinting my eyes against the wind. I took a step toward Elanore, but her winds gusted me back. I had to crouch to maintain my footing. Out the corner of my eye, I could see that Steifan and Tholdri weren't having any more luck advancing on the skin changers.

I gritted my teeth, turning my shoulder toward the wind, making a smaller target to lessen the pull. My braid whipped out behind me. Her winds were so strong they seemed to burn my skin. "You can't keep this up forever, Elanore!"

"You are right!" she shouted. "I am sorry, Lyssandra." Her apology drifted to me on her winds. She closed her eyes and threw back her head.

Wind gusted me so powerfully that it stole my breath. My boots scraped across the stones at my feet. I was forced to drop to my hands and knees, barely maintaining my grip on my sword. I search for something, *anything* to grab onto, but there was only loose stone. The skin changers' trinkets got caught up in the wind, pelleting me with bits of metal, cloth, and what smelled like rotting flesh. Trophies from all their victims.

The wind increased, and I was tossed toward the cavern's entrance. I had lost sight of Steifan and Tholdri in the chaos. My fingernails scratched across stone for a painful moment, then I flew out into the open, tumbling across the ground. Snow swirled around me as I desperately searched for a handhold. I had lost my sword. It had probably gone over the edge of the mountain.

My palms burned as I scraped them across the icy rock. Elanore emerged from the cavern, her figure hardly distinguishable from the swirling snow. She lifted her arms again and her wind hit me. My body careened over the edge of a small cliff. I barely managed to grip the stone as my feet flailed below me.

I gasped for breath, trying to pull myself up, but my hands had gone almost entirely numb. I couldn't lift myself.

Someone gripped one of my hands and I almost instinctually tugged away, then I saw a lock of golden hair trailing above me. Tholdri held onto both of my hands, keeping me from falling, but he had to be laying flat on his belly on the ledge above. He didn't have the right leverage to pull me up.

He gripped my hands tightly, and I was glad at least for the final touch before I broke my neck falling down the mountain.

"Mother! Stop this!" Ophelia's voice carried on the wind, sounding tiny and far away.

Abruptly, the unnatural wind cut off, but there was still enough of a storm that cold gusts whipped my body back and forth. I knew Tholdri's hands had to be freezing, but they felt warm on top of mine. He gripped my hands tightly, then started hauling me up. Once I was far enough, I let go of him to scramble across the stones.

Elanore stood near the entrance of the cavern, a hand over her cheek and shock in her expression. I realized Ophelia must have hit her.

Ophelia looked just as horrified. She huddled away from her mother.

I searched quickly for my sword, but I didn't see it anywhere. I also didn't see Steifan. Dread filled my gut. If he had gone over the edge—Elanore would pay.

Though I felt unsteady on my feet, I charged toward her. I needed to take her out before she could stir up more wind.

I staggered just before her as a clawed hand exploded from her chest. She blinked at me, stunned. Blood speckled her face. Ophelia screamed.

The male skin changer snarled behind her, tearing his clawed hand free from her chest. "Sorry mother, but we need her."

Elanore fell at his feet, dead. Ophelia continued screaming, backing away toward the cliffside. And I was left facing the skin changer without my sword.

He opened his mouth to speak, just as Steifan leapt out of the cavern and lopped off his head. Hot blood sprayed across me, scalding my skin because I was so cold. The skin changer fell beside his dead mother.

I stared at Steifan, stunned. Blood poured from a wound at his hairline. He must have been temporarily knocked unconscious inside the cavern.

I wasn't sure where the female had come from, but before I could blink she was shrieking toward Steifan, holding out grotesque hands turned to claws. Reacting purely on instinct, I tackled Steifan out of the way. I rolled off him, claiming his sword before he could react.

Tholdri met up with me as I chased the final skin changer to the edge of the cliff. I knew she could turn into a mouse at any moment, but for some reason, she wasn't. Instead, she wept. She wept for her dead brother, and perhaps even her mother.

Snow swirled around her, lifting her matted crimson hair as she reached out toward me. "He said we would all be family. You and I!" she sobbed. "We would be true family!"

Her tears froze on her face. Her dirty hands were just hands again, cradled before her like I actually had something to offer.

"Family?" I asked. My hair had mostly pulled free of my braid. It swirled around me. Bright red amongst the white of the snow.

She nodded, her eyes pleading. "Family. He said you would come to understand. That's why he wanted you to come here."

It was a lie. Eiric knew I would kill them. They had served their purpose. I stepped toward her.

Her eyes widened. Hopeful.

I shoved Steifan's sword through her gut then up through her chest. The movement pulled her closer to me. She stank of rotted flesh.

"Don't you know?" I whispered. "All of my family is dead."

I withdrew my sword, splashing more blood across my clothing. The skin changer toppled backward, and then was gone, her body flying down the edge of the mountain.

I took several ragged breaths, but couldn't seem to calm myself. Tholdri gripped my shoulder, pulling me back from the edge.

She had been evil. She deserved to die. But the final look she had given me—

I knew it would haunt me. And Eiric had done this. Every death was his fault.

Maybe he thought *he* was my family too. But it surely wouldn't save him.

CHAPTER TWENTY

We left Ophelia outside with her dead mother while we hurried into the cavern. The skin changers were gone. She should be safe, as long as she didn't freeze to death. The storm had closed in around us, encasing the mountain in solid gray and white.

I shook ice and snowflakes from my hair as we moved through the near darkness. The cavern was in shambles. It was lucky Drucida had been behind Elanore when she cast her winds. She hadn't been disturbed. I was the first to reach her.

I knelt beside her and checked her pulse. Thready, but there, and her skin was warm. There were even a few embers left in the fire at my back since it had been built in a concave pit. Tholdri set to work adding random pieces of cloth to the glowing coals, trying to revive them.

Steifan knelt next to me as I slowly rolled Drucida over. There were slices across her neck—claw marks.

The same blade-sharp claws that killed Elanore. The skin changers could summon them at will.

Her coat was missing, and her dress was shredded, soaked in blood. They had sliced her through the fabric like frenzied animals. Maybe the claws were what they used to skin their victims, but they had treated her differently than the others. The deep gashes would surely damage the skin they hoped to steal. Perhaps they had used other tools. Now, we might never know.

The fire flared to life at my back. I knew the basics of wound tending—I had taken care of myself and others often enough—but I was no healer. Drucida needed a healer, *quickly*. Her clothing was soaked with blood, and there was more drying on the cavern floor.

"Help me move her closer to the fire," I said to Steifan. "We need to keep her warm."

The wounds would need to be cleansed, but at least they had mostly stopped bleeding. Unfortunately, by the light of the fire, I could see more. Her face was a mass of bruises, one eye swollen shut. My clothes were as blood-soaked as hers, but my coat at least could cushion her head.

I balled it beneath her, then sat close. "If she can make it to nightfall, Asher can heal her."

Tholdri glanced at her as he continued to stoke the fire. He had found a few more pieces of wood, and an old book. He tore out the pages one by one. His thoughts were clear on his face. She was in bad shape. She didn't have long. But there was no way we could carry her through the storm down the mountain.

"Why did you come alone?" I muttered, looking

down at her. She knew I would have been able to track the other skin changers in the morning.

I looked up as Ophelia staggered into the cavern. Her hands were coated in blood. Her mother's blood. She shuffled toward us like a sleepwalker, then fell to her knees beside Drucida.

"What are you—"

She cut me off with a sharp look.

I bit my tongue. Her eyes were puffy and red-rimmed, her face pale.

She held her hands over the wounds at Drucida's throat. There was nothing that I could see, but my skin prickled with sudden warmth. I leaned closer, realizing the warmth was coming from Ophelia.

She closed her eyes and was quiet for a long while, holding her palms just over Drucida's skin. Finally, she let out a shaky exhale and her shoulders hunched. She removed her hands.

The wounds were still there, but they looked better, like they'd had a few days of healing. Her eye was a little less swollen.

"I'm still learning," Ophelia muttered. "I'll need a moment before I can try to do more."

I stared at her, amazed. The healers at Castle Helius were skilled with herbs and could stitch a wound well enough to barely leave a scar, but I'd never seen anything like what Ophelia could do.

Her sniffling and her trembling shoulders were the only signs that she was fighting tears, or maybe it was just from the cold. "My mother—" She kept her eyes on her lap, her bloody palms flat on her curled knees.

I waited until she was ready to continue.

She shook herself like a bird settling its feathers, then cleared her throat. "I never knew my mother. Jacques and I were abandoned when we were babies. I didn't understand why Drucida brought us to the fortress until I saw her. The moment I saw her face, I knew who she was."

"You look a lot like her," I said softly.

She nodded with her eyes still closed. A few tears dripped down her face. "I do, but it was more than that. I just . . . knew. I was so shocked, but it was nothing compared to how I felt when she asked us to leave. She told us she had three previous children, and that their father had cursed them to spite her. She claimed the children were dead, but she still feared their father would curse any other offspring she bore."

She took another shuddering breath. "But I refused to leave. And not just because of her. I had the opportunity to learn magic, true magic. I wasn't about to give that up. Eventually, she came around. But she said we had to keep our relationship a secret, if only to keep me and Jacques safe. This was several years ago." She finally opened her eyes, but she stared at nothing. "When Jacques was killed, and she asked for the knife, I trusted her. We were her children. Of course she had our best interests at heart." She let out a bitter laugh.

Finally, she actually looked at me. "When she told me to tell only her if I noticed one of the skin changers, I knew something was wrong. I put the pieces together and confronted her, and she told me the truth. The three skin changers were her children. They killed Jacques. They killed my twin brother, and she still wanted to protect them." Rage flashed across her features. "I apologize. I should have told you when I figured it out, but I wanted to give her the opportunity to do the right thing."

"It's not your fault. We all do strange things when it comes to family."

She nodded, her eyes once again going distant. "I never wanted her to die that way."

"I know."

She was quiet for a while, and I thought she would leave it at that, but then her eyes snapped up to my face. "But they knew you. Who is Eiric?"

I was surprised Elanore hadn't told her. "He's an ancient vampire, the very first vampire. He is the reason I came here. I must defeat him."

"And he sent my mother's children here?"

I chewed my lip. Drucida was unconscious, but it still wasn't something I should admit.

"You can tell the truth, Lyssandra." A voice rasped between us.

We both whipped our eyes downward. Steifan and Tholdri shuffled closer.

Drucida's good eye cracked open. She took a breath that sounded like it hurt. "I know why the skin changers came. You can tell the truth."

My heart tickled my throat. She knew. If we made it back to the fortress, she would immediately toss me out. Or worse.

Her hand fluttered weakly to her chest, assessing the

damage. "Oh light, I should have remained unconscious."

I agreed with her, but I didn't say so out loud. "Ophelia healed you as much as she could. Once darkness comes, Asher can finish the task."

She let her hand fall limply back to her side. "Are the skin changers dead?"

"Yes." I looked across her at Ophelia. "And—"

"My mother," Ophelia finished for me.

"Your mother?" Drucida asked.

"Don't act like you didn't know. That's why you brought me to the fortress, isn't it?"

Drucida smiled softly. "I'm sorry for your loss, child."

"She brought it upon herself."

Drucida started to shake her head, then winced. "No. She loved Alexander, once. Loved him enough to have three children with him. But it was a dark love, and when she fled, he could not let her go. She did not ask for her children to be cursed. She only wanted to protect them." Her eye rolled up to Ophelia. "And you."

It wasn't my story to interrupt, but I had to know. "Is Alexander still alive?"

"I do not know. He could be, though I imagine if he were I would have heard tales of him. A powerful blood witch." She aimed a weak but meaningful look my way.

"I hope he's rotting in a ditch," Ophelia said. "And I hope his soul is just as cursed as the creatures he created."

"I hope so too." Drucida rolled her eye back toward me. "But Eiric. He's worse, isn't he?"

I wasn't sure what to say. I glanced at Steifan and Tholdri, then back down at her. "More dangerous, at least."

"The light sent you here for a reason."

I furrowed my brow. She knew. She knew why the skin changers had really come. "Eiric attacked your people so you would let me in. He wants me to learn magic. I do not know why."

"It may be what your enemy wants, but it also is what is supposed to happen. I see that now. I didn't want to accept it, but I see it."

"I don't understand."

Drucida sighed and closed her functioning eye. "I found Illya's final tapestry. It was still raw, the edges unfinished, but she knew she was in danger. She hid it before she was killed. She knew I must see it."

My wide eyes met Ophelia's. "And what did the tapestry depict?" I asked Drucida.

"You," she breathed. "You were reading from an ancient tome, casting a ritual. The sky behind you was dark. Everything—so dark."

My heart sputtered in my chest. "What does it mean?"

"It means you will access your full abilities, Lyssandra. Whether I help you, or not, you will do it. I must make sure you use your power for the right reason."

"You don't trust me to do so?"

Her good eye slitted open again. "No one can be trusted where blood magic is concerned. Just look at what it did to Alexander."

Anxiety rippled through me. So much talk about the

corrupting influence of blood magic, and yet, I still knew so little about it. To curse the blood running through a child's veins . . . it was abhorrent. Unthinkable. But to curse the blood running through Eiric's? It had possibilities.

"I don't like that look on your face, Lyssandra."

I gave Drucida my best innocent expression.

She didn't buy it for a second. Her eye narrowed. "Yes, I believe I'd much rather be your ally, for now."

"That's good enough for me."

Tholdri had moved toward the mouth of the cavern to look out at the storm. "I can't tell how long until dark," he called back to us. "But Asher and Cael might have trouble finding us through the snow."

"They'll find us." I looked at Ophelia. "But it might be a while. Do you think you're up for another round of healing?"

She didn't look like she was. She looked frail, devastated, and cold. She nodded. "I can try."

Drucida gave me one last look, then closed her eye. "Thank you, child."

"One more question," I said.

Drucida hardly shifted. "Hmm?"

"Why did you come alone?"

"Ophelia wasn't the only one to figure out Elanore's secret. I had hoped to spare a mother the grief of killing her children. But I overestimated my power. And I didn't know there would be two of them."

I leaned closer. "But how did you track them?"

"I am high witch, Lyssandra. Do you think yourself more skilled?"

"That doesn't answer my question." If she could track things too, there hadn't been a need for me to bleed all over several corpses.

She sighed heavily, then winced at her own movements, her eyes still closed. "I *saw* the cavern. Just as I can sometimes see other things. I wasn't even sure the skin changer would be here, but I thought it worth investigating."

"There, was that so hard to admit?"

She frowned. "Go away, Lyssandra."

I stood, then moved to join Tholdri at the cavern's entrance. The world outside was solid white. Normally we would have burned the bodies, but at this rate, we'd never find them. And I'd never find my sword. The thought left a hollow ache in my gut. I'd grown rather attached to it.

Tholdri moved close enough that our shoulders were touching. "One step down, Lyss."

He was right. The skin changers were gone, and Drucida had gotten past her reservations about teaching me. *Truly* teaching me.

I looked out into the snow. "Now we just have to survive the storm."

"Are you speaking literally, or metaphorically?"

I shook my head as I turned away to sit back by the fire. "Both."

Though we couldn't really see when darkness fell, I sensed it. After several sessions of healing, Drucida had finally been convinced to rest. Ophelia curled up next to her, lost somewhere in the depths of a bad dream. She whimpered in her sleep, tiny pathetic sounds.

I tried to ignore them, but it was difficult.

I moved to the cavern's entrance where Steifan kept watch. Tholdri lounged on the other side of the fire. His eyes were closed, but I could tell he wasn't quite sleeping.

Steifan turned as I reached him. He looked as exhausted as I felt, but he was still standing. And he was the only one of us who still had their sword. Tholdri's had been lost over the edge of the cliff, just like mine.

Steifan's muted blue coat only had a few blood splatters. When he had beheaded the male skin changer, most of the blood splashed toward me.

He looked back out toward the snow. He no longer seemed so terribly young to me. He had seen enough now. He understood the life of a hunter. "I wonder if Markus has recovered."

"I doubt he'll be marching up the mountain to find us. He'll probably be running in the other direction as soon as he can."

He wrapped his arms around himself, his eyes haunted. "He won't, Lyss. I don't think he can."

"What do you mean?"

"The bond for him, it's not like what is between you and Asher. You were able to stay away from Asher for years. I don't think the same will be true for Markus."

I moved closer and lowered my voice. "What do you mean? He was able to stay away from his previous master."

"I know, but something about this is different. Every day it seemed to get worse for him. He didn't speak of it, but I could tell. He was panicked. He *needed* to find you."

Suddenly my pulse was hammering in my throat. "He seemed fine when we met you at the gates."

"That was the most relaxed I had seen him in a week. It was because he found you, Lyss."

I shivered at his words. It felt nice to be around Asher, but I had never been panicked without him. I had fought the pull between us for years. "That is the absolute last thing I wanted to hear."

"I know, but it's true. And I thought you should know."

"Thank you for telling me. Though I'm not sure what to do about it."

He nodded back toward the sleeping witches, then gave me an encouraging smile.

I crossed my arms, mirroring him. "Is this your way of telling me I should ask for help?"

He simply smiled.

"You've spent far too much time around Tholdri."

"He says he needs to counteract *your* influence so I don't become a surly nightmare."

I heard a soft chuckle back by the fire. As I'd suspected, Tholdri wasn't asleep.

"Just don't start primping in the mirror all the time. Tholdri's favorite sight is his own reflection."

"Well it is a beautiful sight," Tholdri muttered, just loud enough for us to hear.

In that moment I couldn't argue. He looked far

better than me, with my loose hair tangled and blood staining my clothing and skin. I smiled at Steifan. "Let me know when you get tired. I'll take over for you."

Steifan nodded, and I walked back toward the fire, leaving him to guard the entrance. I would ask Drucida for help with Markus, once she was well. I would have to tell her how the bond was formed, but it seemed a small matter compared to everything else I had admitted to. She already thought me capable of countless atrocities. What was one more? At least without my sword, I couldn't create a servant bond with anyone else.

CHAPTER TWENTY-ONE

The vampires found us shortly after darkness fell. Cael hesitated at the entrance while Asher approached, his eyes only on me, taking in the blood on my clothing. He wore his usual black coat over a black shirt. The white dusting of snow on his shoulders matched his hair. The ice on his eyelashes made him seem ethereal, somehow unreal. The look in his silver eyes, however, was something I knew well. He was shielding his worry, but he didn't like seeing blood on me.

Still seated by the fire, I lifted my hands. "Before you get overprotective again, none of the blood is mine." I wrinkled my nose. "For once."

He looked down at my arm where my sleeve had bunched up, revealing part of my newest cut, crusted over with dried blood.

"Alright, just a little bit of it is mine." It was healing, but more slowly than usual. I had reached the end of my energy stores—maybe the end of my magic stores too.

Ophelia sat up, rubbing the sleep from her eyes. She blinked at the vampire, then huddled a little closer to Drucida, shaking her lightly.

Drucida grunted in response, but after a few more light shakes, her eyes opened. With Ophelia's continued healing, the swelling in her face was nearly gone. Seeing Asher standing on the other side of the fire, and Cael beyond him, she motioned for Ophelia to help her sit up. While her wounds were all now more than halfway healed, she was still exhausted and in pain. She would be for quite some time.

"I take it the skin changer has been dealt with?" Asher's attention remained fully on me.

"There were two more, actually. Not just one." I stood. "It's a long story. One I'll tell you later. Would you be willing to help Drucida heal? She suffered much at their hands."

Drucida cleared her throat. "That will not be necessary. Ophelia has done enough."

I looked over at her. "You're being foolish."

She lifted her chin. There was still a light dusting of bruises turning her flesh from brown to purple. "Even I am entitled to a foolish moment every now and then."

I frowned, but let it go. If she wanted to feel awful, that was her choice. She was no longer in danger of losing her life. Let someone else carry her off the mountain.

Tholdri remained lounging by the fire. "How bad is the snow outside?"

"Treacherous," Asher answered, still looking at me. "Where is your sword?"

"Lost." I averted my gaze. "Can you help us get back to the fortress?"

Cael finally stepped forward. He'd stayed far enough from the fire that snowflakes still clung to his crimson hair. His shapeless black clothing cast eerie shadows behind him, reminding me of the living shadows he could summon. I hadn't seen them in some time. I wondered if they only came when he was in his other form. "We barely made it up here ourselves. It is far too dangerous."

I tilted my head. I was absolutely starving, and covered in congealed blood. "We can't just stay *here*."

He lowered his chin and gave me a look that reminded me so much of my grandfather that for a moment, I had no words. "I will fetch you some supplies and let Elanore know what has happened."

I winced, glancing back at Ophelia. That they hadn't noticed Elanore's body showed just how bad the snow had gotten. I had seen it piling up at the entrance, but hadn't looked further outside since my chat with Steifan.

"Another long story," I said when Ophelia just stared at her lap. "But Elanore is dead." I turned back toward Cael. "And if you're capable of fetching supplies, you're capable of helping us off the mountain."

"I could not risk dropping you." His words were for me alone, though he did spare a slight glance toward Drucida.

"He is right." Asher moved closer to me. "It is too dangerous. We will fetch you supplies from the fortress, and in the morning you can assess things for yourself."

"I'll go," Cael said to Asher. "I can let Charles know what happened. You stay here with Lyssandra."

I glared at both of them. "When did you decide to band together against me?"

"They're trying to help you, Lyss," Tholdri said behind me.

I crossed my arms and turned my back on them. "Insufferable vampires."

Drucida was smirking at me.

I wrinkled my nose at her. "Don't worry, I still find you insufferable too."

She grinned, though it looked like it hurt. "Don't fret, Lyssandra. If travel is still an issue in the morning, I can go down myself."

I had forgotten about her impressive cold tolerance. "You know, that doesn't make me feel any better."

Asher touched my shoulder, and when I turned back toward him, Cael was already gone.

"I don't remember *agreeing* to stay here," I growled.

He guided me back toward the fire.

I stepped into the circle of its warmth, relaxing, a little. "Cael better return with enough food to feed an army."

With his hands still on my shoulders, Asher lightly pushed down until I sat. Then he sat behind me so I could lean against his chest. If he was bothered by me being covered in blood, he didn't show it. I leaned against him, his presence relaxing me further.

Tholdri was looking at him wide-eyed. "You've done it. You've tamed the mighty beast."

Steifan lifted a hand to hide his silent laughter.

"Let us hope Cael brings a bottle or two of wine with the supplies," Drucida chuckled. "I think we all need it."

Ophelia finally smiled. Drucida patted her leg.

Just one big happy family. At least for the night.

"It makes sense." Asher absentmindedly rubbed his hand up and down my arm. "The witches were still incredibly powerful back when I first heard tales of the skin changers."

We had waited for Cael to return with supplies before we told them everything that had transpired. I had a full belly, and a half-empty bottle of wine in one hand. With the fire fully stoked, my insides were as warm as my outsides.

I leaned against Asher, oddly content, though I still stank of blood. "So it must have been an old curse. Something another blood witch used before."

"Hopefully not on children," Ophelia muttered.

Asher stopped rubbing my arm and lightly gripped it instead at her words. "We can only hope. And we cannot say what other monsters were created in the same way."

I shivered at the thought. No one should have the power to alter someone's blood—to change them into something else. And yet, that power rested somewhere within me.

I took a swig of wine, forcing the thoughts out of my mind. There would be time enough to worry about such things once we were back in the fortress. For now, even in the vile den, it felt like I had a reprieve. We were cut off from our troubles.

I looked around the circle at my companions. No one seemed to want to sleep anymore, probably because we had discussed how many parts of people had ended up in the cavern. Elanore's winds had swept away much of the smell, but some of it inevitably lingered.

Drucida eyed the bottle of wine in my hand. I wasn't much of a drinker, but being a vampire's human servant had its perks. My mind felt slightly fuzzy, but that was it.

"You might want to save some of that for when we face Charles," she said.

Cael had seen Charles at the fortress, and had warned us we'd be in for an earful whenever we made it back.

I took another sip. Asher's hand started running up and down my arm again, relaxing me. "I don't understand why you must go to such trouble to convince him of anything."

Cael's voice echoed from back in the shadows. "The fortress has always been divided. Some gifts are entirely different from others, especially between men and women. Women are usually more powerful because they are more in tune with the earth and its elements. Men sometimes grow . . . prickly because of it."

Drucida smirked. "Prickly is one way of putting it." She turned her attention back to me, her face glowing in the firelight. "Most of the men within the fortress follow Charles. Not all, but most. If I do not work with him, we would become too divided. Together, we are stronger."

Ophelia's hands fidgeted in her lap. "Even Jacques wanted to learn from him. He took after our mother with the gift of air, but he was nowhere near as powerful. We know nothing of our father, but we do not believe he had magic."

"And what is Charles' magic?" I asked.

Drucida looked down at the flames near her boots. "Fire. Charles' gift is fire. You wouldn't know it from looking at him, but he is one of the most powerful male witches I have ever encountered."

I tried to picture Charles controlling fire like Elanore controlled wind, but I couldn't quite manage it. It was impressive to think of though. Such gifts could easily turn the tide of battles both large and small.

"And what of Illya?" I asked. "Before her death, it seemed you needed to consult with her as well."

Drucida nodded. "Seers. Those with more subtle gifts. Many hoped to learn from her."

I kept my mouth shut about how worthless the tapestries still seemed to me. Even though one had finally convinced Drucida to teach me true blood magic.

"Aren't you a seer as well?"

She shrugged. "I sometimes have visions, but not like Illya. Half her life was spent *seeing*. When a tapestry needed to be made . . . it was like she had no choice in the matter."

"It doesn't sound like a very nice life," Steifan commented.

"It wasn't," Drucida said without looking at him. "I

will take care of Charles," she continued, her eyes still on me. "You will learn, and we will try to locate Eiric. Whatever he is doing now, it cannot be good."

I glanced at Steifan and Tholdri before I could help it. They were both already looking my way.

Steifan nodded at my silent question.

"Actually," I sighed, "we do know one thing he is doing."

Drucida picked up the other half-empty bottle of wine and took a swig, then motioned for me to continue.

"We believe he is controlling Gregor Syvise, the man who has taken control of the Helius Order. He has convinced the other hunters that I killed my grandfather. They will hunt me, if they can." I said the words without allowing myself to feel them, but the aftertaste was still unbearably bitter.

"Syvise?" She looked at Steifan.

His cheeks reddened. "Yes, my father."

"Eiric can control even the minds of hunters?"

"He can cloud our minds," I explained. "I'm not sure about control. Probably not, or he would have done it already. While he's of a proper bloodline, Gregor was never trained as a hunter. He simply funds the Order with his coin."

Drucida's attention went back to Steifan. "And you agree that your father is being controlled?"

He fidgeted, then raked his fingers through his black hair. "He was most certainly not himself the last time I saw him."

Cael finally stepped closer to the fire. "Eiric wants

Lyssandra strong, but cornered. Though we are not sure why."

"I can think of one reason," Asher said behind me.

I leaned away enough to look back at him.

"What does a mother bear do when it is cornered?"

I lifted a brow, not sure where he was going with this. "She destroys anything that gets in her way?"

He nodded. "Eiric wants you powerful, capable of destruction, but also cornered."

"But what does he want to put in my path?"

He shrugged, and even seated, the movement was graceful. "I cannot say. But with the Helius Order after you and your hunter allies, and with young vampires targeting the ancients . . . "

My eyes widened. "He's threatening all of my cubs, isn't he?"

"I'm not sure I appreciate this analogy," Tholdri cut in.

I ignored him. Eiric had been backing me into a corner without me even noticing. He knew I would have to act eventually. The only question was, what did he want me to do?

"It is only a theory."

I realized he was sensing my sudden panic. "It's a good one."

"It makes sense," Drucida agreed. "But it doesn't tell us what he'll do next."

Asher's eyes were still on me, gauging my reaction. "I believe his next move will be something more grand. He's been putting all of his pieces in place for quite some time."

Tholdri sighed. "Well that's comforting."

Asher took my hand, rubbing small circles against the back of my palm with his thumb, but there was no comforting me now. We had discovered Eiric's smaller machinations, and many had died because of them. Just how many would die before his final plot was revealed?

And who, if anyone, would survive?

CHAPTER TWENTY-TWO

The morning trek down the mountain was filled with curses and frozen feet. The sky was a clear, pale blue, and the snow had settled enough to make the journey possible, but that didn't mean it was comfortable. Only Drucida seemed unfazed, if slightly winded.

I had kept an eye out for any glimmer of my sword on the way down, but saw nothing. Perhaps someone would come across it when they returned to properly dispose of Elanore's body, but that wouldn't happen until spring. According to Drucida, now that the first snow had fallen, it would continue to pile up through autumn and winter.

We reached the gates to find Charles and Markus already waiting within. Markus stared at me unwaveringly. Any questions I'd had about how he might feel were answered. He was furious. But . . . he was still here. His skin and short hair were clean, and he'd shaved the stubble from his strong jaw, so he'd regained at least enough energy to take care of himself.

Charles wore a heavy coat with white fur at the collar, the soft pelt a few shades lighter than his silver hair, combed once again to perfection. It was difficult to tell if he was frowning beneath his heavy mustache, or if it was just his constant expression. It hadn't changed much since I'd first met him.

"I see Cael spoke the truth." His eyes lingered on the blood on my clothing.

Drucida stepped around me, partially shielding me with her body. "The skin changers are dead, and we have much to discuss."

I peered around her at Markus, meeting his angry gaze.

Charles nodded up at the sentries, then the gates began to open. I was so intent on Markus that I was a little too slow with stepping out of the way. Tholdri had to yank my arm back just before one side of the gate would have hit me.

I finally lowered my gaze from Markus' face as we walked into the fortress, and I found myself frozen yet again. He stepped toward me, then extended my sword.

I stared at the naked blade in his hand. I had been too busy observing his expression to notice it. "How did you get that?"

"It came with a letter," Charles said caustically.

We all waited for him to go on, but instead he looked at Drucida. "I told you letting them in would be the ruin of us all." He turned and walked away.

"What is he talking about?" I asked Markus.

He was still holding my sword out toward me. "Follow him. Read the letter for yourself. I already have." His expression gave me nothing, not even anger. I couldn't tell what he was feeling at all.

I took my sword, sheathed it, and started walking. My blade stayed quiet, granting me no answers. But *someone* had found it on the mountainside. Someone had been watching us the entire time.

Tholdri hurried to walk at my side. "The skin changers were just the first part of his plan."

I nodded, ignoring a pair of women bundled in heavy coats looking our way. "Yes, and I think we are about to learn part two."

Greetings, my kindred.

It has been so very long since I walked this earth. The witches I once knew are little more than dust. Even my beloved half-sister, Lavandriel, is lost to me. Of course, she is the reason I was locked away, so perhaps it is no great loss after all.

I suppose she cannot be blamed. My allegiances were divided, as they are still. The Blackmire line lives on. Blood of my blood. My past, present, and future.

On the other side of my dark coin, the vampires. My creations. I have spoken into the minds of my children, and they have awaited my arrival. While it pains me to cut ties with my past, we must all move forward.

At the equinox, my kindred, I cordially invite you to war.

—Eiric Blackmire

I LOWERED the letter in my hands, my steaming mug of tea forgotten on the table before me. Drucida, Charles, Markus, Tholdri, and Steifan were seated around me. Ophelia had been sent home. We were back in Illya's room of tapestries. It seemed oddly fitting, being surrounded by events of the past, present, and surely some of the future.

Drucida had fetched the unfinished tapestry. My likeness was indisputable. The surrounding darkness... ominous. Neither she nor Charles recognized the tome in my hand. My other hand would have been lower, where the tapestry was unfinished. Maybe I was holding something there too. We might never know.

Steifan was the only one looking at me and not the tapestry spread out across the table, anchored by candles. "It's what Karpov was talking about from the start, isn't it? The vampire war."

"But not vampires against vampires." I couldn't seem to put the letter down. My eyes scanned the words again. "Vampires against witches. That must be what Eiric means."

"Then why target the ancients?" Tholdri asked.

"To get them out of the way, so he can control the young ones. Who can say how long he has been speaking into their minds?"

"Karpov wasn't young," Tholdri countered.

I hung my head, finally placing the letter on the table. I should have been exhausted. Instead, I just felt numb. "No, but he craved power, *dominion*. Eiric's plan would have appealed to him."

Charles was glaring at all of us. "The vampires should never have been any of our concern. Cedrik and Cael left us with their own vendetta in mind. It has nothing to do with us."

"And this has nothing to do with them." My fingers traced my likeness on the tapestry. "This only concerns me. He is doing this all to use me in some way."

Charles smiled cruelly. "Then perhaps you should leave us in peace."

"That is no longer an option," Drucida cut in before I could reply. "Eiric is a danger to us all. He sent the skin changers after our people, and that act cannot go unpunished." She eyed Charles defiantly. "Or do you not mind our enemies killing our people whenever they please?"

He stood, slamming his hands on the table. "The vampires will attack us because of *her*." He whipped an accusing finger my way.

Drucida stayed seated. *Calm.* "And we will be ready for them, with a blood witch on our side."

Charles looked like his soul left his body for a moment. He inhaled sharply. "You still plan to teach her?"

"I find I have adequate motivation."

"This is madness."

She finally stood. "She can help protect our people, Charles. You know teaching her will give us our best chance at survival. A blood witch against vampires."

He was close enough that I could hear his shallow breathing and his pounding heart. I couldn't blame him for his reaction. He was absolutely terrified. "It's not too late to send her away."

"They are coming for us on the equinox, Charles. Whether she is here or not."

I wasn't entirely sure about that, but I didn't argue.

Charles slowly lowered himself into his chair. "We should have exiled the entire Blackmire line from the start."

Taking his insult for agreement, Drucida turned toward me. "Do you still believe Eiric's human servant is nearby?"

I shrugged. "Seeing that I lost my sword during the day, and it was delivered with the letter, I think it's likely."

"Good. I believe we should capture him."

I nodded. "I agree. But it will not be easy." I looked at my three fellow hunters. Eiric could cloud our minds, but we at least seemed to have *some* resistance to his control.

Though he was still angry with me, Markus nodded at my unspoken question. "Leave that to the four of us. Everyone else should stay safe within the wards of the fortress."

I was surprised he even knew about the wards, but I didn't argue. It was a sound plan. The four of us with hunter blood would find Xavier and bring him back to the fortress.

"Lyssandra," Drucida said tiredly. "You have to stay here and learn."

"I can't let them hunt him without me. He's dangerous."

She glanced at Charles, then back at me. "We have no other choice. By the equinox, you must be ready. I want you able to boil the blood in every vampire's veins."

I shivered at the thought, my mind searching for any argument that wouldn't leave Tholdri, Steifan, and Markus vulnerable.

"She's right, Lyss," Tholdri said. "This is the reason you came here. You need to focus on defeating Eiric. Leave the rest to us."

I knew I couldn't argue, but I couldn't quite bring myself to agree. Instead I stayed quiet, looking once more at the tapestry. The tome in my hand seemed oddly familiar. I could have sworn I had seen it before, but I wasn't sure where.

All I could say for sure, was that I would see it again.

CHAPTER TWENTY-THREE

Three days later...

Ian stood in front of me in the empty dining hall, smiling.

I flexed my fingers at my sides, trying to picture the blood flowing through his body. I had tossed my newly acquired black coat across the nearest chair. The dark gray one was ruined. The new coat had black on black embroidery forming intricate patterns at the cuffs and collar. I liked it. Plus, the long split hem made it easy to move. I hadn't asked Drucida where she'd found it. If it came from one of the skin changers' victims, I didn't want to know.

"You're not focusing, Lyssandra." Drucida stood a few paces away, arms crossed.

Today was the first day I had seen her in breeches instead of a gown. Dark gray with a black tunic on top. I wasn't sure what her choice of attire said about what my training today might entail. The other hunters had left at dawn two days prior. Steifan had donated blood to Cael the night before they left. That issue was taken care of for now, but I was otherwise on my own. At least until Asher woke each night.

Drucida started tapping her boot on the floor.

I frowned at Ian's smiling face. "I'm trying."

"You're *not* trying."

"But what if I hurt him?"

Drucida walked up to Ian's side, facing me. "He volunteered for this, Lyssandra. And you're only trying to warm him a little bit. He'll be fine."

I wasn't so sure about that. When I had warmed Asher, I had been using my blood as a connection. Now, I was trying to use Ian's, and I had no idea what I was doing.

"Try closing your eyes," Drucida instructed.

My frown deepened, but I closed my eyes.

"Now sense him in the room."

That part was easy. I was good at sensing people nearby. I had always thought it was normal that I could feel whoever else was in a room. Just as I could feel someone sneaking up on me. Apparently, it wasn't. Asher had been right. My instincts were not built on external cues alone.

"Now make a connection. It should be easy since he is willing. You'll have a harder time doing the same with your enemies."

I flexed my hands again. "I can sense him, but that's it."

"It is as I feared, then."

I opened my eyes to find Drucida with a gleaming dagger in her hand.

Great. More cuts. "And what exactly is this fear of yours?"

She stepped toward me, dagger held at her side. I was glad to have my sword back. It let me know she wasn't about to get rid of me because I'd proven useless. I didn't really believe she would think that way, but caution had kept me alive a long time. Long for a hunter, at least.

She extended the dagger, hilt first. "This is all new to me as well. I don't know blood magic. I had hoped you could hone your skills through will alone, but you might need a little more to work with." She looked down at the dagger, then nodded back toward Ian.

I ignored the offered weapon. "You want me to cut him?"

"I think it's necessary."

I looked past her toward Ian. "And you're alright with this?"

He was still smiling, but it had wilted slightly. "She let me know it was a possibility from the start. I still want to help."

I pinched my brow and shook my head. This was madness.

Drucida was still holding the dagger out toward me. "If a bit of his blood can be the catalyst to save us all, it's worth it."

She was right, but I didn't like it. Ian was a willing participant, but he wasn't like me and the other hunters. Blood and pain were an integral part of our lives. I didn't know his past, but the situation was likely more frightening for him than it would be for a hunter.

My hands felt clammy as I took the dagger from Drucida. The least I could do was make the wound myself. I wouldn't mess up and cause him to lose too much blood. Someone else might.

He looked a little green around the edges as I approached him. He was shorter than me, but young enough that he might still have a final growth spurt.

"How old are you?" I asked.

His dark brows lifted, disappearing behind his shaggy bangs. "Eighteen."

Light. He was only a few years younger than me, but the gap between us seemed like centuries. "Can you push up your sleeve?"

He did as I asked, pushing the sleeve of his white shirt up above his elbow. I could feel Drucida's eyes boring into my back. She might act apathetic, but she didn't like the idea of me slicing up one of her people.

I gripped his wrist with my left hand. His skin felt a little cold. He trembled slightly. I had never wanted to wound anyone less.

"Do you like working in the kitchen?" I asked.

His brows lifted again, then he gave me the slightest smile. "It's nice. Even with other people around, it's distracting enough that I don't always focus on their energies."

"I can imagine that's helpful. What's your favorite thing to cook?"

The questions were useless, but they had their desired effect. His body relaxed. The trembling subsided. "Silverfish baked with cream and boiled eggs. It takes a while to prepare, but it's a comforting dish. I like to make it around the solstice, though we can't always get silverfish. It comes from one of the villages over the mountain, so availability depends on how much they are willing to spare—"

Maintaining eye contact, I sliced the dagger across his skin.

His breath hissed out of him reflexively, then he blinked at me, lowering his gaze to the blood welling across his forearm. "Oh, that wasn't so bad."

"Distractions help." I stepped back, glancing at Drucida.

"Same thing," she instructed. "Try again."

I pursed my lips, looking down at Ian's arm, but his blood just seemed like blood. There was nothing magical about it. *No pull.*

"I think I need more."

Ian cringed, but I shook my head.

"No, not from you. I think I need a connection."

There was no blood on the dagger, but I wiped it on my black breeches just the same. Then I pushed up my sleeve and sliced it across my forearm. Blood-borne illnesses were rare, but possible. Fortunately I didn't have to worry about them. Vampires couldn't catch them, and neither could their servants.

Ian watched me, wide-eyed. Drucida remained silent at my back.

I closed my eyes, focusing on my own blood, my wound the twin of Ian's. I could hear his blood dripping on the floor. I could feel mine, but I couldn't hear it.

Then I realized our blood was flowing at the same rate, falling at the same time.

My breathing quickened. Ian's did the same.

I focused on my blood, warming it slightly.

Ian gasped.

Wanting to be sure, I chilled my blood—only the portion pooling across the floor. I didn't want to give Ian hypothermia by mistake.

My eyes flew open as his teeth started chattering. His skin looked slightly blue. My blood had frozen to the floor.

"Cut off the connection, Lyssandra." Drucida rushed past me.

The dagger, forgotten in my other hand, clattered to the floorboards. I took a step back, my pulse racing, then swayed on my feet. Dizziness washed over me, rooting me to the spot.

Drucida took Ian's coat from the chair beside mine, wrapping it tightly around him. Her eyes were wild and panicked like a spooked horse as she looked over at me. "Go into the kitchen. Fetch him some hot soup. We need to warm him up."

I had the brief thought of warming him with my magic, but it wasn't worth the risk. I might boil him instead. My cheeks burning, I rushed into the kitchen, still feeling unsteady as I searched for a fresh bowl. Finding one, I rushed to the stove, burning my fingers as I flung a lid from one of the massive pots. There were chicken bones boiling within, making broth. It would do.

I dunked the bowl halfway into the broth, then ran

out into the dining hall, dripping broth across the floor as I went.

Drucida had lowered Ian into a chair. He was visibly shivering, which was good. It meant his body was trying to warm itself back up.

I approached and handed him the broth. He took it with a weak smile.

"I'm sorry, I didn't mean for that to happen."

He kept the bowl in his hands, letting the steam warm his face. "I figured. It's okay. But this is good, right? You've learned something new?"

Drucida gave me a dark look. "Yes, now if she slices herself as well as her enemies, and if they are either weak of will or willing participants, she can make them really cold."

I scowled. "We could try it on you. Then we'll know if the participant needs to be *willing*."

She wrinkled her nose. "I'd rather not."

Ian sipped his broth, watching us.

Drucida stood. "I'm going to look for another volunteer. You shouldn't try anything else on Ian today." She took a step away, then looked back. "Don't kill him while I'm gone."

My scowl deepened. I didn't want to try again, on *anyone*. But there was no other choice.

Once she was gone, I took the free seat beside Ian. "Again, I apologize. I was just trying to chill the blood outside of you, not inside of you."

He sipped more broth. He was looking better by the moment. No permanent damage done. "It's alright, I volunteered. I knew the risks."

I rubbed a hand across my brow. Now that my nerves had faded, fatigue was hitting me. We had been practicing for days, draining my energy, but accomplishing nothing. I slouched further in my chair. "Why *did* you volunteer?"

He shrugged. "Drucida said it was important. She said there was nothing more for you to learn without someone to practice on."

I watched him out the corner of my eye.

Noticing, he gave me a half smile, then extended the broth toward me. "You look like you need this more than I do."

My stomach growled in response. He seemed to have recovered, so I took the broth. "Well I appreciate you trying to help, even if I failed."

"Can I ask you a question?"

I stiffened. My instinct was to say no, but he *had* just risked his life helping me. "Go ahead."

"What is it like carrying a vampire's energy around with you?"

I sloshed some of the hot broth over my fingers, then cursed under my breath. "I wasn't expecting you to ask about *that*."

He looked down at his lap. "You don't have to answer."

"It's fine." I held the bowl in one hand to flick broth from my fingers. "It's . . . I don't quite know how to describe it. Asher shielded me from our bond for a long time."

"Really?"

I looked at him, wondering why he was so interested. "Yes, really. He saved my life, but I wasn't ready to accept being a vampire's human servant."

"And you are now?"

I sat up a little straighter. "You sure do ask personal questions, don't you?"

"You asked me about seeing energies. That's *personal*. At least to me."

"Fair enough." I shrugged. "I don't think I'll ever be fully accepting of it, but I'm not an actual servant. He has no control over me."

"So you entered into a romantic relationship with him willingly?"

I set the broth aside before I could spill it again. "Who told you I am in a romantic relationship with him?"

He gave me another half smile. "It's kind of obvious."

"Why do you care?"

He looked away, and after a moment I realized it was to hide his blush.

"Oh. I see." I sighed, leaning back against my chair. "Truth be told I had never planned on having *any* relationship with him. It just sort of happened. Circumstances brought us together."

"Are you ever frightened of him?"

I closed my eyes. Practicing on Ian had drained me. I was ready for a nap. "I used to be."

"But not anymore?"

I smiled with my eyes still closed. Coming from most anyone else, I would have found the questions irritating, but Ian was genuine enough that I didn't mind. "No, not anymore. He would never hurt me."

I paused at my own words, realizing they were true. Asher would never willingly hurt me. I could only say the same for a handful of people.

I could feel Ian watching me, but I was too tired to open my eyes.

"Would you like some actual food?" Laughter tinged his voice.

"Yes, please."

I listened to his movements as he stood and walked into the kitchen. My smile slowly faded. Yet another innocent caught up in my mess.

I would do whatever I could to protect him—to protect all of them. Ophelia, Ian, even Drucida. They had all suffered so much already.

From the outside, we seemed incredibly different, but we weren't really. When their blood spilled, it was just as red as mine.

I RETREATED TO MY LODGINGS, sore and exhausted. I wasn't sure why Drucida had thought it wise to bring in Charles as my next *victim*. She had wanted someone unwilling, I suppose, and she had found him.

And all I had gained from the experience were a few fresh wounds. With Charles actively working against me, I hadn't managed a single feat of magic. I suspected he only agreed at all because he wanted to humiliate me.

We were back at the beginning. I needed a real teacher who knew blood magic, but as far as we were all concerned, one did not exist.

I removed my sword and leaned it against the bed, then flopped down across the mattress. The cottage felt too quiet without Tholdri around. I wondered what he was doing now. And if they had safely made it across the mountain.

I closed my eyes. It wasn't quite suppertime, but I was exhausted. My magic, as unimpressive as it was, was too much for my body. I couldn't keep up.

My breathing slowed. My body felt cold, but I was too tired to reach for a blanket. All I wanted was for the pounding in my head to stop.

I laid quietly for a long while, until my thoughts were distracted by the crackling of a fire. I sat up and looked around. Had that fireplace always been there? I thought of the old enchantments on the cottages, rubbing my face to chase away my confusion.

I froze when I realized there was someone else in the room. I lowered my hand and opened my eyes.

Eiric stood before me.

My heart sputtered in my chest. He looked just like he had the night he was freed. Crimson ringlets draped the sleeves of a billowing cream colored shirt. His pants were black velvet, tucked into shiny black boots. He smiled at me, but there was something not quite right about it. Madness danced in his green eyes.

I pushed past my shock, staggering to my feet then backing away. I still wore my boots and coat. I had fallen asleep with everything on. "How are you here?"

It was pitch black outside my windows, but there should have been hours left until darkness. I knew I couldn't have slept for so long.

He stalked toward me. "Do not fret, Lyssandra. This is merely a dream."

"A dream?" I flexed my hands, glancing around for my sword. I'd had such dreams of Asher before, but that was different. We had a connection.

"Blood of my blood." He backed me against the wall, then stopped right in front of me. I couldn't find my cursed sword. "I could find you anywhere."

"Why are you here?" I could believe it was a dream. My sword was missing, and there was a new fireplace in my cottage. But that didn't mean I wasn't in danger.

"I've come to see how your training is going." He smiled. "Will you be ready by the equinox?"

I wasn't sure what to say, so I settled on no answer at all.

"I can smell your wounds. The cost of blood magic is high, is it not?"

"What do you know of it?" I growled.

He leaned forward. He was too close, but there was nowhere for me to go unless I wanted to stumble over the bed. "You mean you haven't figured it out yet?" His voice was a low hiss. "No one told you why I died?"

"You had a wasting disease. You took your own life." Amarithe had told me as much, and she knew him personally.

"I do love a good story, but no." He stepped away, and my heart climbed back down from my throat into my chest. He paced toward the fire, stopping so close to it that his velvet pants glowed orange. "I enjoy watching the flames. They remind me of the sun. The sun that was stolen from me, so very long ago." He glanced over at me. "It could happen to you too, you know. It *will* happen, eventually."

I debated going for the door, but if this really was a dream, there was no escape until I woke. "What could happen to me?"

He turned his gaze back down to the fire. "I didn't have a wasting disease. My magic corrupted my blood. I used too much. My death was the final price."

A lump formed in my throat. We were of the same line, I should have considered the possibility. "You had blood magic?"

"It was a different time. I was strong. I could do almost anything." He turned his head toward me. "You are lucky, Lyssandra. Being bonded to a vampire has slowed the progression for you." He smiled abruptly. "I guess you have me to thank for that. Without me, your master would not exist."

It was actually Cerridwen that I had to thank, but I kept quiet. "Is there a reason you're telling me this?"

"I'm giving you the warning I never had. And when it becomes too much for you to bear, I will help you. You will come to me. You will beg me to save you."

"I'd rather die."

He smirked down at the fire. "And you will, Lyssandra. If you don't ask for my help, you and your master will both die."

"Is that why you wanted me to learn magic? So I'll need your help?"

"It would have come to you eventually either way. You would have needed my help regardless."

"Then why attack the witches?"

He laughed, startling me. "Why attack those capable of sealing me away? The ones who kept me trapped in a little box for centuries?" He laughed again. "*Why* indeed."

He gave the fire a longing look, then turned toward me again. "I look forward to seeing what you are capable of, Lyssandra." He tilted his head, draping his curls across his shoulder. "You look so very much like my half sister. I do wonder if your gifts will be as great." He turned away, laughing, the sound tinged with madness.

His laughter echoed in my ears as I sat up in bed, gasping for breath. The fireplace was gone. The sun was just going down outside my windows. My sword leaned against the wall beside my bed, its eye open, watching me.

"Thanks a lot for the warning," I muttered, rubbing my eyes.

Eiric had possessed blood magic. It had killed him. Unless he was lying to scare me. It was a possibility.

I unraveled my messy braid, raking my fingers through my hair so I could tie it up more neatly. It was also a possibility that blood magic would kill me too. I tied off my hair, then stood and grabbed my sword. Blood magic was just one thing on the long list of threats. It could get in line.

Cael and Asher found me in our usual spot on the mountainside. I had known it wasn't wise to wander out alone, but I needed space. Lots and lots of space. Space from Charles and Drucida. Space from my too quiet lodgings. And especially space from my own thoughts. The howling wind helped with that.

Asher reached me first. I could sense him just behind me. I huddled in my winter cloak. It had been colder on the mountain since the first snowfall.

"Why are you out here alone?" His words carried to me on the wind.

I turned toward him. Cael stood a few paces back. "I needed a moment to myself."

Asher frowned, but he knew better than to argue with me. Being overprotective would get him nowhere. "I smell fresh wounds on you."

I wrapped my cloak more tightly around me. *"Practice."* I looked at Cael. "I have a few questions to ask you, if you don't mind."

His brows lifted. I hadn't been able to spend much time learning from him since we'd arrived at the fortress. While he'd told me some stories on our travels, I still had many questions. After my dream with Eiric, those questions had become much more specific.

Asher bowed his head toward us both. "I will give you privacy."

In the blink of an eye, he was gone, and part of me regretted it. Our time together was always so limited, and with the threat Eiric posed, I wasn't sure how much we had left.

I shook my head at my own thoughts. It was too soon to give up now.

Cael stepped closer. "What would you like to ask me, Lyssandra?"

I tried to think of the best way to ask. While he usually answered my questions, there were some topics he tended to avoid. "Before you became . . . what you are. Did you have magic?"

A cold breeze swept his red hair back from his face. He left it loose tonight. Even in the moonlight, the color contrasted sharply with his black clothing. His goatee was darker than the hair, framing the grim line of his mouth. "Some. Enough to perform the ritual where I gave up my life. But I was never as strong as those you have met here. My power paled in comparison to Drucida's."

I had suspected as much. He had become what he was to protect our family line. To give us a chance against Eiric, should he ever escape. "And my grandfather?"

"Perhaps even less than me. Our sister was more powerful than us both. When she died—" he inhaled sharply, like the pain was still fresh to him. Maybe it was. He turned his head away, darkness shadowing the hollows of his cheeks. "When she died, we sought to make ourselves more powerful in other ways. We wanted to hunt vampires so that Eiric could not control them. We found the Helius Order, and Cedrik knew exactly what he needed to do."

"He climbed through the ranks," I finished for him. "At some point, he had a daughter, and she married a hunter and had me. Did my mother have strong magic?"

"Some, but she was forced to hide it her entire life. She was not granted a chance for her skills to flourish."

"Had she lived, would my grandfather have made her a human servant to get rid of her magic?"

He frowned.

"I'm going somewhere with this, I promise."

His brow creased, almost like he was in pain. "That was not something he did to cover up your magic."

"I know he did it to make me stronger. But he *did* want to hide my magic."

He moved closer, lifting his hands toward me, but not quite touching. "He only wanted to hide your magic until you were strong enough. And while becoming a human servant helped in that regard, that's not the only reason he did it."

I blinked at him. That had been my grandfather's plan with me, Markus, and perhaps others. He wanted to strengthen the Order.

"He did it to save your life."

I stared at him. "I don't understand."

"Your grandfather didn't know that you had blood magic, but he suspected. I'm sure Drucida has told you that blood witches often . . . *lose* themselves."

I wrinkled my nose. "Yes, she made that abundantly clear. But I still don't understand what that has to do with me becoming a human servant."

"Markus was turned before you," he explained. "With him, yes, the intent was strength. But it was experimental. Cedrik suspected that strong hunter bloodlines might stand a chance of maintaining free will despite the master servant bond, and he devised a way to amplify the effect."

Goosebumps prickled up my arms. I told myself it was from the cold. "How? And why am I only hearing of this now?"

The pained expression crossed his face again. "I was asked never to speak of this. Your grandfather didn't want you to be afraid of your magic when it came time to access it. He had hoped to eventually teach you himself. Once he was gone, I wasn't sure how to tell you. I wasn't sure *if* I would tell you. But with you trying to learn magic, I think you must know."

"You think I must know *what*?"

"Your grandfather had blood magic, but it was weak. Too weak to use against his enemies. The most he could do was alter Markus' blood. He strengthened his resistance to vampire wiles. Then we set him up to become a human servant. I already had control of my ghouls at that time. We didn't want him to suspect that he was set up."

"And he did the same to me, didn't he? Is that what you're trying to say? That he cursed my blood, just like Alexander did to his own children?"

"But he didn't do it to punish you, or your mother." His tone was sharp, defensive. "He included it in your training to make you willing. He did it to keep you safe."

"To keep me safe from *myself*," I corrected. I remembered that part of my training. All hunters were taught mental fortitude. Not all hunters were taught by the Potentate himself, like me. And he must have done the same to Markus, making us both *willingly* participate.

"Safe from yourself, *and* from Eiric. Cedrik had an ancient in mind for you. Someone who could keep you grounded. Who could help you maintain control. And who would also be a strong ally."

"Who?"

"His name is Geist. As far as I know, he still lives. He was allied with some of the older witch bloodlines. He was our connection to the other ancients."

"Was?"

"After Asher claimed you instead, we lost track of him."

I huddled in my cloak, digesting his words. My parents had lied to me. My grandfather had lied to me. And now, my great uncle had kept this information from me. "You should have told me from the start. It could have saved us time."

"We didn't *know* if you had blood magic. The witches needed to test it."

I stared at him until he finally looked at me. "But you said my grandfather suspected from the start. Why?"

He turned away again. His jaw twitched.

"Tell me, Cael."

"I cannot."

Anger welled within me. So many lies. *Painful* lies. I deserved the truth. "*Tell me.*"

He turned, and my own pain was echoed in his eyes. As I watched, his face thinned out. His skin stretched too tight over his bones. His other form was peeking out.

If he hoped to scare me away from my answers, he

had picked the wrong woman. "Tell me why he suspected I had blood magic."

His shoulders hunched. His crimson hair turned gray and stringy. Shadows swarmed around him, and still I did not back down.

My instincts screamed at me to run, but I stood at the edge of the shadows. And I knew through my sword that he meant no harm.

His voice was like jagged claws on stone. "You killed your parents, Lyssandra. You didn't mean to, but you were angry with them, and you twisted their blood."

I staggered away, feeling like I had been punched in the gut. I wrapped my arms tightly around myself, my heart racing. "You're lying."

He watched me, his eyes floating in hollow, rotted sockets. "I set the fire to cover it up, but they were already dead."

My breath hissed through my teeth. "That's not true."

"After it happened, you moved to Castle Helius. Your grandfather kept an eye on you, watching for signs of your magic, but it was like you had sealed it away. You were so traumatized by your parents' deaths."

I blinked back tears. I remembered being mad at my parents right before they died. I had wanted to live at Castle Helius with Tholdri, but they said I was too young,

"I was angry." My words came out a guttural sob, though I had meant to speak evenly. "I remember being angry, but I never would have hurt them."

Shadows swarmed his face, leaving only his eyes visible. "You didn't mean to."

I turned away from him. I couldn't stand his knowing eyes on me.

I sensed him reaching one skeletal hand toward me, but I didn't want him to touch me. Biting back tears, I ran.

CHAPTER TWENTY-FOUR

Tholdri

Markus' long fingers curled around the edges of his boiled leather mug. He hadn't touched his ale, though I couldn't blame him. It tasted like it had come straight from a goat's bladder. Anxiety rippled off him. He tried to hide it, but it was there. Steifan was right. The longer Markus was away from Lyss, the more agitated he became.

Usually with Lyss, things worked in the other direction.

I smiled at the barmaid as she brought us another round. She frowned briefly at Markus' mug, then returned my smile. I was just being friendly at this point. We had already questioned half the village. This woman didn't know anything.

Situated at the base of the mountain, the village was fairly isolated other than a small trade route leading to the nearest port. Drucida had claimed this village had few dealings with the fortress on the other side of the mountain. In fact, most would claim such a fortress did not exist.

She'd been right. The villagers didn't know about the fortress, Xavier, or anything else. If vampires were hunting the area, they had been discreet. No bodies or bites. Usually it was a sign to move on, but something felt . . . off. Perhaps Lyss' keen intuition was rubbing off on me.

Steifan returned from exchanging a few coins with the barkeep. He pulled out a chair, then slumped into it. Though we had brought our horses, most of the journey had been too treacherous to ride. Our feet were frozen and blistered. I would count us lucky if none of us ended up losing a toe.

Steifan pulled his half empty mug toward him. He cringed every time he took a sip, but he kept doing it. "The barkeep says we can sleep in his hayloft. He claims that's the best we'll find unless we continue east for another few days."

Markus' fingers flexed around his mug. "Xavier isn't here. We should move on."

He was probably right, but . . . *something* was off. I noticed a young woman watching us. She had to be only seventeen or eighteen. Thick black lashes rimmed eyes almost as dark. Raven hair cut just below her chin framed a round face. She noticed me looking, then turned away. Her dress was simple, the linen sky blue, covered partially by a heavy cloak.

It wasn't as cold at the base of the mountain, so the heavy cloak struck me as odd.

I realized Markus was still watching me, waiting for an answer.

I stood. "We will take the hayloft tonight, allow the *horses* to rest. If we find nothing come morning, we'll move on." I glimpsed the horses through the nearest window. No one had tried to steal them—yet. But we would keep a close eye on them.

I stepped away from the table, intent on questioning the young woman, but she had slipped away somewhere. I caught a glimpse of just the hem of her cloak as she stepped through a doorway behind the bar. A hint of night air rushed in, then the door closed.

Dismissing the option of charging past the barkeep, I went for the front door. Steifan and Markus watched me, but neither questioned where I was going.

I stepped out into the night. It was early yet. Candles and lanterns glowed in the windows of surrounding homes. Low voices and clucking chickens formed a comforting din.

I circled the small tavern, focusing on the things I couldn't hear. I noticed an unusual scent. A prickling along my skin told me there was a vampire somewhere out here.

I kept my hands loose, ready to grab my sword as I walked between a small garden and the side wall of the tavern. I turned another corner. The door the girl had exited through should be right ahead.

I expected to see her somewhere. She had only gone

outside a moment before, but I was met with only darkness. The stables were to my left. We hadn't boarded our horses yet, wanting to keep them in our sights, but there were a few other mounts huffing and nibbling at dingy hay, their deep breaths fogging the night air.

I walked toward them, searching around for where the girl might have gone. Maybe I was mistaken. Maybe she was just tossing out a bucket of refuse, and had already stepped back inside.

But my senses told me otherwise. My skin prickled again. I turned, spotting a dark shape leaning against the tavern wall. I had just passed by that area, but I knew I hadn't missed him. He had been watching me from somewhere else, waiting for his moment.

"You are far from Castle Helius, hunter." His voice held a thick accent I couldn't place.

I didn't reach for my sword yet. If I could gain information before killing the vampire, I would. "I bear no insignia of the Helius Order."

He stepped out of the shadows. His skin was a bronze that would turn a deep brown if he ever saw the sun. Straight black hair flowed over the shoulders of his burgundy coat. The first word that came to mind was *refined*. The second word was *dangerous*. "It's in the way you move, hunter. I must ask, what brings you to such a remote village?"

He seemed almost human, which meant he was old. Judging by how he snuck up on me, perhaps even ancient. "Most vampires don't take the time to speak with hunters."

One corner of his full lips curled. "The same can be said of your ilk. I'm surprised you have not yet drawn your sword."

"Let's just say I've had an exceedingly strange year."

He stepped closer and I tensed. I might be foolish enough to speak with him, but I wouldn't let him in close. He could tear out my throat in a heartbeat. I'd grown comfortable around Asher and Cael, but I had to remember—most vampires were monsters, at least the ones I'd encountered previously.

"What did you do with the girl?" I asked.

He lifted one finely arched brow. "Girl?" His accent made the *i* sound more like an *e*.

"The one who just stepped out here."

"I know of no such *girl*. Now will you answer my question, hunter? *Why* are you here?"

I supposed it didn't hurt to ask. If he was an ally of Eiric, he was likely to eventually attack either way. "I'm looking for a human servant. He calls himself Xavier."

"A hunter hunting a human servant?" He smiled. "How intriguing." He took another step.

One more step, and I would draw my sword. "Do you know of him?"

"I do not. But I know many other things. There is unrest here, and across the province. I had hoped you had come to investigate."

"Unrest?"

His sigh was long and exaggerated. "Of course the hunters would not notice. You only wish to kill us. You do not concern yourselves with deeper matters."

"Do you mean the young vampires hunting the ancients?"

His face showed true surprise. It was rare that one could surprise a being so ancient. Because he *was* ancient. He felt too much like Asher to be anything else. "That is precisely what I mean."

"Oh, I can tell you all about that. But first, where is the girl?"

"I do not know to whom you refer."

I blinked, and suddenly he was closer. I reflexively drew my sword, angling it between us not quite right. A gift from the witches, the weapon was unfamiliar, a little shorter than the blade I'd lost on the mountain.

So close, I could tell that he was about my height. He held one slender hand to his chest. "Dear hunter, you *wound* me."

"Come any closer, and the wound will not be metaphorical."

He lowered his hand. "I do not know of any girl."

"Then this conversation is over."

"You will not attempt to kill me?"

Still holding my sword out, I shrugged one shoulder. "Like I said, I've had an exceedingly strange year."

"You and I both, it seems." He stepped back.

I made to go after him, intent on finding out what he'd done with the girl, but he was already gone.

I blinked at the space where he'd been. *Definitely* ancient. He might have been lying about Xavier, but I didn't think so. Which meant we should move on.

I did a final search of the stables and the surrounding area, then returned to the tavern. The girl wasn't anywhere inside. It was as if she had disappeared into thin air.

I hoped she had simply gone to bed, but I didn't think so. Something was wrong, but maybe it wasn't the something I thought.

CHAPTER TWENTY-FIVE

Lyssandra

I slipped in and out of wakefulness. Asher was curled up behind me, his arm around my waist, his face nuzzled into the back of my hair. He'd found me near the gates, though I hadn't run directly there. I had run blindly until my chest ached, and my body was ready to collapse from exhaustion. After that, I had staggered toward the gates, seeing no sign of Cael.

Asher had escorted me back to my cottage, where I fell into a fitful sleep. Every time my body tried to wake, I forced it back under. I didn't want to think. I just wanted to rest.

But my mind finally won out. I opened my eyes to the soft glow of candlelight. Asher had lit them, something about not wanting me to wake in darkness.

I rolled over in his arms, putting us face to face.

His eyes were open, meeting mine.

"He told you?"

He searched my face. "Your pain was like an icy dagger through my chest. I didn't give him much choice."

"And?"

His hand skimmed the side of my waist. I'd removed my sword and coat, leaving only my thin shirt and woolen breeches. "And what?"

A lump formed in my throat. I forced my words out around it. "I killed my parents."

"You were a child. You did not mean to."

"That doesn't make it any less awful."

He watched me silently, offering no comforting words, nor condemnation.

"You were right. Amarithe didn't unlock my magic. It was there all along. I just refused to look at it. Part of me knew what I had done, and I sealed it away when I was just a child."

"I apologize. I never should have pointed it out."

I tucked my chin against my pillow, averting my eyes. "You had every right to. I've been a fool." I bit back tears. "I—" I swallowed. "I cursed their blood. How could a child do that?"

"You are Blackmire. You should have been trained. Instead, you were left with no knowledge of your capabilities. You couldn't have known what would happen."

"Like I said, it doesn't make it any less awful."

He lifted his hand from my waist to stroke my hair, pushing it away from my face. "Does this change your plan going forward?"

I hadn't thought that far ahead. I still longed for the blissful ignorance of sleep. "No. Eiric must be defeated.

For Steifan and Tholdri." My breath shuddered out of me. "And for you."

"And for you," he finished.

"I can't say I'm terribly interested in my future at the moment. I'm not even sure a future is possible."

Sensing a tingle of panic from him, I sighed. I could tell him the truth. I owed him at least that much. I told him about my dream with Eiric, and what he'd hinted about my imminent demise. And I told him what Cael had told me, about my grandfather's plan to save me.

Asher pulled me close, settling my cheek in the crook of his shoulder as he shifted onto his back. "Your grandfather believed a bond with an ancient could stabilize you. He wanted to strengthen you beyond the physical."

"Yes, though he had intended me for another. Geist. Do you know of him?"

"I do not. Though oddly, I would now like to kill him."

I smiled before I could think better of it, but it soon wilted.

"I can do what your grandfather intended, Lyssandra. I will not let you fall."

I closed my eyes, pressing against him. "Or I'll just bring you down with me."

"I could think of no finer reason to die."

I let his words settle into me. I knew that he meant them. I *hated* that he meant them. I did not want to be his downfall.

I wrapped my arm around him. "I feel so tired."

"Then rest, Lyssandra. I will be here."

"Only until morning."

"Yes, only until morning." The pillows hissed as he turned his neck. He laid a soft kiss on my forehead.

My breath trembled, but I would not cry. I allowed his presence to soothe me, and eventually I drifted back to sleep. He whispered something to me as I drifted off. Words I was still not ready to acknowledge, now more than ever.

I pretended not to hear, and it broke something within me. Something that had once hoped I could possibly say them too.

I WOKE ALONE with morning light streaming through my window. My entire body ached, but it was nothing compared to the pounding in my skull. I knew I needed food after all the energy I had expended the previous day, but my appetite had left me.

I slid out of bed, ending up seated on the floor. My parents—

I chased the thoughts away. Eiric's attack would come soon. *Too* soon. I couldn't let the fortress fall just because I was wallowing in self-pity. I had work to do. The pity would come later.

I got ready for the day, wearing the same clothes as the previous day since they were still fairly clean. The embroidered jacket tugged against my healing wounds. My healing was slowed again from using too much energy. The pain was almost welcome. It meant I was still alive, for now.

I strapped on my sword and left the cottage, walking numbly between the other vacant dwellings. My shoulder blades itched like there were eyes on me, but there was nothing there. The small street was quiet, contrasting with the distant bustle of the rest of the fortress. I turned abruptly, thinking I saw someone in one of the windows, but then I realized it was only my reflection. The almighty hunter, jumping at shadows. It was almost laughable.

With a heavy sigh, I looked skyward. Judging by the position of the sun, the morning meal was over and done with. *Perfect.* I could find Ian and beg a cup of strong, steaming tea to chase away the ache in my head.

I was only halfway there when Ophelia found me. She presented a clear picture of what I probably looked like, though I had avoided any actual mirrors. Her green eyes were hollow, her skin ruddy and pale at the same time. Her hair was limp, unwashed. Only her apprentice robes appeared relatively clean, though there was dust on her sleeves.

I stared at her as she approached, unsure of what to say.

"I was just coming to your cottage." Her eyes didn't quite meet mine and she reached me. "I've been going through my mother's belongings. I found something you might want to see."

I nodded. "Show me."

"Right now?"

"I could use the distraction."

She smiled softly. "I know the feeling. This way."

She led me to Elanore's lodgings. The last time I had

been inside had been to question her. Now that she was dead, I felt a little bad about the encounter. Although she *had* been hiding something. Drucida had been right.

Ophelia led the way inside.

I halted just across the threshold. The place was in shambles, papers pulled out of drawers, clothing piled up on furniture, and little trinkets tossed across the rug.

Ophelia gave me a nervous smile. "I might have been a bit feverish when I started searching. I just wondered—"

"If she had lied about anything else?"

She seemed relieved to not have said the thought out loud. "Yes. Without Jacques, I feel alone. And angry. I should feel sad, but I just feel so very angry."

"You have every right to be."

I walked further into the space. I had my own anger to deal with. Anger at a lifetime of lies, but I knew what it really was. Anger to cover up my pain. Same with Ophelia. I wouldn't point it out if she wouldn't.

She walked toward the desk, then lifted a leather-bound journal off the top of a pile. She turned toward me, journal in hand. "I never knew that my mom kept journals. I found them in an enchanted drawer. I nearly lost a finger trying to get it open before I found the key."

She held it out toward me.

"No offense, but I'm not terribly interested in your mother's diaries."

The journal remained extended. "This one is about her time with Alexander. Not in the beginning, but the end. I thought—" She looked down. "I thought you might find it useful."

For a moment, I thought my heart might have stopped beating. Another blood witch corrupted by magic, and right in front of me was a firsthand account of the process. I didn't want to read it. I really didn't want to know. But I had to. Morbid curiosity was my fatal flaw. One of many, I was beginning to learn.

I took the offered journal. "Thank you."

"No, thank you." She met my eyes. "If my mother had her way, I think the rest of us would have died that day. She would have protected her children to the bitter end."

"You were her child too. She wouldn't have stood by while they harmed you."

She shrugged. "Perhaps. I just wish she could have protected Jacques."

"I'm sure she wished it too."

"Were you close with your parents?"

My hands clenched around the journal as a sick knot formed in my stomach. "I thought I was." I looked away. "I need to go. Thank you for the journal."

I walked toward the door before she could say anything else. I'd leave her to paw through her mother's things. We all had to grieve in our own ways.

"Lyssandra?" she questioned before I could escape.

I turned back toward her.

"I hate to ask, but I was wondering, could you show me how to use a sword?"

I blinked at her. "Why?"

"I am a healer. I can help those who have been harmed, but what good will it do if I can't protect myself?"

I lowered my hand from the door. "You're worried about the attack?"

"Shouldn't I be? Everyone is preparing, but there's nothing for me to do. I just—" she hesitated. "I have lost much, but I don't want to die. I want to stand at least a chance of protecting myself."

I nodded. I understood. "Let's go."

"Now?"

"Food first. Then I'll teach you."

It seemed she couldn't decide whether she should be frightened or relieved. She wrung her hands, her shoulders hunched, but finally, she nodded. "Yes. Let's go, thank you."

I turned away again, and found myself looking forward to it. It had been a while since I'd sparred with anyone.

We all had our own ways to grieve. This was mine.

"What about your blade?" Ophelia held the short sword awkwardly, even though I had corrected her grip several times. We had left the journal in my cottage, exchanging it for a few daggers I would show her how to use later. The short sword was from the fortress armory.

I stood in a defensive stance. I'd removed my sword and leaned it against a small boulder. We were on the grassy expanse near the old temple. It was the first place I'd thought of with enough room for me to teach her. "Most vampires were just normal village folk once.

They don't know how to wield a weapon any more than you do. But they also don't have motivation to learn. They *are* weapons."

A crowd was gathering around us. I noticed Ian and Teresa amongst them. It was the first time I had seen Teresa in a while. Drucida had mentioned that she'd fallen ill after Illya's death. I hadn't thought much of it—finding your mentor murdered had to be traumatizing—but now I remembered what Ian had said about her. No energy. While everyone else shrugged it off, it still struck me as odd.

I focused on Ophelia. She only had a short span of time to learn, and I wanted her to know what to do should she be attacked.

I darted to one side and she followed me with her sword, keeping it between us.

I nodded at her. "Good. Never let them get close. If they get too close, it's over."

She put her shoulders back, gaining confidence. "But how do I attack?"

"You don't." I dropped into a roll, skirting around her then coming up behind her.

She moved too slow, her sword drooping.

I sighed. "You would have been dead there."

Her sword drooped further. "But you moved so quickly."

"Not as quick as a vampire."

She gnawed her lip, frustrated, but when I gestured to her sword, she lifted it, holding it correctly. "So I'm just supposed to follow them around and keep a sword between us?"

"No. You strike at the opportune moment. They will smell your fear and think you an easy victim. You will use that to your advantage."

She followed me with the tip of her blade. The crowd started murmuring around us.

I would have liked to prepare her for how truly fast a vampire could move, but I felt like death walking. Even after a meal, I was exhausted, my movements sluggish.

I darted in again and she reflexively flicked her blade. It sliced across my arm, easily cutting through my shirt and the flesh below.

I winced. I really was too tired.

"Oh no!" She dropped the sword, rushing toward me.

I held up one hand. "It's fine. I'm just not at my best."

Murmurs from the crowd increased. Ian and Teresa ran toward us.

I gripped my bleeding arm and straightened. "It's fine, really. I'm not as rested as I should be."

"At least let me heal it." Ophelia stepped closer, then practically pried my fingers from my bleeding arm.

She tore my sleeve further, revealing the wound.

Teresa gasped.

"It's not that bad," I assured her. And it wasn't. I'd suffered far worse.

My skin warmed as Ophelia began her healing, her eyes on my wound. "That's strange," she muttered under her breath.

"What's—"

She gasped, then her eyes rolled back in her head. She fell to her knees.

I glanced reflexively at my arm. My flesh was entirely healed. A wash of energy coursed through me. No, not just energy. *Magic*.

Ian knelt beside Ophelia. I wanted to help, but I couldn't look away from my blood on her fingers.

Oh. Oh no. "Ophelia, I'm sorry."

She blinked rapidly, clinging to Ian. "What was that?"

I winced. "I think I stole your energy. I apologize. I'm not quite in control of . . . things."

But there was more to it than that. I could still sense her magic. My vision blurred, and as it refocused, a soft green light formed around Ophelia. Ian had something similar, but pale yellow. When I looked at Teresa, I realized what had happened, because there was nothing around her. Just as Ian had claimed. I was seeing what Ophelia and Ian saw when they looked at people.

I staggered, feeling dizzy. I knew there were still people watching us, but I couldn't focus on them. It was too overwhelming. Instead I looked at Teresa. She was giving me an odd look, no longer frightened.

I saw it in her face as it dawned on her that I had just figured out her secret. It wasn't that she didn't have energy. It was that she was hiding it behind a glamour. "You're Sidhe," I gasped. Then the world went black.

CHAPTER TWENTY-SIX

I woke in my bed. It was still light outside. I hadn't lost much time. I sat up, groaning as I rubbed my aching head. Sensing a presence beside me, I turned.

Drucida had moved a chair next to the bed. With Ophelia's help, all of her wounds had healed. The gashes across her neck were now pinkish mounds of scar tissue. She still wore her tunic and breeches, along with a look of judgement.

"Teresa is Sidhe." My voice cracked, my throat too dry.

"She is, though I wish you had not said so out loud. I promised to keep her secret."

"You knew?"

She leaned against her chair, tilting her head back to gaze at nothing. "I brought her here. Of course I knew. She's not pure-blooded, but close. Her mother died when she was small. She grew up in the care of a neighbor, all the while hiding what she was."

"But you could tell?" I asked. Glamours were tricky. Most people wouldn't know what they were seeing unless they knew exactly what to look for. That was why neither Ophelia nor Ian had figured it out.

"I knew another Sidhe once, long ago," she explained. "I told Teresa she could live here. It was her choice to continue hiding what she is. Illya was the only other person who knew."

"Is that why she was apprenticed to her?"

She crossed one leg over the other, settling in more comfortably. "No. Most Sidhe have the gift of sight. Teresa was working to develop hers."

I sighed, flopping back against my pillow. "And now I've shared her secret. I was just so stunned—"

"You mentioned previously that you know of another Sidhe?"

"Yes."

"Can you tell me their name?"

I thought about it. "No, I don't think I can."

She gave me an inquisitive look.

"I once swore an oath to not share her secret. I no longer consider her a friend, but that oath still stands. Of course, Asher and the others know too, and they swore no such oath."

A small smile curled her lips. "I'll keep that in mind. Now, I'm not here to discuss Teresa. What you did with Ophelia—"

I draped a hand across my eyes. "I know. I stole her energy. I didn't mean to."

"You also stole her magic."

I lowered my hand and turned my head toward her. "She could tell?"

"She thought you might have. And with you realizing what Teresa was . . . " She shrugged. "I put it together. Ophelia's magic helped you recognize the glamour because you've seen glamours before. Ophelia and Ian simply didn't know what to look for."

"Well it was only temporary. I can't see your energy now."

"Still, this is progress. You're learning."

It sure didn't feel like progress to me. "It feels like I'm losing control, more and more."

"It happens when one begins developing their gifts. Once your mind comprehends what's there, you must learn to align yourself with it. I imagine it's hard to believe you could ever control such power, but that lack of belief is a hindrance. Fear can also make things more difficult."

Fear. Of course. I knew a little bit about that. After what I'd learned the previous night, I was more terrified of my magic than ever.

I felt her watching me. "You've thought of something."

"It's not something I share easily."

She straightened in her seat, then turned fully toward me. "If it can help you learn, Lyssandra, then I implore you to share it. We are running out of time."

She was right. I needed to get past my fear. Ignoring it was doing me no good.

"Cael told me I killed my parents." I forced the words out, not allowing myself to feel them. They were just words. And if Drucida could help me prevent such things from happening again, they were worth sharing.

She blinked at me, stunned.

"Yes, it's awful, and I don't want to talk about it. But I'm afraid. I am afraid of what I might do next."

"I'm surprised you would tell me."

I sat up again. It didn't seem like a conversation to have lying down. "Trust me, I didn't want to, but you *are* trying to teach me. After what happened with Ian, and now with Ophelia, it seemed important for you to know what I can do."

She nodded at my words. "Well, I appreciate your trust. And this also answers another question."

"Which is?"

"Why you didn't feel your magic for so long. How you were able to ignore the signs. Our inner knowing is such a strange thing. Oftentimes, we don't realize our own knowledge."

"I was wondering if that was it," I sighed. "That deep down, I knew I had hurt my parents, and so I shut my magic away."

"I think it's quite likely. There were probably other signs of your magic, but you ignored them. You could sense things, but you blamed it on instinct, or later on your bond with Asher."

It was exactly as Asher had suspected. Amarithe didn't unlock my gifts. I was simply put in a position where I could no longer ignore them.

I couldn't quite look at her as I asked the next question. "Is the only reason I have lasted this long because I haven't been using my magic? If blood magic corrupts all users—"

"Yes. I believe that's the case."

Brutal honesty. Usually I appreciated it, but now? Not so much. "Cael told me that the real reason my grandfather wanted me bonded to a vampire was to stabilize me. He thought an ancient could help me maintain control."

She blinked at me. "Cedrik *wanted* you bonded to a vampire? I had assumed it was an accident."

I winced. I had forgotten that she didn't know *everything*. She knew I was bonded to a vampire, but not why. "Yes, he did. I was intended for another, but by a simple trick of fate, I ended up with Asher."

"I suppose it makes sense, though it was a risky endeavor."

"He tested it out on someone else before me." I leaned against my headboard. "Oh light, it's too difficult remembering what I have and haven't told you. I may as well start from the beginning."

By the time I finished explaining everything that had happened with Markus, we had made tea and moved to the small table near the window.

Drucida sipped from her cracked mug, pondering my words. "Well, much more makes sense to me now. Cedrik always did take too much liberty with the fates of others."

I looked down into my steaming mug. I knew it was none of my concern, but— "What was my grandfather to you?"

She lowered her mug, then tapped her fingers on the table, considering her next words.

"Oh come now. I just spilled all of my darkest secrets."

She smirked. "I suppose that's true. Cedrik was my first love." She lowered her chin. "Not my last, mind you, but perhaps my greatest."

I grinned. "What happened?"

She reclaimed her mug, wrapping her fingers around its warmth. "He changed after his sister died. He became so . . . single-focused." She smirked. "A trait he has passed on to you."

I rolled my eyes.

"When he decided to leave, he asked me to go with him. He asked me to join his cause. But I was content where I was. I had already lost much. I dedicated myself to finding others in the same position."

I slipped my tea, absorbing her words. "Do you ever regret not going?"

She shrugged. "Sometimes. I regretted it when you told me he was dead."

"I'm sorry."

"So am I. I *might* have let my regret color my treatment of you."

"I've experienced worse." I set my mug aside. "Don't worry about it."

She watched me for a long moment, and I knew what was coming next. "The equinox is almost upon us."

"I know." I looked her up and down, at least what I could see of her above the table. "I imagine you have a dagger hidden *somewhere*."

"I hate to make you practice now, so soon after learning what happened to your parents."

I stiffened at her words. I couldn't think about them. I simply didn't have the strength. Not yet. "We have no choice. I will not let the fortress fall."

"You are a braver woman than I."

She had no idea. After everything Eiric had revealed . . .

My magic would corrupt my blood. Even with Asher to keep me strong, it would eventually be the death of me.

But even without my armor, I was a hunter of the Helius Order, and I would fight to the bitter end.

Drucida got me something more to eat while I tidied myself up. By the time we left my cottage, I was full, warm, and somewhat clean. We still had a few hours before darkness. Far too much time to practice. I wondered how much more blood I would lose.

As we walked between the vacant cottages, I was overcome by an eerie feeling. Drucida didn't seem to notice.

"Why have the cottages remained vacant all this time?" I asked as we walked. "I know, the enchantments, but you would think they would be a good thing."

Drucida wrinkled her nose, keeping her gaze forward. "Because Blackmire witches don't like to share." She gestured to one of the more nicely preserved cottages, not really looking its way. "The stronger enchantments have preserved some of the cottages. and they keep the gardens growing, but they also keep others out."

I looked at the cottages again. "You mean you can't go in some of them?"

Drucida stopped walking, turning to face me. "No, I cannot."

I grinned and shook my head. "That must be infuriating for you."

"What's your point, Lyssandra?" She crossed her arms and tilted her head.

My grin widened. "You don't even know what's in them, do you?"

"I'll ask again, what is your point?"

"Why don't you just tear them down?"

Her eyes rolled upward for a moment. If I didn't know any better, I'd say she was counting down in her head to keep from snapping at me. "Because the rest of the enchantments will wear away eventually. They have to. Then, the remaining cottages will be usable. We don't need the space currently, so there's no use wasting resources."

I searched her face, suspecting a different motive. The enchantment on the secret spring had lasted since the fortress was first erected. It wasn't practical at all to wait out such things. "Did my grandfather live in one of these cottages?"

She pursed her lips, and I knew I was right. "Yes, once."

My heart did a nervous flip. "Which one?"

She pointed behind me. I turned. It was the same

cottage where I had been startled by my own reflection. I stared at it, picturing my grandfather and maybe Cael living there as young men. I wondered if their sister had lived with them, or if she'd had her own dwelling.

"Come to my home when you are ready," Drucida sighed behind me.

I turned toward her with a hopeful expression.

"The door won't be locked. There's no point. You're the only person who can go in."

"Thank you, Drucida."

I turned away from her, walking toward the cottage, both excited and anxious. My grandfather had left intentionally, with ample time to pack. I might find absolutely nothing. Or I might find a trove of information about the man I had hardly known. At least not in the way one should be able to know their own family. And Cael . . . maybe I would learn something more there too. There had to be a reason he hadn't mentioned the cottage, unless it was simply too painful.

Drucida was gone by the time I put my hand on the door. I felt the white washed wood for a moment, wondering if I could sense the enchantments.

I sighed. I could feel *something*, like when I passed through the gates. But I wasn't experienced enough to tell what that something was.

Holding my breath, I opened the door and crept inside. Sunlight streamed through the windows, giving me plenty of light to see by. Everything was clean and perfect. A small dining table was beneath the window, circled by four chairs. I jumped at a sudden sound, then realized a fire had come to life within the stove. How strong Blackmire's magic must have been once, to maintain everything so perfectly.

Seeing nothing of interest, I continued on down the main hallway. This dwelling was bigger than mine, with several doors bordering the hall. I opened the first door, then peeked inside. A bedroom. I walked around the neatly made bed to check the small dresser, but all the drawers were empty. I looked under the bed, already knowing what I would find. Nothing.

I stood, disappointed. My grandfather and Cael must have taken all of their belongings with them.

I searched another room and the water closet, coming up with nothing. I knew I was wasting my time, but I couldn't leave the final room unchecked. I walked the rest of the way down the hall, then opened the door, quickly realizing that this must have been their sister's room, my great aunt.

I was elated when I opened the dresser to find neatly folded clothing. They had left just after she died. They must not have had the heart to clear her things away. Feeling itchy with excitement, I pawed through her clothes, then opened the rest of the drawers, finding nothing more than a few anonymous trinkets.

I dropped to the floor, searching under the bed. At first I didn't see it, but there, in the shadows at the head of the bed, a small trunk.

I pulled it out, then sat back on my heels, placing the trunk on my lap. I smoothed my hands across the aged wood, tracing carvings of vines and tiny birds. I reached for the latch, then hesitated, remembering Drucida's enchantments. Would I lose a finger if I tried to open the container?

I glanced back at my sword over my shoulder. "What do you think?"

The only answer was a shiver up my spine. Oh well. I was already covered in fresh scars. What was one more injury? I flipped the latch, and nothing happened. I waited a few heartbeats, but all was still.

With my pulse beating at my throat, I opened the trunk. Within was the grimoire from the tapestry, or at least a replica. My hands trembled slightly as I lifted it, more from shock than anything else. I ran my fingers over the leather casing. It really was the same tome. The intricate embossing formed a swirling pattern of runes I couldn't read.

I stared at it, finally remembering where I had seen it before. It had been on a shelf in the Potentate's study. A time or two, I had seen it on his desk. But then, how was it here? It should still be back at Castle Helius.

I opened the tome, skimming the first few pages. It read like utter gibberish, and some of the words were spelled strangely, but I knew what they must be. They were all rituals. In the tapestry, I was casting a ritual, at least according to Drucida. Whatever Eiric wanted from me ... was it in this book?

I went through a few more pages, but I couldn't figure out what anything meant. I considered burning the tome, but couldn't bring myself to follow through with the thought. Even if whatever Eiric wanted was within the pages, maybe they also held what was needed to beat him. With my magic not coming along quickly enough, the rituals could possibly be key to our survival—or to our destruction.

I slammed the book shut and stood, casting a final glance around the room. Why was this the only thing left besides clothing? And why was it here? Was it perhaps a replica of the tome back at Castle Helius?

As always, too many questions. I would bring the tome to Drucida. Maybe she could figure out what Eiric wanted from me. And if she couldn't, I wasn't sure if anyone else could. I might have just been wasting time looking around for relics of the past.

Shaking my head, I braced the tome under my arm, then left the room behind. As I walked down the hall, my eye caught on a flicker of movement, a glimmer of crimson hair. I skidded to a halt, once again realizing it was just my own reflection, this time in the mirror hanging in the water closet.

I stared at myself, barely recognizing the tired creature before me. I could almost understand why blood witches always resorted to taking energy from others. The magic wasn't sustainable otherwise. We were almost as bad as vampires.

Shaking my head at my own thoughts, I continued onward. Drucida was waiting, and night wasn't far off. I hoped to at least accomplish *something* before darkness fell.

CHAPTER TWENTY-SEVEN

I didn't accomplish *anything* before night fell. Drucida had confirmed that the grimoire appeared to be the one in the tapestry, but she had no idea why it was in the trunk, nor what Eiric would want from it. She was going to read through all the rituals, but it would take time.

Despite my lack of accomplishment, I had much to tell Asher when he found me at nightfall. With my energy drained, and no skin changers to hunt, we retired to my cottage. We had stoked the fire in the woodstove, and sat on the small rug in front of it. Once we had exhausted our discussion of the grimoire, I told him about Teresa.

"She's clever." Asher's body curled around mine. He braced himself up with one hand on the rug. "To not only disguise her own scent, but create a new one. It's remarkable."

If I didn't know any better, I'd say he was a little irritated that he hadn't realized what Teresa was.

I smirked, though with him curled around my back, he couldn't see it. "If there's one thing I've learned about Sidhe, it's that they can fool *anyone*."

His free hand went to the side of my waist. I'd had just enough time for a proper bath before darkness fell. I'd washed the drying blood from my wounds, and changed into soft tan linen pants and a loose green shirt. The shirt had delicate pearl buttons—another gift from Drucida. I was beginning to suspect one of the skin changers' victims was not only my height, but had excellent taste in clothing.

"I haven't seen Cael since you spoke with him," he said out of nowhere.

I froze. "And?"

"He was in a poor state. It's . . . troubling."

My breath felt shallow in my lungs, a mixture of anger and worry. "He should have told me about my parents sooner."

"I'm sure it was not an easy tale to tell."

"It was far more difficult to *hear*," I snapped.

"If he loses control, he will become too dangerous."

He didn't have to finish his thought out loud. We both knew what it meant. If Cael had no master, no one to help him remember himself, we would need to kill him.

"You're right," I sighed. "My anger cannot be a priority. We should find him." I leaned back against him, horribly tired.

"Tonight, you should rest."

"That only leaves four more nights. I want you both

inside the fortress before Eiric comes. I won't let him use you against me."

He pulled my loose hair aside, then leaned in and kissed my neck. "Then I will find him before the night is through."

My breath sighed out of me as he kissed further down my neck.

"You should rest," he breathed against my skin.

"You know, you keep saying that, and I never agree."

"I keep hoping you'll become more reasonable."

I turned onto my other side, facing him. "Do you?"

He leaned in close, draping his hair around his face. "In *some* regards." He picked up the edge of my sleeve, revealing a fresh cut.

"Practice," I said tiredly.

"I do not think this *practice* is entirely practical."

I frowned. "Drucida is doing all she can to help me learn."

"At least let me give you blood. You'll heal more quickly."

"I won't let you grow weak again."

He kissed me lightly. "Please."

I pulled away enough to look into his eyes. "I accidentally stole Ophelia's energy today, just like what I did with Markus. I can heal on my own." Plus, I didn't relish the thought of drinking blood, even if it would make me stronger.

"We cannot say what tomorrow will bring. I worry for you."

I kissed him, pressing closer. I lowered my shields,

letting him feel *my* worry. He hadn't fed again since the day Xavier stabbed him.

His arm looped around me, pulling me up to straddle his lap. "Your worry is not just for me. Something else is wrong."

I gnawed my lower lip, wondering if I could distract him with more kisses.

He gave me a look that said he knew exactly what I was thinking.

I pursed my lips. "You're coming a little too close to reading my mind for my liking."

"What else happened?"

There were too many things I didn't want to say, so I started with the easiest. "Ophelia gave me one of her mother's journals. She claims it details Elanore's final days with Alexander, before she was forced to run from him. I'm yet to bring myself to read it."

"You are worried you will become like him."

"Everyone seems to think I will." *Including Eiric.*

"You don't have to read the journal." His hands smoothed across my hips, pulling me closer.

"But I should. I should be prepared."

"You are not like Alexander. *Or* Eiric."

I wished I could agree with him, but there was no way for him to know for sure. I had killed my own parents, for light's sake. I could be too dangerous. Just like Cael.

"You are not like them," he said again, lifting one hand to stroke my cheek.

I leaned against his hand. His fingers were colder

now. He'd need more blood soon. "You should feed. I won't hardly feel another cut."

His hand stayed where it was. "Not tonight, Lyssandra."

"But—"

He lifted my palm from my lap, then placed gentle kisses across my callouses. He pushed up my sleeve, revealing a few fresh cuts. He kissed those too.

I closed my eyes. Sleep tugged at me. Even after stealing Ophelia's energy, I was not at my full strength. Not even close.

My sleeve slipped back over my wounds, then Asher wrapped his arms around me, lifting me easily with my legs still straddling him.

I leaned my head against his shoulder as he carried me toward the bed. "You really should feed," I muttered.

He laid me across the bed, then pulled a blanket over me. "Not tonight, Lyssandra," he whispered next to my cheek, ending his words with a chaste kiss.

I wasn't sure how long it took me to open my eyes again, but when I did, he was gone, off to find Cael. I rolled over on my side. I wasn't used to sleeping so early in the night, but I could fight it no longer. I checked to make sure my sword was still leaning against the bed, then I was out.

AT FIRST WHEN I saw Eiric, I thought he had invaded my dreams again, but then I realized this vision was different. It was a vantage point I had experienced before, seeing through the eye of my sword. I was pretty sure the blade was leaning against a bed, just like it was in the present time.

Eiric had his back to me, but I would recognize those crimson ringlets anywhere. His style of dress was different, the clothing less fitted and the natural oatmeal color of linen. His tunic was lighter than the pants, wrapped at the waist with a wide blue sash.

At first the vision was silent, then words filtered in.

"You're not yourself. You don't know what you're doing." A woman's voice. One I recognized. *Cerridwen*.

"I have a purpose, my love. I was brought back to this life for a reason. I cannot ignore it."

She stepped around him, coming into view. "You were brought back because of me. *I* brought you back." Long skirts dyed a vibrant green swirled around her legs. Her hair was long and dark.

"And don't you want me to *stay* with you?" Eiric implored.

Cerridwen's eyes widened. "There's no reason you can't."

He stroked her cheek, but there was no tenderness in it, no love. Madness hadn't quite taken him yet. He didn't seem quite like he did now, after centuries of imprisonment, but he had already been twisted beyond repair. First by the blood magic, then by death.

"I want Lavandriel to perform a ritual, but only *you* can convince her."

She shook her head. Tears glistened in her eyes. "She knows what you've been doing. She knows you've killed people."

He straightened, lifting his chin. "She only suspects. And I am her brother, she loves me. If we both convince her together, she'll do it."

Cerridwen looked right at me. Forgetting where I was, I started to panic, but then I realized she was just looking at the sword. There was a certain knowing in her expression. She knew what Lavandriel planned to do, at least in part. Soon, they would use the sword to seal Eiric away.

The eye I was looking out of blinked, then I woke with a gasp, clutching a hand to my chest. It was still dark outside. The woodstove pumped heat into the room, but everything else was quiet. Asher had not yet returned.

I reached for my sword leaning against the bed, pulling it into my lap. Its eye was open, watching me.

"Why did you show me that vision? What ritual did Eiric want Lavandriel to perform?"

The sword didn't answer. It stared at me, and I stared back. Eiric wanted me to learn blood magic—the same magic both he and his sister had possessed, so I could perform some ritual from the tome. And he wanted me to have my sword, otherwise, Xavier would not have returned it.

Whatever the ritual was, it was ancient, and *horrible* judging by Cerridwen's reaction. If Lavandriel had not been willing to cast it, I would most certainly feel the same. I wished I could talk to her, just once. According to Amarithe, she had lived a long life. I didn't know how she died. Surely the magic finally got her. But I would trade much to last just a few more years.

As I watched, my sword shut its eye and went dormant. It had nothing else to share with me. I curled up and tried to go back to sleep, but visions of ancient vampires and dark rituals swirled in my mind. I wished Tholdri was still with me. He always knew how to cheer me up. But even more, I simply hoped that he was well, and taking good care of Steifan. They were probably better off being far away from me. Painful, but true. I didn't want to be alone with my thoughts. But it was better for everyone if I was.

CHAPTER TWENTY-EIGHT

Tholdri

The tavern was mostly empty. Only the few most devout drunks remained, most of them slumping over in their seats. Markus hadn't liked the idea of staying another night, but when morning came and I still could not find the girl, I'd made it my mission to convince him.

Now, it seemed we were at a dead end. No one knew of the girl, which was strange. In such a small village, everyone knew everyone. Perhaps she was a traveler just passing through. All I knew now was, she was probably dead.

I leaned back in my seat. We'd had an unappetizing meal of tough, chewy goat meat with a lumpy brown sauce. I had a feeling I would pay for it by morning, in the worst possible way.

"I'll take one last look outside, then we'll rest. Get an early start in the morning."

Steifan's brows knit together. "The equinox is only a few days away. We're running out of time."

He was right. We couldn't afford to venture much farther, and we had accomplished nothing. I would shoulder the blame of that myself, trying to find a girl who might not ever be found.

I stood. "Four more nights left, plus the following day. We can make it to one more village if we travel swiftly."

Markus swirled one finger around the rim of his full mug of ale. "Not if there's more snow in the mountain pass. We'll need the extra travel time."

"We'll just have to hope for the best." I turned away, wanting to avoid an argument.

Markus had been far too quiet during the day as we searched for the girl. All of that anxious energy trapped inside him would boil over eventually. I wanted to return him to Lyssandra before that could happen. Not that she wanted him, but he was her responsibility, not mine.

I stepped outside. There was a man leaning against the wall next to the door, staring out into the night. His short brown hair was streaked with silver, matching a bristly beard. He didn't so much as glance my way, but I had a feeling he was watching me. He was far too alert, his body tense.

Keeping an eye on him myself, I stepped away, then did a wide circle around the tavern. Once the man was out of sight, I heard the soft hooting of an owl coming from his direction.

I reached for my sword, the tiny hairs prickling at the back of my neck.

"That won't be necessary." A woman stepped around the back side of the tavern. Short black hair, large eyes, round face.

"Not dead after all," I muttered to myself, lowering my hand from my sword.

Her brows lifted. "You thought me murdered by a vampire?"

I frowned. "You knew I was looking for you?"

She stepped closer, wrapping her blue cloak around herself. She was far smaller than me, but she could be hiding a weapon under all that fabric. And this entire situation felt *off*.

"You're a hunter. Your kind are always sticking your noses into other peoples' business."

"And what is your *business*?"

She smiled. She seemed a bit older now that I had gotten a better look at her. I'd been thrown off by her size. "The safety of my village, and all who dwell here." She extended one arm, exposing a bit of her dress beneath her cloak. No weapons, at least nothing large.

"*Your* village?"

"*My* village. Now tell me what you want, hunter. Why are you here?"

"There is an ancient vampire in the area. He may be hunting *your* village."

"I assure you, he is not."

This conversation was getting stranger and stranger. "You know of him?"

"I was coming to meet him last night, before you so rudely interrupted us."

"Do you also know of a human servant named Xavier?"

"I've never heard the name before." She glanced to her right, and a moment later, I realized why.

Off in the darkness beyond the small garden stood a lone, tall figure. The vampire I'd met the previous night. "You're not a human servant." I said to the girl.

"I am not."

"And yet you are . . . *friendly* with a vampire?"

"Allies need not be friends." Her voice was closer now. My attention had been on the vampire. "I'll ask you one last time. Why are you here?"

"A group of vampires are planning an attack. The servant I'm after, Xavier, is an integral part of the scheme."

"You wish to stop this attack?"

"I do."

I glanced at her just long enough to see her smile. "Well, hunter. You should know, your answer just saved your life."

The vampire still standing in the shadows chuckled. I felt the sound deep in my bones. No, I might not have Lyss' intuition, but I could surely feel when the tides of fate had shifted.

CHAPTER TWENTY-NINE

Lyssandra

Days passed, and before I knew it, the equinox was only one more day away. Tonight was the final night. The witches had prepared the best they could, and I had been working with Ophelia on her swordwork. It wasn't much, but fortunately she would not be on the front lines. Those with healing magic would be stationed at the old temple. She would probably do a lot more good than I would.

I hadn't learned to control my magic. We hadn't found Cael. And Drucida had learned nothing from the grimoire. But at least she had been reading it. I still hadn't read Elanore's journal. It sat on the table in my cottage. Every time I looked at it, my fear and anticipation renewed.

But I was running out of time. Drucida's teachings

had failed. If there was any information that could prove useful to me, I needed to have it.

I paced back and forth, passing the table several times before I forced myself to sit. I flipped open the journal, then read the first entry. It seemed normal enough. Elanore mentioned the twins being sick, but just with something minor, and she had plenty of healing herbs.

She spoke of her home with Alexander. A storm that shook the walls. Her own blossoming magic . . .

And Alexander himself—a witch of the Blackmire line. Even after six years together, she was still proud that he had chosen her.

My gut twisted as I forced myself to turn page after page. The entries became more dark. Alexander was not acting like himself. He had fits of temper. A strange look in his eyes.

I continued skimming the entries until I found what I was looking for. I hardly blinked as I read over Elanore's hastily scrawled words.

I've done it. I finally left him. He was no longer the man I knew, and I feared for my children's lives. I hope later they will come to understand the choice I made. I did it for them. It would only be a matter of time before one of Alexander's victims was not a nameless stranger. Only a matter of time before it was one of us. He took everything from them. Worse than a vampire. He stole the magic and life from their veins, just to make himself stronger. The Blackmire witches are abominations. I hope now that my children will be safe.

I flipped to the next page, but it was the final entry. The rest of the pages were blank. Her children must have been cursed at that point, and she'd had no desire to continue writing. Yet, she had kept the journal all this time. I wondered if it was so she could read through the happier times at the start. Or if she simply wanted to remind herself of all she had lost.

I shut the aged journal, then stared at the worn leather binding. Elanore had not been a foolish woman. Her love for Alexander had been real, and I thought it likely that his love was real too, until the magic twisted him.

And here I was, doing everything I could to strengthen my own magic. How long would it take before I was no longer myself? I hadn't felt any shift, but maybe I just hadn't noticed.

I sat there for a long while as the sun began to set outside my window. The witches were busy with their preparations. They were strengthening the wards in the walls and reinforcing the gates. While the walls were impressive, the fortress had not been built to withstand siege. An army was never supposed to find it. But I had no doubt that Eiric would. Whatever enchantment kept people from seeing the fortress unless they knew what they were looking for did not apply to him.

I sat back in my chair, waiting for darkness. This would be our final night. Tomorrow night, the vampires would come, and whatever Eiric ultimately planned, would be revealed.

Asher found me still seated in the same spot. I knew instantly that he had not found Cael. I had chased away our greatest weapon. Tholdri and the others were also yet to return, and part of me hoped they would not make it. I hoped the weather would keep them far away from the battle to come.

I looked up at Asher as he shut the door behind him. "Drucida let you through the gates?"

He approached the table, his eyes on the journal. "The sentries did not question my arrival. You read it?" His eyes lifted to mine.

I nodded.

"Was it useful to you?"

"No."

He stepped around the table, then took my hand, guiding me from my seat. He pulled me into his arms. "The witches are stronger than you believe. Even without your magic, we still stand a chance."

I pressed my cheek against his chest, breathing in his scent. "Eiric won't kill me, but he'll kill everyone else. It's somehow worse."

He stepped away enough to look down at me. "But

that's not what you're worried about. What was in the journal?"

"Exactly what we knew would be there. His magic twisted him. He started killing people for power. Elanore fled. In her final entry, she thought she had escaped him."

I kept my eyes averted, but I could feel him watching me. "There is more. Something you are not saying."

"I hate it when you do that."

His hands slid around my hips. I knew he was waiting for me to look at him, but I was not inclined to oblige. He would read too much in my expression.

"Alexander is just one man. One man driven mad by power. Why does his story disturb you so?"

"Because he's not the only one," I snapped. "I told you about the dream. The same thing happened to Eiric." I finally met his waiting gaze. "And you know what? I almost considered his offer. Perform whatever ritual he wants, and he claims he can prevent me from going mad."

He stared at me for several heartbeats. My heartbeats, not his. I didn't think he was even breathing.

"Say something," I demanded.

"You cannot trust him."

"I'm not a total fool. Of course I cannot trust him to help me, but I believe him. He didn't die from a wasting disease. He corrupted his own blood. The same likely happened to Alexander."

"Neither of them were bonded to a vampire. I will protect you from such a fate."

I glared at him, though he wasn't the one I was angry

with. I wasn't sure *who* I was angry with. Lady Fate, I suppose. "You'll try. And I might twist your blood too."

"So be it."

"That's not acceptable."

With his hands still on my hips, he leaned closer. There was something dangerous in his expression. At one time, it would have made me nervous, but not now.

He lowered his voice. "As I have told you before. If you go down, I go down. If you turn into a monster, then I will become a villain at your side. I will *not* lose you, Lyssandra."

I wanted to hit him, or scream at him. It wasn't alright. I would not hurt innocent people. I would never let it get that far. Instead of giving in to hysterics, I took a deep breath. "I'm going to speak with Drucida tomorrow. If I become a monster, I want her to be prepared to kill me."

His fingers dug into my hips. "You will *not* do that."

I narrowed my eyes. "Do not presume to order me around."

"I will kill Drucida myself before I allow her to harm you." His emotions leaked through. Emotions I wasn't used to feeling from him. He was always so calm. Now he was panicked, and angry. So very angry.

"Don't threaten her."

"Lyssandra," he said lowly. "If anyone attempts to harm you, I will *kill* them. I don't care if it's Drucida, Cael, or even Tholdri. I will not let them hurt you, even if you wish it to be so."

I pulled away from him, then stood with my arms crossed. "It is my choice, not yours."

In the blink of an eye, he closed the space between us. He towered over me, close enough that our bodies were almost touching. He leaned his neck down toward me. "And you would allow me to order someone to kill me?"

"That's different. I would die too."

"And if you would not? If I were the only one who would perish?"

My throat went dry at the thought. I glared at him.

"Tell me the truth, Lyssandra."

"You can ask anyone whatever you want," I spat.

He leaned even closer, draping his hair around us. "And you would let them kill me?" His tone was even. All emotions cut off. The anger I had felt from him just moments before was like a distant dream.

I glared up into his silver eyes, and knew he had me. Even if his death wouldn't kill me, I wouldn't let anyone harm him. "They wouldn't get within twenty paces of you," I spat.

And it was the truth. He was in the very small group of people that I would never allow to be harmed, no matter what. Principles and oaths be cursed.

He gripped my arms. For a moment I feared feeling his anger once more, but it was gone. He pulled me close, then he kissed me deeply.

My body responded in kind. I plunged my fingers into his hair, pulling his mouth more firmly against mine. There was something desperate within us both. Something that knew we might not be alive much longer.

I jumped up and he caught me, cupping his hands

across my butt as I wrapped my legs around him. I fed at his mouth, feeling a sharp sting as I cut my lower lip on his fang. I groaned deep in my throat, too far gone to care.

Still kissing me, he walked us toward the bed. I could feel the shape of him against my inner thigh through our pants, and all thoughts of death and blood magic left me. He laid me on my back, smoothing himself over me.

My thoughts spiraled. How had I found myself here, wanting to protect a vampire over any other? It came to me then, what he had whispered to me on a previous night, when I had pretended to be sleeping. So soon I would face death, and if not death, madness. And yet I was more afraid of a few simple words.

He kissed me again, using one hand to deftly undo the buttons of my shirt. My body lurched as each button came undone. His slow restraint was admirable, but I had none to offer in return. I reached up and undid his buttons so quickly that a few popped off his shirt. I gripped his open collar, then pulled him over me.

Our mouths met, hungry and desperate. So desperate that our shields came crashing down, and I could feel a different type of hunger. I could feel his bloodlust so carefully shut away deep within him. Tomorrow night, Eiric would come, and we needed to be strong.

I cupped his jaw, deepening our kiss. My lip had already stopped bleeding. I pulled away just enough to say, "You need to feed. It must not be put off any longer."

He hesitated, and I knew I was right. I hadn't given him much the day Xavier attacked him. He was beginning to grow weak again.

I looked into his eyes. "I am offering, Asher."

"Offering what?"

"*Everything.*" And I meant it. We might not have long, but for the time being, he could have everything I had to offer. He had earned my trust, and so much more.

"Are you sure?"

"I wouldn't offer if I wasn't sure." And he already knew I was. My shields were still down. He could feel everything I was feeling.

He lowered his face to kiss down my neck, and my body throbbed with need. "Only if you will take blood from me afterward," he whispered against my pulse.

"Doesn't that defeat the purpose?"

He nuzzled against my neck. "No. It is not in the blood itself, but the energy exchanged. We will both be better for it."

I still didn't like it, but if it would convince him to feed... "Alright."

His body shuddered against me. With him still between my legs, I reacted, lifting my hips to meet him.

He brought his mouth back to mine, removing the sleeves of his shirt one by one as he kissed me. My open shirt and undergarment went next. He cradled my breasts, teasing my nipple with his tongue before pulling more of the flesh into his mouth. I groaned as his fangs grazed my skin, but didn't draw blood.

His fingers undid my pants before my mind could

even register his movements. Then he leaned away to tug them over my hips.

My body throbbed with every small movement. The idea of him biting me, which had seemed so unthinkable before, was now a source of warm anticipation. I wondered what it would feel like to have his fangs plunge into my neck while he was inside me.

He stood, gazing across my body as he undid his pants, then slid them down. His body was as ready as mine was.

He crawled over me, partially kneeling between my legs to kiss down my stomach. His fingers slid slowly inside me, stealing a moan from deep in my chest. He moved his face further up, his fingers sliding in and out of me. The desperate edge between us had worn away, leaving only heat and anticipation.

He held his chest just above mine, bracing himself with his free arm so his mouth could find my ear. "I love you, Lyssandra. Even if you can never truly feel the same, I love you more than the night itself."

I closed my eyes and turned away, my chest shattering from the inside. I wanted to say it, but my mouth couldn't form the words, and I didn't know why.

He kissed the pulse in my neck.

I turned my face toward him. I couldn't quite say the words, but I could let him see the darkest recesses of my soul. I dropped my shields fully, until there was nothing of them left. No hiding.

His mouth found mine as he lowered himself over me. He slid into me, sending a wave of pleasure through my body.

I pushed my hands through his hair, wanting to drink him down. I wanted more. *Everything*.

One moment his mouth was at my neck, the next, he pulled out of me and effortlessly rolled me onto my stomach. His hands gripped my hips as he eased his was back inside.

"Asher," I gasped, the pleasure too intense.

He pulled out a little, his fingers running through my hair and down my back. Then slowly, he drew in and out of me, eliciting small whimpers from my throat. I didn't think I had ever made such sounds before, but the feeling of desperation had returned. I wanted to give him all I could, for we did not know what the next night might bring.

He held himself over me as his rhythm quickened, his own pleasure melding with mine. He thrust so deeply it was on the edge of pain, but he knew my body well. He could tell exactly where that thin line was drawn. His fingers dug into the flesh of my hips as I pushed against him.

Feeling my body close to climax, I turned my head, pushing my hair back to bare my neck.

He leaned across me and kissed my hot skin. I moaned, rocking my hips back against him. His tongue darted across my flesh just before his fangs sank in.

I gasped at the sharp sting, but it was quickly drowned out with the feel of him inside me. He drank from the wound, every pull of his mouth echoing the thrust of his body. Pleasure built within me, the sensation of him at my neck building the heat between us.

I writhed beneath him as I was sent over the edge,

and still he drank me down, his body becoming almost as warm as mine.

He thrust deeply, spasming as we both cried out.

My hands dug into the mattress. I could feel my blood within him like molten gold. I could feel his strength returning.

He collapsed on top of me, pinning me to the mattress, but I didn't mind. I enjoyed the weight of him as I tried to remember how to breathe. How to be a separate entity apart from all that heat.

He slowly drew out of me, then turned me over. His hair was a silken shroud around my face. I ran my fingers through it, pushing it behind his back and over one shoulder so I could stroke my hands down his bare flesh.

He shuddered again, bracing with his arms to look down at me. I realized his eyes were on the fresh punctures he had made. "Was it painful?"

I smiled, though he wasn't looking at my mouth. "In a good way."

He lifted his gaze to my eyes. "It is your turn now."

I frowned.

"You promised."

"Fine. But I have no fangs." I smirked.

He smiled. "No fangs, but plenty of daggers."

"Including one underneath my pillow."

I could tell he didn't quite believe me, but he reached under the pillow beneath my head, then came out with a sheathed dagger.

"A lady can never be too prepared."

He shook his head at me. "No, Lyssandra. I believe this is a quirk exclusive to you."

He rolled off me, propping himself up on the extra pillow beside me. He gestured with his free hand for me to come closer.

Suddenly, I was terrified.

He watched my expression. "You've had my blood before, Lyssandra."

"Yes, but I was bleeding out at the time." Despite my words, I moved closer.

"Do you trust me?"

"Yes."

"Then come, lean against me." He extended one arm.

I sidled closer, allowing him to wrap his arm around me, pulling my back over one side of his chest. Once I was situated, I relaxed.

Asher drew the dagger across his forearm, not so much as flinching. Blood welled across his pale skin.

I realized his shields were still down as his calmness washed over me. My heartbeat slowed, matching the rhythm of his.

"The bond," I muttered. "It's more than it used to be."

"Yes, Lyssandra."

"It scares me. It scares me more than anything else."

"I know."

With trembling fingers, I pulled his offered arm toward my mouth. I pressed my lips to his skin and drank. And it didn't taste just like blood. It wasn't repulsive.

It tasted like him. It occurred to me that we had

crossed a line that could not be uncrossed. There was no going back. No gaining more distance.

I closed my eyes and relaxed against him. Tomorrow, I could be frightened. But this moment . . . it was just for us.

CHAPTER THIRTY

I hadn't quite fallen asleep when Asher sat up in bed. "Someone is approaching the door."

I sat up beside him, feeling renewed for the first time since I'd discovered the cost of my magic. Our clothes were still strewn across the floor and the foot of the bed. I lifted a hand to my neck, feeling the healing bite marks there, before moving my fingers into my messy hair. The hair would cover the bite, for now. With vampire blood in my system, it should be healed by morning.

I stumbled out of bed, quickly pulling on my underthings and breeches, but I couldn't seem to find my shirt, and the rest of my garments had been taken away for cleaning. With an apologetic shrug, I stole Asher's shirt and slipped it on, buttoning it as I walked toward the door. I opened it a crack, just as Ian was about to knock.

He stared at me for a second, then lowered his hand,

huddling in his heavy coat. "Drucida sent me to find you."

I opened the door a little further, though not far enough to reveal Asher in my bed. "What's wrong?"

"Tholdri and the others have returned."

I wasn't sure whether to be relieved or disappointed that they had returned just before the equinox. "So what is the issue?"

"There are two others with them." His eyes widened, and he looked over my head, prompting me to realize Asher was now standing right behind me. Shirtless, since I was wearing his.

"What others?" I asked.

Ian didn't seem to hear me.

I removed one hand from the door to snap my fingers, drawing his gaze back down to me. "What others?"

"You should probably just come and see. Drucida wants your opinion before she lets them in."

I glanced back at Asher.

My shirt dangled from one of his fingers.

Fighting a blush, I snatched my shirt, then turned back to Ian. "Tell Drucida we'll be there shortly."

He inhaled sharply, as if only then realizing he had been gawking. "Yes, very good." He turned and walked stiffly away down the dark, narrow path.

I closed the door and leaned my back against it, glaring up at Asher. "You didn't have to make such a spectacle of yourself."

He pouted, attempting to look innocent, but innocence was one thing ancient vampires really couldn't pull off. When I continued staring, he settled on a small smile. "He likes you."

"That's neither here nor there." I walked past him, removing his shirt so I could put mine on.

I felt better once I was fully dressed with my boots laced up to my knees and my sword at my back. I was curious about Tholdri's company, but it was always worth taking the time to be fully prepared. I never knew when I might need to run, or fight.

Asher had put his shirt back on, watching me all the while. "Tholdri would not bring a stranger here without good reason. He knows Drucida's rules."

I tugged a final tangle from my hair, started braiding it, then stopped. I'd need it to cover the bite, for now. I fluffed it around my shoulders, then turned to Asher. "I honestly have no idea who he'd willingly bring. Let's go find out."

He stopped me with a hand on my arm before I could walk past him. "You're feeling better?"

"You can't tell?" But I already knew he couldn't. I had put all my shields back into place. When he only looked at me, I sighed. "Honestly, I don't know how I feel. But for now, it doesn't matter. Everything has already been set into motion. Tomorrow . . . we will do what we can."

He watched me for a moment longer with his hand still on my arm. Finally, he nodded. "Very well."

I hesitated. "I would like you to stay here during the day. I don't want you outside of the fortress when Eiric comes."

He inclined his chin, still watching me steadily. "As you wish."

I pulled away and walked toward the door.

Silently, he followed.

I had learned long ago to not hope for the best, but still, something within my chest fluttered. Tholdri had brought someone to us, someone he deemed important. Maybe someone who could help. I wasn't sure in what way, but I would take it. With Cael still missing, we needed all the help we could get.

Tholdri

I wondered just how angry Lyss would be that we had brought a vampire here. We had no idea if we could actually trust him—he might be in league with Eiric—but I didn't think so. My gut told me he was telling the truth. He was an ancient, long allied with some of the older witch lines, and he had known our Potentate. He had answered enough questions that we knew it was true.

At least we had now been let inside the gates to wait for Lyss. The new fortifications the witches had worked on were impressive, but they wouldn't be enough against vampire strength and speed. I hoped their magic was far more impressive, or we were all probably going to die tomorrow night.

I looked over at the vampire. Markus and Steifan kept their distance from him, though I found myself oddly more worried about the witch, Merri, the woman

I had thought was a damsel in distress. *That* illusion has been thoroughly shattered.

The village we had visited was home to a hidden clan of witches. They guarded their secret with their lives, and now it had cost them. People had started disappearing around the same time that we came to the fortress. I didn't think it was the skin changers. I thought it was Eiric. The disappearances were enough to motivate Merri to join us.

Merri ignored me, but the vampire looked my way. Noticing my attention, he smiled.

"You know, it's creepy when you look at me like that."

He shrugged, crossing his arms and smiling a little wider, his dark eyes dancing with laughter.

Drucida watched us with an air of open condemnation. And Charles . . . I couldn't quite tell what he was feeling, but he didn't seem as angry as I'd thought he would.

My shoulders relaxed when I spotted Ian jogging back toward us. The moon was bright enough for me to notice a flush on his face. Maybe it was just from cold and exertion, or maybe Lyss had embarrassed him in some way. The lad had taken a liking to her, and tact was not her strength.

He reached Drucida, his breath fogging the night air. "They are on their way."

I smirked. Of course Asher was holed up in her cottage with her. I knew I should have been bothered—such a union would undoubtedly end badly for one or both of them—but I was glad Lyss was enjoying herself. She did so rarely.

I noticed the pair coming our way. Markus visibly straightened, his eyes glued to Lyssandra, who was looking irritated and disheveled with her hair frothing around her shoulders.

Her stern expression relaxed a little as she spotted me, then her attention turned to Merri and the tall, smiling vampire at her side. She stopped beside Drucida, more at ease than she would usually be. Something had shifted between the pair. Perhaps they had realized that their temperaments were almost identical. To truly hate each other, they would have had to hate themselves.

They exchanged a few low words while Charles glared at them, then Lyssandra and Asher approached us.

I opened my mouth to explain what we had learned, but the vampire, Geist, stepped smoothly around me.

Lyssandra tensed, but didn't go for her sword.

Geist bowed his head, draping his long black hair around his face. Even bowed, he was a good deal taller than her. "Lady Yonvrode, I have heard much about you. My name is Geist."

Her eyes widened, and she took a step back. "*Geist?*"

Asher was between them in the blink of an eye. "What is the meaning of this?"

Merri watched them with amusement, making no move to intervene. Markus seemed rooted to the spot, and Steifan was looking to me for guidance.

I stepped toward Geist. I didn't like getting near him,

but Asher seemed about ready to tear his head off. I held my hands out in a soothing gesture. "Let's all calm down. Do you two know each other?"

"No," Asher hissed. "But he knew your Potentate."

I had never seen Asher so angry. He rarely showed *any* emotion, anger or otherwise. "Yes, I'm aware of that. That's why I brought him here. He and Merri are sympathetic to our cause."

Drucida snorted. "I thought you wiser than this, Tholdri."

"I know he's a vampire—"

"Not him." She rolled her eyes. "*Her*. She's a necromancer."

I opened my mouth, then shut it, looking at Merri. So that was it. That's why she felt . . . *off*. "Oh," I said, unsure of what else to say.

Geist gave me a bemused look.

Merri crossed her arms. "You can pretend I'm a villain all you please, Drucida. It won't change the fact that you need my help."

"I need nothing from your kind," Drucida snapped.

This was all going far more poorly than I had expected—and I hadn't expected much. I stepped toward them, ready to smooth ruffled feathers, but Geist cleared his throat.

He was still face to face with Asher, smiling. "We have been aware of young vampires gathering for quite some time. When I heard news of a plot to destroy the ancients, I came to these parts, hoping my old allies would know more of it. Instead of information, I found missing witches, and a *hunter* with a strange tale to tell."

He tilted his head, raising an eyebrow at me. "He told us what is planned for the equinox. We have come to help."

"Why?" Asher demanded. "Why would you help?"

Geist sighed. "I am assuming by your demeanor that you are aware she was meant for me. You stole her moments before I would have found her."

"And now you hope to claim her?" Asher's words were sharp as broken glass.

Geist chuckled. "I wouldn't dream of it. You smell of her and she of you. It's no secret what you've been up to tonight."

I lifted a hand over my mouth, unsure if I should laugh, or prevent Lyss from killing him.

Geist forged on. "Regardless of what she could have been to me, that opportunity has passed. I am more interested in thwarting Eiric's plan."

"And you?" Drucida asked, still glaring at Merri.

Merri gave her a pleasant smile. "Several of my people have gone missing. I believe what Tholdri has told us. Eiric is a danger to us all. Our best chance of defeating him is to act now, *together*, before he can pick us off one by one."

Lyss finally stepped around Asher. Her cheeks were red, but her expression was resolute. She looked up at Geist, meeting his eyes as only a vampire or human servant could. "My grandfather trusted you a great deal, and that is enough for me. We will accept your aid."

"*Lyssandra*," Drucida gasped.

She turned toward the high witch. "You know I'm right. He is an ancient. If he fights alongside us, he could save many lives."

Drucida looked a bit like a dying fish. "And the necromancer?" she finally managed to say.

"You know my name, Drucida," Merri sighed. "And it is not just my help being offered. I have a summoner as well. Her name is Liliana."

"A summoner?" Drucida balked.

That, at least, I knew a little bit about. Lyssandra had told me about the summoner, Matthias. Dangerous, and a bit mad, but incredibly powerful. Useful in a fight, as long as they were on our side.

"Yes." Merri smiled. "Are you irritated that I've kept her hidden so close by? You are not the only one capable of setting illusion wards."

Lyssandra placed a hand on Drucida's arm. "Before you go insulting anyone, I think you should consider her offer. We need the help."

Drucida straightened her spine. "A necromancer and summoner could just as easily be in league with Eiric."

Lyssandra looked once more at Geist. "They are not. My grandfather chose this vampire for me for a reason."

Asher shifted, but didn't interrupt.

Drucida's expression softened. She gave Lyssandra a nod before turning her attention back to Merri. "Fine. We accept your offer."

Merri's brows lifted. "Really?"

Drucida lifted her nose a bit. "You're not the only one allied with vampires, Merrilyn."

Merri watched her for a long moment, then nodded. "Those willing to fight are already on their way. They will reach the fortress by morning."

"You have our thanks."

This seemed to surprise Merri even further.

Drucida turned to Lyssandra. "I have much to do before morning. You may make use of the Blackmire cottages with broken enchantments." With that, she turned and walked away.

It was only then that everyone seemed to notice Charles standing a few paces behind her. Surprisingly, he was grinning. It was the first time I had ever seen him grin, and it was aimed at Merri. "Welcome back, Merrilyn," he said, then turned and strode away.

Nervously standing apart from the rest of us, Ian hurried after him.

Once Charles was out of sight, I asked, "Did he get possessed while we were away?"

Lyssandra seemed just as shocked. "I honestly have no idea."

But Merri didn't seem surprised. "Charles is my uncle. When I devoted myself to necromancy, he was forced to go along with my exile, but that didn't stop him from sending other lost witches my way." She smiled. "Unbeknownst to Drucida."

Markus cleared his throat. "We should rest while we can." His attention being solely on Lyssandra made it seem like he planned on resting *with her*. I didn't believe that was his intent, but by the looks Merri and Geist gave him, it was implied.

Lyssandra turned toward me. "You know where the cottages are. Just make sure you choose the more decrepit ones."

At my lifted eyebrow, she sighed. "I'll explain later."

Then she looked at Geist. "Might we have a word alone?"

Geist bowed his head, seemingly unsurprised.

"Let's go, kids," I joked, waving to the others. "Let the adults have a chat."

No one seemed to think I was funny, but I was used to it. Hunters could be a humorless lot, and it seemed necromancers were the same. Nevertheless, Steifan, Merri, and Markus followed, the latter mumbling under his breath.

I was beginning to wonder if the bond with Lyssandra might prove too much for Markus—if it might slowly drive him mad. He was insufferable at times, but I had a feeling madness would make him even worse.

Lyssandra

I watched Tholdri leave with the others. I didn't miss the number of times Markus glanced back at me. I had no idea what I was going to do about *that*. Drucida hadn't known either. The master and servant bond was something she knew little about.

"You should take better care of your servant," Geist commented.

I scowled. "I don't know you well enough to take your advice." I looked at Asher, who'd moved closer to me. "I would like to speak with Geist, *alone*."

"He is ancient. We do not know if we can trust him."

"But we're going to." I waited until he looked at me. "I'm not going to be able to ask him the questions I want while you're looking at him like you want to kill him."

"I *do* want to kill him." He gave me a small smile. "Though perhaps that is irrational."

"It is," I agreed.

He gave Geist a final look. "If you upset her in any way—"

Amusement danced in Geist's nearly black eyes. "*Upset* her? Not *harm* her?"

Asher gave him a mocking smile of his own. "She is entirely capable of killing an ancient. It is not her *safety* I am worried about. Do not *upset* her."

Geist gave him a little bow. "You have my word."

With that, Asher turned and walked away. Though I knew he wouldn't go far.

I turned my attention to Geist, suddenly wildly uncomfortable. The sentries above were quiet, but I knew they would be listening. I gestured for Geist to start walking.

With one dark brow lifted, he obeyed.

I matched his long strides down the cobblestone street, trying to figure out where I should start. When Cael had given me his name, I never thought I would meet the vampire in person, let alone so soon.

I decided to start with the most simple of questions. "Why did you agree to my grandfather's plan? Why were you willing to take on a servant who would not obey you?"

"I thought it was an interesting plan from a powerful

ally. And you were to remain separate from me. It would not have cost me much."

Reaching the edge of a small, quiet square, I stopped walking and turned to face him. "There has to be more to it than that."

His smile was utterly charming. I had to admit, he was pleasant to look at, but I surely would have hated him just as much as Asher at the start. "Your grandfather told me what he suspected of your magic."

I crossed my arms, increasingly uncomfortable. "That doesn't answer my question."

"Who would turn up the opportunity to have a Blackmire witch as a human servant? Even as a servant with free will, you would have been yet another powerful ally." He leaned a little closer. "One who would not be able to kill me."

"I hunted Asher for many years with the intention of killing us both."

He laughed. "Perhaps fate spared me, then. Why don't you ask me what you really want to know, Lyssandra?"

"Is it really a coincidence that we would meet here of all places? *Now* of all times?"

He straightened. "Just as suspicious as your grandfather, I see."

I waited for him to answer my question.

"And that same cold stare." He chuckled. "It's like seeing Cedrik again." He searched my face, his mood sobering. "Your grandfather sent me a letter just before his death."

I narrowed my eyes, not sure if I could believe him.

My sword was silent. I didn't think he had any ulterior motives, but— "Cael said they lost track of you. How would my grandfather know where to send the letter?"

"We had a plan in place, should things become dire. He sent the letter to a friend in Ivangard whom I visit periodically. He told me that should he perish, you would be sent here. I went to Merri first to see if she'd heard of you. We were preparing to send word to her uncle when Tholdri arrived."

"Why did my grandfather want you to find me?"

"To make sure you learned the truth. He wasn't sure how Cael would fare, and since I do not see him here, I assume Cedrik was right to worry."

Perhaps I should have explained to him about Cael, but I really wasn't sure what to say. "Even if your story makes sense, I don't understand why you care."

He leaned a little closer, bringing with him the faint scent of turned earth that clung to all vampires, young and old. "One must care about others, otherwise there is no point to such a long life. Haven't you ever wondered why some of us go mad, when others, like your master, do not? Blood and power can only satiate for so long. Cedrik was my friend."

Friendship. Now there was a novel concept. "Did he tell you about what happened with my parents?"

He went utterly still, only his eyes moving slightly as he observed me. "Yes. It is why he was so worried about you."

"And you weren't worried that in becoming my master, I would do the same to you?"

"You could try, but magic works better on those

either unsuspecting, or weak of will. I had enough faith that I could kill you if I needed to."

"You would kill your *friend's* granddaughter?"

He lowered his voice, leaning close again. "Lyssandra, if it came to that, if you lost your mind, my *friend* would want me to kill you. If only to spare you."

"You may still have to do that." I turned and walked away.

Without a sound, he caught up to my side. "So it is true? You have found your magic again?"

"Some of it." My boots sounded loud across the cobblestones compared to his silent steps.

"And that is why Eiric wants you?"

I nodded without looking at him.

"Tomorrow will be very interesting."

It was a vast understatement. It would be even more interesting now that he and Merri had arrived. But at least now, I had a way out. If I needed to die, I was pretty sure Geist would kill me. And he might even survive Asher in the process.

"What will we do now?" he asked after a moment of silence.

"We will prepare for battle, of course."

"Ah," he chuckled. "I must admit, I haven't missed living in lands where hunters dwell."

"Neither have I."

CHAPTER THIRTY-ONE

At first light, Markus, Tholdri, Steifan, and I stood atop one of the hastily constructed lookout towers, not far from the sentry posts near the gates. The tower had one tall ladder leading up, and railing around the platform to keep anyone from falling. No one would be able to see very far at night, but that wasn't really the tower's purpose. The purpose was to protect more powerful witches while they rained destructive magic upon their enemies. The base of the tower was already warded. Any who tried to topple it would be in for an unpleasant surprise.

"There." Markus had his back to me, peering off in the distance. He pointed at a small group of people coming over the mountain pass, barely visible from our vantage point. "That will be the rest of Merri's people, including the summoner."

I was more intrigued than frightened by the idea of another summoner. Matthias had lived for centuries before his magic had twisted him. According to Merri,

Liliana was only eighteen. It was brave of her to come. Brave, or stupid. Either way, she was willing to fight with us. And if she was as powerful as Matthias had been, she could simply use her summoned shadows to escape.

Steifan stood close to my shoulder, wearing his hunter armor for the first time since he'd arrived at the fortress. To my surprise, the flaming crossed sword insignia did not weigh on my heart. It was just a symbol. It didn't change who he was, nor did the lack of it change me.

"So witches in the towers," he said. "Archers at the walls."

"And the rest of us in the streets," I finished. "Ready, should they break through the gates."

"And what about you?" Tholdri asked.

At the question, Markus turned to face me. "I will be at your back."

"Tholdri fights at my back," I said instantly.

Markus' jaw tensed. His short brown hair shimmered in the early morning light. "You are Eiric's ultimate target, and I am the strongest fighter amongst us."

"That might not be true anymore," I countered. "You are no longer a vampire's human servant."

"No, I am servant to a blood witch who can steal my life force with a thought."

I knew the argument was coming eventually, but did it have to be now? "Then why would you want to guard my back?"

"Because I need to keep you alive, and out of the clutches of a psychotic ancient vampire."

"And you think you're suited to the task? When I will have two other ancient vampires protecting me?"

He stepped forward, making the wooden planks creak beneath his boots. "You cannot rely on Asher and Geist alone. They are not accustomed to battle."

The thought of Asher being a soldier once came to mind, but it was not my story to share, and it was a long time ago.

"He can take your back, Lyss," Tholdri interrupted. "He's right. I've seen him fight. I want the best behind you." He looped an arm around Steifan's neck and pulled him close. "Plus, I have to make sure this one doesn't get into any trouble."

I watched them. My heart beat evenly, but it was painful. I didn't want to take them into this fight. But I nodded. There was no going back now.

"Someone is coming up the ladder," Markus said, dismissing the argument now that he had his way.

"I know." My tone was childish, but I couldn't bring myself to care. I had heard someone climbing up, someone small and thoroughly out of breath.

A moment later, Teresa's head appeared above the platform's edge. She huffed, her face bright red, her hands searching for a place to pull herself the rest of the way up.

Chuckling, Tholdri stepped past us and grabbed her arm, hauling her onto the platform. He kept hold of her as she swayed slightly on her feet, her blue apprentice robes whipping in the cold breeze.

"Why are you here?" I asked. Drucida had assigned her to the temple. She was to help the healers.

She blew a sweaty lock of hair from her face. "I want to help. Now that my secret is out—" She hesitated, glancing at each of the men before settling on me. "I think I should help. My glamours are not strong, but they are enough to fool some lesser minds."

"Sidhe usually only care about other Sidhe." There was no malice in my tone, just a statement of fact.

She straightened her small shoulders and lifted her pointy chin. "Drucida took me in, knowing fully what I was. This is my home now. I *will* protect it."

I smiled. "Good girl. You can go to one of the towers near the dining hall. Be part of the last line of defense."

Her shoulders slumped back down. "The *last* line?"

"Your glamours will do the most good there. Let those with destructive magic take out as many as they can first."

Steifan smiled and nodded encouragingly.

She didn't seem entirely convinced, but she nodded. "As long as I get to help. I want to protect Drucida."

I didn't tell her that if the vampires made it to the dining hall, Drucida would probably be dead. Her magic was strong. She would be one of the first lines of defense.

To my surprise, Teresa stood on her toes and threw her arms around me. "Thank you for letting me help." She pulled away quickly, seeming embarrassed. Her cheeks red, she took a step back, then tightly gripped the railing, peering off at the approaching witches. "Do you think there are more necromancers among them?" She sounded worried, but she was worried about the wrong thing. Necromancers could summon ghouls, and perhaps control lesser vampires, but it was nothing like what Eiric could do.

"They are on our side," I soothed.

"For now," Tholdri finished.

We all watched the witches coming. I hoped they would be enough.

"We haven't talked about our contingency plan," Tholdri muttered. "What do we do if Eiric takes you?"

A knot formed in my chest. Eiric claimed he wanted vengeance on the witches. He wanted to kill anyone strong enough to seal him away again. But I knew if he had the opportunity to take me, he would. He believed I had learned enough, or else he wouldn't kill the people who were supposed to teach me.

"You don't get anywhere near us," I said. "I don't want to give him anyone to use against me."

"We won't be able to keep Asher away."

I took a deep breath, trying to still my racing heart. There was no reason to get worked up. There would be plenty of time for that later. "If Eiric wants to use me, he won't be able to kill Asher."

"And what about Cael?" Steifan asked. "Where do you think he went?"

"I don't know. I think he ran."

Markus furrowed his brow. "But why?"

I continued watching the witches coming over the mountain. "Because he told me I killed my parents."

I could feel everyone staring at me. I hadn't planned on telling them, but I was tired of keeping secrets. Tired of hiding what I was.

"Lyss—" Tholdri began, but I shook my head.

Everyone was deathly silent. Teresa stared at me with wide, innocent eyes.

Most of the witches had made it across the pass. They would be at the gates soon. I looked at Tholdri. "How did you find them? How did you know what they were?" He had been around a witch all of this time, and had never known it.

He swiped a palm across his face and shook his head, his golden locks lifting in the wind. "Pure dumb luck, Lyss. Nothing more."

I looked past him in the direction of the gates. It was early yet, but night would come quickly. "I hope you have more of that dumb luck to spare, Tholdri."

"So do I, Lyss. So do I."

Darkness came, and we waited. Asher and Geist both woke. They stood with the rest of us in the streets. A nervous buzz of energy surrounded us. Torches blazed, casting long shadows and sending ribbons of smoke toward the hazy moon.

"Nothing yet." Markus watched the sentries at the gates for their signal.

We had no idea what was to come. In the blink of an eye, the vampires could be upon us. The wards were strong. They would keep the weaker ones out, for a while. But Eiric had been planning this long before he was released. He wouldn't attack if he didn't believe he would win.

The first line of defense would be the ghouls

summoned by Merri. They lurked just outside the gates, obedient to her command. They wouldn't last long, but they could provide a warning while taking out some of our weaker enemies. Archers and witches with more far reaching magic would do all they could to keep the vampires from breaking through the gates.

A few murmuring voices were the only thing to cut the silence. Witches with little to no magic held a variety of weapons. I wondered how many actually knew how to use them. At least Ophelia and her short sword were back at the temple. If the vampires made it there, she would be the only one to hold them off. While many of the children had been taken down the mountain on what was sure to be a dangerous and long journey, there were other innocents who either couldn't, or wouldn't leave.

Some of the witches glanced at Asher and Geist, likely wondering if they would turn against us once the time came. Bloodlust could easily consume younger vampires, but not two ancients. Of course, the surrounding villagers didn't know that.

A ghoul squealed, its shrieks echoing across the mountain.

I drew my sword, waiting.

Another squeal, ending abruptly with a wet gurgle. I could hear the sentries moving around in their posts, but they weren't giving us any information. For some reason, they couldn't see anything.

"Wait here." Geist was gone in an instant, merging with the shadows closer to the gates.

I could feel Markus not far behind me, ready to go

into formation. Tholdri and Steifan were within sight. We were the only four souls in the fortress with ample experience killing vampires.

I kept my attention on the gates, though we could no longer see through them. They had been reinforced with solid steel, melded together with magic.

Another squeal, then finally shouts. The first vampires must have been moving too quickly for the sentries to comprehend what was happening. Now, the twang of arrows being loosed was almost deafening.

My heart beat evenly as I waited. There was always anxiety leading up to a battle, but when it actually occurred, I was calm. My instincts took over. I was ready to fight.

A bone-shaking *boom* drowned out everything else. I swayed on my feet. The gates exploded inward in a wave of blue fire. I barely registered Asher's hands on my arms. He yanked me aside, shielding me with his body. Instinct alone kept my hand around my sword.

I staggered away from Asher, blinded. Flecks of ice stung my hot skin. Drucida was putting out the blue fire, but what had caused it?

Asher pulled me further back, and the feel of ice on my skin ended.

I heard Geist's voice too close. He was right next to me. "Ivangard witches. I recognize a few of them."

Slowly, my vision returned to take in the chaos. At least what I could see beyond the narrow alley Asher had pulled me into. The gates and one of the sentry towers were no more. Fire and ice from the witches on our side obscured my view of the vampires flooding into the fortress.

"Tholdri." I gasped, choking on smoke.

"He fell back with the others," Asher said right behind me.

I peered out, needing confirmation of his words, but the fighting had started. I couldn't see beyond the first few bodies. We were trapped in the alley between the magic onslaught, and the fighters beyond.

I gripped my sword. I needed to get out there and fight, but I also needed to know what we were dealing with. "Who are the Ivangard witches?"

Geist still stood too close, but there was no other choice in the narrow space. "They live as *priestesses* in the high temple of Ivangard, but they are actually witches. Every last one. I've had issues with them before, and now it seems they have sided with Eiric."

"But why?" It didn't make any sense. Eiric would have nothing to offer them.

"I don't know." Geist stepped back as a wave of blue fire shot past the entrance of the alleyway. "But they are here. The light preserve us." With that, he was gone, darting out during a lull in the magic, leaving me alone with Asher.

I turned toward him. "We need to regroup with Tholdri and the others."

I spun as another wave of blue fire exploded across the main street, followed by the chill of ice.

Asher leaned near my shoulder, looking outward. "They have fallen back around the dining hall. I don't think we can reach them."

"Well we can't just do nothing," I hissed.

The next thing I knew, his hands were on my hips, and he was hoisting me toward the nearest rooftop. I tossed my sword onto the thatching, then pulled myself up. Asher came up right behind me.

I sheathed my sword, then stayed low, creeping across the rooftop to get a better view. Sensing another vampire, I turned just in time to see Asher breaking a young man's neck. The vampire must have seen us coming up and followed.

Poor choice.

Asher nodded, and I crept onward, dropping into a crouch as soon as I had a good view.

Bodies littered the streets, both vampires and witches. I didn't let my gaze linger long enough to recognize any of them. The fighting had moved well beyond the gates. Out on the mountain was only darkness. I didn't see Eiric anywhere.

"Looking for me?"

Asher and I both turned. At the far edge of the roof stood Eiric. And he wasn't alone. Cael stood beside him.

CHAPTER THIRTY-TWO

Tholdri

My skin burned. Cursed fire magic. None of us had been expecting it. Now the witches had backed us into a corner. Markus and Steifan stood in formation with me, but we had lost Lyssandra. I could only hope Asher had gotten her to safety when the first blast hit.

A female vampire darted toward us and I swung my sword, lopping off her head. None of these vampires were older than a few weeks. They were hardly faster than humans, and they didn't know how to fight. They were cannon fodder, nothing more. I didn't know if Eiric had created them, or if he simply controlled them. Either way, he didn't care if they all died. They were only a distraction.

Which led me to believe he was going after Lyssandra. Tonight. *Now.*

"We need to clear a path!" I shouted back at Markus. "We have to find Lyss!"

He impaled a male vampire on his blade, then tossed the body aside like it weighed nothing, even though the man had been as tall as either of us. Being servant to Lyss instead of an ancient vampire hadn't weakened him in the slightest.

He turned his blood spattered face toward me. "I will go. It will be easier for me to find her on my own."

"We'll all go!" I shouted.

One of the witches spouted that blue fire straight from her hands toward Steifan. I gripped him by the collar and tugged him out of the way, though to his defense, he was already moving.

"We can't let them get past us toward the temple," Steifan huffed, his eyes wide. "Everyone there will be slaughtered."

Curse the light, he wasn't lying. A shadow creature darted past in the periphery of my vision. I turned just in time to see it turning one of the enemy witches into nothing but bloody ribbons.

My stomach churned. I was glad the summoner, Lilliana, was on our side, but she definitely blurred the line between ally and enemy.

I turned to face another vampire, holding my sword between us. "Don't let me down!" I shouted back at Markus.

But he was already gone.

Lyssandra

Eiric clicked his tongue at Asher as he moved in front of me. "That will not be necessary. I mean her no harm."

I stared at Cael. It had to be an illusion. "What are you doing with him?"

He was still in his more monstrous form, his desiccated skin stretched tight across the bones of his face. Shadows swarmed around him, agitated. "I am doing this to help you, Lyssandra. I believe it is the only way."

"Then you know nothing," I snapped, drawing my sword.

Eiric watched me curiously. His curls floated in the smoke-filled air. The battle still raged on further in the fortress, but he paid it no mind. "You know I can cloud your senses with a single thought, Lyssandra. It will go better for you if you don't fight me."

My fingers ached around my sword, I was clenching it so tightly. "What is the ritual you want me to perform? What is all this for?"

I blinked, and he was closer, halfway across the roof, leaving Cael back in his shadows. Eiric's loose white shirt billowed around him, tucked into the same velvet pants I had seen in my dream. "With your help, *Lyssandra*," he said my name like it was something poisonous, drawing out the *ss* in a long hiss, "I will once again walk in the light. I will rid the world of my creations, so that only I remain."

He took another step and Asher moved more in front of me, for what good it would do.

"Why?" I demanded.

The corners of Eiric's lips curled up. I couldn't exactly call it a smile. It was far too twisted. "I will have the life that was stolen from me. And you, Lavandriel's descendent, will be the one to give it back. Poetic, is it not?"

"If that's all you want, then why attack the witches?"

"I already told you. They are my enemies. I will not allow them to put me back, *ever*. When I come to rule this realm, they would try to topple me."

It was difficult to stand still. I wanted to attack him, or jump off the roof, anything to end this horrible anticipation. "And what of the Ivangard witches?"

He shrugged. "Powerful allies, for now. You mortals are so easy. You think you know what you want, and the second someone offers, you jump at it, regardless of consequences."

Asher abruptly yanked me aside, and a moment later I realized why. Eiric now stood right where I'd been, just a heartbeat before. He was too fast. I would never be able to fight him. I needed my magic.

But how? The most I had managed was a weak connection when both I and my opponent were bleeding.

Blood of my blood, a whisper slithered through my mind.

My fingers twitched around my sword hilt. That was right. Our connection might be distant, but Eiric and I shared the same blood, and my sword knew it. It knew him well. It had been his weapon once, after all.

Eiric looked down at the blade like he had heard its voice. "Such a funny blade. When Xavier brought it to me, it *rejected* me." His words were so sharp I half expected them to slice through my skin.

"Is that why you gave it back to me?" I asked.

His eyes lifted to mine, and we looked at each other for just a moment until I lowered my gaze to his nose. I was immune to most vampire wiles, but not to Eiric. Not that he needed me to look at him for him to cloud my mind, but it was foolish to risk it.

He smiled again. "I was going to have to give it back to you eventually. You'll need it for the ritual. You're not powerful enough on your own."

Blood, my sword repeated in my mind.

Again, Eiric's eyes went to my blade. "Does it speak to you?"

"Sometimes." I'd had enough talking. If Eiric grabbed me, it would all be over. I lifted my left arm, making my sleeve bunch up around my elbow, then I sliced my sword across my skin.

Cael inhaled sharply, reminding me of his presence. But his bloodlust was no longer my concern.

Eiric tilted his head, observing me. "What are you up to, Lyssandra?"

The fighting was growing more distant. Had the fortress already fallen? "Blood of my blood." He wasn't bleeding, but it had to be enough.

I focused on the connection between us—searching for the traces of shared blood in our veins. The connection nearly staggered me. His energy was pure darkness. I felt his dark blood in mine like ink swimming through water.

I thought of heat. I willed my blood dripping on the roof to boil.

Eiric's eyes widened. "You have learned well." His breath steamed the night air.

I wanted to keep my attention on him, but more than anything, I needed to focus. I closed my eyes, willing my connection with Eiric to deepen, and I boiled my blood. I could hear it sizzling where it had soaked into the thatched roof. The magic grew, climbing up to the blood slicking my skin. My breath hissed out as my own blood burned me. Then it moved inward. Heat pulsed inside me painfully, like the worst possible fever.

"Lyssandra." Asher tried to shake me, then quickly released me. I smelled burned flesh. Just touching me had burned him.

My eyes felt dry and gritty, but I forced them open. Eiric was on his knees. His eyes had gone blood red with broken capillaries. "You will pay dearly for this, witch." He lunged toward me.

I couldn't move, I could barely breathe, then Asher was there, shoving Eiric away.

Eiric toppled across the roof, nearly going over the edge. When he staggered to his feet, he was bleeding from his nose and eyes. His fingertips had turned black. The skin further up blistered, like an invisible fire was burning him.

He set his sights on Asher. "Harming you will harm her just as easily."

His movements were too fast to follow. One moment he was burning alive from the inside, the next, he had Asher pinned against the roof. He struck with one hand, sinking his fingers through Asher's stomach.

I cried out, then fell to my knees, barely bracing myself with my sword. Asher's agony coursed through me, overwhelming the burning pain already searing through my body.

I didn't think Eiric would do it. I had thought he wanted the ritual performed so badly, that he would never hurt Asher. I had been wrong.

Using my sword like a cane, I pushed myself to my feet. I staggered toward them, trying to lift my blade, but my strength was leaving me.

"Do it now!" Cael hissed.

I distantly realized someone had been hiding in his shadows. Someone small. Teresa stepped into the moonlight. She held up the ring that should have been on a cord around my neck. I was too weak to even check for it. Then I remembered her hugging me on the watchtower. And I remembered the brief warning from my sword the day Teresa had come to find us, right after Illya died. Teresa's glamour wasn't weak. It was as strong as Ryllae's—*stronger*. She had not only hidden what she was, she had hidden her intent from both me and my sword.

Teresa extended the ring in her small fingers, pointing it not at Eiric, but Asher. "Do not kill him yet," she said calmly to Eiric. "We must sever the bond first."

No. If Asher and I were separated, he would die.

Seeming to come back to himself, Eiric withdrew bloody fingers from Asher's abdomen. Beyond the blood, his entire hand had turned black.

Asher gasped, still alive, but blood was pouring from the wound in his stomach. Eiric had practically disemboweled him.

I tried to focus on my magic. It might kill me, but if I could take Eiric down with me, Asher might live. Eiric's young vampires would no longer have a master. If any of the witches were still alive, I could save them too.

Teresa stepped closer, extending the ring while chanting under her breath. Dizziness overcame me. Asher's already weak life force was draining away.

I couldn't lift my sword. I could barely stay up on my knees. "Please," I begged, my eyes on Teresa. "Please, stop. I will do anything."

The girl who looked back at me was not the one I had met. She was no longer timid. She was entirely sure of herself, and her purpose. "Break the bond, Cael."

Eiric had managed to stand. He was already healing, while Asher was dying at his feet.

Blood steadily leaked from my nose. "Eiric, I will perform the ritual—" I coughed. Blood flew from my mouth across the roof. "Just don't—"

He sneered down at me. Blood coated the lower half of his face, pouring down to soak his white shirt. "Your love for him is a weakness. You will learn that, in time."

I was so close to losing consciousness that I thought the figure creeping toward us was just an illusion. Then I saw Markus' face.

Cael turned first, his shadows surging around him, just as Markus slashed his sword. It sliced across Cael's abdomen and he shrieked.

"Break the bond!" Eiric ordered, moving to intercept Markus.

I fell beside Asher. All of the heat I had summoned was gone. My skin was so cold. I reached bloody fingers toward his. "I love you," I gasped, but my words were too weak, and they died on the wind.

With Eiric occupying Markus, Cael knelt over us, his eyes bobbing in hollow sockets. "I'm doing this for you, Lyssandra." The words sounded wrong with a voice meant for a creature straight from the grave.

"I will kill you," I rasped. Blood splattered from my lips.

He put one skeletal hand on my chest, and one on Asher's, then closed his eyes and bowed his head.

Teresa watched us, ring still in hand.

"What are you—" But I couldn't finish the question. My vision darkened.

Cael chanted, old words I did not recognize.

The bond pulled tight, then snapped. What was left of my heartbeat plummeted. I could no longer feel Asher at all. For all I knew he was dead, and I would soon be too.

I heard Eiric curse, but I no longer cared what was happening. I didn't even flinch as fire washed across the roof. A man shouted for Markus to move. It was Charles, but he was too late.

I watched through blurry vision as the shadows of Cael and Teresa fled from the flames, while Markus stood at the edge of them, closer to me now. His hair and clothing singed as he shielded us with his body, his eyes wide and panicked. Blood dripped from his nose, and I knew he must be weak. I was killing him too.

He was saying my name over and over again. Maybe I looked like I was already dead.

I opened my mouth, and despite the blood, my throat was horribly dry. I could barely speak. Fire washed around us.

"Get Asher off this roof," I croaked.

Markus' eyes went wider still.

"Get him off this roof. That is an order." A spark of magic flared within me, and I knew he had to obey. He was my servant, after all.

He clenched his jaw, then slid an arm under Asher's shoulders.

My eyes fell shut. The fire burned my skin and singed my hair. I didn't blame Charles—he couldn't let Eiric escape his flames. If he burned me alive, then good riddance. At least then, Eiric couldn't use me. If the only way for me to thwart him was to die, then so be it.

I had almost lost consciousness when arms wrapped around me, and someone picked me up like I was a child. I felt air, and momentum, and then all was solid darkness.

CHAPTER THIRTY-THREE

Tholdri

Steifan and I limped toward the temple where everyone was regrouping. Battles were never as long as the histories made them seem. People died quickly. And when the attacking force is about to lose, they retreat.

The same had happened with the enemy witches. Most of the baby vampires were dead. The cobblestone streets were awash with blood. The buildings that hadn't burned were coated with soot and ash. The moon hung above us, casting everything in harsh relief.

Steifan kept glancing toward the gates. One side of his face had been slashed by a witch's blade from temple to chin. Even with healing, he would wear a deep scar for the rest of his life, however long that might be.

"I still don't see her anywhere."

I kept walking. "Either Markus found her, or he didn't."

But it wasn't how I truly felt. I wanted to run through the streets searching for her, but I could barely walk, and we needed to regroup in case any enemies lingered.

It was Geist who found us, halfway to the temple. There was blood on his hands and face, but no visible wounds. "You need to come."

He had fought alongside us, and had helped turn the tide of battle. Without him putting down so many of the young vampires, we might not have survived.

I nodded, fully trusting him now. We followed him back down the street, toward the gates, stepping around bodies and debris. Nothing else moved. Everyone still living had gone toward the temple.

He led us to where the first blast of blue flame had occurred, then down a narrow alley. There was a seated figure leaning against one wall, and another dark shape sprawled out at his feet.

Once we were close enough, I recognized Markus beyond his charred skin and burnt hair. He cradled one arm, the bone likely fractured. At his feet lay Asher, unmoving.

"I gave Markus blood," Geist explained, pressed in near my shoulder, "but he is too weak to donate blood himself. Asher is close to being lost to us, forever."

So he wasn't already dead. He most certainly looked it. And that would mean Lyss—

"Where is she?" Steifan asked. "Where is Lyssandra?"

Still leaning heavily against the wall, Markus turned his neck to give us a dark look. "Eiric took her. She ordered me to get Asher off the roof."

My heart plummeted. But if he took her, at least she was still alive. I crouched beside Asher, withdrawing a spare dagger from my boot. I had lost plenty of blood myself, but I didn't hesitate before pushing up my sleeve and slicing my flesh. I held my bleeding arm over his mouth, but he didn't move. Blood pooled around his lips, then dripped down his face.

Geist squeezed past to kneel at Asher's head. "He must drink, or he will die. And if he dies, Lyssandra—"

"Cael broke their bond," Markus muttered. "Cael and Teresa. I don't know how. Necromancy . . . and something else."

I didn't know what it meant. When Amarithe tried to break their bond, Asher would have needed to die. But he wasn't gone, yet.

Geist gripped Asher's jaw and opened his mouth. My blood dripped down his throat, but he still wasn't swallowing. If he didn't swallow soon, it would start pooling up in his mouth.

Curse the light, even if Lyssandra really was no longer bonded, she would never forgive me if I let him die. "Drink, dammit." I held my arm closer, nearly pressing my flesh to his lips. "Lyssandra still needs you. So you have to stay alive for her. You have to help us find her."

I thought his throat might have convulsed, but it might have been a trick of the eye. I met Geist's heavy gaze as we waited. I looked him right in the eye, something I had never done with any of the undead. I had never expected to see such a sympathetic expression from a vampire.

Asher's bloody and burned hand reached weakly upward, gripping my arm and pulling it to his mouth.

I winced as he sucked down my blood, but I let him have as much as he needed. He could have it all, if it meant he would save Lyssandra.

By the time he finally released me, I felt dizzy and not quite able to stand. I looked down at him as he struggled to sit up. The look in his eyes was something dangerous, *inhuman*. I knew by that look that everyone involved in Lyssandra's abduction was going to die.

WE MADE our way toward the Blackmire cottages just before dawn. There were already hints of blue and purple light in the sky, made hazy by the lingering smoke. There was no time for Asher and Geist to seek alternate shelter.

Markus had filled in some missing information for us on the way. Asher had not spoken at all. I didn't think any of us had seen Cael's betrayal coming, but Eiric must have planned on using him from the start. He needed a necromancer to break Asher and Lyssandra's bond.

But the bond ...

I glanced at Asher, then quickly looked away. How was he still here? Traditionally, to break the bond, Lyss would have needed to die. With a necromancer and the ring, Asher should have needed to die. But they were both still walking, according to Markus.

We reached the string of cottages and even Geist had

to stop and stare. A few were blackened, but others were entirely untouched. All while the neighboring buildings had burnt to ash.

"How is this possible?" Geist asked.

Markus looked like a demon with his blood and soot smudged skin, and his burnt hair. At least his wounds were healing with Geist's blood, and his arm seemed better. "The enchantments," he observed. "They still remain."

I stared at the unharmed cottages. "Those must have been *some* enchantments."

"At least I know which cottages to avoid," Geist breezed past us, going for the nearest damaged, but still standing cottage.

I realized the sun was almost up, but Asher wasn't moving. He was just staring at the far cottage where Lyss had been staying. It had no lingering enchantments, but it was far enough from the street that it bore no damage.

I found myself reluctant to touch him. He was no longer bonded to my best friend. I knew he loved her, in his own way, but what might he become without her?

I tensed as he looked at me. There was no emotion on his face. "At nightfall, we hunt them."

"We?" I glanced past him at Steifan and Markus.

Asher was so still, I didn't think he was breathing, though he had to be at least taking in enough air to speak. "I will need eyes during the daylight hours." He glanced at Markus. "And I will need you to track her. I cannot feel her any longer."

Rage danced in Markus' eyes. Whether it was

because Lyss had been taken, or because now he would be forced to get her back, I might not ever truly know. He gave Asher a slight nod.

It must have been good enough for the vampire, because he turned those cold eyes back to me. "Be ready."

I barely saw him move. He was suddenly just gone. My blood had worked wonders for him, apparently.

I pinched the bridge of my nose, trying to ward off the steadily building ache. "Let's go to the temple," I sighed. "See who else is still alive." I looked at Steifan again. "And you need to get your face stitched up."

He had been uncharacteristically quiet through it all, and now answered me with a nod, only slightly more enthusiastic than Markus'.

With an invisible little ache in my chest, I turned and led the way. I had grown to like the witches, and hadn't had the heart to look too closely at any of the bodies. For once, dawn's light was cruel, because it illuminated all of the blankly staring faces as we walked past.

We found Drucida at the temple, tending the wounded with Ophelia. Charles was there too. I'd have to thank him for saving Markus and Asher later, though that likely hadn't been his intent. His intent had been to kill Eiric, and he had failed.

Drucida spotted us as we walked through the open doorway into the dim, candlelit interior. The stone walls were just as crumbled as they were on the outside, though all debris had been swept away.

She approached us. Her tunic and breeches were torn and soaked with blood. "She's gone, isn't she?"

I nodded.

She looked at Steifan. "Go to Ophelia. She has no magic left to heal your face, but she can at least clean your wound and stitch it up."

Steifan did as he was bade, and Drucida gestured for Markus and I to step outside with her.

I felt better once I was back out in the light. The grass was trampled, but there were no bodies here. Soon, the witches would need to start building pyres.

"How were those other witches so powerful?" I asked. "What was that blue flame?" Geist had called them Ivangard witches, but that hadn't really explained anything.

Drucida peered off toward the horizon. "I don't know. I have heard whispers that the priestesses of Ivangard have magic, but I have seen nothing like it. Charles can summon fire, but not like that."

The memory of those burning flames crept across my skin. They had destroyed so much. If it had just been vampires, they never would have made it so far into the fortress. So many would not have died.

I glanced at Markus, then back at Drucida. "You should know, Teresa is a traitor. She stole Lyssandra's ring and attacked Asher with it. I imagine she is with Eiric now."

"Teresa?" Her tone was pure disbelief.

I nodded.

"But how? *Why?*"

I glanced at Markus again. He was the one who'd seen it, he should be the one explaining it. When he made no move to speak, I sighed. "I don't know, but Markus saw her. She assisted Cael in breaking Lyssandra's bond with Asher."

I expected further shock at the mention of Cael, but she simply shook her head. "Cael would not have done that without good reason. He must have a plan."

My temper flared. Cael had betrayed Lyssandra. He was her only remaining family, and I knew what she must have felt in that moment. "He is a monster. There are no excuses."

I could tell she wanted to argue, but her mouth sealed into a grim line instead. "What will you do now?" she asked finally.

Markus surprised me when he actually deigned to speak. "Find Lyssandra. We leave at nightfall, once the vampires awaken."

"Asher and Geist?"

We both nodded.

"I suppose they are the best to hunt her now." She looked down at her joined hands for a moment. "There's something you should have. It may be a mistake, but I feel the light has ended my role in this endeavor, for now. Wait here."

She walked away without further explanation, and we were left standing in the blossoming sunlight. It would be a warm day. Far warmer than we had seen since we arrived at the fortress. I wondered how far away Lyssandra was, and what was being done to her.

"She's not being harmed."

I turned to look at Markus, but he was still watching the sunrise.

"I would feel it if she was being harmed. She's not."

"Thank you for telling me."

He nodded, still not looking at me. "She feels different now. Breaking the bond with Asher didn't make her weaker. It just made her . . . different."

I followed his gaze, watching the salmon pink glow expanding across the sky. "Different how?"

"I don't know."

Silence surrounded us as we watched the sunrise. Eventually Drucida returned.

She approached our backs, then came to stand between us. She handed me a leather tome. It looked just like the one Lyssandra held in the tapestry. "I think you'll need this. Keep it safe."

I took the book gingerly. I could feel its age, and something else. Something that made my skin crawl. "What am I supposed to do with it?"

"I believe it is part of a pair," she explained. "That's why I can't make sense of it. The rituals are cut in half. Lyssandra told me there was a similar book in Cedrik's study. I would not be surprised if Eiric has it now."

I looked down at the book. It did feel vaguely familiar. I'd had the same thought upon viewing the tapestry. "If Eiric wants it, then it should be destroyed."

Drucida shook her head. I only then realized that some of her long hair has been burned away. "No. It may contain the ritual Eiric desires, but I believe it also contains something that can destroy him. I feel it in my bones."

While I didn't understand Drucida's special way of *knowing*, I was in no position to question it. I braced the book beneath my arm.

We all turned together and watched the sun. I never thought I'd see a sunrise that wasn't a relief, but apparently there was a first time for everything.

CHAPTER THIRTY-FOUR

Lyssandra

I was floating. My body felt impossibly light, but also numb. I could tell I had been very cold, but I didn't feel anything anymore. I wasn't sure how long I had been floating in that dark, cold space.

When I finally opened my eyes, I saw a woman I recognized. Familiar, but . . . I knew I had not met her before. Strange. And I wasn't floating. I was on a cushioned carriage bench. Heavy curtains kept us in near darkness. I could hear the gentle clopping of horses' hooves outside.

"Who—" My words scalded my throat and I started choking.

The woman offered me a water skin. Her hair was dark, shining like fine silk. I knew her face, but—
"Drink slowly."

I sat up against the cushions, my burned hands

screaming at me. I obeyed her instructions, trickling water down my throat. Every swallow was agony.

When I couldn't stand any more, I lowered the water skin. I wished there was more light. "Who are you?" I rasped. "Where are you taking me?"

Her smile was mocking. "You don't recognize me? Just yesterday, we shared an embrace."

It was only then that I noticed her loose blue robes. Her features were still sharp, but there was more age to them now. I closed my eyes and took a shallow, aching breath. "Teresa. Even your appearance was a glamour. You knew as a child we would all trust you more."

I opened my eyes to see her nod. Now that I knew who she was, I could see the similarities. The big brown eyes, the fine, pointed chin. "It was Eiric's idea."

"He spoke into your mind too, while he was still trapped."

She tilted her head. "He wanted me to arrive at the fortress well before you. I needed to be trusted before you could arrive."

Everything had gone according to Eiric's plans. *Everything.*

"Asher?" I couldn't look at her as I asked it.

"Your bond is broken, but beyond that I do not know his fate. I believe Cael tried to spare him. Being both a vampire and a necromancer, I believe he is the only being who could manage such a feat."

The bond. It really was gone. I couldn't feel him at all. All I felt was a yawning cavern of darkness within, but I would not let it consume me. Eiric was still alive. When I was done, he wouldn't be.

"Where are you taking me?"

"To Ivangard. There, you will be well protected. No one will be able to reach you until you can perform the ritual."

I hadn't expected her to actually answer. Ivangard would be roughly a week by carriage. Not as far as I'd dreaded. If Markus was alive and willing, he would be able to track me. But who else was left? And what condition was Asher in, if he was even still alive?

An iron fist gripped my heart at the thought. He had to be alive. Cael tried to spare him, and I knew Markus had at least gotten him off that roof.

"Why would you do it?" I asked. "Why would you ally yourself with such a monster?"

"What wouldn't I do for the man I love?"

Love. Of course. He had played her, just like he did with Amarithe. "You're a fool."

Her smile reached her eyes. "You're so much like her. Like my beloved Lavandriel."

"What do you know of it?" I hissed.

She settled against the cushions, smug. Her face looked a little different now, glowing and beautiful. Was it more glamour leaking away, or new glamour being put into place? Either way, she was somehow more familiar now, not less.

She watched me trying to recognize her, and her smile widened. "I promised Eiric I would release him once I found a way to break his curse. *You* are that way, Lyssandra."

My jaw dropped as I realized where I had seen her before—in the visions provided by my sword. I hadn't put it together because it shouldn't be possible. "You're supposed to be dead. The shadows killed you."

"They were rather terrifying." She leaned forward, bracing her elbows on her knees, pooling the loose blue fabric in her lap. "But I am a necromancer, and of the old blood. I am not killed so easily."

"You should no longer have glamour. How did you do it?" When she gave up her blood and her life, she should have become something else. The gifts of her people should have been lost to her.

"You do not know of the old blood, Lyssandra. I am far different from your good friend, Amarithe."

"You could have released Eiric yourself."

She smiled again, and it was lovely. I wanted to slice that smile from her face. "He didn't want to risk you killing me."

"There's still time for that."

She shook her head slightly. "No. No, Lyssandra. He will never let that happen."

I leaned forward, mirroring her, though it pained me. I had no weapons, and I was horribly weak, but it didn't matter. "Before this is all over, you *will* die, Cerridwen. That is a promise."

Her smile widened, but I didn't miss the flicker of hesitation in her eyes. Part of her believed me. *Good.* I tried to never break my promises.

I FELL asleep at some point. I hadn't wanted to, but I needed to heal. I needed to be strong. Without the bond, it would take time. But there was something else now. I could feel my magic coursing through my veins. I had been right from the start. The bond *had* dulled my magic, it simply hadn't cut me off from it entirely.

My body hurt so much it was difficult to breathe, but I managed to sit up. It was dark outside now. Only dull moonlight shone from beneath the heavy curtains in the carriage. And once again, I wasn't alone.

I leaned heavily against the cushions and glared at Cael. He was back in his more presentable form, crimson hair combed away from his high cheekbones. Neat goatee framing full but stern lips. Shadows cut across his features.

"Why did you do it?" I asked.

He straightened his shoulders. His sleeves were burnt at the edges from Charles' fire. My clothing was singed too, along with the end of my braid. "I did it to protect you, Lyssandra. You must believe me."

"I do not."

He sighed, slouching down in his seat. "Eiric found me the last night we spoke. He told me his plan. I could either help him and try to spare Asher, or I could let him sever the bond in the way he intended. He had Teresa watching you. When you couldn't learn in the way you were supposed to, he knew you needed to be freed."

My throat felt tight with the need to scream at him. I held it in, but my words trembled. "That explains nothing. And don't call her Teresa. Her name is Cerridwen."

He bowed his head in acknowledgment. "Yes, it is

truly her, alive all this time. As for the rest, Eiric already told you what he wants you to do."

"He wants to walk in the sunlight, and kill all vampires and witches. That still does not explain why you betrayed me. It was not only to spare Asher. You could have fought with us. You could have stopped any of this from happening. Now tell me *why*."

"Because being a human servant made you *weak*," he hissed. His face thinned out with his words, stretching across his bones. "And you must be strong. If you want to beat him, this is the only way. You must have full access to your magic."

"You fool," I spat. "You think as a prisoner I am strong? You have given Eiric exactly what he wants."

"He wants you to reach your full potential. And *I* want you to use that full potential against him."

"If you truly wanted Eiric dead, you would not be allowed in this carriage with me right now."

He leaned back, his face returning to normal. "I am here because they need me. And their need for me will allow me to protect you until you're ready."

"Why should I believe a single word you say?"

"I am your family, Lyssandra."

"My family is dead." I flexed my fingers, realizing there was something around my wrist. I lifted it to the sparse moonlight. Silver glinted against my skin. It looked like a strip of impossibly fine chainmail, fitted perfectly to my wrist. "What is this?"

"It's enchanted to keep you from accessing your magic until we are in Ivangard."

I tried to push it toward my hand, but it wasn't just

perfectly fitted to my wrist, it was *melded* into my skin. Panic tickled the back of my throat. "Get it off of me."

"I cannot."

I glared at him. I wanted to tell him to go rot in a swamp, but there was still one very important thing I needed confirmation on. "Asher, he is alive?"

"He was when Markus toppled off the roof with him. Beyond that, I cannot say."

I tugged at the bracelet again, but it wouldn't move. "You'd better hope he made it, for your sake."

"You are no longer bonded to him, Lyssandra. You are free."

I gave him a cruel smile. "I love him, and I *will* fight for him. Though that is something you know nothing about."

He didn't seem to know what to say to that.

I shook my head. I didn't want to hear what he had to say regardless. For now, I would believe that Asher was alive, because to believe otherwise . . . I could not afford to break down. Not now. If Cael insisted on remaining by my side, I would find some way to use him against Eiric. And if I had to go to Ivangard to do that, then so be it. Those witches had killed many. They must pay for their crimes.

And I would carve that payment out of their flesh.

EPILOGUE

Asher

Trapped. Trapped by daylight, when she is being taken farther away from me. We were only able to travel so far by night, and I didn't want to rest for the day. I didn't want to depend on Markus. If I had it my way, I would brave the sunlight to find her. But . . . I cannot *feel* her. The place where she'd been is a hollow cavern. I must wait. Markus can track her. He *will* find her. I will not give him a choice.

I put a hand over my face, longing for true darkness, but whenever I close my eyes, the scene becomes fresh once more. Her pain. Her magic. Her final order to Markus.

And those words.

She loved me. I had longed to hear her say it. But now . . . it didn't matter. Those words did not change what I would do. Because even if her love was hatred instead, I would still find her. From the very start, I had been willing to burn the world to keep her safe.

And now, that is exactly what I will do.

Time drags on too slowly, until finally, another night begins.

The three hunters are already waiting atop their horses when I find them. The spare mount—Lyssandra's mare—is tied by a long tether to Tholdri's saddle.

They say nothing as I reach them. They have learned to stop speaking to me.

I have nothing to say to them. My purpose is all-consuming and absolute.

And . . . Geist does enough talking for the both of us. I'm not sure if he has joined us because he actually cares for Lyssandra's safety, or if he only desires to thwart Eiric. Perhaps it is simply because he has taken a liking to Tholdri. Sometimes, when you live so long, you will take any chance to shift the tide of your life.

I should know.

We only wait moments before Geist steps into the small clearing where the hunters had made camp during daylight.

"We travel north." Markus' eyes are hollow—his gaze dead. But I know it is simply a mask. He is growing more panicked by the day.

"Lead on," Tholdri says, because it is all that is left to say.

Only Markus can track her. I will willingly follow him to the ends of the earth. Too many years I spent hiding away, causing little harm. That is over now. If anyone harms her . . .

They will be as dust. Empty, meaningless dust falling dead at my feet.

NOTE FROM THE AUTHOR

Dear reader,

I hope you enjoyed the third installment of A Study in Shadows! Thanks so much for reading. I hope you'll continue on for a sneak peek at my new book, The Mage's Bargain. I know we left Asher and Lyssandra on a bit of a cliffhanger, but they'll be back soon :). I also have many other series which are listed at the end of this book if you'd like to check them out.

SNEAK PEEK AT THE MAGE'S BARGAIN

COMING WINTER OF 2023!

THE MAGE'S BARGAIN

The mission? Steal a bushel of fireroot from Mage Lycus Pendragon's garden. The plan? Wait until all his wolves fall asleep, snatch the root, and run like the Dark Mother's shadows are nipping at my heels.

I knelt in the tall grass, peering up at the castle. I had already scaled the imposing stone walls, and had made it to the garden fence without being detected. Now I just had to get past an entire pack of wolves, Mage Pendragon's creature to call. Rumor had it that under the full moon, the mage would transform into a wolf himself and run with the pack. They were only stories though, made up by the nervous minds of villagers. Everyone feared Lycus Pendragon.

I had decided that he wasn't so scary when I agreed to the job, but now I was doubting my own good sense. I made enough coin picking up tasks where I could—and also picking a few pockets—did I really need an entire pouch?

No, I didn't. But I had been half drunk when I

agreed, and I had boasted about the job in front of Tadrick of all people. There was no going back now. Not without the fireroot.

I shifted my stance as one of the wolves rolled over onto its back, aiming its belly toward the warm sun. Its tongue lolled out of its mouth, giving it the appearance of a harmless puppy, though I knew it could tear me apart in seconds. I had brought my bow to defend myself, but if it came to using it, I was as good as dead. I could never take down all the wolves in time.

I peered toward the garden beyond the wolves, spotting the towering tufts of fireroot. The long crimson leaves tipped with orange were lovely to look at, but the leaves weren't what I was after. No, I wanted the roots reaching deep into the ground. The roots that were worth a whole pouch of coin to the right bidder. They were so rare that I might be able to get even more than I was promised from someone else.

The final wolf flopped onto its side. Within minutes, it was snoring. Now was my chance. I crept a wide circle around the slumbering wolves, slowly edging toward the low garden fence. I glanced at the wolves again as I reached it. They hadn't moved. Maybe this would be easier than I'd thought.

I gripped the low iron fence, lifting one leg over it.

"You know, there's a gate," a man's voice said just behind me.

I froze with my leg still in the air. *Oh please, let it just be a servant.* I dared a glance over my shoulder.

He was tall and imposing, with dark reddish-brown hair falling in wild waves past his shoulders. Stubble lined his strong jaw. My gaze crept upward toward his eyes. *Wolf eyes*. I had managed to catch the attention of Lycus Pendragon himself.

I lowered my leg back down, then stood straight, tugging my worn forest green tunic over my tan pants. I had chosen the colors to blend in with the woods. "My apologies, everything is so overgrown here I didn't notice the gate."

His eyebrow twitched. There were long scars lining one side of his face, slicing through the brow. "Are you aware that you're trespassing?"

Let's see, I was dressed for stealth with a bow slung over my shoulder, creeping past a pack of wolves within the castle walls. My heart tickled the back of my throat. "I had absolutely no idea. I'll leave at once."

He stepped in front of me before I could flee. One of the wolves had woken, and crept toward us with its hackles raised. "What were you after? A garden seems an odd place to commit a robbery."

I pressed the back of my legs against the fence, wondering if I would be quick enough to snatch the fireroot and run. I knew the buyer wanted it to suppress a curse. He had run out, and was growing desperate enough to hire a simple thief. I wouldn't be able to grab as much as he had asked for, but he would still pay dearly for a small amount, I'd wager.

"Ah," Lycus said, following my gaze. "Fireroot. A curse of the heart, but which one?"

"I don't know what you're talking about." And I really didn't. I personally knew nothing about curses. I had never suffered from one, unless you counted barely having enough coin to get by.

He leaned closer, bringing with him the rich scent of cinnamon and woodsmoke. "Who cursed you? One of the Ladies of the Wood?"

He thought I was the one with the curse? I supposed that made sense. Sneaking into his estate had been a rather desperate act. The wolves were creeping closer, and my heart was beginning to pound. "I need the fireroot for my family, alright? We were all cursed. Can I have some?" If it was for a whole poor family, surely he'd give me enough.

He leaned away, his eyebrows raised. "You came here to steal from me, and now you would ask a favor?"

The wolf beside him growled, as if to emphasize his words.

I was starting to feel like I might faint, but I managed to reply, "You have plenty of it. You don't need it all."

He stared at me. Silent moments ticked by with my heart pounding in my ears. I balled my hands so tightly my knuckles turned white.

"How do you know what I *need*?"

My throat tightened. I had no idea what to say to that. The wolves were close enough to touch. I suspected I was about to die. "You are a mage. You already have everything you could possibly want."

He blinked at me, as if surprised by my words. Finally, he laughed. "What is your name?"

I tensed at his laughter. I wasn't sure if he was

mocking me, but I was really in no position to defend myself.

"Your name?" he asked again.

I saw no reason not to tell him. From what I knew about mages, they couldn't use your own name against you. "Kaida." I tossed my dark brown hair behind my shoulders. "A proud daughter of the Oakvale clan."

His brows lifted further. "A proud thief, you mean? You villagers always have such ridiculous names."

I scowled despite my fear. "If you say so, *Lycus Pendragon*."

He smirked. The nearest wolf laid down beside him, losing interest in the conversation. "Well, Kaida Oakvale, I cannot reward a thief, but I can offer a thief a bargain."

My breath hitched. We all knew the tales of what happened when foolish girls made bargains with mages. "I'm not a fool."

He tilted his head, draping his hair across the shoulder of his fine gray coat. His scars stretched when he smiled. "You must need the fireroot quite desperately to have come here."

I forced my hands to relax at my sides. Let him believe what he wanted. He would probably be far less inclined to help me if he knew I was only after coin. "Why would you offer me a bargain?"

He shrugged. "Perhaps I'm simply bored."

Of course he was. He was a wealthy man with powerful magic. He didn't have to work for anything, so what else was he supposed to do? If he wasn't going to give me the root, I only needed to keep him talking long enough for me to plan my escape. "What do you propose?"

"You will work for me, and in exchange I will give you what you need to cultivate fireroot so your family will never run out. You can use as much as you need while you are here."

I blinked at him. Here I'd thought I was about to die, and now I was being offered a job. I preferred to be paid in coin, but cultivating fireroot could prove far more beneficial in the long run. Curses of the heart weren't exactly hard to come by, but fireroot was. "You want me to be a servant?"

"Do you have something against it?"

Considering I made most of my coin through petty thievery and sometimes hunting gophers in people's gardens . . . I opened my mouth to answer, but couldn't quite bring myself to say yes. I didn't like being indebted to someone when I could make do by other means.

"I will need the fireroot, *and* I will need to be paid." I could scrub floors for fireroot *and* coin. He probably had far more to pay me than the other villagers.

"Very well."

I blinked at him. I couldn't believe he was actually agreeing. Part of me had been hoping he would simply send me on my way.

"Well?" he pressed.

"You want me to stay for more than a month?"

"If the bargain suits us both, then yes."

This had to be a trick. Things had shifted too quickly for me to follow. "How often can I visit my family?" I asked, stalling. I had no family to visit, other than my sister who I didn't actually want to visit, but I wanted to make sure I wasn't trapped here.

"As often as you please, but only once you have earned the first batch of fireroot. I won't have you skipping out on your half of the bargain."

As if I could. We all knew what happened when you broke a bargain with a mage. "So I work here, and you pay me and give me fireroot. That's it?"

He leaned a little closer, making me tense. "Yes. That's it."

Oh gods, something told me I was going to regret this, but I *needed* that root. Not only for the payment, but because I had bragged to everyone that I would get it. Just the first shipment would do. "Fine, but there better not be anything hidden in this bargain. I'll do tasks a *normal* servant would do. I'll serve your meals, dust your trinkets, and launder your clothes. Nothing funny."

He tilted his head, smiling at me. "As you wish."

"And this isn't a long-term bargain," I added. "This is on a month-by-month basis."

"Trust me, I have no intention of keeping you permanently."

I glanced toward the castle, the pale stone seeming to soak up the sunlight. I wondered what sort of strange things were concealed within. It was the domain of a mage, so there would most certainly be many oddities to behold. It was terrifying, but I had to admit, it was also intriguing. I was being invited inside, an opportunity that would surely never come again.

I held out my trembling hand. "We have a deal. I'll be your servant, doing normal servant tasks, nothing *funny*, and you'll send fireroot to my . . . family." I pulled my hand away before he could grab it. "*And* the first shipment has to go out today." My buyer wouldn't wait forever.

"You have not yet worked for it."

"Those are my terms, take them or leave them." I extended my hand again.

The wolf beside him watched on as Lycus wrapped his large hand around mine. "The bargain is sealed. We'll begin today."

I thought I heard thunder echoing, but the sky was blue and peaceful. Goosebumps erupted across my arms. "I have to go home to tell my family what happened first," I lied. I couldn't just have to root delivered without collecting payment.

"You will write them a letter. The courier will take it with the fireroot."

I tugged my hand away. "That's not good enough. I need to actually see that they get the fireroot."

"They may write you a letter in return. The courier will wait for it."

"Why can't I go home first?"

He sighed. "Do you want the fireroot, or not?"

I gritted my teeth. I had come here knowing I might never return home, but I'd thought it would be because I was in a wolf's belly. This was preferable, but still. Now I'd have to somehow rope my sister into collecting my payment.

"As I suspected. Now come." He turned away and started walking.

My jaw agape, I looked down at the wolf still watching me. It was frightening having it so close, but it no longer seemed aggressive. "Is he always this demanding?"

The wolf tilted its head. I took that for a *yes*.

I gave the wolf a wide berth and followed after the mage. I tried to step only where he had stepped, fearing traps in the tall grass, until we reached the circular cobblestone expanse at the front of his estate.

There were no carriages waiting, no signs of life at all. If I didn't know any better, I'd guess he lived alone, but that couldn't be right. The castle was absolutely massive. At least compared to the buildings I was used to.

He approached a set of dark wooden doors, twice as tall as he was. It was the only entrance I could see from the front of the castle. I gasped as the doors opened without him touching them. Inside, there was only darkness.

"Was that magic?" I asked, my feet suddenly frozen in place. There was no one inside. No one had touched the doors.

He smirked back at me, and there was something roguish about it. "You'll get used to it."

I shuddered. I didn't *want* to get used to it. "Are there any other surprises I should be prepared for?"

"Nothing here will harm you without my permission." With those not so comforting words, he stepped into the darkness, leaving me alone on the cobblestones outside.

I debated making a run for it. It might be my last chance. Something bumped into my lower back and I let out a high-pitched *yip*. I spun around, finding a wolf had snuck up behind me. Judging by the pale patterns in its fur, I suspected it was the same one from the garden.

The wolf sat, watching me.

I looked down at its sharp teeth as it opened its mouth in a wide yawn. "I imagine if I try to run from this bargain, you will chase me?"

The wolf grunted, then licked its chops.

I hefted my bow more securely over my shoulder, then turned and marched toward the doorway. *Fireroot. Think of the fireroot.* If I could pull this off, the village would tell tales of my cunning for years to come, and I would be so rich, I wouldn't even notice. This was the only way.

I walked into the darkness, finding that once I was inside, it was no longer absolute. I could see well enough in the barren entryway, though I didn't see the mage anywhere. The doors closed behind me with a resounding *thud*, sealing the wolf outside.

I stepped lightly across the stone floor. Hallways went off in either direction, and just ahead was a wide stone stairway. Narrow windows lit my path, accompanied by the golden glow of candlelight. I looked upward, expecting a chandelier, but there was nothing cradling the glowing orbs bobbing along the ceiling, gently lighting the room.

I was staring at them with my jaw hanging open

when a throat cleared behind me.

I jumped, then turned to behold one of the most beautiful women I had ever seen. Her thin face looked as if it had been carved from porcelain. Her eyes were large and shimmering silver, matching the silver streaks in her long blonde hair. She wore a plain white shirt that should have dimmed her regal demeanor, but instead it emphasized her slender body and long legs, clad in matching pants. I was looking directly at a princess from a fairy story.

"Are you just going to stand there like an idiot, or are you going to get to work?"

My eyes flew wide at her tone. "W-work?"

She crossed her long arms. "You made a bargain, did you not?"

"Well yes, but—"

"No buts," she cut me off. "I will show you to your chamber where you can leave *that*." She eyed my bow with disdain. "Then you can start by assisting the cook in the kitchen."

Regaining my composure, I crossed my arms, mirroring her. "Now wait just a moment. I was promised a shipment of fireroot would go to my family today. I'm not lifting a finger until that happens."

"It's already on its way," she scoffed, breezing past me. "Now hurry up."

I hurried after her. "But I never even said where to send it."

"You claimed to be of the Oakvale clan, did you not? That is where it will go."

I cursed under my breath as I followed her down a

long hall. I couldn't believe I had been stupid enough to give the mage my true surname. Now the fireroot would be delivered to my sister. She was the only Oakvale left, besides me. And just how had the mage communicated everything so quickly?

I stopped as we reached a flight of stone stairs. "But I was supposed to write a letter to go with it."

She turned toward me, clearly irritated. "You can write it in your chamber. It will catch up."

Puzzled by her words, I simply stared at her.

She shook her head as she turned away, then marched stiff-backed up the stairs. She never peeked over her shoulder to see if I followed.

I glanced behind me, wanting to run if only to spite her, but I wasn't quite willing to give up on this strange new opportunity. At least, not yet.

So be it. I could endure a measure of poor treatment if it meant never picking another pocket. At least it seemed my new employers intended to keep me alive.

My mind made up, I hurried after the woman, quickly reaching the top of the stairs. I spotted her at the end of an adjacent hallway, her arms crossed and foot tapping next to an open door. She looked at me, then nodded toward the doorway.

I lifted my chin, then walked confidently toward her. I might have made up my mind to become a servant, but I wasn't about to scurry under her watchful gaze. I reached her, then looked into the room, well lit by daylight. I was instantly disappointed. Such a grand castle, and yet my new chambers consisted only of a tiny bed, a side table, and a soot-stained hearth.

"Had you been expecting luxury?" she asked.

"Hardly." I entered the chamber and leaned my bow against the bed. I didn't like leaving it behind, but I couldn't very well lug it around while helping in the kitchen. I dusted my hands, then turned back toward her.

She suddenly had parchment, a quill, and a pot of ink in her hands. I had no idea where they had come from. She held them out toward me expectantly.

I cautiously approached, taking the offered implements from her.

She crossed her arms. "Hurry up now. You must be quick if you want the letter to catch up with the shipment."

I hurried toward the bed, uncorked the ink, and sloppily jotted down the details of the bargain I had made. My sister might be puzzled by the mention of *our curse*, but she would know the letter came from me by the terrible handwriting alone. She knew of the job I had taken, hopefully she could figure the rest out. And if she tried to steal my hard-earned coin, I would wring her deceitful little neck.

Once I was finished, I walked back toward the woman, handing her the still-drying letter. "Will you at any point be giving me your name?"

She lifted one finely arched brow as she took the letter. "Why?"

"So I can curse you in my dreams," I said sarcastically. "Or maybe I just want to know what to call you."

"Silver." She turned away without further explanation. "Now come."

I glanced back toward the bed, realizing I had forgotten to cork the ink, but both the ink and quill were gone. Flummoxed, I turned toward the door just as Silver disappeared down the hall empty-handed, leaving me wondering just where my letter had gone.

I took a deep breath. Alright, I was in a fairy story, being led by a fairy princess. Sure. I could deal with that, though the shiver down my spine begged to differ.

I stepped out of the chamber and hurried after Silver, wondering at her strange name and the disappearing implements, and also wondering how the mage had arranged everything so quickly. Was the fireroot really already on its way to my sister? Had the letter already *caught up*? Our village was the only one nearby—she wouldn't be hard to find—but this was all so strange. I wouldn't do an ounce of work until I knew for sure that the root had been delivered.

Silver led me through another hallway, then down a different flight of stairs. She opened another door, leading further down into pitch darkness, then stepped aside.

I stood at her shoulder, for the hundredth time wondering if I should run. The darkness did not look in the least bit inviting.

"Here."

I turned toward Silver to find she held one of the glowing orbs in the palm of her hand. No, she didn't quite *hold* it. It floated above her pale flesh.

"What am I supposed to do with that?" I hated the breathiness of my voice. Everything was happening too quickly. And where had that cursed mage gone?

"Hold out your hand."

Her tone left no room for arguments. I held out my hand, putting every ounce of effort into not letting my fingers tremble.

She plopped the orb onto my palm.

I gasped, my skin suddenly feeling icy instead of warm like I would have thought. The orb hovered just above my outstretched hand. "How does it work?"

"They are a part of the castle. You can take them from anywhere and use them as you need."

That didn't really answer my question, but I had a feeling I wouldn't truly understand an actual answer regardless.

"This leads to the cellar." She gestured toward the dark abyss in front of us. "Bring up a basket of apples, one brick of butter, and a sack of flour. The cook has everything else she needs in the kitchen."

"We're making an apple pie?" I guessed, surprised.

"Obviously. Fetch the items. The kitchen is that way." She crossed her arms and nodded over her shoulder. "You can't miss it." With that, she turned and marched away.

I was left staring after her. She never even gave me the opportunity to ask where I could find the mage.

No matter. I would find him myself. I waited until I could no longer hear Silver's footsteps, then I shut the door and went searching in the other direction.

Apple pie could wait. I wasn't going to be tricked into working before I knew for a fact that I had been paid.

ALSO BY SARA C. ROETHLE

TREE OF AGES

Finn doesn't know what—or who—uprooted her from her peaceful tree form, changing her into this clumsy, disconnected human body. All she knows is she is cold and alone until Àed, a kindly old conjurer, takes her in.

By the warmth of Àed's hearth fire, vague memories from her distant past flash across her mind, sparking a restless desire to find out who she is and what powerful magic held her in thrall for over a century.

As Finn takes to the road, she and Àed accumulate a ragtag band of traveling companions. Historians, scholars, thieves in disguise, and Iseult, a mercenary of few words whose silent stare seems to pierce through all of Finn's defenses.

The dangers encountered unleash a wild magic Finn never knew she possessed, but dark forces are gathering, hunting for Finn and the memories locked away in her mind. Before it's over, she will discover which poses the greater danger: the bounty on her head, or a memory that could cost her everything.

Books in the Series:
Tree of Ages
The Melted Sea
The Blood Forest
Queen of Wands
The Oaken Throne
Dawn of Magic: Forest of Embers
Dawn of Magic: Sea of Flames
Dawn of Magic: City of Ashes

THE MOONSTONE CHRONICLES

The Empire rules with an iron fist. The Valeroot elves have barely managed to survive, but at least they're not Arthali witches like Elmerah. Her people were exiled long ago. Just a child at the time, her only choice was to flee her homeland, or remain among those who'd betrayed their own kind. She was resigned to living out her solitary life in a swamp until pirates kidnap her and throw her in with their other captives, young women destined to be sold into slavery.

With the help of an elven priestess, Elmerah teaches the pirates what happens to men who cross Arthali witches, but she's too late to avoid docking near the Capital. While her only goal is to run far from the political intrigue taking place within, she finds herself pulled mercilessly into a plot to overthrow the Empire, and to save the elven races from meeting a bloody end.

Elmerah will learn of a dark magical threat, and will have to face the thing she fears most: the duplicitous older sister she left behind, far from their home in Shadowmarsh.

Books in the series:
The Witch of Shadowmarsh
Curse of the Akkeri
The Elven Apostate
Empire of Demons
Legend of the Arthali
Gods of Twilight

THE WILL OF YGGDRASIL

The first time Maddy accidentally killed someone, she passed it off as a freak accident. The second time, a coincidence. But when she's kidnapped and taken to an underground realm where corpses reanimate on their own, she can no longer ignore her dark gift.

The first person she recognizes in this horrifying realm is her old social worker from the foster system, Sophie, but something's not right. She hasn't aged a day. And Sophie's brother, Alaric, has fangs and moves with liquid feline grace.

A normal person would run screaming into the night, but there's something about Alaric that draws Maddy in. Together, they must search for an elusive magical charm, a remnant of the gods themselves. Maddy doesn't know if she can trust Alaric with her life, but with the entire fate of humanity hanging in the balance, she has no choice.

Books in the series:
Fated
Fallen
Fury
Forged
Found

THE THIEF'S APPRENTICE

Liliana is trapped alone in the dark. Her father is dead, and London is very far away. If only she hadn't been locked up in her room, reading a book she wasn't allowed to read, she might have been able to stop her father's killer. Now he's lying dead in the next room, and there's nothing she can do to bring him back.

Arhyen is the self-declared finest thief in London. His mission was simple. Steal a journal from Fairfax Breckinridge, the greatest alchemist of the time. He hadn't expected to find Fairfax himself, with a dagger in his back. Nor had he expected the alchemist's automaton daughter, who claims to have a soul.

Suddenly entrenched in a mystery too great to fully comprehend, Arhyen and Liliana must rely on the help of a wayward detective, and a mysterious masked man, to piece together the clues laid before them. Will they uncover the true source of Liliana's soul in time, or will

London plunge into a dark age of nefarious technology, where only the scientific will survive?

Books in the series:
Clockwork Alchemist
Clocks and Daggers
Under Clock and Key

Printed by Amazon Italia Logistica S.r.l.
Torrazza Piemonte (TO), Italy